MAGDA
 # REVEALED

MAGDA REVEALED

A Novel

URSULA WERNER

SHE WRITES PRESS

Published 2025
Printed in the United States of America
Print ISBN: 978-1-64742-864-8
E-ISBN: 978-1-64742-865-5
Library of Congress Control Number: 2024920685

For information, address:
She Writes Press
1569 Solano Ave #546
Berkeley, CA 94707

Interior design by Stacey Aaronson

She Writes Press is a division of SparkPoint Studio, LLC.

Yet everything that touches us, you and me,
brings us together like the stroke of a bow,
drawing from two strings a single voice.
On what instrument are we strung?
And which violinist holds us in his hand?
O sweet song.

—RAINIER MARIA RILKE

—

For Julia, Anna, and Emily.
Always.

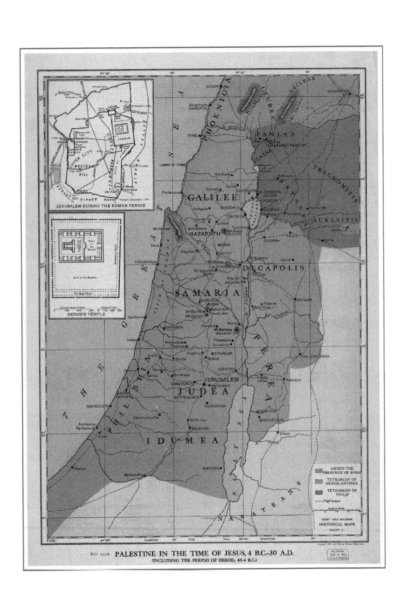

PALESTINE IN THE TIME OF JESUS, 4 B.C.–30 A.D.
(INCLUDING THE PERIOD OF HEROD, 40–4 B.C.)

PROLOGUE

*C*all me Magda.

You know me by other names: Mary Magdalene, Miriam of Magdala, the Magdalene. But those are the names they gave me. They are not mine. Everyone who ever loved me called me Magda.

Clear your mind of everything you think you know about me. And while you're at it—this will be much harder, I know—clear your mind of everything you think you know about Yeshua, or Jesus, as you call him. Because there's been a lot of misinformation about me, about him, about us. Two thousand years of misinterpretation, cover-up, deception, and yes, outright lies. One of men's most abiding and successful power plays, set into motion by Peter and Paul.

Oh, I know you think of them as saints. But you don't know the whole story, the *true* story, the one where they pushed me off into the Mediterranean in a tiny boat with one sail.

You're raising an eyebrow. "*True* story?" you ask. "If you know the *true* story, why haven't you told it before now?"

Look, I tried. I spread our story as far and wide as I could. I went all the way to southern France in that tub. I wrote my own gospel, setting forth Yeshua's truth as I understood it. And once I saw what Paul and his church were up to, I hid copies of my gospel so that my truth and Yeshua's truth might survive.

But there's a longer answer to your question, a multi-millennial answer.

When I came Here, after my death, I was exhausted—ready to check out, eager to bask in Yeshua's spiritual presence and the all-nurturing energy of the Source. I hushed into a deep, transcendental silence. But silence has consequences, especially when it lasts two thousand years. Back on Earth, Peter and Paul and the Roman Catholic Church they created hijacked our story. They told it *their* way, muzzling all opposition. They focused on Yeshua, cutting me out entirely. They spread lies about me, said I was demonically possessed, called me a prostitute and a whore. In short, they screwed me. That's what people with power do.

Did I fight back? No, I was done. I let all of you go, despite my love for you. In my lifetime, I had tried showing you a better, more connected way to live, but in the end, I lost you to Paul. You've always been susceptible to mass manipulation. Paul knew that. The Church he built is based upon it.

Now Yeshua wants me to step in again, go back to your world. I'd just as soon run screaming in the opposite direction, but it's hard to say no to him. Because Yeshua is a gem, isn't he? He's the Hope Diamond of love and loyalty. He swirls threads of promise and trust throughout the universe, spreading sweetness and optimism like spiritual cotton candy.

He's been following you from up Here, you know. For two thousand years, Yeshua has been poking his spiritual finger in your terrestrial pie, waiting for the right moment, watching you evolve. (He uses the word "evolve" with a straight face.)

"The moment is ripe," he says.

"What? Now? Why now?" I ask.

"Time is running out, Magda, for Earth and all its people." He points to your greenhouse gases and melting glaciers. And he's right, I can see it, you're all headed toward oblivion. You have to change, and change radically, or your species will die.

Yeshua says the truth will make a difference. "This is our last chance," he says. "And it must begin with setting the record straight. Tell people what really happened, what our time on earth was all about. Until you share the truth, we can't save them, we can't take the next step."

"What next step?" I ask.

"You still have work to do," he says.

"What work?" I ask. "What on earth can be done that I didn't try to do two thousand years ago? That wasn't wiped out by the Church, by banishment, burial, or burning?"

He talks about seeds. (Always the agricultural metaphors with him.) How the seeds we planted way back then can still be watered today. How fields that are burned to the ground become more fertile than ever. How they foster new growth. How everything can be—you guessed it—reborn.

And there it is, the ace up his sleeve. Resurrection. Who can argue with that?

MAGDALA

I

The day was rainy and cold, typical spring weather. The library was damp, because our home, like so many others in Magdala, was built to keep desert heat out, not in. I sank into the folds of my father's woolen tallit. The prayer shawl carried a hint of his scent, a comforting mixture of hemp and brine that swirled into the aromatic spice of the papyrus I studied. Spread before me was the *Shujing*, Confucian's Classic of History, translated into Greek. Marcus Silanus, my father's emissary in the eastern caravans, had acquired this precious scroll for me a week earlier.

I read aloud, pondering each word: "Heaven sees as my people see, heaven hears as my people hear." Did that mean God in heaven heard my weeping every night? Did God see the blood that stained my bed and shamed me?

"Yes."

The voice that answered my unspoken question was deep and unhurried, a cello's low *C* drifting idly through the air. I looked up, surprised because I had not heard anyone approach. My father's reassuring frame hovered in the doorway, but before him, already several paces into the room, approached a man I had never seen before. I shrank back into the pillows of my reading corner.

Nothing in the outward appearance of this man suggested he was anything other than ordinary. In fact, he looked shabby, in his worn-out, weather-ravaged linen tunic and cloak. The tunic covered a lean, athletic frame, which I would later learn owed its fitness and strength to manual labor and extensive walking in the hilly Galilean terrain. The cloak was pulled over his head because, as his followers later told me, you never knew where King Herod Antipas's goons were going to pop up.

Because of the cloak, I couldn't really make out his hair and face until he got close. When he did, I saw a surf of thick, dark curls cresting his shoulders. (Who knows where that hair came from? No one else in his family, including his mother Maryam, had anything like it.)

But what caught and held my attention were his eyes. Deep dark chocolate. The ebony bark of an olive tree after a rainstorm. His eyes drew me in, gently and immediately.

Have you ever seen a raindrop resting on a flower petal? Round and whole, a world unto itself, all its water protected from disturbance by its perfect unbroken surface? Imagine being inside that raindrop and you'll begin to understand the sense of peace and refuge I experienced when Yeshua's eyes enveloped me. For two years, I had not felt safe, conjuring dangerous men behind every shadow. Fear had lived in every bone, every muscle, and every nerve of my body, and had kept me in a constant and extreme state of physical tension. But in that moment, I was suddenly released from its grip.

Unexpectedly, I wept.

The man named Yeshua sat down next to me.

"Your tears cleanse your body of pain." He said, gently brushing my wet cheeks with his thumbs. His skin was as soft as the belly of a newborn lamb.

I startled and pulled away from him, casting my eyes downward. "Do not touch me, Rabbi. I am unclean."

"No, Magda." Somehow it seemed right that he should use my familiar name. "This is not true. It is a fiction that others have created about you. You are in pain. I shall bear that pain with you. In sharing it, I lift some of its weight off your shoulders and your soul." A shadow clouded his gaze briefly. "You will do the same for me one day."

My father, still perched in the doorway, did not say a word. Later, he told me that he and my mother had gathered every piece of information they could about the miracle worker from Capharnaum. Yeshua was their last hope. They were so desperate for me to be well that they agreed not to interfere with his healing, the only condition he placed on his assistance.

"I was skeptical," my father told me. "But the moment Yeshua touched you, I felt your destiny shift. I knew you would be well." He smiled at me wistfully. "I also knew that he would take you from me." He was right. My lifelong journey with Yeshua began that morning.

When I had spent all my tears, Yeshua stood up, ready to depart.

"Come with me, Magda. You have work to do."

Mutely, I followed him to the front entrance of our home, where my mother stood with my mantle, battling her instinct to grab my arms and hold me back. A stern look from my father reminded her of her promise not to interfere, and she gave me a quick kiss on both cheeks. On the doorstep, I hesitated, overcome by a familiar wave of panic.

I had not left the house in two years. The outside world, my childhood playground of joy and adventure, now felt terrifying and dark. A few months after I was attacked, in the early days of my self-imprisonment, my mother tried cajoling me to come to the market with her. I hyperventilated the moment I stepped outside, collapsing on the front threshold, clutching my throat in panic, and wheezing for breath.

That kind of behavior didn't do my reputation any favors. Nor did our elders' declaration that I was banned from the town synagogue as long as my womanly bleeding remained unpredictable. The elders' edict, together with whispers about what had really happened to me, led to rumors that I was a woman defiled.

Through whispers and innuendos, the town concluded that I was possessed by demons. Crazy idea, right? But remember our ignorance—we didn't have two thousand years of scientific discovery to explain the world around us. Natural phenomena that you don't think twice about today used to terrify me and my people—eclipses and comets sent us scurrying into caves, microbes and viruses and the diseases they wrought mystified us.

Demons were easy scapegoats. Did you have an incessant violent cough? Probably a demon pressing against your lungs. Was there an oozing sore on your leg? Might be the outward manifestation of some dermatological demon. Were you subject to sudden seizures and convulsive fits? Definitely a demon, the worst kind.

Mental disease was especially confusing and thus particularly demonic. Today, people might be diagnosed as schizophrenic or bipolar, but back then we were slapped with the label "demon-possessed," just because we didn't behave as others did. In my case, it was my complete withdrawal from the outside world that sealed my diagnosis.

"The world awaits," Yeshua said that morning, resting a hand on my shoulder. At his touch, instantly and inexplicably, my fear receded. I stepped outside.

Keeping my head shrouded and my cloak pulled close around my face, I followed Yeshua through the drizzling rain across town. Past the synagogue, its heavy stone muting the dissonant morning chants of some worshipper seeking comfort. Past the harbor and its fishing boats, now empty and abandoned for drier indoor shelters, where people could find warmth beside hearth fires or in fermented tavern brews. Past my father's fish-salting and pressing factories, which processed the fish caught in our lake, creating pastes and sauces that could be sold abroad and providing a generous income for our family.

I was glad the rain kept people indoors, for I didn't want to be recognized. Grateful too that the day's wetness tamped down the stink of fish oil and seaweed that normally oozed through Magdala's streets. Everything had been washed clean by the spring rain, and as I breathed in the fresh air, I thought, ever so hesitantly, that it smelled of hope.

Soon we passed the last stone building marking the end of Magdala proper and veered off the main road onto an overgrown path. Now I knew where Yeshua was taking me.

Out here, to the west of town, the hills began rising into mountains, carpeted by billowy undulations of rockrose shrub. That cover was pierced by dark erratic spikes of thorny broom, and more occasionally, by the ramshackle huts of goatherds who used these wild pastures and cliffs to feed their flocks. As a girl, I used to roam the neighboring fields to the south, gathering blooms from a sea of anemones that announced the onset of spring each year. My mother would not let me run in the western hills, because of the path we were now on. It led to the lepers.

When I was very young, our servant Lydia and I used to pass an old beggar-woman on our way to the market. A compassionate soul, Lydia always purchased additional bread or fruit and, on our return, she would place the food on the small plate in front of the woman's cracked and calloused feet. One day, the hunched woman wasn't in her usual spot. When Lydia learned that Roman soldiers had taken the woman to the leper camp, she was terrified that she herself might have contracted the disease. My mother became hysterical, peppering Lydia and me with questions: Had Lydia ever let me touch the woman? Had I ever placed any food on her plate? How close did I get to her? My father, ever the voice of faith in our family, said we must all pray for God to spare us this scourge.

God did spare us. So did *mycobacterium leprae*, the bacteria scientists now hold responsible for this terrifying illness. But back in my time, there was no understanding of what leprosy was nor how it spread. We had none of the antibiotics you use today to cure it. Instead, we could only watch in horror the disfiguration it brought to its victims—fingers and toes fused together, noses collapsed into faces, bodies that were ongoing eruptions of skin ulcers and unsightly lumps.

Panic prevailed over sympathy. Anyone who was suspected of having the disease was sent off to live with other lepers, in makeshift settlements like the one at the end of this dirt path.

As we began our journey up that trail, my fear intensified. With each step forward, I fought an instinct to turn and run. Then I caught myself. Who was I to flee from a band of lepers? Was I not equally unclean, equally defiled? Had not the town's elders banished me from our synagogue? Did not the people of Magdala shy away from me? Perhaps that was why Yeshua had brought me here. Perhaps this was where I belonged.

Before my attack, I had thought of myself as a lucky and privileged only child, pampered by both parents, especially my father, who rescued me from the domestic chores my mother tried desperately to teach me every day. "You'll be my business partner today," he'd say, pulling me away from the threshing stone or the bread oven, over my mother's meek objections. I loved accompanying him around town, visiting fish factories, merchants, and clients, and getting rudimentary instruction on how his business operated.

Perhaps he intended me to follow in his mercantile footsteps, for my father also insisted on giving me a classical education. Believe me, that was no small thing at the time. None of the other girls in Magdala were learning how to read or studying the Torah—for them, Hebrew and Greek were indecipherable scribbles on a page. But I was given tutors—crusty and humorless old men—patiently crouching over me as I learned to read, first Hebrew, then Greek. These scholars came from nearby synagogues and were paid handsomely for their efforts and their discretion. Over the years, I learned history, religion, literature, and even rudimentary mathematics.

What would I have done without that blessing of literacy?

I've thought a lot about this—why it was that Peter and the others had such a hard time understanding Yeshua's message. Why, later on, when I tried to explain it to them, Peter called me a liar. I've concluded that basically, it comes down to their illiteracy.

Before I met Yeshua, I had spent two years reading spiritual treatises from all over the known world. When I heard Yeshua preach, the themes sounded familiar. I could see how his message fit into what I had been reading. I heard echoes of their eternal truths. But Peter and the others had no context for the lessons Yeshua gave them. They didn't have that intuitive understanding because they couldn't read. Even worse—because this deficiency would ultimately doom the authenticity of Yeshua's legacy—they couldn't write.

Think about it. Why did Paul's version of Yeshua's message and his identity come to be the accepted view of the early Christian church? When Yeshua died, those of us who had actually lived with him, who had heard his message day after day and knew him as we knew our own hearts, tried spreading his message in person. But it was Paul—who never met Yeshua, who claimed to have seen him in a vision on the road to Damascus (a vision, by the way, that no one else in Paul's caravan corroborated)—whose teachings about Yeshua's ideas became the foundation of the Roman Catholic Church that you know today. Why?

Because Paul knew how to write. He wrote nonstop, letter after letter, to the Corinthians, to the Romans, to the Galatians. So what was left, when the Romans killed all the rest of us, or when we crept into caves and died of old age? What was left, when there was no longer anyone from our original group to spread Yeshua's truth face-to-face, no one with the authority of having known him personally?

What was left were Paul's letters. And a Church that made sure they were the only written records around.

My own ability to read—more specifically, my proud recitation of the Torah on that fateful day I turned sixteen—led directly to the dirt path I was now taking up to the leper camp. Because what happened on that day affected my life so profoundly, I might as well fill you in, however much it pains me to remember.

Magdala

2

The year I turned sixteen, my birthday fell on the Sabbath. It was late spring, a time when the olive trees stitched a milky white and creamy pink tapestry into the Magdala hills. The morning was exceptionally fair, sending a light warm breeze to kiss my cheeks as my mother and I left the house, heading to synagogue. We left earlier than usual, for it was my father's turn to read from the Torah.

I loved our town synagogue. My father took me there every day to pray when we completed his daily rounds of visits and errands. It was he who taught me how to enter the building. "This space is sacred, Magda," he told me. "It is your time to be alone with God. Leave everything unimportant on this threshold here, so it does not clutter your mind." I tried following his advice. When I stepped over the marble threshold, I imagined all my petty worries and resentments slowly drifting out of me and into the thick stone walls. When I sat down on a stone bench, I pictured the air moving more slowly inside this holy room than it did elsewhere. I took longer, deeper breaths. In a short time, my heart slowed to a contemplative beat. Back then, I did not put a label on this calming discipline. But I can see now that my meditation practice—which Yeshua would help me develop and which would balance and center me for the rest of my life—began in that room.

On the morning of my birthday, my mother and I stepped over the temple threshold and shuffled across its grand mosaic floor. The undulating sea of gold, cobalt, and cinnabar tiles was the creation of the most talented tile setter in town, Maccabee the Younger. Meant to commemorate Jerusalem's annual Feast of Dedication, it took over a year to complete, and drew appreciative visitors from as far away as Sepphoris.

We chose a bench to the left of the large Torah stone, behind which my father already stood. Settling down as townspeople drifted in, I let my mind wander to my favorite subject, one that incited both excitement and fear: Now that I was sixteen, would my parents finally seek my betrothal? They had been delaying for years, telling me they wanted to keep me to themselves, and I did not object. I was in no hurry to give up my relative freedom. At the same time, I was eager to begin my life, whatever shape it might take. I sat there, casually considering whom I might marry. Ignoring the background buzz of neighbors greeting neighbors, I floated possibilities: Jonah, the baker's son, who snuck an extra honeycake into our order each time he saw me? Meir, the fisherman, whose muscular build enticed me to the harbor every morning?

Suddenly, a hush fell over the room. I looked up to hear my father loudly greeting some visitors from his station on the raised bimah. Following everyone's gaze to the southwest corner, I saw an unfamiliar group of eight young men shuffle into the room. They were dressed in the telltale cloaks of white linen that identified them as theological students from the nearby town of Gabara. We had had such students visit before: they came to experience the diversity of worship in different villages.

The tallest of the men acknowledged my father's invitation with a nod, then swept his eyes over the congregation like a lion scanning the prairie. The close-cropped bristle of black hair edging his cheeks and chin resembled the mane of an apex predator. When his gaze reached the bench where I sat with my mother, it paused. Now, there are things I cannot remember at all about that day, but I do remember that look. It was extremely unsettling. It felt invasive. Disrespectful and dangerous. I quickly took my veil, which had been draped loosely over my shoulders, and pulled it over my head.

My father opened the Torah and began reading the story of Ishmael, first-born son of Abraham. You remember Abraham, don't you? Tested by God to come within an inch of slitting his son Isaac's throat? Told by his barren wife Sarah to violate her slave Hagar so they might have a child? Forced to banish Hagar and Ishmael, the boy Hagar bore, because Sarah became so jealous of them? I had always felt sympathy for Hagar and Ishmael, never suspecting that I too would one day be expelled from my home because of someone else's fear and envy.

Reading slowly and sonorously, my father reached the passage where Ishmael is dying of thirst in the desert, and a messenger from God appears to reassure Hagar:

"What troubles you, Hagar? Fear not, for God has heard the lad's voice where he is. Rise, lift up the lad and hold him by the hand, for a great nation will I make him."

My father stopped and cleared his throat. I waited for the rest. I knew God was going to make Ishmael the father of many tribes, from Havilah to Shur. But my father didn't resume his recitation. He looked straight at me and smiled.

"Sixteen years ago," my father said, "I too received a gift from God. A gift that has manifested itself as the greatest blessing of my life." His voice broke slightly on the word *blessing,* and he lowered his head, blinking his eyes. "I speak of my beautiful daughter Magda. Today, to honor God's beneficence and goodness, and to mark her sixteenth year as a member of this synagogue, I would like Magda to complete the reading."

I was stunned, as was everyone else in the room. Nothing in our oral or written traditions forbade a woman from reading the Torah in public, but it was hardly ever done. Certainly, there had been learned, literate females in Jewish history—Huldah the prophet and Deborah the judge were two of the more famous ones. Yet the only female who had ever stood behind the Magdala Torah stone to open the sacred scroll was Rebekkah, wife of Rabbi Eleazar, from Sepphoris. Her recitation years earlier had caused quite an uproar at the time.

Rabbi Eleazar had come to Magdala to see our famed mosaic floor, and our elders asked him to lead the Torah reading. But a last-minute cold took his voice, so right before the Sabbath service, he asked his wife to read in his stead. The elders objected loudly. Fuming, Rabbi Eleazar stood up and slammed his fist on the Torah stone. He pointed out, in a whisper so faint that people held their breaths to hear him, that if a woman had the ability to read, why should she not read God's word? And why should she not read in public? Did not God want *everyone* to worship him, illiterate as well as literate? Would not God want *any* literate person, man or woman, to share His truth with others when the occasion arose, when there were ears that could hear? No one had an answer to that argument. After the service, even the elders had to admit that Rebekkah's reading had been flawless and her learning excellent.

On that Sabbath birthday morning, I was terrified. But I never considered disobeying my father. I looked at my mother, who smiled and patted my back. "Go," she said. Reluctantly, I stood up. Every part of me shook so hard that I could barely put one foot in front of the other. It wasn't the reading I was afraid of—there were parts of the Torah I loved so well, I practically had them memorized. What I feared was reading aloud, in this cavernous room, before all these people, many of whom still resented the precedent Rebekkah had set, and who were now undoubtedly murmuring disapproval under their breaths.

When I arrived at the Torah stone, my father took my right hand. "Start here," he whispered, placing my finger on the text in the scroll. "You will find strength in the words themselves, Magda. Let God's words fortify you as you read them aloud."

I began hesitantly, my voice faltering. "And God opened her eyes and . . . and she saw a well of water, and she went and filled . . . filled the skin with water and gave to the lad to drink. And God . . . God was with the lad, and he grew up . . . ." Slowly and painfully, I continued. Word by word, sentence by sentence, I improved. My voice became louder and more confident. My father was right—I felt empowered reading aloud and delivering God's word with my own voice to a group of believers gathered to hear them. Some energy animated me, shaping my tongue, opening my diaphragm, clarifying my speech, and making the message echo across the room. In that moment, I believed more truly than I had ever believed before—in God, yes, but also in myself. By the time I got to the end of the reading, I was so immersed in the flow of God's words, the slightest breeze might have carried me off to live with the angels.

Practically floating with joy, I drifted back to my seat. The rest of the service was a blur. I was too pleased and wrapped up in my performance to hear it. Afterward, friends and neighbors came up to my parents to congratulate them.

"I had no idea your Miriam was so accomplished," said Lemuel the scribe. "Her Hebrew is excellent, as fluent as Rebekkah's, if I remember correctly."

"Magda is a quick learner," said my father, "with a great facility for languages."

"I have also learned Latin and Greek," I called down from atop my pink cloud, heedless of my boasting. My mother gave me a sharp look.

"Is that so?" said Lemuel. He grinned and slapped my father on the back. "You know, Shimon, you might have to go farther afield than Magdala to find an appropriate husband for this young lady. I don't think our young men can keep up with her."

I blushed deeply, out of embarrassment and pride. Honestly? My egotism that day was through the roof. I can protest all I like about wrongfully being called an adulteress or whore for all these years, but I have to own up to the sin of pride. And isn't pride an even greater sin than adultery? Isn't it possibly the greatest sin of all? Yeshua and I had many conversations during the weeks of my healing, about whether the pride that I felt that day was the kind that would be considered sinful. He thought not. He told me that what I had experienced was not only pride in my own achievement, but pride in honoring my parents and God by reading well from the Torah. He reminded me of the commandment, "Love your fellow man *as yourself*."

But in the two dark years that followed that day, I looked back with a critical eye. I tried desperately to make sense of an event that was nonsensical, tried to understand what I might have done to deserve what followed. The one thing that stood out was my own runaway arrogance in that Torah performance. And I saw what happened later as the severe correction I had earned, even though I remembered very little of it.

They say memory loss is normal after a traumatic experience. It's a protective mechanism of our brains. Maybe my partial amnesia saved my sanity in the long term. For the sake of this story, I'll try recalling what I can from that afternoon.

After our midday meal, I remember my parents going up to their bedchamber to rest, as was their custom on the Sabbath. I took a stroll through the olive groves, to mull over the many things on my mind: whether my parents would seek my betrothal, and if so, when; whether they would search for my husband in Magdala or beyond. Once more, I got sidetracked in thinking about whom in Magdala I might accept as a husband.

I thought again of Meir, the fisherman, youngest son of a man named Ehud whom I had befriended when I was a little girl. For years, Ehud used to let me help him sort fish while our servant Lydia was at the market. That was how I came to know Ehud's five sons. My earliest friendship was with Ehud's eldest boy, Judah. Judah taught me how to identify catfish, which were terefah, or "unclean," and how to sort them into baskets for Gentiles. By the time I was old enough to pay attention to boys, Judah had married, and now he had a young baby. Undeterred, my school-girl's crush shifted to Judah's youngest brother, Meir.

Meir was now eighteen and oh, so handsome! Sometimes, I asked my father to walk along the harbor, claiming that I wanted to hear the waves and feel the wind on my face, when what I really wanted was to watch Meir sort fish. Those powerful arms. That wild untamed mesh of tresses bouncing on his shoulders like buoys bobbing in a gale.

In the middle of this fantasy, I realized that I had walked all the way through the olive orchards and back down to the synagogue. Here's where my pride really misled me: on a moment's whim, I decided to go back inside and relive the morning's triumph, revisit the scene of my success, as it were. The sanctuary was empty and silent as I entered. Tiptoeing across the mosaic floor, I went to the bench where I had sat with my mother and took a seat, bowing my head in prayer.

I don't remember what I prayed. Most likely, I was too caught up in the memory of my Torah reading to properly give thanks to God. Pride again. But my prayer was soon interrupted by footsteps and the chatter of other worshippers. I looked up.

It was the students from Gabara, all eight of them strolling noisily into the temple, showing no more deference or respect than they would in a public market. The tall one, who had made me so uncomfortable earlier and who seemed to be their leader, saw me immediately.

"Look who's here! Our little Mistress of the Torah," he mocked. He whispered something to the two men closest to him. They grinned and separated, walking around either end of the bench I sat on. Now I could no longer watch all of them—six men still approached me slowly, led by the tall one. And two others had just slipped out of my peripheral vision, one to the left, the other to the right. What were they up to?

My curiosity and confusion were suddenly replaced by fear. Something was not right about this situation. I should go. Immediately.

I was about to leap up out of my seat when my arms were grabbed from either side and pressed tightly against the back of the bench.

"What . . . ?" I tried freeing myself, but the men holding me intensified their grip. "What do you want? Let me go!"

"It will be more pleasant for you if you don't struggle," the tall one said.

In the black void that follows, I remember strange details: the brown piece of fig skin stuck between the tall man's front teeth; his low, gravelly voice, rasping like a scythe cutting through wheat stalks; and what he said, as he stood over me.

"It seems to me that a young woman who dares to read from the Torah ought to know what she is talking about," he said, untying his sash. I twisted and turned against the stone, rubbing my skin raw. He tried grabbing my legs, but I kicked like a wildcat, so several others stepped forward to hold me by the knees. Someone clamped a large hand over my mouth. It stank of sweat and dirt.

"Hagar was forced to lie with a man. Shouldn't you know, shouldn't you *understand*, exactly what that means? How that feels?" The tall man pushed up my tunic and bent down to breathe in my ear. "Ah yes, I will teach you. I will teach you what it means not to be pure."

The rest of that afternoon is lost, deeply buried in the recesses of a brain I put to rest long ago. I have no desire to go digging for it.

MAGDALA

3

*I*f you're a survivor of any kind of physical assault, you know what it feels like to be shattered. You used to be a whole person, but the violation of your body blasted you into little pieces. No matter how hard you try to patch yourself back together, you remain a fraction of your former self: the wounded, cobbled-together you rests over the whole you that used to exist. Maybe you try adding things to the numerator of that fraction—therapy, hypnosis, drugs, alcohol—to bring the ratio closer to one. Maybe some of those alternatives help for a while. But you can never *quite* get rid of the sucker-punch deep within you, that oozing creep of shame and blame that will perpetually keep you from feeling whole.

I can't say how often I was raped—maybe it was only once, maybe it was many times by the same person, or maybe it was all seven men. All I know is that eight men approached me in the synagogue, and only one had the courage to carry me to my home afterward. I'm assuming he didn't participate and that he felt bad about the crime, though clearly not bad enough to prevent it. To explain my unconsciousness, this young man told my parents I had had a seizure, and then he ran. My father immediately called for a physician, who discovered that I was bleeding and bruised in the genital area.

My parents never asked me any questions. The doctor told them all they needed to know. From my physical wounds, they knew I had been sexually violated, perhaps multiple times. From the identity of the young man who brought me home (whom they immediately recognized as one of the rabbinical students), they knew who was responsible. Unfortunately, they also knew that they would never get justice against the perpetrator, because no one would believe that a young girl, who couldn't even remember the event, was raped in a holy space by holy men dedicating their lives to God. It was unfathomable; therefore, it could not have happened.

I was lucky in one respect: my parents did not blame me. They could have, because now that I was no longer a virgin, I was practically unmarriageable. That must have been a heavy blow to them. But they did not turn their faces from me in disgust, as so many other families would have done.

That day in the synagogue was a turning point in my life. Before then, I was a smart, strong-willed girl who was used to getting her way, who did pretty much everything a boy did, who looked at the world with a fearlessness and bright-eyed wonder that, in first-century Roman-occupied and impoverished Galilee, could only come from economic privilege.

After that day, I was a pariah, to myself and to the people of Magdala. No one blamed me more for my defilement than I did. Actually, *defiled* is a mild word to describe my self-perception. When I first heard others whisper that I was possessed by demons, I thought, Yes, that's perfect. That's exactly who I am. Evil, evil to the core. Evil and filthy and foul.

The day I followed Yeshua up to the leper camp, I quivered on that knee-jerk impulse of fear and self-loathing. By the time we saw the collection of patchy goatskin tents that marked the end of our route, I was terrified, but I resolved to accept the fate that I convinced myself I had earned.

On the edge of the encampment, we came upon a small clearing buzzing with gnats and flies. Swatting at the pests, I quickly saw what attracted them: a food depot. To the right of the path, plates and platters piled with fruit, bread, and cheese and covered loosely with linen had been left in the dirt. To the left, a jumble of empty dishes and trays sat awaiting collection.

"Provisions for the afflicted, brought by family and friends," Yeshua explained. He knelt next to one of the trays on the right and lifted the linen. "I am hoping someone will have left a supply of . . . ah, yes! Excellent." He withdrew a small cruet and replaced the cloth.

I followed him into the tiny settlement, staying close to his side, unsure what to expect. I call it a settlement, but really it wasn't much more than a ragtag collection of tattered and element-battered animal skins pulled over a makeshift framework of tree branches. (Think of your modern-day tent cities, homeless people squatting under highway ramps. Different time, same societal purge.)

Because of the rain, people huddled under a jujube tree with great thick limbs that extended up and horizontally over the group. As Yeshua approached, the lepers shrank back in a reflex of fear habituated by years of rejection. Undeterred, he walked forward, making sure to touch lightly the hand or shoulder of anyone within arm's reach. When he reached the base of the tree, he stopped.

There, in a shallow bed of dirt that had been smoothed out between the tree's roots, lay a woman with her eyes closed and her mouth contorted in pain.

She was gaunt and shriveled, a dried fig of a human being. It was impossible to say how old she was, because disease had completely blotched her skin and ravaged her limbs and face. Two younger women crouched by her head, stretching a piece of linen between them to shelter her face from raindrops.

"Come," Yeshua beckoned to me. He knelt down at the woman's feet, and I did the same, trying hard not to recoil in horror.

"Let us give our sister some relief," he said.

Yeshua reached for my hands and turned my palms up. Then he cupped them together and poured a measure of olive oil from the flask he had taken. "You have been instructed in the art of anointment, yes?" he asked.

I hesitated. My mother was the expert in anointment, not I.

My mother's hopes for my future evaporated when I was raped. With every drop of blood on my bedsheets, there went her dreams about my marriage, perhaps to the son of some merchant in Bethsaida or Tiberias. With every excruciating cramp of my womb, there went her fantasies about grandchildren who might play in her courtyard. I had grown up too quickly to satisfy all my mother's nurturing instincts, and if she had placed her hopes in becoming a doting and loving grandparent, those too were suddenly erased.

Nevertheless, ever resilient, my mother poured her instincts into taking care of me. She sang to me and fed me soups and stews, though I had very little appetite. And she practiced a skill that proved indispensable to my recovery. Indeed, it would later become vital to my identity. Anointment.

Judging just from what's written in the Bible—a book that, I will remind you, was largely written by men—you might think that anointment was a rite practiced only by, and upon, priests and kings. That it was a ceremony in which one person of high honor applied oil to the skin of another person of equal esteem, in order to consecrate him. (Ceremonial anointment always involved a "him.") And sure, ceremonial anointment did take place, whenever a king had to be coronated or a high priest ordained. But those liturgies were few and far between.

Much more common was the anointment practiced by women in every household. The application of herbal oils to family members who were sick or in pain. The ritual blessing of guests before dinner. The final commemoration of the body of a loved one before it was wrapped in a shroud. Anointment was a tactile ritual handed down from mother to daughter, linking them to grandmothers past and granddaughters to come.

When I was recovering from my attack, my mother called upon the magic of anointment to reconnect me to my body. Twice a day, at dawn and dusk, she came to my bed with a small bowl of oil, which she rubbed on her hands and massaged into my skin, from my scalp to the soles of my feet. Drifting in and out of consciousness, I smelled something sublime, spicy and sweet, wet and earthy, like cassia incense lit inside a damp stone room.

"You are using myrrh oil?" asked the physician one evening, arriving just as my mother completed her ritual and sniffing the air.

"My husband could not get frankincense from our trader. I understand that myrrh also has healing powers," my mother explained.

"Oh yes, myrrh has excellent medicinal qualities," he reassured her. "It greatly reduces pain and inflammation. If you can afford the expense, of course. It is quite dear."

My mother did not answer him. She waited until he left to

bend toward me and whisper, "Nothing is more dear to me than you, Magda. Nothing."

Anointment was revelatory. My mother's oiled fingers, slowly and steadily tracing the contours of my body, coolly brushing through my hair and over my forehead, told me that she cherished me. They recalled me to the sleepy hours I had spent with her when I was a baby, nestled against the warmth and nourishment of her breast, oblivious to every threat or attraction in the world outside, content and peaceful in the cocoon she created.

I was not the only beneficiary of my mother's skills. Her reputation as an expert anointer had brought her to numerous homes in Magdala, whenever someone was ill and needed healing oils, or when someone had died and there was no woman in the family proficient in preparing the body for burial. And when beloved friends visited our home, she sent them off with an "embalming grace"—a few minutes during which she massaged their necks and shoulders with her strong fingers doused in fragrant oil. Though I watched her do this for years, and she had instructed me in the basics of the art, I still felt far from capable.

Yeshua waited patiently for my response.

"My mother taught me how to anoint," I said, "but I consider myself a novice."

"Good enough. Magda, I would ask you to share whatever skill you have with this woman." Yeshua moved back a bit to give me easier access to the woman's feet.

I should have balked. After all, I was being told to touch the body of a leper, which I understood to be a sure and inevitable step toward ending up right here, in this wretched community of outcasts. Yet strangely, I felt no anxiety. Slowly, I rubbed the oil over my hands and fingers, as I had seen my mother do countless times before.

If you are a staunch and devout Catholic, you'll recoil at the thought that Yeshua was asking me to engage in a rite that is, essentially, body massage. Because doesn't that lead inevitably to sexual arousal? Which in turn launches a carnival of depravity and dissolution?

To which I can only raise my eyebrows and ask: Really?

Yeshua would tell you that there is nothing more holy than physical touch, because touch is a palpable moment of together-ness between humans. The whole point of my anointing the woman before me was to establish kinship with her. "She feels alone, completely abandoned by society, unredeemable," Yeshua said to me that day. "In anointing her, you begin removing some of the armor that she has amassed around her soul."

Cautiously, I picked up one of her feet and used my fingertips to stroke and knead the oil into her skin—the heel calloused by rough sand and gravel, the gnarled and misshapen toes battered by small rocks and bits of desert brush. I slowly glided my thumbs up along the softer, more sensitive arch and heard her utter a low groan of release.

"This world has battered her spirit," Yeshua continued, "Years of censure and exile have generated layers upon layers of protection."

I could feel those layers peel away as I shifted next to her hands and arms, taking her clawed knobby fingers between my own.

"By touching her, you take her out of her isolation." Yeshua watched as I moved to the base of her neck and began sliding my thumbs up and down her spine. "She does the same for you."

Walking my fingers along both sides of her head and cradling the weight of her skull, I did indeed feel myself overlapping with her. The vibrations of my pain began resounding with hers. And as her agony gradually diminished, like piano strings hushed by a damper pedal, my own torment receded too. By the time I was done, the woman was smiling faintly at me, and I felt lighter than I had in years.

That was how Yeshua led me to reclaim my life—one leper at a time. Several times a week, throughout that spring and early summer, he and I returned to the small encampment outside Magdala. During each visit, I anointed one or two people, men as well as women. Ordinarily, women in our society would not be permitted to touch the body of any man who was not a member of her family. But these lepers, male and female, had no family members who were willing to anoint them. And Yeshua, I soon realized, did not believe in the segregation of the sexes—in his view, men and women were equal to each other.

Gradually, we came to know everyone in the community. As people relaxed into my hands, they opened up to me, spilling stories of their families, their dreams, and their sorrows. Over time, I stopped noticing their physical deformities. The old man with the caved-in cheeks and clawed hands became, simply, Micah, a tailor from Hamam. The two young girls with mottled faces and arms were Adinah and Yael, daughters of Dalit, who lived in Ginosar and walked two hours every day to see them. People became individuals, not exemplars of disease.

Thus I learned the fundamental principle of Yeshua's ministry, which I now pass on to you: radical equality. That's right, everyone on Earth is equal. No one is better or worse than anyone else. We may look different on the outside, we may come from different cultures, but in essence, deep within, we are all *exactly* the same. Sounds like a simple concept, doesn't it? Ah, but simplicity can be deceptive. Because the human ego is powerful. Because the last thing you want is to be just like someone else, right? You want to be richer, smarter, more powerful, more attractive.

Everyone has their adjective. Everyone wants to be "better than" in some way.

I remember clearly one evening when Yeshua and I stayed long enough at the camp that Yael invited us to share supper with them. It was an animated meal, with joking and laughter that we had not heard when we first arrived. Looking around the campfire, what I saw in the faces illuminated by its flames was hope. I suspect that was what they saw reflected in mine.

At the end of the meal, Adinah brought us cups of chamomile tea and honey. I held the drink in my palms, not trusting my fingers, which were still slippery from the oils I used that day, and I watched the rising steam swirl up into the layers of the setting sun. Yeshua blew across the top of my tea, breaking my trance. "When you are done looking west," he said, "look east." There on the opposite horizon appeared the full moon, its pale-yellow surface dotted with craters. Two orbs, one flaming as it ebbed, one luminescing as it rose.

In that moment, I understood two new things about myself. First, that I was sitting among people who accepted me as I was. Second, that I had, over the past few weeks, become good at anointing.

The first revelation, that I was loved and could love in return, healed me.

The second revelation, about anointment, would transform my life.

MAGDALA

4

*B*ut you want to know more about Yeshua. Maybe you've seen movies depicting his life, maybe you've heard priests or ministers interpret his parables, maybe you've even read the gospels that made it into the Bible, your New Testament. Listen, if you want to know the truth about Yeshua, you can't believe everything you read in those books. First of all, the scribes who called themselves Matthew, Mark, Luke, and John (who knows what their real names were) wrote long after Yeshua had died. None of them were there for the actual events they narrated. I'm not saying they deliberately got things wrong. But some of them had religious agendas, others were concerned about political backlash. They tailored their narrations accordingly. (From here on in, I'm going to call those narrators "the Quartet," because I think of them standing next to a barber's pole with razors and shears, singing their hearts out as they snip and slice pieces of the story to suit their purpose.)

I'll give the Quartet credit for this: they understood the power of a good symbol. Paul started it, Paul and his nascent church were experts in the art of symbol manipulation and exploitation. Take the lamb, for example. Cute pile of fluff gamboling through the grass, white woolen ringlets unsullied by mud—what a compelling symbol of innocence and sacrifice! Thanks to Paul and the Roman Catholic Church, Yeshua's go-to Easter moniker became "Lamb of God." (For the record, I hate that nickname. Reminds me of our last week in Jerusalem, all those sacrificial lambs bleating their little hearts out one minute, bleeding to death the next.)

Then there's the number twelve. Early on, the men who forged Yeshua's story decided he must have twelve special followers, twelve members of an inner circle, twelve disciples. They singled out twelve as a magical number, because it connected Yeshua's story to the Torah. You know—twelve sons of Jacob, twelve tribes of Israel—bingo, twelve disciples.

The problem with symbols is that people come to take them as the truth when they aren't. Because there wasn't a special group of twelve male "disciples" selected by Yeshua to be the unique heralds of his message. Rather, there was a handful of men and women whom Yeshua thought of as confidants, close friends. Peter was one of these. As were John and James, the sons of Zebedee. And I.

The more important point, the one you won't find anywhere in the Bible or in popular lore, is this: Yeshua's followers weren't all men. The *majority* were men, yes, because back then (as now), men had way more freedom to drop everything and run off. Women back then (as now) were too entangled in cookware and washing boards and caterwauling babies to move anywhere freely. But some women *were* able to break away—Yohanna, Shoshanna, and Ilana. Those are the names I remember with love and longing.

I didn't meet these women until later, because Yeshua asked his followers to keep their distance while he was working with me. In the early days of my healing period, I was jittery as a sand cat, ready to burrow into a dune and disappear at the drop of a seed. Everyone in the group respected Yeshua's request. They filled their time by practicing meditation or busying themselves with tasks around the camp they had set up nearby, giving the two of us wide berth whenever we walked outside. Everyone, that is, except Peter.

Now, I know many of you love Peter. The Church tells you he was a saint. He was the first Pope, says the Church. He was a Christian martyr, it says. He chose, when Emperor Nero ordered his execution, to be crucified upside-down because he was too humble to die the same way Yeshua had died. All of that may be true, but it doesn't erase what he did to me—his refusal to acknowledge me after Yeshua's death, his cowardly complicity in my banishment from my homeland.

In fairness to Peter, I'm going to try to be balanced here. He did have some good qualities. He was dependable and loyal to his friends, especially the men in our following. He was a good provider for his family—when he was home in Capharnaum, that is. Which, after Yeshua came into his life, wasn't often.

But Peter was also hugely sexist. "You need to go back to your husband," he would say to Yohanna, "so he can put you in your place." When Ilana got married and became pregnant, he congratulated her for knowing her rightful role. As for how he treated me, well, you'll hear about that soon enough.

To some degree, I can't fault him, because Peter was a product of the misogynistic culture he lived in. And I might have given Peter's sexism a pass, had Yeshua not insisted that women were just as intelligent, capable, and worthy as men. Yeshua's fundamental message to society, a message we heard over and over, in every story he told, to every gathering of listeners, was that vision of radical equality I've already mentioned. You would think that daily exposure to this idea would have tempered Peter's chauvinism.

Nope. If anything, Peter became more contemptuous of women over time, especially me. Women were threats to his relationship with the man he loved. Of course, we all loved Yeshua, but Peter's love bordered on obsession. He wanted Yeshua to himself, and that meant women were dangerous. Because, after all, there were *some* needs a healthy heterosexual male like Yeshua might have that only a woman could fulfill.

Peter began spying on us the first week of my rehabilitation. Whenever Yeshua took me on walks through the hills or along the lake's shore, I had the distinct sense of being followed. More than once, I saw the shadow of a man hiding behind a bush or a tree. For a while, I dismissed it as my own fear trying to beat me down. By the second week, however, the feeling was so acute I could no longer keep it to myself.

"Rabbi," I said, stopping a few paces before the shrubbery of a low-lying plane tree. I was certain that I had just seen the edge of a piece of clothing being pulled under the vegetation. "I believe we are being watched."

Yeshua looked up. He had a habit, when walking with me, of lowering his head so he could focus on the conversation. When I knew him better, I learned this was because he often felt overwhelmed when he engaged the world. "It is so unique," he whispered to me months later, as I placed a drop of honeysuckle nectar on his tongue. "The ability to experience through our senses is extraordinary. There is so much to process, so many beautiful smells and sounds and tastes. What a bittersweet beauty, knowing that it is all fleeting and impermanent."

That day, Yeshua followed my gaze to the plane tree.

He sighed. "Peter. Show yourself."

There was a rustling of branches, as a burly shape pushed its way through the brush. Though he quickly knelt, I could see that the twig-strewn penitent before us was a large man, a good palm taller than Yeshua, and at least three palms taller than I. The bulkiness of his rough clothing suggested brawn and heft. His face had the weathered skin of a man daily engaged with the elements, with brows and lips creased in perpetual vigilance for any sudden storm.

Yeshua stepped in front of me to give me cover.

"Why have you chosen to follow us when I specifically asked you not to do so?" he asked. He didn't sound angry, more curious about Peter's presence.

"Rabbi, I—I feared the coming of a rainstorm," Peter said, eyes shifting briefly to the clear blue sky. "I came out to collect firewood in advance, that we might have a sufficient supply of dry wood."

"Ah Peter, you do not answer my question." Yeshua's gaze was unyielding. "Perhaps you are indeed seeking wood for fire, but that is not the primary reason that you have come all this way, is it?"

"Well, actually . . . ." Peter raised his head. Catching just the slightest glimpse of Yeshua's scrutiny, he quickly bowed it again. "No sir. It is not."

"Return to the others, Peter," Yeshua said, not harshly. "I know why you have come. It is premature. There will come a time for you to meet this gentle woman. That time is not now."

Maybe Peter's antagonism to me arose from that first encounter, in the moment that Yeshua dismissed him and sent him away, choosing me over him. Maybe Peter never forgave me for that.

My "exorcism," as the Quartet refers to my time in Magdala with Yeshua, lasted two months. Seven days a week, for eight transformative weeks. I like to think that Yeshua "healed" me for as long as he did because he saw my potential. I was intelligent and well-read, thanks to those years of isolation and my father's dedication to purchasing scrolls from passing caravans. I had a strong heart and spirit, both of which Yeshua believed could be reclaimed from the muck of shame and self-doubt they were mired in. Judging from the others I was to meet, Yeshua gathered fierce and courageous women.

Our sessions together always included a visit to the leper camp, where I learned to cultivate my skills in anointment. Most days, we also visited the harbor, our starting point for long walks along the shore of the lake or meandering forays up into the hills. The harbor was where Yeshua performed his first miracle in my presence. Not that I knew it at the time.

We were approaching the narrow beach where Magdala's fishing boats unloaded their catches one morning, just as my fisherman friend Ehud pulled in. Seeing us, Ehud dropped his nets and hurried over.

"Magda! Dear girl, I am so happy to see you outside again." Ehud's sea-toughened skin crinkled around his eyes, and his chapped lips widened into a smile. "Come Judah, Moshe, Meir! Come see who has risen."

I cowered into my cloak and took a step back, using Yeshua as a shield against Ehud's enthusiasm. I should not have been afraid of Ehud, for he was my friend, and the only person in Magdala who had dared come visit me during my isolation. Occasionally, he had brought one of his many sons with him, and they filled me in on gossip around the lake, not minding my silence. To them, I was the daughter and little sister that they never had; to me, Ehud and his sons were the boisterous family that I often longed for.

But on that morning, I was not ready to confront him or his sons, not out in the open. Too many men, even if they were friendly and loving. Yeshua raised a hand, and Ehud immediately checked himself.

"Of course, of course, too soon, too soon. Fear not, dear Magda, I will tell them to stay back." Ehud returned to the shoreline, where one by one, his sons were beaching their boats, hauling nets that I could see were largely empty of fish.

"The sea chooses to keep her bounty once again, eh?" I heard Ehud grumble to Moshe, his second-eldest. "Oh Moshe, Moshe, how are we to pay our taxes?"

Taxes. As the only child of a privileged family, I had been sheltered from the harsh realities of Jewish life under Roman occupation. Back in BC 63, long before my birth, the ever-expanding, voracious Roman Empire had marched into Jerusalem and announced itself ruler of our land. Almost immediately, Rome started taxing us, because what was the point of having a colony if you couldn't make money from it? My friendship with Ehud had opened my eyes to the burdens Roman taxation imposed— he once told me his family had to pay half of their income in taxes every year. Half! Unfortunately, that was not an unusual sum for people in Magdala. Rome was determined to squeeze every last shekel it could out of us.

You probably don't know how much we Jews hated Roman occupation. The Quartet completely downplays that critical piece of our history. Indeed, the four gospels don't even mention Rome until Yeshua goes to Jerusalem. Was that an accidental oversight?

No, it's a deliberate omission, made in the interest of self-preservation. You see, all the gospels were written on the heels of a catastrophic Jewish rebellion. In the year AD 66 (thirty years after Yeshua was crucified, and only four years before the first gospel, Mark, was written), Jews decided they had had enough of the Romans. Miraculously, they took Jerusalem back by force and ruled themselves for several years.

Ah, but never underestimate the Romans. In AD 68, Rome returned, with reinforced armies and a vengeance that was swift, ruthless, and total. The Roman army completely sacked and destroyed the Holy Temple. It razed the city of Jerusalem. Unsated, the army erupted into Judea, torching towns and cities all over the land. Whoever wasn't killed was sold into slavery. You've heard of Masada? The fortress high atop a mountain, where almost 1,000 Jews committed suicide rather than submit to Roman soldiers below? Enough said.

Against this historical backdrop, the men who wrote in the names of Matthew, Mark, Luke, and John were terrified of poking the Roman bear again. So the Quartet don't tell you anything about the Jewish struggle under Roman occupation: the heavy taxes, the slow and steady impoverishment of the lower classes. There's nothing in those pages about periodic uprisings by rebels in Galilee and Jerusalem, the inevitable crushing of those rebellions by Roman forces, or the Roman predilection for lining roads with crucified insurgents.

No, the Quartet did everything possible to assure any Romans reading their pages that this new movement of theirs, these teachings, this thing later called "Christianity" was not a threat. It was all about mustard seeds and fig trees, fishermen and little children. No need to worry.

Standing on Magdala's gravelly beach with Yeshua and Ehud that morning, I watched Judah's boat sail in toward us. I hoped he had had better luck fishing, though from what Ehud had said, it would take an enormous aquatic bounty to satisfy his family's tax burden. As Judah approached the shore, I saw that his head was bowed, and his shoulders slumped. Not the stance of a fisherman with a successful haul.

Yeshua walked to the water's edge and bent over to wet his fingers, as if testing the lake's temperature. He lingered there for a moment, then straightened his back and beckoned to me.

"Come, Magda," he said. "We still have much to discuss on our morning walk." Obediently, I followed.

We walked to the end of the harbor, then turned north toward Ginosar. A few black-headed gulls flew overhead, squawking in excitement. I paid no attention to them, for I was listening to Yeshua describe his meditation practice. By the time Judah beached his boat behind us, and Moshe helped him pull in his nets, I was too far away to hear their cries of joy. In those nets, which had been empty just a moment before, there now roiled and churned an immense jumble of fish, far more than Ehud or his sons had ever caught.

MAGDALA

5

I still haven't answered your most burning question, I know. You want me to tell you whether or not Yeshua was God. And you're going to be disappointed because I can't answer that question for you. Everyone has to come to their own conclusion on that issue.

All I can do is tell you what I saw and what I thought. And you know what? I never thought of Yeshua as God, at least not in the beginning. None of us did. We all knew that he could do remarkable things. Some of his followers had been present for the early miracles that made his reputation. What was most amazing to me in the beginning was his ready access to an invisible spiritual realm. If you were interested, as I was, in lifting the veil between this world and that unseen other, he would show you the path. It's not easy. It requires turning inward and shedding all external self-definitions, all attachments to the external world.

He knew the way. Did that make him God? Or just a highly-tuned spiritual teacher?

I can tell you that the Yeshua I knew was very human, and he loved being alive. If he was God, then he was enjoying a magnificent field trip to Earth. He approached the world around him with the openness and amazement of a toddler. You'd think he hadn't been living in a human body for the past three decades, so enraptured was he with what he saw and heard and smelled. The scent of the myrrh oil I used for anointment, for example, made him mildly euphoric. He'd shut his eyes and inhale deeply, holding his breath in deep concentration, trying to isolate and identify the essential *myrrh*-ness of the cloud assailing his nostrils. Eventually, I'd have to wrest the vial away from him.

He took great delight in our long walks around Magdala. Fields of anemones, all blushing different hues of pink and red as they unfurled themselves to the sun, would drop Yeshua to his knees in a prayer of gratitude. Walks along the lakeshore might take twice as long as they took with anyone else, if we were barefoot and Yeshua wanted to feel sand granules sloughing over his toes. Hiking up to Mount Arbel became a full-day adventure, because Yeshua had to stop and stroke the petals of a wild cucumber or test the sharpness of a thistle barb.

And when we did finally reach the summit of a hill or mountain, Yeshua would bask in the view like a parched desert traveler encountering an oasis. We'd sit on a rock ledge and look out over Magdala and Capharnaum to the north, or the shiny new city of Tiberias to the south. In the distance glittered our lake, shimmering sea of holiness, a million tiny halos crowning its waves.

It was on top of Mount Arbel that I first came to understand the depth of Yeshua's spiritual knowledge. Remember, for over two years in my father's library, I had absorbed and pondered the intellectual narratives of other cultures, reading the works of spiritual and philosophical masters that my father, through Marcus Silanus, had bought for me. But there was no one to discuss

them with—my parents were busy with their daily activities, and
although Ehud and his sons were occasional visitors, they were
not deep thinkers. The questions and ideas raised by my studies
spun around and around in my head, where I assumed they
would remain unexplored.

Until Yeshua.

"What is the relationship between Atman and Brahman?" I
asked one morning, calling upon a concept I had read in the
Upanishads. "Are they both God? Is one more God than the other?"

Yeshua laughed, reaching into the pocket of his tunic, and
presenting me with a handful of dates and almonds, mixed with
dried-out bits of grass. Yeshua was a grazer. I shook my head, intent
on my question.

"Is there such a thing as 'more or less God,' Magda?" he asked,
a stem of dried grass hanging from his lips as he chewed. "God is
either everything or nothing. There are no fractions of God. There
can only be impediments that we impose upon our access to God."

And we were off, discussing the soul and the body and ego
and spirit. You don't want to hear all of it, I'm sure. But for people
who dismiss Yeshua as uneducated and illiterate, I'll tell you this:
Yeshua may not have had a formal education, but the man was a
walking, talking encyclopedia of knowledge and wisdom. Every
idea that I raised—whether it was from the Rig Veda or the Upanishads, the Book of the Dead or the Tao Te Ching—Yeshua understood it, as if he had written it himself. He was like Google or
Alexa or Siri, the thing you all have nowadays on your phones and
computers, the source you consult when you want to know what
restaurants are near your hotel, or when Napoleon was defeated at
Waterloo, or where to watch *The Real Housewives of Beverly Hills*.
Except that Yeshua had more than facts at his fingertips. He had
total comprehension. He was Alexa or Siri on acid—he offered

dimensions of perception and judgment that you didn't even know existed.

"Of course he did," you Catholics will say. "He was God."

Maybe so—you'll have to come to your own conclusions, as I said. But if he was divine, that divinity didn't keep him from burping and passing gas at the dinner table, like every other male in our group.

One day, Yeshua mistook a poison sumac shrub for edible sumac, and the rash that bloomed on his arms and hands was a great source of fascination to him. We happened to be sitting at the market near Ehud's fish stalls the morning the rash broke out. I had closed my eyes, mentally stepping away from the hustle and bustle of housewives and servants bartering for the day's wares, when I heard little gasps coming from where Yeshua sat. Looking up, I saw him staring at the rash, his nose about an inch from his skin, slowly pressing on a blister with his fingernail and voicing surprise at the pain he felt when it popped.

Suppressing my laughter, I was about to suggest that we return to my home so I could treat him with some soothing ointment, when a commotion at Ehud's fish stand drew our attention.

"You must go look for him, Ehud! You must!" A petite woman, whom I recognized as Ehud's wife Esther, was pulling on the fisherman's arm. When Ehud didn't move, she dropped to her knees and grabbed his tunic. Her tightly braided bun wept silver-brown strands of hair as she sobbed into the coarse fabric of her husband's clothing.

Ehud knelt down to reassure his wife, awkwardly patting her on the shoulders with his forearms because his hands were covered in the innards of a fish he had just been gutting. "Esther, Esther, it is pointless to go again. I could go, yes, or I could send one of the boys. But we've done that before, haven't we? And to what avail? We never find Meir. All we find are rumors. If Meir is with the Zealots, he'll only be found when he is ready."

I caught my breath when Ehud mentioned the Zealots. This group of Jewish rebels was persistent, organized, and fanatic, known for its violent attacks on Roman convoys and Roman agents. Their short-term goal was to disrupt the Roman tax collection machine. Long-term, of course, they dreamed of freedom from Roman occupation and self-rule. The Zealots survived regular, brutal crackdowns and mass crucifixions, yet always managed to recruit more men willing to risk their lives for their principles. Men who insisted this was *our* land, given to us by God, and that Rome must be expelled, by all necessary and violent means. For frustrated young men who watched their families grow more impoverished year after year, the Zealots's message of "self-rule or die" might indeed look appealing.

Now it had ensnared Meir, Ehud's youngest son.

✍

Ehud and his family weren't the only ones unexpectedly becoming entangled with the Roman state. I didn't know it that morning, but while I was blissfully wandering around Magdala with Yeshua that spring, two Roman officials were taking actions that would change the course of both our lives.

The first was Herod Antipas, tetrarch of Galilee. A man ruled by paranoia and insecurity. Antipas had felt slighted when, after the death of his father, Herod the Great, he was given only a quarter of his father's Judean empire. Aggrieved and vengeful, he spent most of his days scheming how to increase his power, either through the acquisition of new territory or the elimination of enemies, or both.

One of Antipas's perceived enemies was a harmless preacher named Yochanan the Baptizer. (You know this man as John the Baptist.) Yochanan chose to live in the Judean desert and baptize his followers in the Jordan River, and this behavior did not particularly bother Antipas, though he thought Yochanan seriously deranged. But when the number of people who followed Yochanan steadily increased, day after day, month after month, Antipas bristled. Convincing himself that the man was a political threat, the tetrarch had Yochanan arrested and tossed into a dungeon. That decision would have devastating consequences for all of us.

The second Roman thorn in my side was a prelate named Pontius Pilate, Roman governor of Jerusalem. Small man, great ambition. And an even bigger temper. The gossip I heard in the market was that Pilate once lopped the head off a foot soldier who joked about his height. "Now you're just as short as I am," Pilate supposedly said as he walked away. I can't speak to Pilate's size because the one time I saw him—the day he sentenced Yeshua to death—he was sitting on a dais, and I was clawing my way through a throng of unwashed pilgrims.

Officially, Pontius Pilate was a prefect, or regional commander, appointed to manage Judea by a man named Sejanus, head of the Imperial Guard that protected Roman Emperor Tiberius. It was not a plum position. Judea was not the cream of the crop of Roman provinces—all it had to offer was desert, a few semi-fertile valleys, and a bunch of raggedy Jews. And we Jews were difficult. Obstreperous, not easily pacified, not like our tame neighbors to the south, the Egyptians.

In his first confrontation with the "natives" shortly after he arrived, Pilate had reluctantly capitulated to Jewish demands that he remove certain icons—small replicas of Emperor Tiberius's head sitting atop poles—that Roman soldiers had carried to Jerusalem. The Jews complained that icons were forbidden in the Holy City, and after mass demonstrations, Pilate had the icons removed. The concession later tormented him. Pilate was afraid that he had sent the Jews a message of weakness. If he was going to control these people, he needed them to know that he was not someone to be trifled with.

The following year, Pilate learned that Jerusalem was outgrowing its existing water source, the nearby Gihon spring. He decided to build a new aqueduct, one that could bring distant water to the city. To bankroll this expensive venture, Pilate siphoned surplus funds from the city's Holy Temple. He knew that Jews considered money in the Temple treasury sacred, to be used only for religious purposes. But he didn't care.

Up in Galilee, we heard whispers of a protest being organized to oppose the new aqueduct. It was rumored that Zealots were leading the opposition. Still, we had no reason to pay any attention to those reports, until the morning we learned that Meir might be involved with them.

Judah came over to his father's fish stall and embraced his mother. "Imma, if Meir is with the Zealots, then he might be on his way to Jerusalem with them right now."

This statement only fed his mother's panic. "I know! That's exactly what I'm afraid of! Meir is heading into great danger!" Esther waved an accusing finger in Judah's face. "Pontius Pilate is not a good man, Judah."

"Fear not," Judah said. "I will go to Jerusalem to find Meir. Before he can get into any trouble." He forced a smile and looked back at his brother. "Moshe will join me, won't you Moshe?"

Moshe dropped a net he had been mending. "Of course," he said. "Of course. Imma, we will find him."

The next morning, as Yeshua and I sat atop a hill in a field of barley, we watched Judah and Moshe head out on the road toward Jerusalem. The wind whispered through the stalks as we sat in silence. After some time, Yeshua reached for one of the barley heads, plucked off a few seeds, and popped them into his mouth. He chewed and nodded. *"Mmm, so nutty. Want some?"*

I was still sailing on the rustling wind, thinking about all that I had experienced over the past weeks. This man had transformed me. I thought I was irrevocably damaged by my attack, but Yeshua had restored my sense of self. He had given me his respect and companionship and never treated me as if I were anything other than his equal. He listened to every thought or feeling I voiced. He told me I was capable of doing anything. And to my surprise, his expectations became my own. Respect and confidence have that kind of generative power—when someone consistently showers you with them, you come to believe you are worthy.

Yeshua also gave me his friendship, which I returned whole-heartedly. In fact, after eight weeks of daily interaction, something more than friendship grew in my heart. I was, I realized that morning, slowly falling in love with the man sitting by my side. We were kindred spirits—we understood each other completely, we vibed. And he was beautiful—your quintessential tall, dark, and handsome hero. This fact about Yeshua isn't well-known, because none of your artists have been able to conjure an accurate image of him. But I daresay that Michelangelo, if he had been living in my time, would have been drawn to Yeshua as a subject for sculpture. Forget David.

Yeshua dropped the seeds he held and reached for my hand. He grasped it tightly and squeezed it. "You are done, you know. Cured. I can't find a single bit of demonic residue within you."

I opened my eyes to his playful smile and squeezed his hand

back. I could live happily ever after in this moment, just sitting here in the sun and wind, touching him.

"You know," he continued, "after this week, I will be returning to my ministry."

"What?" I plummeted from my dream cloud.

"Magda, you are healed now, I must move on." For once, the gentle tone of his voice did not soothe me. Each word he spoke constricted my throat more tightly with anticipatory loss. "You have cast away your demons and reclaimed yourself."

Had I? I had no memory of grappling with demons and sending them forth from my body. But I did feel more peaceful. More content. More loved. For the first time in my life, I believed I had something significant to give to the world. True, I still had moments of fear, I still startled at sudden unexplained noises or movements. But my time with Yeshua had taught me a fundamental lesson—that I would be taken care of, no matter what happened. That even if my body experienced pain, or my soul experienced sadness, I would be all right. Because I was not alone.

I couldn't tell you *who* or *what* would take care of me. Before my assault, I had taken God's existence as a given, even though I had absolutely no personal experience of that fact. After my assault, my perceptions of God vacillated wildly. In one moment, I felt like the lowliest of sinners, to have deserved such extreme punishment. In the next, I felt betrayed and abandoned by an entity that saw fit to allow arrogant, supposedly spiritual men to commit such violence, and then wander around untouched.

All of that mental turmoil disappeared with Yeshua's arrival. With Yeshua at my side, I felt whole and secure. I felt seen and loved for who I truly was, even if I myself couldn't describe that person yet. And it was Yeshua who brought me the certainty that everything would be all right.

I was not ready to let him go.

"Where will you go? Who is going with you?" I asked.

"I will travel around Galilee," he said. "And Judea. Perhaps Syria." His brows furrowed. "Soon, I will go to Jerusalem again."

"With . . . ?"

"With the followers outside Magdala who have been waiting for me." He reached toward my left shoulder for the edge of my veil and pulled it down so he could see my face uncovered.

Oh, those eyes of his, when they looked straight at you.

"And with you, Magda, if you'll join us."

As if I had a choice in the matter.

MAGDALA

6

Neither of my parents put up any resistance when I told them I wanted to join Yeshua's ministry. They already knew I would never have a normal domestic life. My father had made clandestine inquiries into possible mates for me and discovered that everyone thought of me as "the fallen woman." Not someone you'd want for a daughter-in-law, no matter how much wealth her father offered.

And while my mother would have been happy to keep me at home indefinitely, she had to admit it would not be the best life for me. Still, she kept her dream of my future domesticity alive, insisting that I take with me a small amphora of frankincense oil. "If you ever have occasion to anoint a king," she said, winking. "Or, if you want to attract one."

Over the next week, I made my modest preparations to leave Magdala, packing up a few belongings—change of clothes, blanket, oils—in a satchel I could carry easily. My father also gave me money and bank drafts that I might redeem in the larger cities, so that I could remain independent. Had it not been for the latter gift, I would never have been able to maintain my independence and establish my own ministry after Yeshua died.

As my departure date neared, I realized I could not leave without saying goodbye to Ehud and his family. My father had a routine of going to the poorer section of town once a week and bringing caramelized honey drops to the children that played in the streets. It was his way of consoling himself for having only one daughter, for he loved children and was drawn to their laughter as an eagle is drawn to currents of wind. On the day before I was to depart, I joined my father on his weekly outing, crossing through the marketplace to a neighborhood where stone homes gave way to structures made of mud and straw bricks. We walked through the narrow dirt streets, past goats and sheep loosely tied to iron rings hammered into the outside walls of dwellings, for the families here had neither space nor money to construct separate barn shelters. Small children ricocheted wildly around us until one of them recognized my father and called out his name. Instantly, they swarmed him for candy. My father pulled a small bag of honey drops from his pocket and tossed them into the air by the handful, sending dozens of feet scurrying in all directions. He smiled, watching them zigzag through the streets.

In the midst of that laughter, we heard wailing coming from the small compound of buildings where we headed—the house that Ehud shared with his extended family. A low-pitched keening cleaved the air, calling us to Ehud's front door. By the time my father lifted his hand to knock, my heart had contracted into a hard pit furrowed with fear.

Moshe received us. I didn't know he and Judah had returned from Jerusalem. In the living space beyond the entranceway, curtains were drawn over the windows, and a dark cloth covered what I assumed was a small mirror on the wall. A candle burned steadily on the large flat rock that served as a table, and pillows were scattered around the floor for visitors to sit on. A few of these pillows were occupied by friends and neighbors. Some of the women—Ehud's wife Esther and her daughters-in-law—were crying quietly, while the men stood or sat nearby, looking stupefied. I had a brief glimpse of Ehud, who was trying to comfort his wife. He appeared confused, like a shipwrecked sailor washed ashore in a foreign land.

"My God, Moshe, what has happened?" my father asked.

But we already knew, from the dark caves around Moshe's eyes, the stubble on his unshaven face, and the tear in his clothing, right over his heart—someone had died. "My little brother Meir," Moshe whispered, hesitating to speak loudly, as if the volume of his speech could affect the truth of his words, "is dead."

"Worse than dead!" Judah quickly rose from the floor in the other room. His tunic had been violently torn and now clung barely to his shoulder, its mangled threads of linen drooping over his pale skin. "Murdered! Cruelly, horribly *murdered!*"

"But how . . . how is that possible?" my father asked.

Moshe sighed. "You know the Zealots? That group of troublemakers in Galilee? Meir is . . . *was* . . . attracted to them. He went to join them. We all tried to keep him at home, but . . . ."

Judah broke in angrily. "He was stubborn, stubborn as a goat. Back when there was that big to-do about the soldiers carrying standards into Jerusalem, Meir was all fire and brimstone, wanted to head to Caesarea straight away to protest with the others. I had to take him on a fishing trip for a week, just to keep my eye on him. But this time, I failed him. I failed." Judah's voice broke into a moan, and he dropped his head against Moshe's chest, weeping.

"Meir left in secret," Moshe explained, "The Zealots all went to Jerusalem to protest Pilate's new aqueduct. You've heard about Pilate's plan to take money from our Holy Temple?"

My father nodded.

"Last week, Judah and I traveled as quickly as we could to find Meir. But the Zealots had too much of a head start. By the time we got to Jerusalem, it was all over."

Moshe swallowed hard and leaned his hand against the door to steady himself. "We looked everywhere for Meir, but nobody was talking. Everyone was terrified into silence. We eventually had to bribe a soldier for the story." He paused, looked back at his parents, and lowered his voice. "Apparently, a crowd of people gathered in the plaza outside the royal palace to protest the aqueduct. Pilate ignored them for days. Maybe he hoped they would go away on their own, maybe he thought they would get bored or hungry. But every day, this soldier told us, their numbers increased. Finally, Pilate had enough. He addressed the crowd from the top of the palace steps. If everyone dispersed quietly, Pilate said, he would forget the entire incident."

"Nobody moved," Moshe said. "Pilate reminded them that Roman law prohibits unauthorized assembly. He again asked them to leave. At that point, someone shouted that if anyone should leave, it should be Pilate himself. Someone else yelled that since Pilate was so small, how would they know he had left? There was laughter. And that set Pilate off."

"Pilate was treacherous," Moshe continued. "The soldier we spoke with laughed when he described the scene to us. He bragged that no one noticed Pilate's men because they were hidden in the crowd, disguised as common people. One hundred of them! When Pilate gave his signal, they suddenly revealed themselves, swinging cudgels and swords, which they had kept underneath their robes. And they . . ." he stopped. "Well, you can imagine what they did."

He wiped the corners of his eyes. "At least Judah and I were able to retrieve Meir's body. We brought him home just now."

I had been listening to the story in mute horror, feeling small and useless until Moshe mentioned Meir's body. Instantly, I knew how I might help. All Jewish bodies must be buried as soon as possible after death, but custom dictated that they be anointed first. "Oh Moshe," I said. "Let me run home to get my herbs and oils. If Meir has not yet been anointed, I would gladly do that for him. For your family."

"No. No!" Judah howled like a tormented animal.

Moshe grimaced. "It is kind of you to offer, Magda, but Meir's body cannot be anointed. We were told that two soldiers backed him against a wall, so he could not escape. They bludgeoned him with great force. His head and body are crushed. We had to . . . ." he lowered his gaze. "We had to . . . *assemble* him into the shroud to carry him here. It was not easy."

Dear Meir. I thought back to all those mornings that I watched him pull boats to and from the lake, coils of ebony hair bobbing around his face like floating seaweed, lips full and soft, shaping a mouth filled with laughter. I turned to my father and wept.

Two days later, we buried Meir's body in the southern caves.

The day of the funeral, Ehud and his five sons bore the litter holding Meir's wrapped remains up the road that led from Magdala to the burial crypts in the southern cliffs. Ehud and Judah walked like golems at the front of the procession, looking straight ahead, stone faces hammered by sorrow. Moshe, Natan, Uri, and Yoav kept their heads bowed to hide their free-flowing tears. Esther and four daughters-in-law followed in a wave of wailing and crying, while Moshe's wife Yiska shuffled behind them, ripping the cloth of her dress, and throwing dust everywhere. My parents walked together, my mother leaning onto my father for support, perhaps imagining herself in Esther's place.

And I followed them, with Yeshua at my side. I had not had

time to tell him anything about Meir's death, yet there he was, with all his followers. They waited for us at the fork in the road from town before it bore south toward the caves. It was the first time I saw his group of devotees, the fellowship that I was about to join. There were about twenty in all, mostly men, and a handful of women. As our procession passed them, Yeshua stepped in next to me and took my hand, and the rest of them filed in silently. A cluster of female voices, whispering softly and in unison just behind me: "We pray for Magda and all who mourn . . . your peace that passeth all understanding." The refrain was a cool cloth on my grief-fevered brow, and when I turned to glance at the women offering this benediction, I saw Yohanna for the first time. She happened to look up at the same moment, pushing a lock of flaming red hair back under her veil.

Sea foam eyes, soft and temperate. A warm beam of a smile, inviting and inclusive. Her gaze dashed left to right, indicating the women at her side, and from that tiny gesture, I felt gently but surely embraced, like a starfish swept into a protective tide pool, kissed by the flowing arms of sheltering anemones.

Up close, the cavern that was our destination looked like the gaping maw of a beast. Inadvertently, I gripped Yeshua's hand more tightly.

"Do not fear this place, Magda, " he reassured me. We followed the litter into the cool darkness.

"But Meir—" I began. My throat tightened as I watched Ehud and his remaining sons place the wrapped body in one of the ledges that had been hollowed out of the cave wall. Leaving Meir here alone in the darkness, surrounded by other skeletons in varying stages of decay, was disquieting.

"Meir is not here," Yeshua said softly, as if reading my mind. "His *body* will be here, but he no longer has need of it. He is free."

I imagined Meir's spirit floating through the air. He had been dead for almost a week, because it had taken days to transport him from Jerusalem. Perhaps he had already traveled past our moon. Or maybe he was resting near a distant star, marveling at his new mobility.

One by one, Meir's family drew near to say a final farewell. Judah was last. He knelt on the stone floor and bowed his head against the rock ledge holding the remains of his brother.

"Meir, my Meir," he whispered. "I loved you. I loved you, and I failed to protect you." He wept silently, shoulders shaking, until at last Ehud stepped forward to help him up. Judah shook off his father's hand, rising quickly. Turning around, he spoke steadily and purposefully, "His death shall not go unavenged."

We watched Judah walk out of the cave and stand on the edge of the cliff, which dropped off sharply next to the path we had just ascended. He looked west, toward Caesarea, where Pontius Pilate made his headquarters. And yelled out, in a voice sharpened by bitterness and despair: "His death shall not go unavenged!"

It was over fifty miles to Caesarea. Judah's threat petered out somewhere in the scrub brush of the canyon below.

⸙

After the emotion of the preceding week, I felt both spent and relieved when the morning of my departure finally arrived. Yeshua said he would come to my house to accompany me to the road to Capharnaum, where his followers would meet us. I stood in the doorway between my parents, awaiting him. We were all teary. Our breakfast that morning had been bittersweet. My mother had prepared a honey cake, my favorite, and decorated it with fresh figs and a lemon glaze. I savored every mouthful, even as my throat already tightened with homesickness. We reminisced, each of us telling our favorite stories—the time my mother stitched my father's tunic to the rug, when he refused to take it off so she could fix its sagging hem; the time my father insisted he knew how to smoke a beehive to get to the honey, and he ended up nursing dozens of bee stings; the time I thought a bright green chafer beetle was a piece of candy and tried eating it (I was very young). I mentally tucked this family folklore away, as you might today hold a keepsake family photo in your wallet.

The air around our front entrance was cool and heavy, weighed down by a blanket of dust that had blown in overnight from the Egyptian desert. Through the thick haze, I couldn't see farther than the pillars defining the boundaries of our front courtyard. How many times had I walked through this courtyard as a child, helping Lydia carry baskets of goods from the market, or bringing freshly-picked wildflowers home for my mother's admiration? How many times had I brushed aside the grape vines crowding our front door, plucked a fruit from their clusters, and savored its juice on my tongue? How many times had I sat on this threshold, looking out and wondering what my future might hold?

Now, that future was approaching. Squinting into the distance, I made out Yeshua's shape as he slowly emerged from the nebula, indistinctly at first, then ever more clearly, as his radiance chased away the shadows.

Seeing the three of us huddled together, concern crossed his face. "You all look very sad," he said.

"Surely, you didn't expect us to rejoice in having to say farewell to our only daughter." My father stepped forward to embrace Yeshua. Then he reached his arms around me and hugged me close. "You are my heart, dear Magda," he confided. "The very essence of my being."

My mother kissed both my cheeks in silence. When she moved away, my father drew her shawl over both her shoulders.

"Do not worry for Magda," Yeshua said, as he shouldered my bag and took my hand. "I will keep her safe."

"If we did not already know that, she would not be going with you," my father said. His gentle eyes met mine one last time, and suddenly, a small frisson of panic stopped my breath. For a split-second, I did not want to leave, I wanted to run back to my father and crawl into him, sit right inside his heart, where he said I belonged. But I shook the instinct off, laced my fingers into Yeshua's, and walked away.

I would never see my parents again.

CAPHARNAUM

1

*W*e did a lot of walking, that day and for the next year. It's probably hard for you to remember, in your modern world of cars and motorized scooters and Segways, that feet are a means of transportation. Some of you keep track of your daily steps with plastic bracelets. You want to walk ten thousand steps a day? Try forty thousand. You want to massage your feet with peppermint lotion and paint your toenails in "cha-ching cherry" polish? We wanted calluses. Better yet, calluses upon calluses. Because the only way to protect your feet from sharp pebbles and tough grass blades on a path through desert scrub brush is to develop the tough leathery skin of an elephant.

That first day, I had no idea what awaited me or my feet. But I was happy to get started, eager to meet these other followers of the man who was changing the direction of my life. When we met up with them, they were huddled together in a fog of levitating sand at the crossroads northeast of Magdala. Upon seeing us, the women—Shoshanna, Yohanna, and Ilana—swarmed around me like honeybees to milkweed.

"We've been waiting *forever* to meet you and talk to you, you know," Shoshanna said. "But *he* was adamant. 'No, no, no,' he yammered. 'She's not ready for you.' Like you were some kind of delicate shrinking orchid!" She guffawed loudly.

Yeshua rolled his eyes.

Shoshanna was a force, a sturdy athletic figure with the arms of a stonecutter. I had never met a woman with short hair before, and I stared at her pixie cut in awe. Though she had the unmistakable shape of a woman, she stood before me like a man, legs wide apart, hands on hips, and head held high. There was a veil draped around her shoulders that I can honestly say I never saw her use, in all the time I knew her.

Shoshanna came from a family of hard-talking brawny men, an upbringing that gave her a coarse tongue, which took some getting used to. Somewhere in her midtwenties, she had already been married and widowed, having shrewdly asked her father to match her with an aged husband. Her hope and expectation, she confided, was that an older man would make fewer physical demands of her in the bedroom. More importantly, she expected him not to live terribly long. She got both wishes and found herself widowed within five years. Luckily for her, her husband had no surviving family, other than the daughter his first wife had given him before she died in childbirth.

"Ilana!" Shoshanna called to a figure hiding behind the other adult woman. "Stop skulking around Yohanna and meet our new friend."

A petite girl shyly approached. She appeared to be quite young, but Shoshanna later told me she was fifteen years old. Fifteen and already drop dead gorgeous: thick coal hair tumbling past her shoulders, lustrous lashes framing eyes the color of a halcyon sea. Her beauty was all the more arresting for her diminutive size. "Tiny" was the word that came to mind, as the girl stood before me, the top of her head barely reaching my shoulders.

"I have made something for you," Ilana said, "but you'll have to bend down." When I knelt, she placed a wreath of wildflowers on my head.

"Oh!" I said, gingerly touching the floral crown. "I did not expect to be coronated."

Ilana giggled, and her cheeks flushed coral.

"Ilana believes all wildflowers ache to adorn women's hair," Shoshanna teased. "She knows my head is off limits, so she's always looking for new victims."

"*Victims* seems a bit harsh," said a new voice. "I, for one, welcome the perfumes of my botanical tiara." The third woman, Yohanna, now stepped forward. As she folded her arms around me in welcome, the scent of lavender drifted from her red hair, and I recognized her as the woman who had smiled at me the day before, during Meir's funeral procession. "But come." She took my hand and Ilana's. "Peter is getting impatient."

"What else is new?" Shoshanna grumbled.

I thought we would be heading straight to Capharnaum, a town at the northern end of the lake, where Yeshua first started his ministry before he came to Magdala. Initially, we did follow the path north along the lakeshore, but around midday, after stopping for refreshment at a meadow with hidden springs, Yeshua decided to take a circuitous route up into the hills. This was, I soon learned, his default approach to any journey—detour whenever possible, because a meandering itinerary allows you to reach more people. Over time, I realized that following Yeshua meant abandoning all expectations of where you were going and when you would get there.

The day had a dreamlike quality, as I adjusted to the strangeness of being on my own, unaccompanied by mother, father, or servant. I expected to be homesick, and a bit of melancholy did weigh down each step that distanced me from Magdala. But I didn't dwell in that sadness, because I was distracted by new, complex feelings: freedom, independence, and confidence, mixed with a smattering of power. I felt like a sand racing snake, wriggling off an old skin that had become too small, cautiously stretching into a shinier, stronger self.

For most of that day, and the many others that we traveled on foot, I walked and talked with Shoshanna and Yohanna. We chattered about our lives and our families and the people in our hometowns. We pondered such deep questions as whether it was tastier to season lamb with rosemary or coriander. And during those blissful moments of rest, when the day's heat threatened to flatten anything that moved, we sometimes braided each other's hair, often using the lovely and remarkably patient Ilana for experimental hair sculptures.

I came to learn just how different Shoshanna and Yohanna were. The one thing they had in common was a fierce love for Ilana. As we were heading up a hill late in the afternoon, Shoshanna told me that Ilana was the reason she had embarked on this journey. The two of them had lived in Sepphoris in the years after her husband died, and she watched her stepdaughter flourish and bloom with both wonder and fear. Sepphoris abounded in urban temptations and shameless men, neither of which would allow an attractive young girl to grow in peace. Shoshanna wanted to give her stepdaughter the opportunity to know herself and develop self-confidence. So when Yeshua first passed through Sepphoris—with his messages of equality and inclusion—she was intrigued. When she learned that his plan was to visit the lesser-known and smaller towns of Galilee, she eagerly joined his fellowship.

"Ilana is totally flourishing here," Shoshanna confided, when

Yohanna and Ilana were out of earshot, delighting in a patch of nearby poppies. "And Yohanna is an added blessing. She loves Ilana, for she has no children. And Ilana responds to her in a way that she does not respond to me. I'm not the gentlest or most patient person, as you might have guessed."

I said nothing. Her statement didn't surprise me, but her self-awareness did. "I've always worried that my harshness won't give Ilana the kind of gentle mothering she seems to need," Shoshanna continued, somewhat wistfully. "Yohanna brings that missing piece."

I knew what she meant. In the short time I had known her, I already felt Yohanna's warmth and tenderness, quiet complements to her blazing mane of red hair. She had a way of drawing people to her, much like my father. But my father attracted others by making them feel as if they were captivating him, laughing heartily at their jokes, and encouraging their stories. Yohanna's magnetism was more serene. That gentle force would, in less than a year, save me from an abyss of grief and despair.

I imagined that the combination of Yohanna's pacific nature and exotic hair had lured many suitors to her childhood home in Tiberias. In the end, the lucky fellow who won her hand was a man named Chuza, an official in Herod Antipas's palace.

"Your husband lets you travel around Galilee alone?" I was astonished.

"We have been among Romans for a very long time," Yohanna explained. "Some would say their cultural freedoms have sullied our Jewish morals."

Shoshanna sniffed contemptuously. "The only good thing about the Romans is the freedom they give their women."

"Well, Herodias certainly takes advantage of that."

"Herodias . . . ?" I knew I should recognize the name.

"King Herod Antipas's wife," Yohanna reminded me. "I hesitate to call her a friend, because of whom she's married to. But for some reason—maybe she was bored, maybe she wasn't getting enough of Antipas's attention—she has taken an interest in me. She has been so kind, while my husband Chuza is . . . well, he . . . ." she faltered.

"Chuza is a jackass," Shoshanna growled. "It's not enough for him to have one beautiful woman. He has to have his prick massaged all over the palace."

Yohanna put her hands over Ilana's ears and frowned at Shoshanna.

"Protect her all you like, Yohanna," Shoshanna shook her head, "but the sooner she learns about the world she lives in, the better off she'll be."

"In any case," Yohanna continued, "when Herodias saw how unhappy I was with my husband's infidelities, she encouraged me to leave, to take a break from him. And she pressured Antipas to make Chuza release me." A bitter laugh escaped her. "I can hear that conversation now, Antipas saying, 'Hey Chuza, let her go. Think of the freedom! You've only just begun pressing all the flesh in this market.'"

Ilana bent over to pluck a bright red poppy from the side of the path. "You're happier here with us anyway." She offered her flower to Yohanna.

"Yes I am, Ilana, no question about that." Yohanna tucked the bloom behind her ear and kissed Ilana on her head.

"I'm trying to convince her to divorce the snake," Shoshanna said. "But she's a loyal one, our Yohanna."

"For now, we are still married, though I am here. We'll see what happens when I go to Machaerus for Antipas's grand birthday celebration." Yohanna sighed, as if exhausted by the very thought of that event.

I was about to ask her what Herod Antipas was really like, when a sparsely-bearded young man came hurrying toward us from the group ahead.

"*Rabbisayswewillstopsoon,*" he sputtered. Barely were these words out of his mouth when he pivoted and ran back.

"What was that?" I asked.

"Oh, that's Levi," Yohanna laughed. "Our tax collector. He's afraid of women, so Rabbi Yeshua tries as often as possible to increase his exposure to us. He just said we're about to stop for the day."

The clearing Yeshua had chosen for our overnight camp was at the top of the hill we had been climbing. As everyone began preparations for the evening meal, I took a moment to step away. I wasn't used to so much uninterrupted society, and I felt a bit overwhelmed.

With the sun low in the sky behind me, I looked east, out over the lake. During our journey that day, the sea water had lain calm and smooth, glistening like the facet of a sapphire polished by the morning's fine sand. Now a slight breeze was blowing ripples into the reflected rose and plum palette of the sky. Closing my eyes, I let the commotion of the day seep into the wind. The fine grays of evening began creeping in, blending dusk into the fissured stone of a distant wall of mountains.

I took a moment to appreciate the sense of certainty that I had felt all day long. This was where I was supposed to be. These were the people I was supposed to be with. The man I had chosen to follow had ideas that I believed in, ideas that I could help others understand. Ideas about equality and kindness, forgiveness, and love. Spirituality through communion with others. His message echoed the words of the many masters I had read.

While the last rays of sunlight warmed my back, something

shifted in the air, and I opened my eyes to find Yeshua standing next to me. He was looking east at the expanse of cliffs rising from the distant desert. His lips tightened into a stern line as he moved his gaze toward the south.

"Golan in Bashan," he said ponderously. "Ofakim, Sderot, Kfar Aza. Gaza. So much blood." Sadness and uncertainty brooded over him. "We can bring our message, Magda, but will they understand?"

I had no idea what he was talking about back then. Now I do, because today I know what he saw. He was looking far into the future, when the plain beyond that cliff would see a fierce battle in the Yom Kippur war. And farther south, where much later, terrorists would ravage peaceful settlements, and a traumatized nation would exact its revenge on innocent civilians.

Two thousand years ago, we didn't know that people wouldn't get our message. Wars and violence had preceded us, but we hoped that our message might put an end to them. How wrong we were.

Is war always inevitable? Is war a necessary part of history, past and future? That's the million-dollar question, isn't it? And we'll never know the answer. We'll never know what might have happened if you had gotten our message; if you had fully grasped what Yeshua and I were trying to teach you. Why? Because the Roman Catholic Church suppressed our message. It shut down the voices that spoke our truth. It executed "heretics" who disagreed with its own accepted canon and burned all "blasphemous" treatises that didn't tow its line. Then, it set up a power structure of priests, bishops, and cardinals, topped off with one purportedly omnipotent, appallingly inaccessible Pope. Whose heavy golden ferula and bejeweled tiara would make Yeshua laugh and cry at the same time. How could that pomp and hierarchy be reconciled with Yeshua's vision of a truly egalitarian society?

How were you supposed to believe his message of peace and love, of turning the other cheek, when the Church built in his name instigated some of the worst slaughters in history? When the Templar Knights blessed by the Pope rode across this land to slaughter all the "infidels" whose lands the Pope coveted? The Knights never feared for their souls, despite the barbarous acts they committed behind the cross-bearing shields they carried, because the Pope had promised them absolution. Because the Pope "spoke for" God.

That evening, looking over to the mountains and flooding with compassion, I reached for Yeshua's hand and pressed it against my heart. I wanted to counterbalance his uncertainty with love and conviction.

"I will help them understand," I said.

He gazed at me, and for once I wasn't immediately lost in his eyes, for they were glazed with tears. Placing his hands on my cheeks, he pulled me toward him. And kissed me.

That was a surprise.

Also a surprise—I kissed him back.

I hadn't realized until that moment how much I wanted to. Ever since my attack, I had suppressed anything that felt like a sexual instinct. Even though Yeshua made me feel completely safe in his presence and his touch, I hadn't allowed myself to think about romance. We had a spiritual kinship that I cherished, and I didn't want to imperil it by seeking something more. Also, I didn't want to presume that I was special to him. He had so many admirers. They all loved him, and he loved them back. Who was I to think I was unique in some way?

The kiss was his decision. Maybe it happened because he

was asserting love against the canvas of violence he had just seen. Maybe he was looking for a life vest on the sinking ship of humanity. I don't know. I didn't care. The instant his lips touched mine, I was lost in the immediacy of his breath. I couldn't stop to think about what the kiss meant—for me, for him, for our relationship, for his ministry. No, I was like your fabled Alice in Wonderland, tumbling down the rabbit hole, and it didn't matter where or if I landed.

CAPHARNAUM

2

*Y*ou're wondering, how could Yeshua have kissed her, if he was celibate?

Yeshua was not celibate.

You probably find that hard to swallow. You think Yeshua was all chaste and virginal because the Catholic Church wants you, no, it *needs* you to think he was asexual.

Look, the Church has to admit that Yeshua was a man. So it has to acknowledge that, as a man, he had physical needs for food and rest. But sexual needs? *Oh no, no, no, no, no.* Yeshua could not have had sexual desires, because if he did, then how could the Church justify telling its priests not to engage in sexual activity? (Let's not get into the utter failure of that directive.) And what would happen to the abstinence movement? Especially since the Pope has declared all "artificial" birth control sinful—if Yeshua wasn't celibate, then the question "What would Jesus do?" might lead to the biggest baby boom since the 1940s.

Some things don't lie—a woman can tell when a man's sexual appetite has been stirred, no matter how many cloaks and tunics he wraps around his waist. So I can tell you from firsthand observation that Yeshua had sexual desires. But just because Yeshua had a sex drive doesn't mean he was a Casanova. When he met me, he was as much of a sexual ingenue as I was.

The average Jewish man, in my day, had plenty of opportunities to practice his sexual skills and satisfy his needs before he got married. Nothing in the Torah proscribed premarital sex for *men*, and though Jewish girls from reputable families might be off limits, there were other alternatives—servant girls, concubines, prostitutes, to name just a few. But Yeshua didn't spend his teenage years in the company of men who might have introduced him to such pleasures.

The world knows nothing about Yeshua's adolescence, because the Quartet skips over that part of his life. In fact, as he told me later, those years were a time of withdrawal and learning for him. He spent some of that time with the inspirational preacher I mentioned earlier, John the Baptist. Rabbi Yochanan, as we called him, was a nomad who lived off the land, spreading the word of God and the coming of the Messiah. Dragging along a small ecosystem of seeds and insects in his unkempt hair, Yochanan wandered along the Jordan River, baptizing countless pilgrims in its cool, cleansing waters. He baptized Yeshua.

"I consider him a brother," Yeshua told me one night, as we lay together beneath his cloak, looking up at a glittering sweep of stars. "He knew long before I did what my purpose on Earth was."

"He told you your purpose?"

"Yes."

"And what is that?" I was curious.

Yeshua lips curled into a half-smile. "I cannot tell you that. Not yet."

I groaned. "Well, what *can* you tell me about your time with Yochanan?"

"I ate a lot of locusts."

"Ugh! Not what I wanted to hear."

"Locusts are surprisingly tasty." Yeshua propped himself up on an elbow and slid an inch or two closer to me. "Very earthy in flavor. Good with honey."

"I don't like my food to jump off my plate."

He traced the outline of my lips with his finger. "Then you have to bite their heads off quickly."

Rabbi Yochanan took a vow of celibacy. Yeshua did not.

When Yeshua kissed me, it was my first indication that he was physically attracted to me. That night, the revelation continued.

He came to me when everyone else had gone to sleep. As I was drifting off, listening to Shoshanna's light snoring, I heard footsteps shuffling closer. Next thing I knew, Yeshua was lying beside me. I felt his torso warm against my back, and he whispered into my hair, "May I lie here with you, Magda?"

My body reflexively stiffened, an involuntary legacy of my attack. Before I could answer, he reached his arms beneath and around me, holding me gently. "I only want to be near you, Magda, if I may. Nothing more." His soothing voice reinforced the sense of warm security already washing over me like a tide. All resistance was swept away.

Thus began the final stage of my healing. There was, you see, a lingering rift between my body and my spirit, a fracture that had been created during my sexual assault. When my attackers spread my legs and forcibly parted my thighs, and when savage loins slammed my body into the hard stone bench of our synagogue, my spirit flew. It could not bear to experience the physical and emotional trauma my body was undergoing. My internal self quickly disconnected and hurried away. It fluttered nearby, waiting for safety. Years later, it was still waiting.

My mother saw this schism and tried to heal it. Her daily anointment of my body taught me that physical contact with another human was not inherently dangerous. But I still experienced a knee-jerk feeling of detachment every time someone else touched me. When Yeshua kissed me earlier that evening, I welcomed the kiss, but a small part of me disengaged to watch its unfolding, like a dispassionate voyeur. "Look, there you are falling into the rabbit hole," observing Magda chattered inside my head. "Do you care that you are falling? Do you care about the consequences? No, you don't care."

After that first night, Yeshua and I lay together as often as circumstances allowed. Sometimes our bodies were still, and we talked quietly before falling asleep in each other's arms. Other times, our voices were still, and we slowly explored each other with hands and fingers and mouths, always gently, always respectfully. I wanted to go slowly to reawaken my body and teach myself how to feel pleasure. Yeshua wanted to go slowly because he wanted to savor the pleasure he felt. We were like two children—one who was scarred by hot caramel exploding from a kitchen stove, the other who had never tasted sugar—suddenly finding themselves outside a candy shop with the doors wide open.

We were both looking for the same thing, but for different reasons. I sought to reunite my body and spirit, to feel whole. Yeshua wanted to understand the human struggle with temptation and the power of our bodily instincts. He also just liked to be touched.

If I thought Yeshua's preference for my overnight company would go unnoticed, I didn't know the women I was traveling with. Shoshanna and Yohanna pulled me aside after the first night.

"We don't want to pry . . ." Yohanna began.

"But do you know what you're doing?" Shoshanna interrupted. "By which I mean, the how and the what of being with a man? Because we can help you with that if you need it. There are ways to make it easier, even pleasant for you."

Extreme heat in my cheeks and ears made me lower my eyes. "Oh no, thank you, no. He and I aren't . . . we're not . . . ." I couldn't think of the right words.

"No need to be embarrassed, we've seen it all," Shoshanna assured me. "We know how it works—or in my case, with my aged husband, more often how it didn't."

"No, I . . . we . . . ." I tried willing my blood to recede from my face. "We are not together like that. Or at least, not yet."

"Oh." Shoshanna looked disappointed.

Fortunately, Peter was a deep sleeper, because if he had noticed Yeshua's nighttime wanderings, his jealousy of me would have skyrocketed. When he learned much later that Yeshua was visiting me at night, Peter decided he must be coming to me for sexual release. That was all Peter needed to confirm the rumor he had heard in Magdala, that I was a whore.

Yohanna warned me about such consequences, the morning she and Shoshanna confronted me.

"Consider your reputation, Magda," Yohanna said gently.

I laughed at her concern. "Oh, Yohanna! Really, that's the last thing in the world I need to worry about. After everything that's happened to me, I'm not sure I even have a 'reputation' worth considering."

"Don't underestimate our world," Shoshanna said. "It can always bring a woman lower than where she already is."

Wasn't that the truth?

CAPHARNAUM

3

We spent a week in our first camp, on a hill that the Church has now majestically labeled the "Mount of Beatitudes." It's where Yeshua gave one of his most famous sermons. If you want to know what Yeshua was really trying to teach humankind, if you want to understand the gist of his message, you'll find it in that talk. Matthew and Luke both documented the "Sermon on the Mount" in their gospels.

I'll save you a trip to your Bible and summarize it here: You are all the same, Yeshua said, so love one another. And be humble. Nobody is "better than" anyone else. You. Are. Equal. If there was anything that got to Yeshua, it was one person's attempt to exercise power or authority over another. He spent his life trying to convince us of our fundamental internal sameness. Seek that sameness in yourself, Yeshua urged, find it in others, and you will intuitively know how to live your life.

It's a pretty simple message, but boy, has it gotten mangled over two thousand years. Partly that's because ours was an oral society. Stories were passed down from one person to another, told over campfires or at dinner tables. Each time a story was repeated, it differed just a tiny bit from the original version, maybe with a dramatic embellishment or two. Unlike your approach to history today, our people prided themselves on making a story uniquely their own when they told it. There was no premium on getting to "the truth." In fact, there was no "truth," there was just the story, being told by a particular storyteller.

Keep in mind too, as you listen to any tale, that you're never getting all the angles. Even a firsthand witness has her limitations. Remember when I told you that Yeshua came to Magdala because my father had sent for him? That's what I thought at the time, but I learned there was more to the story.

"I had heard about you, you know," he told me one day as we were walking together in the hills. "Before I came here." He pulled a stalk of wild oat from the ground and began examining its leaves.

"You heard about me?" I was dumbfounded. "Where? When?"

"When I was with Rabbi Yochanan. About two years ago. Gossip and rumors make their way down the Jordan pretty quickly."

"Rumors? What rumors?"

"Well, I know now it wasn't a rumor, but when Yochanan and I first heard it, we were amazed. We heard that a young woman had stood before an entire congregation and read from the Torah. No stumbling, no tripping over words, she read clearly and purely, and her voice rang out as if straight from God." Yeshua tossed the oat seedlings into the air and watched as the wind scattered them.

I should have felt moved, because wasn't that a flattering description of my recitation that fateful day? To be heralded by others as speaking with God's voice? Instead, I found myself getting angry. *Two years ago*, he said, he had first heard about me.

"Why didn't you come?" I demanded.

"What? I did come. Here I am."

"No, no, why didn't you come *back then*, when you heard the news? If the story was so amazing, why didn't you come to meet me *then*?" My voice rose in pitch. I stopped walking. Suddenly, I needed more air.

"Magda, I . . . ."

"*No!*" I screamed. "If that was such an extraordinary event, if I was such a marvel, to be speaking with God's voice, weren't you curious about who I was? Didn't you want to see me in person? *Why didn't you come!?*"

Yeshua was speechless. He reached a hand out, but I slapped it away.

"Because if you had come when you first heard, if you had shown *any interest* in me, we would have met earlier," I cried. "What happened to me would still have happened, but I wouldn't have spent *years* in terror. I wouldn't have spent *years* holed up in a small room, too scared to leave the house, too traumatized to speak to anyone. I wouldn't have spent *years* . . ." Hyperventilating now, the tears came so fast, I stopped trying to wipe them away. I subsided into hiccups and sobs, and in that brief interim, he stepped forward and pulled his cloak around me.

"I wouldn't have spent years watching my life slip away," I finished quietly, my voice muffled in his clothing.

"Dear Magda," Yeshua shushed. "Dear, dear Magda. I am sorry for all your pain. I wanted to come to you, I did, but it wasn't time yet. Your life was shaping itself during those years. Slowly, painfully, I know, but you were growing through all that pain."

"It didn't feel like I was growing," I said between hiccups. Calming now, breathing in his smell through the linen threads of his tunic, I wanted to keep him talking so we could stay close. "But I suppose you had to go grow your own ministry."

"Yes, for a short while, I went to Capharnaum. I began

teaching and healing people. But then Yochanan was arrested, and Herod Antipas received news of my so-called miracles in Capharnaum, and soldiers began popping up all over the city. I was considering whether to go into hiding when your father's message arrived. And I knew the time had come to meet you."

In Yeshua's mind, our meeting was predestined. It could not happen any earlier than it was supposed to happen. He came to me, in part, because he had to escape Antipas's radar.

Now, Yeshua was prepared to pick up his ministry where he had left off.

The Sermon on the Mount, as Christians today know it, was the talk that relaunched that ministry. It attracted quite a crowd, despite the fact that it was held in the middle of nowhere. How did we manage that, you might wonder? We didn't have social media or television or even billboards to advertise the event. Ah, well, your modern televangelists would be envious of our door-to-door spiritual sales tactics.

When we entered a new town or village, Yeshua immediately introduced himself. "People are more likely to listen to a friend," he rationalized, "than a total stranger." He'd go to the poorest neighborhood in town, knock on a door, and invite himself in, to the bewilderment of the family living there. Explaining that he was traveling around Galilee to get to know its people, he'd sit down on the floor, or on a chair, if one was nearby, and he'd ask the residents to tell him about their lives.

Can you imagine? A complete stranger barging in and planting himself in your home? Your instinct would be to grab a club and chase him into the closest pile of nettles, right? But before you could move a muscle, Yeshua would, I guarantee you, mesmerize you into inertia and compliance.

It was his being. His energy. His voice. I knew from my own

experience that, when Yeshua asked you to talk to him, it was impossible to refuse. His low measured murmur, like a gently rocking boat on a placid lake, reassured you that all was good, all was calm. His spellbound attention convinced you that whatever you had to say was fascinating. And his eyes brought you into a space of suspended reality, where it was just the two of you, one talking, one listening, and you had all the time in the world. Invariably in these homes, stories of pain and hardship gushed forth, like the waters of a flooded river exploding through a dam that finally wearied of holding them back.

Meanwhile, some of us would head over to the marketplace, to spread the news of Yeshua's arrival and to purchase food. The plan was not to strain the hospitality of an already impoverished family, but to bring them a meal that we might share with anyone who showed up.

Yeshua loved these communal meals. I never met anyone who relished food as much as he did. His eyes would light up with pure delight, maybe even a touch of gluttony, when he saw a feast table spread with exotic dishes and delicacies.

The meal was vital to his ministry. Wherever we went, whatever house we entered, Yeshua made certain there was a shared meal of some sort. He deliberately and thoughtfully brought people together to eat with each other, people who might otherwise never eat side by side—fishermen and bankers, beggars and tax collectors, prostitutes and Pharisees. Not that he could always achieve such diversity at his table, but he encouraged us to invite everyone we encountered. Whether or not they attended was up to them.

The point was to nourish our bodies with food and our souls with community. Because a common table erases the differences that society places on us.

"It is hard to snub someone on the street, when you have shared wine and laughter with him the day before," he reasoned.

Of course, it's one thing to bring people together for a meal, quite another to expand that spiritual communion into a transformation of society. Had he lived longer, Yeshua might have begun building the "kingdom of God" he envisioned. As it turned out, that task would fall to me.

The crowd that assembled for the Sermon on the Mount numbered more than I had ever seen gathered for any speaker. Yeshua sat under the shade of an enormous black mulberry tree that was buzzing with dragonflies and cicadas. Peter had urged him to stand on a large stone that he had rolled over from a nearby rockfall, so that Yeshua could look out over the crowd as he spoke. But Yeshua chose to sit, inviting his listeners to do the same. It was not his inclination to tower over others. Nor did he need to—his voice, its tone and inflection, his choice of words, they all conveyed authority.

I wish you could have heard him that day. I was to hear many sermons that Yeshua gave over the next year, but in my memory, this one surpassed the rest. You can read its essence in the Quartet—Matthew got the gist of it, adding some nice poetic flourishes to the Beatitudes—but it isn't the same as hearing it, let alone being there in person to listen. If you can't understand how one man was able to inspire an entire population with his message, it's because you weren't there to experience him directly. Yes, Yeshua was charismatic and charming, but when he delivered a sermon as he did that day, his energy and conviction were infectious.

Remember the "I Have a Dream" speech by Martin Luther King? On paper, its words are poetic, moving, and powerful. But listen to a recording of Dr. King delivering those words, and you will experience something more—an electric tingling at the back of your neck, a sharp contraction of tiny muscles in your skin, a thrilled quickening of your heart. You'll remember the exact intonation of Dr. King's voice when he called out, "I have a *dream* today!" And if you had the extraordinary fortune of being there in person (as I did, because Yeshua pulled me out of my reverie up Here, to go back to Earth and hear it), you would have felt Dr. King's intensity, you would have known the kind of revolutionary energy that can take root and grow in a crowd of rapt listeners.

Yeshua had that kind of power. I stood with Yohanna, under the mulberry, some distance behind him. Words poured out of him like raindrops pattering onto a parched earth, in a melodious, hypnotic cadence. The whirring insects overhead were an ensemble of lyres and cymbals singing with him, swelling and ebbing from piano to forte and back again. Straggling audience members who arrived late stood at the outer perimeter of the listening circle. They edged in slowly, drawn by his voice, compelled to get closer.

Under the mulberry, we swayed to the rhythm of Yeshua's voice. Yohanna reached for my hand. You might laugh at this, since the two of us had known each other for a little less than a week, but our rapport blossomed that afternoon into a friendship that would last a lifetime, through that mutual grip and the anchor of Yeshua's connective truth. We were the salt of the earth and the light of the world. We would turn our cheeks and give our cloaks. We would swear no oaths and store no treasures and serve no master but God. And we would love—oh yes, we would *love*—

each other, of course! And our enemies? It might be difficult, but we would try. We would try, and we might succeed, because we had each other. We *were* each other. In fact, by the end of the speech, Yohanna and I felt so much a part of one another that we were breathing in unison.

Yeshua ended his talk with a lyrical litany of blessings, drawing out and repeating the word *blesséd* a dozen times. Everyone basked in the spread of grace and benediction, so that when he fell silent, nobody moved.

After several moments, Peter broke the spell, standing up and calling out to the multitude.

"And now, Rabbi will heal those who need healing. Please form a line, right . . . here." Using his left foot, Peter scratched a horizontal bar into the dirt, several yards away from where Yeshua was sitting. People in the crowd rose reluctantly, looking awed or bewildered, still processing what they had heard. Peter, acting every bit the proud lieutenant at Yeshua's side, began organizing the supplicants into a row under the tree.

I was still holding Yohanna's hand, thinking about what a treasure it was to have a like-minded female friend, when loud shouting interrupted my thoughts.

"But will the Romans be destroyed? Will God smite them down and annihilate them?"

Impatience propelled someone through the throng of petitioners.

"Judah!" I was surprised to see Ehud's eldest son, so soon after Meir's burial.

He didn't turn his head when I called out. Judah wasn't here to engage in social pleasantries. He was here, it appeared, to bait Yeshua. "What will God do for *us*, if we do what you say?" he demanded.

Yeshua did not bite. "All God asks is that you do what should be done today and not worry about tomorrow. Let God worry about tomorrow."

This was not what Judah wanted to hear. "Yes, yes, yes, I know, I heard that." He shifted his feet uneasily, pacing back and forth next to the trunk of the mulberry tree and shaking his head. "I heard you say that I should love my enemy. But how am I to love my enemy if my enemy has murdered my little brother?" Judah stopped before a cleft in the bark, dug his fingernails in, and tore off a large swath of the outer wood. Fiercely, he crushed the husk between his two hands, then dropped the pieces onto the ground. "How am I to love my enemy if he has beaten my beloved brother's body to a pulp? How am I to love him if he has crushed my brother's bones and cracked open his skull?" He stared at the pile of wooden splinters in the dirt. "Tell me that, Rabbi!"

Yeshua watched the display without moving a muscle. When Judah finished, he rose from the rock he had been sitting on and stepped over to pick up the bits of bark at Judah's feet. Holding them in a pile in his palms, Yeshua walked over to the exposed space on the tree and placed his hands on the trunk, feeling the edges of its wound. When he stepped away, the bark was again whole, fused together. Even the fissure that had existed before was now sealed.

Amazement stole Judah's passion and voice. He stood gaping at the mulberry tree.

Yeshua placed a hand on Judah's shoulder. "What God asks is not always easy. But it is the only way."

"Rabbi, what . . . ?" Judah blinked his eyes a few times and gazed at the spot on the ground where he had dropped the mulberry splinters. Yeshua waited patiently for him to finish the question. But Judah's head remained bowed, and he said nothing.

After a few moments, Yeshua stepped onto the rock and looked out over the entire gathering. "God's way is the only way," he repeated. "The only way to a lasting peace. Peace for your country. Peace for your families. Peace for yourselves."

"Rabbi, Rabbi!" Now Judah knelt, raising his hands in supplication above tear-stained cheeks. "Rabbi, please . . . will you teach me? May I follow you, so that I may learn?"

Yeshua gazed gravely at the man before him. "I have been waiting for you."

CAPHARNAUM

4

*H*umbly, quietly, without fanfare—the healing of the mulberry tree is a perfect example of how Yeshua tried to accomplish his miracles. Most of the people who heard the blessings Yeshua spoke in the Sermon on the Mount had no idea that anything extraordinary had taken place, not unless they happened to be standing near Judah. And the Quartet doesn't mention it.

No, the Quartet preferred big-ticket transformations. Healing was only noteworthy if it involved humans. They wanted drama, paralyzed people being lowered through rooftops, demoniacs frothing at the mouth one minute and being restored to gentle sociability the next. Miracles with a capital *M*.

Some of you cringe at the word *miracle*, I know. There are always doubters. Doubters who say that all of Yeshua's so-called miracles have rational explanations. Doubters who insist that, when Mark, Matthew, and John tell the story of Yeshua walking on water toward Peter's boat, it only *appeared* that he was walking on water, because it was nighttime, and there was a storm, and the rough waves disguised the fact that the water was shallow.

Doubters who say that anyone who claimed to be healed by Yeshua was never really sick or blind or paralyzed in the first place.

You've uncovered so much about the world you live in, so many scientific *facts*, your instinct is to dismiss all the observations of people who lived two thousand years ago, people who, in your opinion, knew absolutely nothing.

But why not allow for just a glimmer of mystery in your world? Why keep your heart on such a short leash?

"There are more things in heaven and earth, Horatio, than are dreamt of in our philosophy," Hamlet says. Insightful man, that Shakespeare. In the vast cosmos of universes among universes that exist beyond the atmosphere of your Earth, do you really think that the one tiny speck of life you know as mankind could come to understand everything there is to know about *everything*? The Greeks called that hubris. I call it arrogance.

But I'm not here to debate. I'm here to tell my story, a story that has been stifled for far too long. Had my story been allowed to spread from the beginning, had Yeshua's vision been conveyed and launched in good faith, unimpeded . . . well, it might all have been different.

✢

I didn't see most of the miracles that made Yeshua's reputation. The walking on water, the multiplication of fish and bread and wine, the raising of people from paralysis or illness or death, the sensational exorcisms—those miracles took place in Capharnaum and around Galilee before he came to Magdala to meet me. I have no doubt that they occurred, because they got Herod Antipas's attention. Jittery Antipas barely had a moment's rest after tossing Rabbi Yochanan into his dungeon, before he started receiving reports of a new prophet performing wondrous feats on the shores of Galilee.

You might wonder why Yeshua began his ministry in Capharnaum, a fishing town on the northern tip of the lake. Why didn't he start his teaching in Nazareth, where he was born and raised? Well, the truth is, he did try his hometown first. But the people of Nazareth wanted nothing to do with him. As far as they were concerned, Yeshua was and always would be a bastard son conceived out of wedlock, no matter what fantastic tales about doves and angels Maryam and Yosef conjured up. To Nazareth, Yeshua was a carpenter, not a prophet. When he returned to them after being gone for over a decade, spewing incomprehensible parables and stories of God's kingdom, the Nazareans decided he was crazy and chased him out.

So Yeshua performed his early magic elsewhere, in Capharnaum and surrounding towns, eventually drawing Antipas's anxious eyes and lethal gaze. Antipas immediately sent troops to Capharnaum to investigate. Much as he loved Rabbi Yochanan, Yeshua did not want to become Yochanan's cellmate, so he took that opportunity to answer my father's plea and came to Magdala.

✣

I had never been to Capharnaum. To hear Peter tell of his hometown's many splendid attributes and diversions, you'd think it was as grand a metropolis as Sepphoris or Tiberias. But those cities had been planned, with thoughtfully considered municipal points of interest. Capharnaum was different: it owed its existence to an Eastern trade route. Its ramshackle collection of structures had been cobbled out of the desert two hundred years earlier, primarily to accommodate and exploit the nearby *caravanserai* of desert traders and the commerce they offered.

By the time I visited, the town was comprised of upstanding citizens—mostly merchants, fishermen, and stonecutters who worked the dark basalt rock that paved the marketplace and walled the buildings surrounding it. For every long-term resident, however, there was another person just passing through. Traders and camel-drivers and other caravan hangers-on roamed the streets, released from arduous slogs through deserts and mountains. They arrived with nerves frayed by weeks of spitting camels and jittery passengers fearful of bandits.

A few of these transients sought peace and quiet, and found their way into our synagogue, which was open to all. Far more of them craved entertainment and pleasure-induced oblivion. For such people, Capharnaum offered the "Wolf's Quarter," a collection of run-down buildings and shacks of ill repute reached by narrow channels of foul-smelling alleys. In the Wolf's Quarter, you could find any manner of diversion, for however long it took to relieve you of all your money.

We passed through this neighborhood as our group entered the city, a few days after Yeshua's sermon. The stench of stale ale and urine wafted around us, and rats scampered quickly into piles of rotting trash as we hurried past. Yohanna, Shoshanna, Ilana and I pulled our veils tightly against our faces and tried not to breathe through our noses. When we emerged from the stink, I saw that a small feeding frenzy of men trailed us. It took me a moment to realize that the lure was Ilana—her beauty was calling them out like chum to starving sharks. I watched hungry eyes flicker over us, settle on Ilana, and lock into focus. Shoshanna noticed them too.

"Reprobates," she grumbled. "I've half a mind to smack the one with his tongue hanging out."

"That would not accomplish anything," Yohanna said, pulling Ilana's shawl over her head.

"Maybe not, but I would feel so much better."

An old fear gripped my heart. "We must find a way to protect Ilana when she goes outside. She'll need company," I said. "A man."

Our discussion was cut short by our arrival at the town synagogue. A modest, square structure, with a two-pillared porch and arched entryway, the building looked more like a residence than a place of worship. The only indication to a passerby that this structure might be something other than a dwelling was its large round dome. Constructed from the same gray basalt rock as other buildings in the city, the dome was unadorned, as was the rest of the synagogue, save for a white marble frieze running between the cylindrical columns on its front porch. This simple embellishment depicted scenes of ordinary life: fishermen, farmers, and merchants at work.

A wide, flat step made of identical marble invited passersby to the door. As I stepped onto it, I noticed an inscription at its base: "He is within." It made me smile.

"You like it," Yeshua said behind me, placing his hand between my shoulder blades. Instantly, the tension I had been holding from our passage through the city melted away.

"It's perfect," I said. "Simple and precise."

"Castus did an excellent job."

"Castus?"

"Gnaeus Cornelius Castus, commander of the local garrison of Roman soldiers that protects Capharnaum. He built this temple for me, as a gesture of thanks. Perhaps your father told you that I had done some healing before I came to you?"

My father had told me very little about Yeshua, perhaps wanting me to come to my own conclusions. But Ehud, when he came to visit me during those dark years, had passed along rumors of

Yeshua's miracles. One of the stories Ehud had shared was that Yeshua had helped a Roman officer who came to him because his slave was dying.

"I heard that a centurion asked you to heal one of his servants," I said. "Was that Castus?"

Yeshua nodded. "Technically, Castus is not a centurion, but he has plenty of authority nevertheless."

"And his servant was ill?" It was strange that a Roman soldier would appeal to a Jewish healer for assistance. Stranger still, that a Roman would care so much about a slave.

"Well, the man who was ill was not a slave. He was . . . ." I watched Yeshua's face soften with compassion, as he searched for the right word. "He was someone whom Castus cared deeply about."

"He was a *sodomite*," Peter scowled, coming to look for us.

Yeshua frowned. "Peter, we have spoken about this. What have I said about love?"

"You have said many things about love."

"Indeed, but perhaps if I remind you of what I said about this *particular* situation, it will help you fight the prejudice you hold toward Castus."

"I doubt it," Peter muttered quietly.

"'Where there is true love, there can be no sin,'" Yeshua continued. "No sin, Peter."

"Yes, Rabbi." Peter hurried into the building that would become our home.

I had no particular opinion about homosexuality. Although I grew up with the command that God had given to Moses—"And with a male you shall not lie as one lies with a woman"—what Yeshua had just said about love made sense to me. Also, the Eastern religious texts that I had studied during my isolation did not prohibit love between two people of the same sex. Surely, love was love, regardless of who was doing the loving? It wasn't the first time that Yeshua's statements contravened established Jewish teachings. But everything I had experienced since meeting this man taught me new ways of seeing the world.

Regardless of the origins of the synagogue, Peter was very proud of it, and he animatedly guided our group around the interior. The front door through which we entered led to a large devotional chamber, a circular room with walls that curved upward, merging into a large domed roof. All along the seam between roof and walls, circumscribing the base of the dome like a crown, was a series of flat, open windows. These light-filled apertures saved the chamber from the atmospheric gloom the dark stone would have cast. Now, at the height of day, sunlight crisscrossed the room in shifting rays of illumination. I closed my eyes and basked in its drifting shafts, listening to Peter half-heartedly.

"The local Roman commander, Gnaeus Cornelius Castus, felt indebted to our Rabbi and wanted to demonstrate his thanks by building this edifice," Peter explained.

"Why is there a Roman garrison here at all?" Shoshanna asked.

To my surprise, Levi stepped forward to answer her question. Over the past week, I had barely gotten to know this shy member of our group, other than to learn that he had been a tax collector for the Romans. Every time I approached him, he hurried away.

"The soldiers are here to protect the nearby trade route," Levi said. "Our local tax and customs office is one of the busiest in Galilee. And nothing is more important to Rome than the smooth transfer of money from its occupied territories." His voice contained no hint of sarcasm.

Behind me, Judah scoffed aloud. "Nothing, that is, except the random murder of their citizens." Judah had retreated under cover of his mantle and was clenching and unclenching his fists along its edges. I tried catching his eye, but he avoided my gaze.

Yeshua scrutinized Judah solemnly.

"'Judge not, lest ye be judged,'" said Levi, repeating words that Yeshua had spoken days earlier. Levi placed a reassuring hand on Judah's shoulder, but Judah shook him off and slunk away to the room's perimeter wall. There, he sat down on a stone bench, withdrawing into the gloom.

"Be patient with him," Yeshua had told us, when he allowed Judah to join our fellowship. We could all see that Judah needed our patience. His grief about his brother's savage death had a chokehold over him, yet Judah was too proud to ask for help. Because of our friendship, and the small kindnesses Judah had shown me during my years of isolation, I felt a particular bond with him. On the day that we left the Mount of Beatitudes, I tried rekindling it.

"What do you think of our Rabbi, Judah?" I asked, falling into step beside him. "Were you moved by his words?"

"Of course I was moved, Magda," Judah said. "But . . . ." His face twitched as he tried to reconcile these new thoughts with the old ones in his brain. "I believe in our Rabbi's command to love and be kind to others. I have always tried to live like that. But everyone, Magda? Everyone? Even the Romans?" Judah stopped walking, as if contemplation of kindness to Romans required his full attention. "Maybe, *maybe*, I can be 'kind' to the Roman soldier who does nothing to harm me. After all, he is only doing his job, patrolling our towns. He has no more control over what he is told to do than we do."

"And maybe I can even . . . maybe over time, I could bring myself to 'love' the Roman, though I doubt it." Judah's brows furrowed and flattened as he tried out the two alternatives, Roman as enemy, Roman as puppet. "Again, only if I could convince myself that the Roman was a pawn just like me."

"But not the Roman commanders. No, not *Pilate!*" The prefect's name spewed out of Judah's mouth like a bitter clump of mugwort. "Not the brute who has no understanding of the sanctity of human life! Not the pig who gave the order to . . . to . . . ." Without warning, Judah's entire body quivered, as he tried desperately not to cry. I stood by his side, unsure whether to embrace him and give him comfort.

"Magda, you have not had to collect the 'pieces' of your brother's body and carry them home to your mother," Judah whimpered. "You have not experienced the anguish of looking upon the face of that beloved brother, seeing a mass of flesh that has been beaten beyond recognition, bits of bone, scraps of . . . of shredded skin." He bent over, gripping his chest and breathing shallowly. I hunched next to him and gently rubbed his back. "You have not," he heaved, "you have not had to wash your hands in a spring and watch the water turn pink, knowing that it is your brother's blood that colors it."

"No," I whispered, my hand stilled. "I have not."

"When you see such things," Judah said, "you can never unsee them."

We heard the noisy ruckus of children long before we entered the courtyard of the house Peter and Andrew shared. A group of six boys and girls chased each other around an open patio of flat stone, where tufts of oat grass and bindweed sprouted between pallets. Plant skeletons kept watch from their chipped clay pots like mummified sentinels. As Peter stepped through the front gate, one small boy barreled into him and fell to the ground. Unflustered, the child hopped back up, about to reenter the fray, when he recognized his father.

"Abba!"

The cyclone of small feet halted abruptly, and twelve inquisitive eyes turned in our direction. "Abba! Abba!" Two more boys and a girl ran to Peter, and two smaller girls skipped to Andrew, wrapping themselves around his legs.

The commotion brought a middle-aged woman out from behind a curtain that sheltered the kitchen. Her blood-stained apron wrapped loosely around her long-lost waist, and it was hard to make out her features because the instant she saw Peter, she lowered her head. The adolescent girl who followed her gave us some idea of what the woman had looked like twenty years ago: raven-haired and buxom, with olive skin yet unmarred by the countless small cuts, burns, and stretches that years of domestic activity would bring.

"You are back," said Peter's wife, Rivka.

Had my father been absent from home for as long as Peter had been, my mother would have greeted him with jubilation. There was, however, no celebration in Rivka's voice. Nor was there a hint of rebuke, even though her husband had left the entire care of home and family in her hands for months. While Peter was in Magdala hiding behind shrubbery, Rivka had stayed in Capharnaum, grinding barley into flour for their bread, slaughtering goats for meat, patching leaks in their roof with clay and straw, and spinning and weaving flax to clothe their children.

Peter chose his wife wisely. She was by nature and early upbringing a submissive woman, raised to believe in her unworthiness, as were so many women in our time. Fifteen additional years of living with Peter, catering to his demands and listening to his diatribes, had cemented her understanding of a man's position in the world—to command and direct—and a woman's position—to obey.

Yeshua's voice broke through an eddy of giggles. "Thank you, dear Rivka, for allowing us to intrude upon your home." The children swarmed him, jumping up and trying to reach into his pockets, and he doled out figs from a seemingly endless supply. I did not remember passing a fig tree on our wanderings.

"Oh, it is no intrusion," Peter interrupted, speaking for her. "Rivka, my wife, break out a meal for us, for we are starved. I'll show my friends the guest rooms where they can sleep and stow their things."

But Yeshua refused this additional burden on Rivka. "Thank you Peter, I am sure the men and I will be quite comfortable sleeping on your roof, as we did the last time I was here. And I believe the women in our company would prefer to sleep in the synagogue, which has rooms for traveling pilgrims. They will have more privacy there, and the opportunity for intrusions upon their spiritual practice will be more limited."

Peter looked surprised. I think he expected our small quartet of women to help Rivka with the domestic chores around his home, with child-caring and cleaning and food preparation. By housing us in the synagogue, Yeshua rewrote Peter's expectations—Peter's, and ours too. Had we women stayed in Peter and Andrew's home, I am certain we would have assumed the more conventional duties that society prescribed for us, and our spiritual lives would have been much diminished. Yeshua saved us from that trap. As long as we lived with him, we lived as freely as any man.

It was a gift I did not take for granted.

CAPHARNAUM

5

nexpectedly, I came to love Capharnaum.

The small pilgrim's room in the synagogue where I slept every night was the closest I ever got to my dream of a home for Yeshua and me. It may surprise you, the fact that I dared to dream of domestic bliss with him, given my conviction that, as a defiled woman, I would never marry. The dream crept into my heart gradually, during the eight or nine hours between bedtime and daybreak, every night for the many months we lived in and around Capharnaum. Those were the hours that Yeshua would steal away from the group of sleeping men on Peter's roof to join me. That time was ours alone.

I'd lie awake, waiting for him, listening to the sounds of Yohanna, Shoshanna, and Ilana in their bedchambers, settling down to sleep, straw crunching in their bed mats as they shifted into more comfortable positions, their sighs easing into slow steady breathing as they gave up their mental burdens for the magical dreamscape of their unconscious. Most nights, I was able to stay awake until Yeshua entered the synagogue, despite the pull of my own exhaustion. I sensed rather than heard him approach, for his bare feet made no sound on the stone floor. As he came down the hall, I felt the air around me thin out, lifting and rarefying with each step he took toward me, the denser elements dropping away to leave a pure weightless ether. Reflexively, my breath quickened and shallowed, so that by the time he reached my bed and joined me under my woolen blanket, I was as lightheaded as if I had climbed Mount Sinai.

Spend every night under a blanket with a man, whispering to each other about your childhoods, gossiping about your friends, spooling out your dreams, and I guarantee you'll be in love with him after a few months. I already knew and loved the daytime Yeshua—Yeshua the healer, Yeshua the prophet, Yeshua the teacher. On some nights, that was the Yeshua I encountered, a spiritual master who took me on a mind-bending meditative journey of self-discovery, showing me how to steer past fear and desire to where my true self lived, guiding me to my own soul.

On other nights, I met Yeshua the man.

By this, I don't mean "Yeshua the human being who had a male body with sexual inclinations," though as I've already mentioned, we did learn much about each other in that sphere. What I mean is Yeshua the human being who struggled with emotions and vulnerabilities.

Like many people, Yeshua had a difficult childhood.

Everybody in Nazareth knew that his mother Maryam had gotten pregnant before her wedding, but contrary to what you may believe, it wasn't uncommon in our time for two people of the opposite sex to give in to their physical desires before marriage. Such behavior was tolerated, provided that the couple was betrothed. But when Maryam's belly began swelling almost immediately after her engagement to Yosef, a man who lived in the far-away city of Bethlehem, villagers raised an eyebrow, questioning timing and paternity. Maryam complicated things by insisting that she was still a virgin, right up to the day her child was born. Her additional claim that this "immaculate conception" was revealed to her by an angel led to mockery and the widespread belief that she was not entirely sane. Yeshua told me Yosef married Maryam because he wanted a wife and Maryam was beautiful. Yosef did not question the paternity of his son. But that didn't keep other people from doing so.

"They called me *mamzer*," he said softly. My head was resting on his shoulder, and I felt him tense. "The other boys in the village."

"But you weren't a bastard," I argued. "Your parents were married."

Yeshua shrugged.

"Did they treat you as an untouchable?" I asked, outraged on Yeshua's behalf. I now understood his compassion toward the lepers.

"Not in any formal way. There were childish taunts and bullying. But I was surprised how much it hurt."

"Of course it hurt." I stroked his hair, brushing my fingers through the thick curls, dislodging small grains of sand and bits of hay. My own psychic pain in Magdala rose up like a ghost, faint from neglect. "Everyone wants to be accepted by others."

"They do, don't they?" Yeshua mused. "People want to be acknowledged as part of the group. Yet they still try to place themselves in categories above each other." He exhaled bewilderment. "Humans are a paradox."

Nazareth's opinion of Yeshua didn't improve over time, as those young boys grew into men and heard rumors that Yeshua had gone to the desert to live with a self-proclaimed prophet who plunged people into the Jordan River.

"When I left Rabbi Yochanan to start my ministry, I went

straight to Nazareth," Yeshua told me. "The day I came back, it was the Sabbath, everyone was in the synagogue, and I wanted to share my good news with these people who had known me from the time I was a boy. The words of the prophet Isaiah seemed right. I stood before the townspeople and told them that I could show them the way to freedom from day-to-day oppression."

"They looked at me as if I were a madman." Yeshua's half-smile was pained, and he sighed. "I imagine they thought, 'What does this day laborer, this *mamzer*, know about freedom from oppression?' They wanted proof. They wanted miracles. And when I told them they would never see a miracle until they opened their hearts and eyes, they became confused and angry and drove me out of town."

"Didn't your family believe in you?" I asked.

He shifted onto his side, and I saw yearning in his eyes. How wrenching for him, to carry the human desire to be understood and accepted, along with the knowledge that no one would ever truly understand him. He looked at me with a touch of envy, as if he wished to be a normal person with a normal life. I understood that wish. The longer we were together, the closer we got to our final Passover journey, the more desperately I wanted Yeshua to abandon his ministry and run off with me—to the western lands of Gaul or somewhere along the eastern caravans—where we might live our lives together in peace.

Yeshua brushed my cheek with his fingertips. "My family resides here," he said. "With you, with Peter, with John and James and Judah and Levi, with all our followers and friends. As for my biological family in Nazareth, well, I do not have as close a relationship with them as you do with your parents. My mother loves me, as every mother loves her son, but she will always submit to the men in my family. My brother James challenged my teaching both privately and publicly. Sometimes, I think he was jealous because . . . ." He paused and grew quiet, looking up at the ceiling.

". . . because he couldn't understand how his brother, the one who used to throw lentils at him across the dinner table, got to be the prophet of the family?" I smiled.

Sometimes, in these heavy discussions, all I could offer Yeshua was humor. I tried bringing him my wit and warmth and the unconditional love that he sought, to compensate for the cold shoulders turned against him. I like to think that I helped him accept and explore his humanity. He needed it. Even after thirty years on Earth, Yeshua the man was a mystery to himself.

⁂

The first order of business for our fellowship in Capharnaum was Ilana. She needed a chaperone to dislodge the unruly male barnacles that continued hanging around the synagogue, waiting to catch a glimpse of her. Peter proposed enlisting one of the Zebedee brothers, John or James. Both of them were large and hefty enough to deter mischief. But Yeshua chose Levi, our shy mathematician. He announced his choice to our group after the evening meal one day, before the women headed to the synagogue.

"*Me?*" Levi was shocked.

"*Him!?*" Peter was appalled.

I understood Yeshua's choice. As a longtime tax collector in Capharnaum, Levi had the respect and fear of the townspeople. Even those who hated him for taking their money and giving it to Rome would never have raised a hand against him, because they saw him as an extension of the Roman state.

Ilana kept her opinion to herself until we women were alone, preparing for bed in the double room we used for dressing. Each of us had chosen her own small bedchamber along the hall, but this larger room served as a private gathering place, where we could gossip, laugh, and share intimacies that we dared not voice among the men.

"Levi is a kind man," Ilana said, a shy smile curving her mouth. "I think he will be easy to get along with."

"He's not much to look at, that's for sure," Shoshanna opined.

"Mama!" Ilana chided.

"Well, you have to admit he looks a lot like a salamander— short arms, small hands, flexible torso," Shoshanna was merciless. "His hair has already begun marching backward on his head. Who knows how long it will be before the last strand steals away? And those eyes—"

"Enough, Mama."

"—bulge out from their sockets like overripe berries on a bush."

"You are the perfect person, Ilana, to cure him of his fear of women," I said, trying to steer the conversation into a different direction. "Whenever I try talking to Levi, he runs away from me."

"Ah, Levi in a group of women is like a skittish fawn newly arrived in a strange forest. You cannot make any sudden movements." Yohanna stretched her arms upward.

"Pah! His fear shouldn't be coddled," Shoshanna scoffed. "In fact, one of us should disrobe in front of him." She pulled her tunic over her head, letting her naked torso underscore her next statement. "Take it all off, let him sink or swim!" she sang, shimmying her bare breasts.

"Mama!"

The next morning, we made our way to the synagogue's devotional chamber for morning prayers. Yeshua was already there, sitting on the unweathered edge of a narrow stone bench, patiently waiting in the dust-sifted sunbeams. To his left sat Levi, head bent, feet jiggling rapidly beneath his tunic. Upon our entrance, Yeshua stood. Levi gave us a quick peek and would have remained seated had not Yeshua pulled him up by the elbow.

"Levi, meet your protégée." Yeshua's hand forced Levi's chin upward, so he had to look at Ilana.

What a sight she was for his timid eyes. Levi could not have been paired with a lovelier specimen of womanhood, nor one more humble. Her shape, proportioned like a sculptor's dream; her head draped in rich ebony waves cascading to her hips; her eyes, startling olive green with a dark pupil that pulled viewers in like a black hole. Part of what made Ilana so captivating was that she seemed unaware of her beauty. Wise Shoshanna, foreseeing the danger of vanity, had taught her daughter not to dwell on her own physical appearance, or anyone else's. As a result, Ilana appeared as embarrassed to be seen by Levi as he was to look at her.

She was the first to smile. Levi had no choice but to smile back.

"There, that's done then," Shoshanna announced, giving her daughter a little push between the shoulder blades, making her stumble a few steps closer to Levi.

Yohanna came up with the true icebreaker. "Rabbi, there is a small building next to the synagogue that looks like it might have been an herbologist's chamber, though it now appears abandoned," she said. "We thought we might inventory its contents."

"I am good with inventories," Levi announced. He was so eager to grasp onto something familiar, something that involved counting.

Yeshua understood. "Perhaps Ilana can help you with that job."

"I do not know much arithmetic," Ilana admitted.

"I imagine that Levi could teach you," Yohanna said.

Thus did numbers, ever a refuge and shield for Levi, come to serve as ambassador to the country of love. Over the next few days, Levi and Ilana stood side by side: she retrieved items from shelves and identified them, while he tabulated and catalogued. From time to time, he called her over to the table where he sat, to review his sums and calculations. As she bent over his shoulder, gravity coaxed her untied hair downward to brush his cheek. Intent as Ilana was upon learning how to carry her ones, she did not notice this contact. But Levi did. Every strand of Ilana's hair tantalized Levi's nose with a whiff of lavender. Each tress startled his skin with a tiny current of electricity. At our next Sabbath dinner, he looked more animated than ever. Two weeks later, hair was not the only part of Ilana touching Levi: they sat together, side by side, occasionally brushing fingers. Gravity had nothing to do with it.

To my delight, the herbologist chamber yielded a variety of dried herbs and plants, as well as a supply of tallow and wooden chassis. Determined to put my mother's teachings to good use, I began assembling my own store of essential oils. Yohanna joined me in semi-weekly forages through the meadows that surrounded town, and we gathered whatever we could find—sweet fennel, cassia, fringed rue, and thyme. At the end of the week, we plucked flowers and leaves from stems, and separated the plants into two categories, those for *enfleurage* and those for *effleurage*. The *enfleurage* botanicals would be gently heated in oil until they yielded their scent; the *effleurage* candidates would be pressed into tallow smeared over wooden frames we had discovered.

"I think I become slightly intoxicated each time we are in here," Yohanna said, as we worked together in the small room. She lifted spent rose petals from one batch of tallow and replaced them with fresh ones.

"'Brewing the blooms,' my mother used to call it." I recalled my mother, standing over the kitchen fire hour after hour, stirring a large pot of herb-infused oil, and felt a brief twinge of homesickness. "When she did her cooking, all sorts of people were drawn to our house by the scent."

"Like a shore lantern calling to fishermen in the fog." Yohanna smiled.

After several weeks in Capharnaum, Yohanna was my closest confidante, other than Yeshua. Yohanna, a married woman who had spent her early twenties navigating the intrigues of a Roman palace, had a depth and complexity of life experience that attracted and intrigued me. And a strong will that she was not afraid to exercise when necessary. As when she decided to follow Yeshua.

"I was baptized, you know," she told me on one of our field trips to gather herbs. "My husband Chuza sent me to Jericho a few years ago, to accompany soldiers who were picking up new slave girls for Antipas. I was supposed to make sure the girls were properly groomed and spruced up by the time they arrived at the palace."

I nodded, looking over the expanse of field and sky around me. How lucky I was not to have been born into slavery.

"We traveled along the Jordan River and stumbled upon a prophet; this rabbi named Yochanan. Wild-looking but peaceful. He was standing on a large rock, preaching words of repentance and forgiveness to a group of followers. Our soldiers, mindful of their 'cargo,' decided to avoid him."

"But I snuck away at night when we made camp," Yohanna admitted. "I'd already been married to Chuza for a few years, and we had no children. Chuza told me it was my fault, that I must have committed some sin, and this was God's punishment for it."

"Oh, Yohanna, that's not true . . ." I began.

"I know that now. I didn't then." Her delicate blonde eyelashes dripped tears into a patch of spikenard. "I accepted the discipline and penance that Chuza meted out on God's behalf. Which always took place in the bedroom." Her voice trembled now. "We were married, you see, so Chuza thought he could do whatever he wanted to my body."

And just like that, Yohanna slid open an inner panel, a window in the wall between the two of us. Hearing her confession, I realized that she and I had each been imprisoned in a similar cell of shame and self-loathing by the jailers who had violated us. She was presenting me with an opportunity.

I stepped over to her—she stood no more than an arm's length from me—and folded my arms around her as tightly as possible. "I experienced something very similar," I whispered.

"I suspected as much." Yohanna wiped her nose with a ragged bouquet of rue. "I didn't know for sure, of course. None of us did, when we followed Yeshua to Magdala. But we heard snippets of things from your Magdalan neighbors—you know, the demon stories."

I didn't flinch, impervious now to my reputation for entertaining demons.

"Then Peter . . . Peter came back from the market with a new report." Yohanna hesitated, unwilling to continue.

In an instant, my immunity to shame fell. An unknown insult hovered nearby, on the tip of someone's tongue, someone I loved and trusted. Should I press her for more? What good would it do? I understood that what I would hear would be painful—still, I wanted to know what I didn't know.

"What did Peter hear?" I asked.

"He said he heard you were a whore." Yohanna spoke the last word so softly it was barely intelligible.

The word shocked me. Defective, crazy, possessed by demons—all of these labels had been flung at me, all were pejorative, and I had been able to weather them. But the epithet *whore* suggested choice and agency on my part, a willingness to be physically violated. Slander like that can have a life of its own.

Because the insult is so malicious and has disgraced me for so long, let me here correct the historical record, once and for all: I am not now, never have been, and never will be, a whore. That rumor that was begun in Magdala and perpetuated so casually by Peter has absolutely no basis in fact. It doesn't appear anywhere in your Bible. (I'll give the Quartet credit for that, at least.) Go check it out if you don't believe me.

No, the main reason my name became synonymous with prostitution is that a misguided Pope from the late sixth century couldn't keep his Mary's straight.

Pope Gregory I. Not the brightest bulb in the golden, gem-studded socket they call a papal tiara. Maybe it was all the years Gregory spent in a monastery that confused him. There were just too many women in the New Testament, he couldn't possibly follow them all—the Virgin Mary, Mary of Bethany, Mary of Magdala, and some unnamed female sinner who anointed Yeshua with her tears and hair. A truly dizzying number of females, and most of them Mary's—how terrifying for a former monk!

In 591, Gregory was writing a sermon, and he decided to make everything easier by consolidating all the Mary's into one female figure and giving her my name. And, for added effect, he made her a prostitute. Why a prostitute? you ask. Why not? Gregory answers. It's so much more dramatic—fallen woman redeemed by the Savior, turns her life around, becomes devoted to him.

Voilà! My name was forever afterward associated with sin and depravity.

When Yohanna told me about Peter's insult, of course I dis-solved into tears. The two of us sat down in the field among silvery tufts of hyssop, inhaling the scent of minty licorice and opening our wounded hearts to each other. I had thought that Yeshua was all I needed for companionship, because he so perfectly understood me. But Yohanna offered me the one kind of empathy that Yeshua could not: an empathy born from *actual* experience, in a body that was female, just like my own. Woman-to-woman rapport, like the kind my mother had established with me when I was recovering from my rape, when she stroked my skin with oil.

From that day on, Yohanna and I were accomplices in the herb chamber. On the morning that we were preparing the rose *effleurage*, Yohanna closed her eyes, brought her greasy fingertips up to her nose, and breathed in their floral scent.

"Imagine being a bee," she said, hugging her body and swaying, "and submerging your whole body in this perfume."

I was about to answer when the light in the chamber was suddenly eclipsed. Peter stood at the entrance.

He minced no words. "A carriage is waiting for you," he pointed at Yohanna, "at my house. Sent by your husband—Chuza, I think he's called? Anyway, you are wanted in Machaerus." Then, as quickly as he had appeared, Peter was gone.

"Ugh. Machaerus," Yohanna groaned.

"Herod's fortress? Why is Chuza there? That's farther away than Jerusalem."

"Machaerus is more than a fortress," Yohanna said. "It has a lavish palace, apart from its many dungeons. Herod must have decided to hold his birthday gala there." She came to where I stood and, without wiping her hands, put one on each side on my face and looked straight at me. We had been working in the herb chamber with roses for long enough that my nose was somewhat numbed to their scent, but Yohanna's movement and the proximity of her fingers reawakened my nostrils. Gazing back at Yohanna, sinking into the swirl of rose extract that swept around both of us, I felt my heart quiver.

She kissed me on both cheeks, with reverence and care, and whispered into my ear, "Now I know how Eve must have felt when she had to leave Eden." Retrieving her cloak from a bench near the door, she stepped outside and walked toward Peter's house. She looked about as enthusiastic as Sisyphus in Hades, heading yet again toward his boulder.

CAPHARNAUM

6

*A*fter Yohanna left, I sulked. But Yeshua had other plans for me.

"Come," he said, poking his head into the herbal chamber one morning. I was dismembering a chicory plant more harshly than necessary. Each leaf and flower that I yanked from the stem felt my wrath toward Herod Antipas and Chuza. Those louts had hundreds of palace servants. Why call Yohanna back? Why deprive me of a female friend just as I was beginning to share my secrets with her?

Ignoring my sullenness, Yeshua escorted me down the hallway to the bathing chambers. The Roman centurion Castus, mindful of Jewish religious rites, had constructed an enclave of small rooms, some with baths, for purification, healing, and blessing. Two of them had large stone cisterns dug out of the ground, which could be filled with spring water from a small aqueduct that Castus had constructed to tap into a local spring.

"Take your pick," Yeshua said, stopping before a doorway.

"Of what?"

"These rooms. For healing. To expand our healing practice."

I wasn't in the mood for games. "*Our* healing practice?"

"Magda," Yeshua chided, "after your experience with the lepers of Magdala, you cannot doubt that you have that gift." He smiled. "It is time for you to exercise and develop it. And I could use your help. After all, I am just one person."

Reluctantly, I shuffled forward. Most of the rooms were dark, with one tiny window to combat the inkiness seeping out from their black stone walls. The last room at the end of the hall, however, had three apertures near the ceiling that coaxed in sunlight. Two wide stone platforms provided an ideal elevated site for anointment. I walked in and sat down on a small bench near the door, stroking the fine grain of the basalt stone with my fingers.

My father once told me that basalt came from cooled volcanic lava. I imagined a cauldron of fire and molten minerals bubbling up from the center of the earth. Stone immersed in boiling liquid, subjected to high heat and shifting pressures. Like Yohanna, assailed by the whims of her husband and his royal ruler. Or Rivka, buffeted by the desires and needs of Peter, who came and went as he pleased. Fathers, husbands, brothers—they all constrained women in some way, offering their opinions or mandates on how we should live our lives.

I was fortunate to be free of those limitations, wasn't I? I should not have thought about changing my situation. Yet the more time I spent with Yeshua, the more I wondered, what it might be like to be married. To him.

"So are you imagining yourself surrounded by supplicants?" Yeshua interrupted my reverie. If only he knew.

I blushed. Not wanting to share my true thoughts, I considered his suggestion out loud. "Perhaps I can be of help in healing some people. But surely there will be others who need *your* intervention? People who are lame, or possessed, or blind . . . ."

"Oh, I will still be available," Yeshua assured me. "But the vast majority of people who seek healing will benefit more from what *you* can offer them."

Thus was my relationship with Yeshua transformed, from apprentice healer to uncertain anointress. Every day, after delivering his daily sermon in the synagogue, Yeshua invited congregants who wanted additional blessing or healing to come forward. He brought them to my small back room.

It was what you might call a "bait-and-switch" operation. People thought they were getting Yeshua, but they ended up with me. Surprisingly, no one objected when I asked them to lie down on the stone platform, or, if we were teaching outside in a nearby village, on some makeshift bench. Yeshua stood nearby, always within sight, murmuring barely intelligible prayers that washed over and through the surroundings, like the pulse of an incoming tide.

And what did I do, you might be wondering?

I did the only thing I knew how to do. I anointed people.

I've already told you how I anointed the lepers outside Magdala. How I adapted an ancient practice—an occasional and largely symbolic rite used by priests to give divine legitimacy to kings and princes—to reclaim people consigned to oblivion. How I implemented anointment skills taught to me by my mother, perpetuating a healing art that was, outside the halls of grand palaces and temples, quintessentially female. In the beginning, I had only a rudimentary understanding of the power of this ritual. Back in Magdala, my anointment had forged a connection with the lepers I touched, making them my friends. Healing both their isolation and my own.

In Capharnaum, however, my anointment practice achieved a new, unexpected level of intimacy.

I laid my hands on people. I brushed and rubbed oils into

their muscles and sinews. I pressed my fingers into their skin, smoothing through knots of tension and coils of fear. My touch dove deep, beyond tendons and bones, through organs and blood, spreading release and relaxation.

Back in Magdala, that's where I would stop, when the person beneath my hands was completely relaxed. But in Capharnaum, I allowed the stream of Yeshua's chants and prayers to carry me further. I felt his energy urge me on, becoming the music for my dance with the person beneath my hands. Once I felt someone's limbs sag into the rock, limp in submission, I allowed my hands to travel over their backs, letting my fingers slide along their spines and up to the base of their necks. There, slowly, gently, I gathered and pressed, in rhythm with the soft susurrus of their breath. Nesting their heads in my palms, I drew my thumbs over their temples and down to the base of their skulls—back and forth, out and around, tracing infinity, again and again—until finally, inevitably, I sensed the lift of that final defensive latch. Always, they gave out a deep sigh, an exhalation of relief and absolute repose.

The next moment was transformative.

Somewhere, somehow, I found myself right *with* the person I was anointing, connecting with him or her in a shimmer of eternity. And I don't mean "with" as in standing next to, but "with" as in within, overlapping into. Being as one. It was a moment of spiritual union between the two of us. And to my additional surprise, I sensed Yeshua's energy there as well, a liquid light surrounding and holding us both. The moment was a free-floating rapture that surpassed physical boundaries and divisions, where our energies converged in a rising tide of bliss.

If that sounds melodramatic, it's because it was. In that space, I was freed from the persistent internal chatter that filled my head day in and day out—"we are running low on milk thistle and feverfew, should I purchase goat or pigeon at the market, where did I put my hair comb?" Lifted right out of that endless noise and distraction of life to a place of quiet euphoria, where nothing mattered except *being*, absorbing the warmth and light around me. It was a transcendent place, a kind of heaven on earth.

Now that I've been Here for a number of years, now that I understand a tiny bit more about *everything*, I can look back at those experiences and recognize what they were—a lifting of the veil of reality that overlays the earthly sphere and separates it from the adjoining realm of spirit.

Oh, how some of you are rolling your eyes! Don't think I don't see it. Go right ahead, you don't have to believe what I'm saying. I don't care. I know what I know. And your scientists are getting there, your physicists with their concepts of parallel universes. Except those universes are not light years away, they're right there next to you.

Here was the transformative part of connecting with people through anointment: I felt more whole than ever before. In that alternate continuum where our internal energies united, for that one eternal instant, we were the same. *Exactly* the same. Whoever it was, whatever stratum of society we came from, we knew that we were no different from one another.

In that moment, we both understood exactly what Yeshua was preaching.

It felt revolutionary because it was. The more I engaged in anointment, the more I grasped his truth of radical equality and its profound implications for society.

You're still skeptical, aren't you? But the feeling I've described isn't entirely outside your realm of experience. You get a tiny glimpse of it when you hold the hand of someone you love. If you're open to it, you might feel a tremor of harmony, the two of you as one amidst the sidewalk crowds and city traffic. The honking of cars, the screeching of whistles may not fray your nerves quite as much when you're in that bubble. Spiritual communion, after all, is a spectrum of experience. I was able to reach its endpoint through anointment in Yeshua's presence.

For a long time, I thought the power to reach that place came from him. It was only after his death that I understood it came from me.

Of course, there were some people who needed Yeshua's unique healing skills. People with physical disabilities, for example. Yeshua didn't ignore them, but he was more cautious in where and how he healed. He had learned his lesson from his first ministry in Capharnaum: no more public miracles before large crowds. Now, all his healing feats were private. The Quartet doesn't tell you about these "minor" miracles because Yeshua asked his supplicants not to proclaim them publicly. We didn't need another round of Herod Antipas's hooligans.

One day, after Yeshua's daily sermon, a young woman came into the anointment room with a baby. I recognized her as the daughter of Capharnaum's only doctor, a curmudgeon who attended synagogue with his family every Sabbath and made it clear that he'd rather be anywhere else. He never stood with his wife, nor with his daughter and her husband's family, but fidgeted near the back of the room throughout the entire service. From there, he could hurry away the moment it ended—apparently, he allotted only so much time every week for worship.

With more than a little envy, I had watched his daughter's belly grow bigger and bigger as she stood next to her husband every week. After my attack, the physician in Magdala had told my parents that he feared I might not be able to have children. It was not a verdict I thought about much, until I fell in love with

Yeshua and began fantasizing about our future. So I was particularly drawn to this young woman. It was all I could do to restrain myself from rushing over and placing my hands on her stomach, that I might vicariously experience the thrill of pregnancy.

When her time neared, the young woman disappeared, and we did not see her for several months. We heard from others that she had given birth to a son. Now, here she was before us, huddled over a small bundle of linen, from which muted cries echoed against the stone walls. She shuffled forward hesitantly, quietly hushing her child.

"How can we help you, my sister?" I asked, touching her shoulder. She startled and glanced up from the cave of her hood. Her strained red eyes and taut lips told me that some great pain had entered her world since the last time I saw her. My heart sank in sympathy.

"My father . . ." she began. "He says nothing can be done. He has exercised all his skills. But my boy, my Yechezkel, he remains . . . ." She could not bring herself to say the word.

"Yechezkel," Yeshua repeated, coming toward her from the bench where he had been sitting. "God will strengthen."

She nodded, keeping her head down. "My husband and I, when we saw our baby for the first time, we . . . ." Her voice broke, and I guided her to the bench to sit. "We knew he could have no other name."

"Yes." Yeshua carefully took the baby from her arms and sat down next to her. The wailing abruptly stopped, as he slowly unwrapped the swaddling around the baby's head. I drew closer to see a perfectly round face and pursed lips pumped by a tiny tongue that was searching for something to suckle. Then I saw his eyes—opaque and strangely shiny, reflecting light when they should have been absorbing it. This baby was blind.

"God will strengthen," Yeshua repeated, placing two fingers on each of the child's eyelids.

That was all it took. As with the mulberry tree, Yeshua's restorative touch was simple and silent, unaccompanied by trumpets and fireworks. He handed the wriggling pile of cloth back to its mother, who eagerly peered at her son. Little Yechezkel, seeing his mother's face for the first time, squealed with delight and reached a tiny hand up toward her chin.

"Oh!" she cried out. "Oh, he sees me! Oh, what a wonder, what a man of miracles you are indeed!" She knelt before Yeshua and began kissing the hem of his tunic. "I will tell everyone, I will spread your name far and wide so you will become famous, I will—"

"No." Yeshua stood and drew her up with him. The baby gurgled and squeaked, and he gave the boy a pinkie finger to suck on. "No, my daughter, do not. I ask you to keep this blessing to yourself. I do not want attention."

The woman gave me a confused look, and I said simply, "Rome."

"Ah, yes. I see," she nodded. Bowing toward us both before she left, she whispered into her linen, "God has strengthened."

CAPHARNAUM

7

*W*eeks passed and cold weather set in. I began looking for Yohanna's return. One night, Rivka gave us some woolen blankets for additional warmth, and Shoshanna and I each laid one over our own beds, and another over the bed of those who were absent. Yohanna. Ilana.

Ilana had not physically disappeared as Yohanna had, but psychically and emotionally she was increasingly unavailable to us, lost in her infatuation with Levi. It was hard to believe that this gawky, amphibious man could inspire such devotion, but the two of them were inseparable. Some weeks earlier, flush with love, Ilana decided to forgo our routine evening bedtime chats to spend time "in prayer" with Levi. Skeptical of the devotional component of these nighttime rendezvous, Shoshanna insisted they take place in the synagogue, where we would be just down the hall.

After distributing the blankets, Shoshanna and I sat in silence, unlacing our sandals. When Shoshanna removed her shawl and spread it over her knees in preparation for folding, she paused. She ran her fingers along one of the side seams.

"Did you know this was Ilana's first sewing effort?" she mused. Holding the shawl up to the lantern, she stretched the wool so I could see the stitches. There were four rows of needle-work: two uneven and irregular, zigzagging down from the armpit to the hem and back again, another two neat and precise, following the same path.

I smiled. "Let me guess. You went back over her seams."

"Sure I did!" Shoshanna's laugh evaporated into a sigh. "She was only six years old. So ready to do everything I did. She begged me to teach her. Always wifely duties—grinding barley or churning curd or spinning yarn from flax. Things I hardly cared about. I wanted her to know how to fight. I wanted her to be strong and independent. But what she wanted more than anything else was to be a wife and mother."

"Those may not be mutually exclusive desires," I suggested hopefully.

"In our world? She'd have to have the right man."

"Well, not that I want to make any predictions, but if it were a man like Levi . . . ."

"She'd be lucky, I guess," Shoshanna admitted.

"Yes, she would."

We heard soft giggles down the hall. Shoshanna cocked her head. "*That* doesn't sound like prayer."

She half-rose from the bench, but I pulled her back. "I think Levi can be trusted."

Shoshanna slumped against the wall. In that moment, she did not resemble the woman I had met several months earlier. Shoshanna was tough and robust, as strong as any of our men, but her posture now looked sluggish and defeated. Of course it did—she was a mama bear robbed of her cub.

"She doesn't need me anymore." Her tone was questioning, begging me to refute her.

I thought about my own mother, who must be wondering

when or if she would see me again. Since arriving in Capharnaum, I had asked the town's fishermen to bring me news of my family and to reassure them of my own well-being. But my father quickly established his own method of information-gathering, through the billowing beard of brawn and gusto that was his trader Marcus Silanus. Marcus had arranged for someone to visit Capharnaum every week and report back to him. Invariably, his agents came to the synagogue and sat in on Yeshua's sermons. They were easily recognizable by the sandstorm-beaten turbans they wore on their heads. I always gave them a smile, because I wanted them to know I was healthy and content. Also, I welcomed their presence because it reminded me of my beloved parents, even if it also rekindled my longing for home.

"Ilana will always need you," I thought out loud, "no matter where she goes or who she is with."

Tears blurred Shoshanna's eyes. I was about to hug her when we heard a loud thud down the hall. Shuffling feet and the squeal of wood scraping across stone told us that the synagogue's heavy front door was being opened. Shoshanna and I hurried to the devotional chamber, arriving just in time to see a cloaked man gently release a body onto the nearest bench.

"Marcus Silanus!" I cried out, as the man drew back his hood.

"Judah!" Levi gasped, hurrying over to his friend's slouched form. Ilana joined him, and she cradled Judah's head in her lap while Levi ran off to fetch some water.

Marcus Silanus turned toward me, dark eyes brilliant against the silver curls that forested his mouth and chin. "Ah, here you are, Magda! Your papa told me you'd find a safe place to hide."

"But what brings you to Capharnaum in person? Usually, when you are seeking news about me, you send . . ." I hesitated, unsure which word would best describe his minions.

"My spies?" Marcus Silanus's mustache stretched over his smile. "So you sussed them out, eh? You always were a smart one. What gave them away, the dried camel spit on their faces? Well, it's a good thing I was here this night, doing business in the Wolf's Quarter, or I'd not have found your young friend."

We hadn't seen Judah in several days. The ongoing agony he felt over his brother's death was so intense that he was now regularly seeking oblivion through drink. He visited the taverns in the Wolf's Quarter almost daily. Some days, Judah skipped our morning prayer and meditation sessions; others, he appeared looking weary and disheveled, his breath betraying the residue of too many goblets of wine. Some of us tried speaking with him. Peter gave him a stern lecture about responsibility and devotion to God and Yeshua's ministry. The Zebedee brothers, after acknowledging the attractions of beer and wine and sharing their own youthful escapades, urged him, somewhat insensitively, to grow up.

I tried a more empathic approach. Leaving the temple one morning, I found Judah sitting on its threshold steps. He looked so miserable that I suggested anointment might ease his pain. He grumbled.

"Don't you see, I don't *want* relief from this pain! I deserve this pain, I *need* this pain, because it reminds me of my failures. I fail Rabbi Yeshua daily. As I failed Meir." He pulled on the blue tzitzit at the edge of his cloak, massaging the tassel that was supposed to remind him of God's commandments. "Did you know, Magda, that I can no longer remember what Meir's voice sounded like? Nor can I conjure the lines of his face. I am losing him, bit by bit every day." He took a deep breath and dug his fingernails into the weft of his tunic. "My pain is now my strongest tie to my baby brother. I cannot let go of it. Without it, I'll lose him completely."

I sat down next to my friend. For once, he didn't push me

away. "Judah, you don't need pain to remember Meir. Your bond with Meir is a bond of love. Love transcends pain. And love transcends death. Our Rabbi has taught us—has taught *you*—this truth."

Judah rolled the tzitzit between his thumb and forefinger, puckering his lips in doubt.

"When I anoint people," I continued, "there comes a sublime moment when I connect with them, when I merge with their spirits, so to speak." Judah shot me a suspicious look. "It's hard to describe, but it does happen. I am one with them, somewhere in an entirely different realm. And you know who else is with us?"

"Rabbi?" Judah guessed.

"Exactly. Because he is part of all of us, in that other realm, in that space where love triumphs over all else."

"Well." Judah let go of the tzitzit and fixed his eyes on me. "I don't know about this crazy space you describe, Magda. Sounds like female hysteria to me. And the love you talk about—is it strong enough to change society?"

"If everyone can be brought to it, yes."

"That's a big *if.*"

"It may take time, but—"

"What about justice, Magda? Will that love achieve justice?" Judah's stare felt almost manic.

I didn't know how to answer his question. "Yeshua has told us to turn the other cheek," I began, though even as I spoke those words, they felt inadequate.

Judah scoffed and headed off into the plaza, as if he'd heard enough. A moment later, he whirled around. "The 'other cheek'? When the wrong that has been done to me is the murder of my brother?" He grabbed the flesh of his right cheek so violently that it seemed he wanted to rip the skin off his face. I flinched and stepped toward him, but he held out his arm to keep me back.

"No, Magda. Even if I could get past my anger and my pain, what do you think would happen if I turned my other cheek to Pontius Pilate? If I presented myself to him and said, 'Here I am, I forgive you for killing my brother. Do what you will with me now.'"

Judah fell to the ground, arms outstretched, palms upright, in a mock supplicating pose. "What do you think Pilate would do? Do you seriously think he would recognize the love I was offering him and let me go?"

Once again, I had no answer. Judah stood back up.

"No. Love—even Rabbi Yeshua's unbounded love for everyone, wherever *that* comes from—love is not strong enough to conquer the Romans. They trample on love, grind it into the ground with their heels, spit hate and disdain upon it. We must have justice first. If we can achieve justice, then and only then, can love flourish." Judah looked up at the sky. "Wherever the kingdom of God is, and however it comes about, surely it *must* be predicated on justice."

Thinking back on that conversation, I watched Ilana stroke Judah's hair with loving compassion. Judah belched loudly and groaned. Levi returned with a damp cloth and water, and began cleaning off Judah's face, wiping away flecks of dried blood and spittle. A large bruise bloomed on Judah's left cheekbone.

"He's a lucky one, this one," Marcus Silanus said. "Lucky not to be in a Roman jail tonight. He was drinking with the lowlifes when I came in. I had business in the back room, so I didn't pay him much mind at first. But when I was done with my affairs, I came back out. And I heard him proclaiming. Standing on a table right before every soul in that room, shouting, 'The kingdom of

God is coming!' I knew him, sure, from all the times I met your papa in Magdala. He's waving his goblet up and around in the air, pointing at the only table in that room that had Roman soldiers round it. He yelled, 'And I mean *our* God, not yours!'"

"Oh, that's not wise," I said.

"No, not wise at all," Marcus Silanus agreed. "But luck was with this boy, cuz there was an officer sitting with these men, and he ordered them to stay seated. Others took up the call and gathered around. They knew your friend, they prodded him, they all drank more and more and got rowdy and mean. And then one of them threw a stool at the Romans. And then, well there were more things flying back and forth than when a sandstorm hits a caravan."

"... *Wrrrr* ... red ... ready ...." Judah, awakened by Levi's labors, tried to vindicate himself. "W-we *wrrready fer revvloosh ... rvloooshen.*"

Revolution? Was *that* the message Judah was spreading? Two days earlier, when Yeshua preached, as he frequently did, that "the kingdom of God was at hand," I thought he was using the word *kingdom* loosely. I saw it as a metaphor for the society based on radical love and tolerance that he envisioned. But Judah had been invigorated by that sermon. He had pulled me aside afterward, more energetic than I had seen him for many weeks. He asked me where our supplies were hidden. I was confused about what he meant, and when I told him as much, he acted as if I were trying to keep something from him.

Now it occurred to me that maybe Judah thought we were gathering weapons and secreting them somewhere, for an upcoming confrontation with the Romans.

Shoshanna shot me a worried glance.

"Most of the youngsters are snoring off their brew in the

garrison jail, but I grabbed this one—" Marcus Silanus nodded toward Judah "and vouched for him. Told the officer I'd bring him here, so he couldn't get into more trouble." He laughed heartily. "I didn't expect him to agree!"

"That must have been Castus," Levi said.

"You know him?"

"Rabbi Yeshua knows him," Levi explained. "And Castus knows Judah. From prior incidents." Over the months that we had lived here, Judah had drawn enough attention to himself that Castus knew exactly who he was and where he lived. "Castus is a decent man."

"For a Roman," Shoshanna added.

Marcus Silanus, noticing Shoshanna for the first time, bowed deeply in her direction. "Oh my, oh dear lady! How rude of me! Look at me, blathering on before introducing myself. I am at your service, ma'am. Marcus Silanus, trader of mercantiles to and from the Far East."

Shoshanna laughed at his formality. "No need for airs, I'm not at all offended. But thank you for the apology . . . Marcus Silanus." She spoke his name slowly, savoring its rhythm. "Well, and I am Shoshanna, a . . ." she paused, momentarily tongue-tied. "What am I, Magda? Fading mother? Temple charwoman?"

"You are a friend to all my friends," I said.

"Yes, that's true," Shoshanna said, offering her hand, because it was clear that Marcus Silanus wanted to kiss it. He did so with obvious reverence, touching his lips to her skin like a petitioner seeking knowledge from the oracular Pythia at Delphi. For the first time in all the months that I had known Shoshanna, she colored and lowered her eyes.

Across the room, Levi coughed politely. "Excuse me, sir, could you perhaps help me move Judah to one of the bed chambers?"

Judah was now out cold, still lying on Ilana's lap and snoring lightly.

Marcus Silanus swung Judah's limp body over his shoulder. "If he were awake, he'd mind being taken from this soft berth"—he winked at Ilana—"to the cold slab of rock he's headed to."

"He's fortunate that the cold stone he will be lying on is a bed," Levi said, "and not a jail bench."

Shoshanna followed Marcus down the hall to one of the empty pilgrims' rooms, while I grabbed a blanket. We tucked its woolen edges around Judah's form, as if by cocooning him we might keep him out of further trouble. Marcus Silanus watched our gentle ministrations, his eyes narrowed in thought.

"Woman's touch. Makes all the difference," he muttered to himself.

The next morning, Yohanna returned.

CAPHARNAUM

8

*A*s soon as she stepped off her horse, Yohanna called us together in the synagogue.

"You never cease to amaze me," I teased, after embracing her. "Where did you learn to ride a *horse*? Why did you not take a carriage?"

"I needed to get back as quickly as possible to warn Yeshua," Yohanna said. She buried her face in my hair and breathed, "Antipas has killed Rabbi Yochanan."

※

Before I pass along the narrative about Yochanan the Baptizer that Yohanna passed on to our group that morning, I must, once again, warn you of certain falsehoods manufactured by the Quartet. Always keep in mind, when you read your Bible (or, for that matter, any historical account) that, until very recently, history has mostly been written by men. And men love to create tropes of femininity to commandeer the truth. Specifically, they like to fabricate mythologies populated by archetypes of women as powerful and conniving, or sexually irresistible and dangerous.

Take, for example, the biblical account of what happened at the birthday feast in Machaerus and how Rabbi Yochanan came to die. Two of the Quartet's historians (Mark and Matthew) have concocted a fanciful and damning story that stars Herodias, Herod Antipas's wife. According to their colorful account, during the entertainment portion of the birthday party, Herodias' daughter Salomé walked to the center of the banquet room and stopped right in front of her stepfather, Herod Antipas, the birthday boy. Cue undulating music. Salomé began swaying her hips, then the rest of her body, in an intoxicating, sexually suggestive dance. (How old was she? The Quartet doesn't say, but according to historical records, she would have been ten. *Ten!* Keep that in mind, as you evaluate the truth of this tale.)

Supposedly, the young girl's performance so enraptured and aroused Antipas that he told her to make a wish. "Anything," he said, blood invigorating his nether regions, "I promise to give you *anything* you ask for."

Salomé being meek and obedient—or so say Mark and Matthew, disregarding the inconsistency between this docility and the exhibitionism Salomé had just displayed—the girl went straight to her mother for advice. "What should I ask for?" Salomé inquired.

Now Herodias supposedly held a long-standing grudge against Rabbi Yochanan. Years earlier, when she fell in love with Antipas and decided to marry him, Herodias had to divorce her first husband. This poor stooge happened to be Antipas's half brother, Philip. "Adulteress!" Rabbi Yochanan yelled out from the desert, relying on intricacies of Jewish law that no one else understood.

Why Herodias should care so much about an insult flung at her by a doom-saying desert vagrant crawling with lice is a fair question that Mark and Matthew do not address. They simply tell us that she bitterly resented the label, and that Salomé's dance at the birthday feast gave Herodias an opportunity to get rid of the libelous thorn in her side.

"Ask for Yochanan the Baptizer's head," she told her daughter. "On a platter." (Nice touch, the platter, at a birthday feast.) That's precisely what Salomé did, says the Quartet. And before you know it—*whoosh! thump!*—in marched the servants with the hairy noggin of the desert preacher, resting in a sauce of its own life's blood. Thus did Rabbi Yochanan supposedly meet his end, his execution orchestrated by a bloodthirsty, vengeful woman and her wanton jezebel of a daughter.

Well. That's one version of events. The other version of how Rabbi Yochanan died is the one Yohanna told us the morning of her return. But first, I need to tell you a bit more about the prophet that Yeshua loved like a brother.

According to Yeshua, Rabbi Yochanan was an inspirational preacher. I can't say what he was like, because I never met the man, but I did hear conflicting reports that claimed Yochanan was deranged. After all, here was a man who baptized followers in the Jordan River, ate wild honey and locusts, wore a coat made of camel's hair that he spun and wove himself, and spent most of his adult life living outdoors in a harsh terrain. Imagine what that does to your mental health, being subjected to the elements day after day, with no shelter to protect you from rain or hail or, as more often happened in our climate, the relentless heat of a desert sun.

But personality aside, there's no doubt that Yochanan was a very popular preacher. He promised absolution through baptism to anyone who came to the river—a quick dunk in the Jordan and all your sins would be forgiven and forgotten. Just in the nick of time, too, because Yochanan proclaimed that the Messiah had come, and that the kingdom of God was near. Gratifying message for all of us who suffered under Roman occupation. It should come as no surprise that people gathered in throngs to listen.

Day after day, as Yochanan's followers increased in number, Herod Antipas stewed in paranoia. There on the Jordan was this wildly popular madman, and up north, there was a magical charmer from Nazareth, supposedly performing occasional miracles in Galilee that defied rational belief. Antipas pondered which of the two men to toss into his empty dungeon. In the end, when Yochanan loudly pronounced Antipas and Herodias sinners, he cooked his own goose. Still in the honeymoon stage of love for his new wife, Antipas sent out soldiers to grab the blabby prophet. By the time Yohanna arrived in Machaerus, Rabbi Yochanan had been languishing in Antipas's prison for many months.

🖋

Three days of bumping along Roman roads in a suspension-free, four-wheeled carriage took their toll on Yohanna. Fortunately, Queen Herodias had sent out scouts to watch for her friend's return. As soon as Yohanna set foot in the palace, maidservants brought her up to their mistress's private bathhouse, where steaming water awaited her in a marbled atrium. Sinking her bone-rattled body into that thermal oasis, Yohanna gave a prayer of thanks for her queen. She had just finished her bath and changed into fresh clothes, when Antipas called her to appear before him.

"Tell me, woman," the tetrarch snarled at Yohanna. "How many people are coming to listen to this Galilean preacher of yours, this Rabbi Yeshua? How popular is he?"

Still curtsying before her ruler, Yohanna kept her head bowed so she could think. She did not want to draw unnecessary attention to Yeshua, for there was no advantage in being visible to Antipas. At the same time, Antipas probably had already received estimates of crowd numbers. Lying would not be wise. Her husband Chuza, standing next to her, became irritated with her prolonged silence and jabbed her ribs sharply with his knee. "Answer the man!" Chuza hissed.

"Your excellency, the numbers vary," Yohanna began. "In the synagogue, where he preaches daily, there are perhaps a few dozen. More on healing days."

"'Healing' days?"

"Yes, my lord. Tuesdays and Thursdays are days of healing, when those who are sick or injured or otherwise in need of spiritual attention come to the synagogue. They receive a ritual that Rabbi Yeshua calls the 'laying on of hands,' in which our sister, Miriam of Magdalene, anoints them with holy oils and . . . ."

"Enough! I don't care about your witchcraft rites or the magical potions you use to confuse the idiots around you!" Antipas exploded. "I want numbers! You say dozens in the synagogue. Are there ever more? Does he preach outside?"

"At his most recent outside sermon, there were more but I cannot say how many," Yohanna said cagily.

"Damn these Jews," Antipas complained to Chuza. "I try to warn them. I throw one of their trouble-making prophets into jail, and what happens? Another one pops up to take his place. It's like that Hydra that Hercules killed—cut off its head, and two more appear. What am I to do now?"

"Well," Chuza said. "You could send a *stronger* message. After all, there's a Jewish prophet in your prison right now. And he still has *his* head."

The corners of Antipas's mouth twitched. "Excellent thought . . . excellent."

The next evening, as birthday guests salivated over platters of slow-roasted lamb in the Royal Triclinium, two of Antipas's men tramped down a narrow staircase into the impenetrable gloom of Machaerus's prison. Their lumbering footfalls and blazing torches scattered bats and scorpions down the corridor. A few centipedes crept toward the cell that the henchmen targeted, scurrying under the heavy oak door just before it was unlocked. The door groaned open, revealing a tiny stone grotto, devoid of all light.

Kneeling on the floor in the far corner was a filthy, ragged man, engaged in fervent prayer. Yochanan gave no indication that he was aware of his visitors, for there was no movement in his hunched body, no break in the stream of quiet murmurs that issued from his lips. The assassins placed the torches they were carrying in nearby wall sconces so they would have the use of both arms for their next task. The sudden flood of light into the room disoriented Yochanan, who looked up from deeply shadowed eyes, which blinked and squinted as he tried to make out his company.

"Hello? Who's there? What . . . ?"

But Yochanan's attempt to understand his destiny in these last seconds of life was cruelly cut short. Disencumbered of his beacon, the first torchbearer abruptly grabbed the inmate by his long hair and slammed his head to the floor, pinning it against the cold stone with one knee. Using both hands to pull the poor man's head away from his body, the brute tried to straighten and stretch his neck into position for the newly sharpened sword of his accomplice. That man, the executioner, raised his arms upward, summoning all his physical strength for the deathblow.

Suddenly, for the briefest of spans—two or three seconds at most—the killer's motion was halted. Because the delay was so fleeting, and because he was illiterate, he did not give words to the sensation, which was of an iron clamp restraining his wrist in mid-air. Nor did he recognize that this momentary arrest of time and movement allowed the captive to gasp out one final vision: "See, the Messiah has come! All kings shall pronounce her truth."

In the next moment, the executioner's arm was released, and the blade plunged downward on the exposed neck of the condemned man, cleaving the second cervical vertebra from the third and slicing through each underlying ligament and artery. The force was so great that the severed head bounced up off the stone and fell back to the floor with a crack, an impact the victim was too shocked to register. In the last seven seconds of Yochanan's consciousness, before all the oxygen in his brain was depleted, he watched the room spin, as his head rolled over and over on the ground, finally coming to a stop near the very spot where he had been praying moments earlier.

The executioner looked up, confused, blood dripping from his blade. He stared at the open doorway with apprehension. "What did he say about a messiah?" he asked. "Did the king come down here?" (The words so disturbed this brute that he later shared the story with Yohanna, hoping she could enlighten him, since everyone in the palace knew she was spending time with prophets.)

"What? No, rubbish!" his companion boomed out, retrieving John's head, and holding it aloft for a moment to let the blood drain out. "Man was out of his mind. Lost his marbles. Total jibber-jabber." He pulled a thick sheet that had been tucked into his belt and wrapped it over the head a few times, then twisted the ends together and swung them through the air, as if the entire bundle were a mace that he was preparing to throw. Finally satisfied, he slung the plasma-soaked package over his shoulder. They would retrieve the body later.

No, there was no gory presentation of Rabbi Yochanan's head on a platter—awash in residual blood from gaping carotid and jugular arteries, eyes open in a proclamation of shock and accusation—before Antipas at his birthday fete. There was no steamy dance by an underage harlot trying to extract promises from a licentious king. Instead, as reported to us by Yohanna, there was a lavish gala, replete with acrobats and flutists, roasted parrots and sea urchins, and, of course, gallons of wine. Herodias attended, not as a back-stage orchestrator of doom and death, but as the loving, doting wife of the birthday boy.

Yohanna said Herodias's banquet entrance mesmerized the entire company and completely dazed her husband. Fashionably late, arriving just as the meal was underway—as the two assassins were making their way down to the dungeon—Herodias showed the guests what true royalty looked like. A simple white silk tunic skirted the curves of her body, and she was draped entirely in gold—golden bracelets gloved her arms, gold lace swam through dark waves of hair up to her golden tiara, a golden mesh cinched her waist, and golden sandals ribboned her feet.

She had barely completed shimmering her way to her seat when Herod jumped up. "A toast!" he called out, raising his wine goblet. (In that same moment, one hundred feet below, the ill-fated prisoner was sharply scrunching eyelids against a sudden onslaught of light.)

"To my stunningly beautiful . . . ." (A hard cranium met un-yielding rock in a loud crack, not heard above.)

" . . . always inspiring . . . ." (A large, muscled leg forced a deep grunt from a crushed larynx, too faint to penetrate the ceiling.)

" . . . unquestionably pure . . . ." (A quick swish of metal sliced the air .)

" . . . *wife.*"

In the triclinium, all cups upended to honor the queen. One guest, seated near the corner of a table, accidentally knocked over a flagon of red wine to his left. The silver vessel fell over just as, many layers of stone below, a fierce grinding crunch severed flesh and bone that had been connected for over forty years.

The contents of the pitcher cascaded to the floor and trickled toward the wall in a lazy rivulet. There, the liquid converged over a slight depression in the floor tiles, gathering in a deep crimson puddle that would stain the surrounding grout and underlying plaster, long after the last Roman foot trod over them.

CAPHARNAUM

9

he murder of Rabbi Yochanan was a turning point.

Two thousand years bring incisive hindsight. Today, I can see exactly how Herod Antipas's actions changed the course of Yeshua's life. And, frankly, the course of history. Because if Antipas had never imprisoned Rabbi Yochanan, Yochanan's followers wouldn't have wandered north in search of a new prophet, and Yeshua might have stayed beneath Roman radar. He could have taken his time in spreading his truth. He would have been free to live a normal life. A life with me.

More importantly, if Yeshua had lived a long, full life, he would have created his own church. Instead, in his absence, Peter and Paul created a Catholic Church in his name that he never would have sanctioned. The whole idea of a hierarchical Church—with the Pope as "Supreme Patriarch," presiding over a power structure of patriarchs, archbishops, bishops, and priests—was totally contrary to Yeshua's message. All the Church "leaders" were men, of course. Even today, women are excluded from leadership positions, and the current Pope defends this tradition as a necessary part of the Church's "Petrine principle." The principle of Peter, he means. The principle of misogyny.

Honestly, if Yeshua had lived to spread his message more widely, over time, who knows? Humans might not be in the mess they are in now.

But my hypothetical ramblings don't matter, do they? Because it's all just wishful thinking, it's not what happened. What happened was that Herod Antipas lopped off Yochanan's head and, a week later, he sent a fresh crew of spies to Capharnaum to keep an eye on us. They hardly tried disguising themselves, looking every bit like Roman soldiers: short tunics, ankle-high sandals, leather belts with scabbards encasing razor-sharp swords. Every day, during our daily service, these men stood against the wall at the back of the synagogue. They entered just before Yeshua called people to prayer and left the moment prayers ceased. Yohanna called them "the Arachnids," because they watched and waited like spiders dangling on the edge of a web.

If Antipas thought that Yochanan's death would make people scatter away from prophets, he miscalculated. The atrocity had precisely the opposite effect. As word traveled that the people's beloved and peaceful Rabbi Yochanan had been brutally murdered by the tetrarch of Galilee, Jewish resentment grew, tempers flared, and people demanded change. New crowds gravitated to Yeshua, seeing him as Yochanan's successor. For weeks after Yohanna returned from Machaerus, fresh faces popped up in our synagogue. Eventually, Antipas's spies weren't the only people standing against the wall.

One morning, Ilana pulled on my sleeve as the Torah was being returned to the ark near the end of our morning service.

"Look! They're up to something," she whispered. "The Arachnids!"

Two of the soldiers were pointing fingers in the air and scanning the crowd.

"*Uh oh.*" Levi understood it first.

"What do you think they're doing?" I asked.

"They're counting."

"Counting?"

"Heads," Levi said. "They're trying to determine how quickly our numbers are increasing."

Who knew what number would tip the balance for Antipas? What magical tally of followers propels a paranoid ruler to armed intervention? We dared not wait for the answer.

At Peter's house that night, the weather outside being turbulent, we gathered indoors, along with the family goats. In the courtyard, freezing rain had flattened the sparse vegetation, leaving a plateau of broken, ice-sheathed stems and leaves. The children could not resist these instant popsicles and ran outside to gather them, much to the dismay of Rivka and Andrew's wife Naomi, who were trying to get them to bed.

Only Peter's five-year-old daughter Huldah sat with us. At the beginning of dinner, she quietly slipped off her chair and hid under the table in front of Yeshua, where she meticulously sorted and knotted the frayed threads of his tunic hem. He didn't notice her until he pushed his chair back at the end of the meal. Smiling at the discovery, Yeshua pulled her onto his lap and stroked her head while we all debated the situation with Antipas. Huldah redirected her tatting skills to the narrow cords edging Yeshua's collar.

"We must leave Capharnaum," Yeshua said. "Break into smaller groups and head in different directions. Antipas won't be able to follow all of us."

"Leave Capharnaum? All of us?" My throat constricted. Yeshua glanced over, but I turned my head, not wanting him to see my selfish fear—if all of us dispersed, what would happen to my time with him?

"No, not all of us," Yeshua clarified. "I do not want to abandon our followers here. Perhaps we can rotate in and out of Capharnaum. Some will stay here to continue teaching while two or three groups venture out. We could go west to the Decapolis, or northwest to Iturea."

"The Decapolis!?" Peter scowled. "The Decapolis is crawling with Gentiles and heathens. We cannot teach people who do not believe as we do, Rabbi!"

"Jews are not the only people on this earth with ears. If their intentions are as pure as this beautiful child," Yeshua kissed Huldah's head, "they are welcome."

"But they do not follow our laws. They are unclean!"

"Peter, what is cleanliness? What is purity? Is it based upon laws made by men, or does it come from within? How many times have we sat and supped with people, beggars and lepers, whom the Pharisees would ban from their tables?"

Peter did not answer. He shot me a dirty look that suggested I was responsible for leading Yeshua down this distasteful path. I shrugged off Peter's scorn. I had long ago given up trying to placate him.

"I have no choice but to continue my work, Antipas or no Antipas," Yeshua concluded. "Yochanan did not die for me to falter."

Huldah let go of her threads and perked up. "Who died?"

"Nobody you know, little one," Yeshua reassured her. "A friend of mine. A man named Yochanan."

"That is sad," Huldah frowned. "Will you die, Rabboni?"

Spoken aloud, the fear robbed us all of speech.

Finally, Peter cleared his throat. "Our Rabbi has a long and prosperous life before him." He plucked Huldah from Yeshua's lap, put her on the ground, and gave her bottom a light pat. "Now off to bed with you."

The little girl scurried back to Yeshua and stood on tiptoe, pursing her lips together. He offered his cheek for her kiss.

"No," she pronounced happily. "You shall not die."

"Well," said Yeshua, "that is a relief."

Later, as our small group of women prepared to head back to the synagogue to sleep, Yeshua did something unexpected. He joined us, taking my hand as we were leaving through the front door.

"Good night, then. I shall see you all in the morning," he called out to the men.

I'm sure Peter's jaw dropped. He and the other men had probably long suspected where their rabbi was spending his nights, when he crept away under cover of darkness, leaving them to find his empty bed space in the mornings. But it had all remained hush-hush and circumspect. Nobody said anything aloud about our relationship, for fear of offending their teacher. That night, apparently, Yeshua decided the pretense was over. The world was closing in on him—it was time to seize the day.

I was giddy with joy as the two of us walked openly to the synagogue that night, holding hands. Surely this shift was a sign of his commitment, confirmation that he cared about me. Lying with him in bed half an hour later, all I could think about was the life we might have together. I was even counting livestock and children in an imagined hamlet up in the Galilean hills.

Yeshua was thinking about his future too, but his picture was not so rosy. "We won't have time to do more than a few of these travel forays," he said, gliding his fingers over my back. "Before we have to go to Jerusalem." I felt a light tremor in his touch.

Jerusalem. Passover. Of course we all intended to go, every Jew made the journey, if he or she could. But Passover was still weeks away. I was surprised he was thinking that far ahead.

"It will be good practice for everyone to preach abroad,"

Yeshua mused. "They need to get comfortable with the idea of being without me. Sooner or later, birds have to fly the nest."

"Without you? Wait, where are you going?" A small alarm went off in my head.

"Oh don't worry, I have no intention of abandoning my ministry. But things do change. Eventually, we must all move on beyond this place."

"Okay, sure, it's fine for everyone else to go out and begin preaching. But what about me?" I pulled his body closer.

"You?" Yeshua laughed. "Someday, you will preach circles around all of them. Around me as well."

"But what if I don't want to leave you?" I held my breath. I had never asked him for any kind of promise.

"Magda," he whispered, pressing himself against me, "You will never be rid of me."

That night, Yeshua had a nightmare. It was not his first, but it was fiercer than any others he had had in my presence. In the past, he would shift back and forth in bed and whimper in his sleep, and I could lull him back to rest by putting my arms around him and shushing him. This time was different, a harbinger of night horrors that would come more frequently in the upcoming weeks. Yeshua bolted upright, crying out in imagined pain and real terror. He extended his arms out from his torso stiffly, swatting the air with his hands, pushing at or away from some unseen object that seemed to hold him upright. Sweat drenched his body, and he gasped like a drowning man, as if his lungs could not get enough oxygen.

"My love, my love!" I called loudly to him. But he would not awaken. All I could do was hold him tightly until, after many minutes, his body finally relaxed.

The next morning, as we ate our modest breakfast of yogurt,

nuts, and dates, I questioned Yeshua about what he had seen. He was circumspect.

"Visions," he said tersely.

"What kind of *visions*?"

"The future, perhaps. *My* future," he shuddered lightly, "perhaps."

That was all he would tell me about his nightmare. But I knew him too well. I felt the sense of doom and helplessness that unsettled him, like a gust of wind ruffling the edge of the sea.

I went outside to the rain cistern for some water to clean our breakfast dishes. Dipping my jug into the well, I wondered whether the arrival of Antipas's minions were the catalyst for Yeshua's nightmares. The more successful Yeshua became in his ministry, the more Yochanan's fate loomed over him.

Suddenly, I heard a loud clattering, of metal hitting metal, coming from a large oak nearby. Hurrying over, I peered around the oak's massive trunk. There stood Judah, holding a sword in the air and admiring it, while a turbaned man dragged a heavy sack of clanking objects off in the direction of the market.

The sword Judah brandished was short and curved, about the size of a dagger. He swished it through the air, then carefully brought the blade to his index finger to test its sharpness. An instant later, Judah jerked his finger back and licked the blood from its tip. He looked pleased.

"Not near my Father's house," growled a low voice.

I hadn't seen Yeshua approach. Nor had Judah.

"Rabbi!" Judah threw himself to the ground. "Oh, Rabbi, please forgive me. Please accept my love for you, in the midst of all my failures."

"Rise, Judah," Yeshua said, "there is no need to prostrate yourself."

"But there is." Judah looked up with exhausted eyes, his face a mixture of urgency and shame. Oily strands of hair mopped his cheeks as he shook his head in self-disgust. "I know I have disappointed you. I am not attending services as often as I should. And I don't always say my prayers at night, because . . . well, in truth, in the mornings, I often do not remember what I did the night before."

"Judah, I am not here to absolve you of your shortcomings. You yourself can repent that which you have done," Yeshua said. "Let us instead discuss your future behavior. And please rise."

"Yes, Rabbi, yes." Judah scrambled to his feet and wiped his nose on the sleeve of his tunic. "But Rabbi, I have done *some* good. I am spreading your message."

"Indeed?"

"Yes! I tell anyone who will listen about the kingdom you promise—how the rich shall be poor, and the poor shall be rich, and how the oppressed shall be free and the oppressors smited. Smited! I'm especially looking forward to that." Judah's eyes were wide and glistening, whether from remorse or mild delirium, I could not tell.

"And what do you plan to smite them with, Judah? This?" Yeshua pointed to the sword that Judah had hastily hidden under his tunic. "A *sica*?"

I gasped quietly. The fisherman Ehud had told me about the *sicarii*, terrorists named after the weapons they used. An offshoot of the Zealot movement, these secret killers were known for assassinating Romans or suspected Roman sympathizers. They had recently orchestrated an attack in Tiberias, just outside Antipas's royal palace. The *sicarii* set an oxcart on fire as a distraction, then murdered the three Roman soldiers who tried extinguishing the blaze, before melting into the crowd. I had never seen a *sica*, but

Ehud told me it was an ancient weapon from Illyria or Thrace, with a curved blade designed specifically to get around protective armor.

Judah was silent.

"The kingdom of God cannot be achieved through violence," Yeshua scolded. "You know that."

"No, Rabbi, I do not know that." Judah's eyes were defiant.

"Violence only begets more violence, Judah. It begets neither peace nor forgiveness," Yeshua said.

"Peace?" Judah cried. "I don't want *peace*, I want *justice*. And forgiveness? How can I forgive a murderer? Someone who destroyed my family?" He shook his head vigorously. "No. That is not possible."

"'Not possible.'" Yeshua echoed. "How do you know for certain what is and is not possible, Judah? If you peel the bark from a mulberry tree, is it possible to reattach it? If you have been fishing all night and your nets are empty when you row to shore, is it possible that your nets might be overflowing with fish by the time you reach the sand?"

Judah looked stunned. Until that moment, he had not known how, all those months ago in Magdala, his nets came to be teeming with fish on the day he saw me and Yeshua speaking with his father. He had been drifting to shore, dragging an empty net behind his boat, too discouraged to pull it in and stow it properly. When he saw us from a distance, Judah almost turned his boat around, so ashamed was he of his failure to catch anything.

Then out of nowhere, just as Judah's bow touched the beach, he heard a great splashing commotion at the stern of his craft. Yeshua and I had already walked away, but Ehud and Moshe came running up, crying out with joy and disbelief, asking him where all the fish had come from, what secret fishing spot had he found that they did not know. Judah had no answer for them. He had been totally perplexed.

Now Judah gaped at Yeshua, more mesmerized than he had been on the Mount of Beatitudes. The trick with the mulberry tree might have been some sort of magic or sleight of hand. But the fish? The fish were something altogether different.

"Rabbi, are you . . . ?"

Yeshua ignored his unfinished question. "Judah, do you know why I tell you to turn the other cheek to someone who smites you? It is because I know that lasting change, the sort of transformation that will bring about the kingdom of God—*that* revolution cannot arise from violence. *That* revolution," Yeshua placed both hands on the middle of Judah's chest, one on top of the other, "begins in the heart."

If I had to pinpoint exactly when the seed was planted for the misguided plan Judah hatched later—the plan he would instigate with the Zealots in Jerusalem—I'd say it was after this conversation with Yeshua. Because on that afternoon, Judah became convinced of Yeshua's divinity. If Yeshua was divine, Judah reasoned, there was nothing he couldn't do, including overthrowing the Romans. All Judah had to do was position himself and the Zealots and the *sicarii* in the right place to help him.

Capharnaum

10

wo traveling groups left Capharnaum the following week. The first included Phillip, Levi, Shoshanna, and Ilana; the second, Peter, the Zebedees, and Yeshua. Everyone planned on roaming the hills for two weeks, using goat paths rather than Roman roads, to throw off Antipas's men. Shoshanna's group departed first, with Shoshanna and Phillip in the lead. Hoping to avoid detection, they left after dark had fallen, but Shoshanna's voice broke the air before they rounded the first bend in the road. She prodded Ilana and Levi to make haste. "*Hup, hup,* you two. You can neck all you like when we stop to rest." I knew Ilana was rolling her eyes and thinking, *It's going to be a long two weeks.*

A storm blew in overnight, bringing a riot of clouds and cold air to the morning. Yeshua and his group left after an early breakfast. He had told me they intended to head southeast to the Decapolis, land that was Herod Phillip's territory, not Herod Antipas's. "I can't imagine Phillip holds any love for his half brother Antipas, since Antipas stole his wife," Yeshua reasoned. "We should be safe there."

They took the inland road rather than the shore path, deciding to brave an icy wind instead of the angry waves crashing over the lakeshore's mosaic of pebbles. My eyes focused on the blue woolen shawl that Yeshua wrapped over his head after he kissed me goodbye. I watched that patch of indigo fade gradually into ash, as sheet after sheet of cold rain obscured him from my view.

Of course I would miss him. But I had Yohanna.

"Teach me how to anoint," Yohanna begged. "I so want to learn!"

Growing up in a Roman household, Yohanna had no experience with anointment, other than the one she had experienced beneath my hands. On the evening she returned from Machaerus, she had come to me before bedtime. "Would you be willing to work your magic on *me?*" she asked timidly. "I am feeling so tired and disconnected."

She had not known what to expect, when I began gliding my hands over the curves of her body. Stroke by stroke, she sank into deep relaxation, and when we reached that final moment where our spirits joined, I shared in her surprise and her joy. "So this is you," we said to each other in silence. "How beautiful you are!"

As an anointress in her own right, Yohanna was a complete ingenue and had to be taught the basics. The day we began her instruction, I asked her to stand next to me in the healing room, where our first client, a young mother complaining of lower back pain, awaited us. Guiding Yohanna's hands and fingers with my own, I showed her where and how much to push her hands against the woman's flesh and muscles. I tried explaining as we went along which internal organs were affected by each pressure point she massaged, and how everything was connected together.

Yohanna was a quick learner—by the end of the week, she stood alone at the second healing bench. But it didn't take both of us long to see that Yohanna would never have more than facility with her hands. She knew firsthand what more could be achieved during anointment, and she could not get there.

"That part of anointment eludes me," Yohanna complained after releasing one of her clients. "That limitless space, where you and I met, where we were as one. Why can't I reach that magical place on my own, with the people I touch?"

I didn't have an answer for her. "Maybe it requires more time and practice," I suggested. "Or maybe it requires Yeshua's presence?" Yet even as I said this, I wondered. On the few occasions when I anointed people without Yeshua in the room, I had still achieved that union with them. In fact, I had been delighting in that realm with my clients all week long, while Yeshua was away. Was it possible that my spiritual connections had nothing to do with him? I wasn't used to thinking of myself as having any kind of power, let alone something unique or special, something *spiritual*.

When the traveling groups had been gone almost two weeks, I became anxious for Yeshua's return. Each morning, I walked to the *caravanserai* to ask if someone had seen him on their travels. Each day, I asked Andrew if the fishermen had any news. The rational part of me trusted that Yeshua was safe, but my old foes, fear and misgiving, hovered nearby. What if Antipas's men had followed Yeshua and arrested him before he got to Herod Phillip's land? I hadn't seen the Roman soldiers that used to be a fixture in our synagogue since the day after Yeshua left. Where had they gone?

One morning, while sorting herbs and oils in the apothecary, I dropped a tray of flasks and burst into tears.

"That's it," Yohanna declared. "You can't just stay here and wait. We're going on our own pilgrimage."

"What? But where to?" I sniffled.

"Let's go to Mount Tabor. I've always loved the prophet Debo-rah—why not go to the site of her greatest victory?"

A vivid memory broke through my cloud of self-pity. The story of Deborah, the only female prophet in the Nevi'im, had been one of my favorites too, when I was a young girl. Before bedtime, my father used to wrap me in the folds of his tallit and tell me stories from the Torah. I could hear my father's slow, melodic voice telling me how, after Moses' death, centuries before I was born, the Israelites were tempted away from God.

"Why?" I asked him. "Didn't they love God? Didn't God love them?"

"Oh yes, Magda, God always loved them," my father said. "As God loves us today, no matter how bad we are. No matter how many times our mother has to tell us to get out of bed in the morning." I shrank into his arms, as he laughed and kissed my head.

"But the tribes of Jacob became lazy and forgetful over time," my father sighed. "They were tempted by the gold and jewels of the pagan temples and the precious stones of their idols. They stopped offering sacrifices to God, they stopped observing the Sabbath. They drifted away from their religion and each other."

"Such shortsightedness, such foolishness." My father could never tell this story without bemoaning the stupidity of the an-cient Israelites. "It's a wonder that God didn't abandon us then and there. And he might have done so, had it not been for the great prophet—"

"Deborah!" I was learning about the prophets with my tutor.

"Exactly. Deborah told the tribes that, if they wanted to defeat the last Canaanite king and reclaim the land God had promised them, they must stop their nonsense, return to their God, and reunite their tribes. If they did this, she promised, God would guide them to victory at Mount Tabor. The male tribe leaders were dubious. What if they went off to fight the Canaanites and ended up getting slaughtered?"

"Deborah told them not to be sissies. Donning armor and a helmet, she led the armies into battle. As soldiers fought all around her on Mount Tabor, she commanded through God, enlisting both the stars in heaven and the flood waters below to help them defeat the Canaanites and regain their promised land.'"

I smiled as I stood in the apothecary, remembering what my father whispered into my ear at the end, when he tucked me into bed. "Look out Deborah, here comes Magda!"

Yohanna was right—standing on earth that had once supported Deborah's feet would be the perfect distraction to keep me from staring at the road awaiting Yeshua's return. We quickly made preparations for an overnight trip. Marcus Silanus, upon learning that Yohanna and I were heading to Mount Tabor alone, insisted on sending a bodyguard to accompany us.

"The road is crawling with thugs," he said. "Your father would never forgive me if something happened to you. I'd never forgive myself."

In the end, Yohanna and I were grateful for the guard and his horse when a wall of storm clouds closed in on us the evening we arrived at the mountain. We had just enough time to have our meal and watch the sun rest on its plum pillow of clouds before those clouds darkened and a freezing rain began. Hurrying over to a large oak tree, we saw that the guard had set up a tent for us. He and his horse disappeared to a nearby cliff overhang.

"Oh, my poor feet," Yohanna moaned, crawling into the tent and sitting on a goatskin spread over the dirt. She removed her sandals and frowned. "Capharnaum has made me soft. Look at these blisters!"

I rummaged through the small collection of oils that I carried in my daypack. "Ah, eucalyptus and lavender," I said triumphantly. "Give me those ragged appendages of yours. I will make you forget all your troubles."

Yohanna leaned back into a pillow that the guard had also somehow packed onto his horse. "This man that Marcus Silanus found for us is a marvel. Do you think he is married?"

I laughed, taking Yohanna's left foot in my lap and rubbing oil on my fingers and palms. "Does it matter? *You* are." Gently, I massaged around the blisters on Yohanna's heel and ankle before pressing my thumbs more firmly into the arch.

"*Aah*. So good." She sighed. "Actually, I don't think I'll be married for much longer. Chuza is seeking a divorce."

"What?" I almost dropped her foot. "How can he? You have been entirely faithful to him."

"He needs no reasons, Magda. He lives in a Roman world, remember? And our Jewish law allows divorce too, at least when the man wants it."

"I don't know much about the legal side of these things," I said. "Yeshua considers marriage sacrosanct, except in the case of infidelity. By the woman *or* the man."

Yohanna yawned, and I turned my attention to her other foot. "If that were the law, I would have divorced Chuza ages ago. There's so much more freedom in being unmarried."

"*If* you have money," I reminded her.

"True. But my father gave Chuza a handsome dowry for taking me off his hands. Chuza will owe me." She chuckled. "*That* will not be easy for him. I hope he has to ask his beloved Antipas for the money."

After attending to every inch of Yohanna's feet, I wiped the excess oil off her skin and mine, blew out our lamp and lay down next to her, pulling the woolen blankets over my chin.

"*Brrrr.*"

"You cold? Come here, let me warm you up. It's the least I can do." Yohanna curled into me, belly against spine, resting her arm over my torso. She breathed softly into my hair. "Who needs Chuza when I have you?" We both fell asleep to the tapping of tiny ice darts against the sackcloth overhead.

I dreamed about marriage—*my* marriage, actually. In my dream, it was not clear who the bridegroom was, but the prophet Deborah officiated. She had fiery red hair, much like Yohanna's, and she carried her sword in a baldric studded with rubies and diamonds. My parents were there (their hair grayer than I remembered it, their faces more lined), along with Levi and Ilana (who nursed a newborn baby) and Marcus Silanus and Shoshanna (both sitting on a camel).

Though I tried, I could not see the groom's face. It was hidden behind a heavy veil, secured to his head with a spiked crown made from a hawthorn bush. He was in the process of putting the wedding ring on my finger—his hands were cold as death—when Deborah suddenly pulled out her sword and slashed the air.

"You dare to wed this woman whom God has consecrated?" she cried. "You dare to take her for yourself?" And with one swift swoop, she brought the sword down on his head.

I woke up suddenly, my heart pounding, my breathing quick and shallow. The tent felt suffocating, overly warm, and thick with heavy expirations of sleep. Peeking my head outside, I saw an embankment of haze muting the faint light of dawn. Too alert now to rejoin Yohanna in bed, I grabbed my cape to keep me warm, and decided to hike up the mountain. Perhaps watching the sunrise from the summit would dispel the lingering shadow of my dream. The walk uphill was neither long nor difficult. Frost-dusted shrubs at the mountain's foot gave way to an open woodland of oaks. The overnight ice storm had coronated each tree with its own crown of diamonds, and these shimmered in the breaking light. I ascended into a sparkling cathedral, awestruck.

Approaching the summit, I heard a faint singsong murmur, like small bells jingling underwater. Intrigued, I hastened to the clearing where the music seemed to originate, stopping on the edge of a small patch of land that was encircled by a congregation of oak trees even more ancient than the ones I had just passed. The light filling this open space radiated with blinding intensity, far more than could be attributed to reflective sunlight on ice-clad oaks. Stepping closer, I barely made out the shapes of six men—three standing side by side, three kneeling with their heads on the ground. All indiscernible except the one I would have known anywhere—Yeshua.

He stood directly opposite me, conversing with two bearded men whom I did not recognize. All three of them were dazzlingly illuminated, some inner light source limning the details of their bodies like ink on papyrus. Yeshua's voice sounded entirely normal to me, but the words that came out of the two other men were the source of the strange sound of bells I had heard. Their speech was fluid and otherworldly, a liquefied hosanna.

With a sudden shock, and without fully understanding how I knew, I realized that these two men were Elijah and Moses.

Peter confirmed their identities. His voice rose from the group of prostrate men, which I now knew must also include John and James Zebedee.

"Rabbi." Peter looked up from where he crouched, and I saw he was trembling. "Shall I build three tents, one each for Moses, Elijah, and you? Shall I, Rabbi?"

I giggled out loud, then clapped my hand over my mouth to avoid discovery. What nonsense was this? Classic Peter, talking about building tents in the midst of a glorious vision. Yeshua heard me laugh. He caught my eye and winked. But before I could gesture back, an enormous cloud descended over the mountaintop, cutting off my vision. As bright as the scene had been an instant earlier, now a dark nebula cast a pall over all of it.

I would have felt unsettled had I not sensed Yeshua standing right next to me. His hand intertwined with mine an instant before I registered his presence. Perhaps it was his touch, perhaps his proximity, but I could feel his hallowing illumination seep into me, making my nerves tingle with electricity.

Then came another voice. Not human. Not animal. It was the voice of deep thunder and catastrophic storm, of explosive stars and eruptive volcanoes, of cleansing surf and soughing rain. A voice not of this world, nor of any other.

"This is my child, whom I love," the voice said. "Listen."

The bass echo of those words remained in the air for what seemed like an eternity, then pulsed one by one into the mist. When the tremor had ceased, I realized that Yeshua was no longer nearby, but I could not see where he had gone. To my right, where Peter and the other men had been kneeling, there was nothing but cloud. Yet to my great amazement, the thinning mist to my left revealed the same flaming-haired female I had seen in my dream—Deborah, the prophet.

"Magda." She spoke my name like a pronouncement. I tried to take in the details of her shape and her dress, but her body oscillated in and out of focus, even as her words were absolutely clear. "His time is almost complete. Your time has just begun." My heart tripped over her statement, registering fear before my stunned brain could comprehend it.

"Even when you can no longer feel him, you will always know him." Deborah reached out her hand and lightly touched my ribcage. Then she pulled out her sword, sending eddies and cascades of fog swirling around us. With both hands on its jewel-studded hilt, she drew a large arc in the air, stretching her arms and body outward as far as they could go, the tip of her sword cutting through the vapor. Her sword left a trail of sparkling lights, as a blade of dewy evening grass might draw a procession of fireflies. Somehow I knew these lights were people, but who and where they were remained a mystery. "They look for justice and forgiveness. They look to join him and each other," Deborah said. "You have the power to bring them all. To connect them all. Only you. Alone."

Her last word hit me like a truncheon.

CAPHARNAUM

11

*A*ccording to the Third Law of Motion in physics, for every action, there is an equal and opposite reaction. For example, if the horse that is carrying you back to Capharnaum pushes its hooves against the ground in one direction, that force propels the horse's body forward in the opposite direction. Or if the woman you love wraps her arms around you to keep you on the horse, and presses her fingers against your ribcage, your chest expands into her embrace.

I wonder now, thinking back on everything that happened after Mount Tabor, if the Third Law also applies to emotions and time. If you're happy, does that necessarily mean that you will be unhappy later? Is it true, as it was with me and Yeshua, that the happiest period of your life inevitably leads to one of crushing sorrow?

✺

When I stumbled down the mountain and collapsed in front of the tent as Yohanna was waking up, she immediately piled us both onto the horse and galloped off to Capharnaum. The poor guard was left to pack up our tent and its luxuries and sit in the cold until someone rode back with another horse. Immediately upon arriving home, Yohanna tucked me into bed.

I was not so much ill as overwhelmed. Was what I had seen and heard that morning real? Or had I fallen asleep on top of the mountain and dreamed the whole thing? Real or imaginary, Deborah's message both excited and terrified me. She said I had the "power of connection." I knew that about myself already. But surely Yeshua had that power as well—the power to connect people to himself. I had seen him draw people in and make them feel whole. Why would Deborah single me out? And what did she mean about Yeshua's time being over and mine just beginning? I hoped that Yeshua could clarify everything.

Fortunately, I did not have long to wait for his return. The following afternoon, as we assembled in the synagogue for prayer and the last rays of sun were disappearing through the windows of the domed ceiling, the four pilgrims returned. James and John walked in first, beaming like overfueled lanterns. Peter followed, exuding equal parts restlessness and joy, striding purposefully past the Zebedees and halting in the middle of the room. He clearly wanted our attention.

I kept my gaze to the door, expecting Yeshua.

"*We*," announced Peter with triumph, "have seen a marvel beyond all marvels." He looked at us one by one, stopping when he got to me. John and James stood together behind him, solemn and silent, like those fur-topped Beefeaters who guard your King of England nowadays. "Yesterday, at Mount Tabor, the three of us saw our Rabbi transformed. We saw him hallowed and exalted."

"By God himself," added John, unable to contain himself.

"Moses and Elijah were there too!" James was as excited as a toddler with a new toy.

For a moment, nobody spoke. Then Andrew rose up to confront his brother. "Why would our Rabbi reveal something so magnificent to the three of you and not to the rest of us?"

"I imagine," Peter crowed, "it is because he holds us closest to his heart. Of all his followers, he trusts the three of us the most. We shall be first in line to the kingdom of God." Again, he looked directly at me as he spoke, tossing his words like daggers.

"The last shall be first, and the first shall be last," spoke a familiar voice from the doorway. "Perhaps your rabbi chose the three of you because he fears that, of all his followers, your faith is most wanting."

The waning rays of twilight carved Yeshua's shape into the deepening shadow of the room. Stunned by his words, Peter began back-pedaling. "Rabbi, I . . . ."

"Say nothing, Peter." Yeshua sounded stern and unhappy. "I would have had you say nothing before—indeed, you may recall that I specifically asked the three of you to say nothing of what you saw." All three men hung their heads at this reminder. "Aside from sparing you the shame of being singled out for your skepticism, I asked for your silence because I do not want a ministry of pageantry and pomp. I want a ministry of quiet teaching and sincere action. Everyone else here knows that."

Not an easy rebuke to hear. My heart almost went out to Peter and the Zebedees. Almost.

An awkward quiet settled on us. It was broken by a flurry of cold air, as the temple door was again pushed open, and Ilana ran in.

"We're back! We're back!" she sang out, scampering over to where Yohanna and I sat on the bench and throwing her arms around our shoulders. "You both are the first to know—I am betrothed!"

In Ilana's face, I saw pure unbridled joy. It was an image I would recall often over the next year, when I needed to lift my spirits. She conveyed, in that moment, a certainty that the world held nothing but goodness.

"Is that so?" Yohanna asked. She smiled knowingly.

Ilana searched Yohanna's face. "Wait, did you know? How could you know? It just happened; he asked me to marry him this morning!"

"Apparently, my love, he's had the idea for some time," Yohanna said, "because he asked your mother for permission before you left. And she shared the news with us."

"Also, there was the dowry to work out." Shoshanna came into the chamber, shaking the sleet off her cloak. "He's quite a dealer, your future husband. Getting rid of you was not cheap."

Ilana's face fell. "The dowry?"

But Shoshanna could not continue the pretense. Seeing her daughter's reaction, she pulled Ilana close and laughed. "Oh Ilana, slap me with a donkey's tail! Of course there's no dowry! I mean, sure, there *could* have been a dowry, but Levi said no. In fact, he wanted to pay *me* for the privilege of having you as a wife."

And just like that, the tiny cloud over Ilana evaporated and she renewed her merry babbling. "He is good, isn't he? I hope I can be worthy of him. Oh, there is so much to think about, so much to do! When shall we wed? Springtime would be lovely. It's not far away, I have already seen one or two saffron flowers."

"Slow down, honey, slow down," Shoshanna chuckled.

"My Naamah has been betrothed for well over two years," Peter muttered, unable to muzzle his opinion.

"*Two years!?*" Ilana's face fell again.

Had Shoshanna been standing closer to Peter, she would have kicked him in the shin, or, knowing Shoshanna, someplace more painful. "But Naamah is still a child," she pointed out, curling her lip at Peter while smoothing Ilana's hair. "You are a woman and can be married whenever you like."

"Oh good!" Brightness again. "Springtime then!"

"And you will have a harem of women to help you prepare," Yohanna announced. The three of us held hands in a circle around Ilana. I half expected someone to start up a tune so we could dance.

"I've always wanted to be in a Jewish harem," Shoshanna added.

Yeshua kissed Ilana on the forehead. "You are both blessed. But where is the happy bridegroom-to-be, that we may congratulate him?"

"He has gone to tell his parents," Ilana said.

"Come, let us find Levi," Yeshua told the men, "and leave Ilana to her happy planning." As everyone else dutifully arose, offering Ilana blessings and good wishes on their way out, Yeshua pulled me aside.

"I shall return shortly." He tucked a piece of my hair behind my ear. "Ah, how I missed you."

⁂

I meant to stay awake that night as I waited for him. But my body must have been too eager for sleep, because the next thing I heard was, "I love listening to you snore." He lay down on our pallet, and I sleepily reached for him.

"Snore?" I yawned. "I don't snore."

"All right then," he said. "You sleep *soundly*."

"No, no. I am a lady," I yawned again. "And ladies do not snore or make *sounds* when they're asleep. Are you disputing that . . . ." His lips found mine and stopped my objections. Even though only two weeks had passed since we last shared a bed, it felt like I hadn't seen him for months. Every part of me was hungry to be touched by him. And to touch him. I kissed him more deeply, pressing my body against his and wrapping my leg over his hip.

"Wait, Magda, wait. I have something important to talk to you about."

My heart almost stopped. What could he mean? Had Peter convinced him to leave me? It was a ridiculous thought, I know, but my emotions ran high. Yeshua pushed himself up and reached over me to light the lamp we kept on a nearby bench. I put a hand over my chest to quiet the pounding I was certain he could hear.

"When Ilana made her announcement this evening," Yeshua said, "I felt something. Something new to me. I was, of course, very happy for her and Levi, but this new feeling made me a bit uncomfortable. I realized . . ." He faltered for a moment. "I realized that I wished to be Levi."

What? Confused, I struggled to sit up. Had Yeshua been in love with Ilana all this time? Could I have been so misled?

"No, no, Magda!" Yeshua knew immediately what I was thinking. "I do not want to be with Ilana, not at all. But I do want to marry." He took my hands, which rested in my lap, and searched my face. "I want to marry you."

Now I was truly tongue-tied. Had he just proposed? All I could do was repeat robotically. "You want to marry. Me?"

"Yes, more than anything I have ever wanted in my life. Yes, I do." Yeshua left the bed, and knelt before me, still holding both my hands. My heart was now on a veritable romp. "But," he whispered, "I can't."

"Oh." My heart's celebration ended.

"Do you remember me telling you about my brother James, who helped the villagers drive me out of Nazareth?" Yeshua began.

"James," I echoed, somewhat dazed. "Have I met James?"

"No, you have not. He wants nothing to do with me. But if I were to get married to you, married under our Jewish law, and if my life were cut short, then everything you owned would, under our law, go to James. I know you prize your independence, and your family's wealth has given you that. But if I were to die, that would be taken from you." Yeshua paused, looking pained as he uttered his next words. "Also, legally, James would have the right to marry you after my death."

"Wait, wait." I tried processing this bombshell. Two words he had spoken—"my death"—tolled inside my head again and again, like sledgehammers on gypsum. My tongue felt thick and unwieldy. "You are assuming . . . you said . . . ." I could not utter the words.

Yeshua finished my thought. "My death."

"Yes." I swallowed hard, eyes filling with tears. I wanted this conversation to end. Nothing good came of it. Shaking my head, I placed my palm over his mouth. "Please. No more."

Gently, he removed my hand. "My love, oh how I wish I did not have to tell you this. But I want you to know what I *would* do for you, if I could. And I would marry you, Magda, I would marry you a thousand times over! Before everyone we know and love. If I knew I could be your husband for any normal period of time." He was stroking my cheek and wiping my tears as he continued. "But you see, Magda, I must go to Jerusalem for Passover this year. I must."

We had spoken about this. If Yeshua wanted to spread his message as widely as possible, he had to go to Jerusalem for Passover, though it meant exposing himself to danger. Antipas had no authority in Jerusalem, but who knew what influence he might have with Pontius Pilate? Maybe he would convince Pilate that Yeshua was dangerous and should be apprehended. And if Yeshua was arrested . . . . I shuddered. The memory of Rabbi Yochanan's execution had not dimmed.

I pushed back, desperate. "But must you go, really? Listen to me, listen! We could go elsewhere to spread the message, somewhere out of Antipas's reach. We could go to Syria, or to Egypt. We could join Marcus Silanus and travel east. There are people everywhere whom you could teach, not just here."

As I made my plea, the memory of Deborah's words on Mount Tabor unexpectedly resounded in my head. "His time is almost complete." I sank back on the bed, feeling the finality of that statement. "So what Deborah said is true," I was unaware that I had spoken out loud.

"Yes." His voice was subdued.

Suddenly, it no longer seemed important for me to understand everything that Deborah had said. Suddenly, I didn't want to think about Deborah at all. What I wanted to think about was right before my eyes, right here, next to my bed. And if our time was almost complete, I intended to make the most of it.

WEDDING

The night before Levi and Ilana wed, all the light in Heaven fell to Earth, pulsed its way up through the soil into the roots and stems of every plant, and saturated a vast diaphane of flower petals that was just beginning its stretch into springtime. We awoke to a brilliant blaze of mustard fields.

That afternoon, Yohanna and I wove wild white lilies into a loose braid of Ilana's hair, before Shoshanna kissed her daughter and veiled her face under an ivory lace fringed with filaments of woven pearl thread.

We carried the bride on a litter from our small synagogue to Levi's house, inviting everyone we met to come celebrate under the streaks of a florid sun.

Standing in the courtyard of his home, Levi allowed his eyes to brim with moisture, reflecting the eager flames of dozens of lanterns, as he watched the woman who would share his life walk toward him.

And I stood with Yeshua, called by him to anoint the couple in scented oils, as he bestowed blessings on their union. For Levi, an exotic wash of sandalwood and ginseng that bathed his crown in root and anise, earth and clove. For Ilana, liquid ribbons of jasmine and rose coiled around her collarbone in a thrill of ambrosia.

What did I feel in that moment when I stood next to the man to whom I had devoted my life? To whom I was so close that it sometimes felt we were breathing as one? Who had said he wanted to marry me but could not? How did it feel for me to watch another couple unite?

I was euphoric. Because on that day, I too was getting married. From the moment Yeshua spoke his first prayer praising the sacred and wondrous love between two people, he took my hand and held it tightly. I felt it then—a singular animating force pulsing powerfully between us—and I knew our lives were indelibly joined from that moment on. If there were some celestial book in Heaven, some ledger keeping track of who marries whom on Earth, Yeshua's name and mine would be found right after Levi's and Ilana's. I did not need words to confirm it. When Yeshua uttered his last benediction, he placed his palm on Levi's forehead, still holding my hand with his other, and I placed my free hand on Ilana, thus completing our matrimonial circle.

Afterward, the eager newlyweds hurried off under the glow of a rising full moon, to a small bedroom within the house, while the rest of us erupted in joy outside.

The marriage celebration would last all week long, but on that night we feasted on roasted goat and quail and clapped to the music of cymbals and lyres and flutes. Marcus Silanus was there, having left a caravan bound for China so that he could offer Shoshanna a shoulder to cry on. He brought two camels, one for the new couple, the other for Shoshanna.

"A camel? How ridiculous. What can I possibly do with a camel?" Shoshanna chided.

"The Egyptians say, 'If you love, love the moon; if you steal, steal a camel,'" Marcus replied solemnly. "So I have stolen a camel for love."

Shoshanna blushed and boxed Marcus on the shoulder.

Marcus grabbed her fist and held it in his weather-worn hands. "In truth, I am hoping you will join my caravan." Shoshanna stared at him in open-mouthed surprise. "Now that your daughter is married, you can go on an adventure."

She glanced back at me and Yohanna, lifting her left eyebrow. Yohanna smiled. I winked. Shoshanna shrugged. "Why not? Who wouldn't want to spend months in the desert with a tribe of unwashed men and spitting beasts?" Laughing, she let Marcus reel her into the crowd.

Also making an appearance that night was the centurion commander Gnaeus Cornelius Castus, his muscled arm around the male partner Yeshua had restored to health a year earlier. The two of them were among the first guests to offer their congratulations to Ilana and Levi, when the bride and groom emerged an hour later from the bedroom. With the wedding couple returned to the party, the celebration began in earnest.

I danced with everyone that night—with Yeshua, with Yohanna, with Levi, with Marcus and Shoshanna. I even danced briefly with Peter, though he was so drunk he didn't recognize me. It's not that I love to dance—I'm a terrible dancer, having avoided all my mother's efforts to teach me. But as with everything else that day, it didn't matter. It didn't matter that I had the agility of a wild boar. The air was filled with music, and the guests were filled with wine, and that combination, plus the occasion, made everyone dance.

By "everyone," I mean not only the members of our fellowship and their families—Peter's wife, Andrew's wife, and all their children, Levi's parents and siblings and cousins—I mean practically the entire population of Capharnaum. In the weeks leading up to the wedding, Yeshua had kept away from the town, to keep Antipas in the dark about his whereabouts. We had all missed him and were ready to celebrate. Everyone who had ever supped with him, rich and poor, respected and reviled, came together for this one event. They feasted together, laughed together, and danced together. It was, you might say, a miracle of assimilation.

The accomplishment was not lost on Yeshua. He stood under a portico, watching the assembly, as I reeled past him in Yohanna's arms. There was a look of great satisfaction on his face, and when I finally stumbled up to him, panting from exertion, he smiled.

"It is so beautiful, don't you think?" he said.

"All our friends in one place, celebrating?"

"Yes, that," he laughed and pulled me close. "Also the brotherhood and sisterhood of humankind. The communion of souls, flowing freely."

"And the moon," I insisted, steering him toward romance, because the moon was full and shining down upon us as if it were the last night of the world and it might never have another such opportunity.

"And the moon," he took the bait. "And you. There is nothing more beautiful than you."

He kissed me then, another one of those dizzying kisses that took me so far within that I ended up outside myself. We stole away to a quiet room inside Levi's home.

There, we took the final step in our physical union. I've already told you about some of our romantic explorations when we lay together, but until that night, we had never taken that ultimate unifying step between two people in love.

We knew each other so well by then. He knew exactly where to kiss and touch me, and I knew exactly how to hold and stroke him, so that when we finally coupled and moved together as one, it felt like we were transformed into a different being. We were a magical sinuous creature riding an ocean wave, swelling to greater and greater heights, nearing the crest, flying for a moment closer, closer to the sky than we had ever been, and then . . . bursting onto the sand, reaching out toward the mysterious dunes of earth, stretching forward even as we were pulled back to the world we knew, leaving behind a trail of mother-of-pearl, sparkling in the damp.

Before that night, I had stood beside Yeshua as a healer, and I had been content to let him make all the decisions. But after that evening, I stood beside him as his wife. From that moment forth, I was committed to making a home with him. And a life with him, a long life, full of ministry and healing, possibly even children. After all, he was in the business of miracles, wasn't he?

I tried putting the words of the prophet Deborah out of my mind. Yeshua's life with me was just beginning. I pictured it in my mind so clearly. Surely, he and I deserved that chance. "You have the power. . . . Alone," she had said. But I was not alone. I was married, and I intended to stay that way.

No, as far as I was concerned, Deborah could take her prediction and stuff it. I was going to do everything in my power to keep him alive.

JERUSALEM

1

erusalem. City of Peace. City of Truth. City of Holiness. Lion of God.

I go back to look at it from time to time. Even now, even from the distance of Here, the city's beauty takes my breath away. There's a *je ne sais quoi* about Jerusalem, a spiritual something in its air. Maybe part of that something is the fact that the city's beauty has always lived side by side with suffering. Certainly, that's how I experienced it. For me, Jerusalem was the City of Heartbreak.

Today, I can look back at the events of that last Passover week without emotional disintegration, even if I still don't understand why it had to happen the way it did. But for years, I used to dissolve in a stupor of pain on the anniversary of his death.

Maybe you've read the Quartet, or you've seen one of the countless films about Yeshua's last week on Earth, so you think you know all the details of this part of the story. Believe me, you don't. Much of what the Quartet wrote was completely fabricated. That "triumphal" entry into Jerusalem, where Yeshua sat on the back of a donkey, with the masses celebrating his arrival, fanning him with palm leaves, calling him the Son of David? Didn't happen. The Last Supper, where he broke bread and sipped wine and told our group that in the future we should symbolically cannibalize him? Yes, we all shared a final Passover meal, but no one was told to drink anyone's blood, either literally or figuratively.

And the crucifixion? Well, on that subject, let me remind you that the Quartet couldn't possibly know any details about that event. Their accounts, which are theoretically based on stories told to scribes by the men in our group, can't be taken as true. Why? *Because none of the men were there!* That's right, the moment Yeshua was sentenced to death, right after they dragged him off to be flogged, our men disappeared, fearful that they might be next. They hightailed it to Galilee. Yohanna and I remained. Nobody in those days would think of arresting a woman. Because, of course, we weren't dangerous.

🖋

We approached the city from the east, after walking for three days from Capharnaum, stopping at night to camp and rest. Our small group of women felt vastly diminished without Shoshanna who, it turned out, had been serious about going off on a caravan adventure with Marcus Silanus. The day after Ilana's wedding, we had said tearful goodbyes to her, and watched Marcus lead a camel, with Shoshanna astride, off to the *caravanserai* outside town.

"I'll be back with treasure for all of you!" Shoshanna called out, wiping away tears with the tail end of her turban before tucking it under her hair.

"The greatest treasure will be your return," Ilana whispered.

The last night of our journey, we rested in Bethany at the home of our friend Miriam, an easy walk from our final destination. At the first glimmer of morning, we rose and made our way up the Mount of Olives. Our excitement to get a glimpse of Jerusalem led us to push ourselves, and we were all panting slightly when we finally crested the hill and stopped to take in the view. Straight ahead, across the Kidron Valley, the city wall rose up from the desert, undulating like a muslin veil through the already shimmering heat. Beyond the wall, rooftops crowded their way into the haze, squeezed together all the way to the horizon by the city's maze of narrow streets.

But our eyes did not linger there. They were compelled north, to an enormous expanse of white and gold that blazed in the ascending sun. Our Holy Temple. My father had told me about Herod the Great's dedicated mission to renovate and enhance this sanctuary for the Jewish people. Herod's vision of grandeur for the Temple spared no expense, and the decades of work required to achieve it spared no slave. Call it noble, call it maniacal, here it was, fifty years later, gleaming before us, a majestic compound of bright white stone and blinding precious metal. Tall pristine porticoes established a fortified perimeter around its vast marble courtyard. At the far end of that space, a smaller stone wall surrounded a rectangular building with a front facade of pure gold. The Holy of Holies, with its sacred inner shrine that only high priests could enter.

Emotions were mixed as we all took in that sight. Yeshua, holding my hand tightly, was silent. I felt the faint heartbeat of his anxiety, muffled by his determination to accept whatever lay ahead. During the four days that it had taken us to walk from Galilee, Yeshua had vacillated between excitement and fear. Excitement, for the possibility of bringing his message to a crowd of receptive pilgrims. Fear, for the increasingly clear premonition he had that Jerusalem would be the site of his death.

I, on the other hand, was in denial, flatly refusing to accept the idea that Yeshua's death was either imminent or inescapable.

We had just been joined as husband and wife in every way other than law. My dream of making a home with the man I loved was now at my fingertips. I consciously dwelled on this fantasy life, trying to keep the implications of his visions at bay. The words of the prophet Deborah hovered at the edges of my mind, but I pushed them away. Why should Yeshua die? His death at this point in time not only felt profoundly unfair, it made no sense.

When we lay together at night, I mustered arguments against it.

"Are you seeing any of the details of how you are to die? Or when?" I pestered. "No, you're not. You don't know if it will happen before the Passover feast or after. You don't know if you'll be poisoned or stabbed or stoned or . . . ."

Yeshua stopped my mouth by rolling on top of me and kissing me. Very effective. After all those months of physical exploration, and our recent plunge into total sexual pleasure, he knew exactly how to redirect my thinking. Making love was a welcome respite from the weight of our future, but in the end, the burden did not disappear.

"How I wish I could remain with you like this forever," Yeshua said, as he held me tightly and drifted off to sleep.

Wish granted, I thought. I determined that he should remain with me, vowing silently to do everything possible to keep him alive, even if it meant throwing myself in front of daggers or spears. And I prayed. I prayed that he be delivered from anything that threatened his life. Normally, I would not pray for anything so specific nor for something that so clearly benefited me, but in this case, I justified my prayer as a more general plea for humanity. Because surely it was in the interest of humankind to have Yeshua live, so that he could teach everyone how to live their lives peacefully. I promised God that if Yeshua were allowed to live, I would devote my life to him completely.

Watching the sun burn its way up the Mount of Olives that morning, I fortified my resolve.

On the other side of Yeshua, Peter let out a low gasp of amazement. "Is the Holy Temple not grand, Rabbi? Is it not a palace fit for a King of Heaven such as you?" Out of the corner of my eye, I saw Judah nodding vigorously. Both men were ready to coronate Yeshua that very instant.

"Peter, how can you not know me after all this time?" Yeshua said. "I would rather sleep out in the open under a celestial night sky than in that lonely gold-plated box. Or, even better," he winked, "give me a nice hovel of mud bricks, with friends to warm me."

✍

We entered Jerusalem on foot. The story that Yeshua rode into the city on a donkey is, as I said earlier, a myth. It's a clever strategy, the donkey tale, because if you know your Old Testament, you'll remember Zechariah's prophesy that the king of the Jews will come to Jerusalem on a lowly animal, a symbol of peace. But outside the world of myth and storytelling, prophecies are limited by historical reality, in this case the hard fact that Jerusalem was under Roman control. Remember, it was Passover, and the city was packed with people. To keep those hundreds of thousands of Jewish pilgrims in line, Pontius Pilate loaded the city with Roman soldiers, all on high alert for potential troublemakers. Would we take the chance of calling attention to Yeshua by parading him into Jerusalem on an animal, thus encouraging a frenzy of Zechariah-steeped messiah-seekers? No, we would not.

It would have been nice if Jerusalem up close resembled what it looked like from a distance—peaceful, floating in a mist of prayers and piety. Instead, the Holy City at Passover was a stew of roughly managed mayhem. Imagine thousands of pilgrims, each one dragging a dusty and reluctant goat or lamb, intent on bringing it to the temple's sacrificial altar so his family could be purified. Or, if the family was too poor to forfeit a goat or lamb, they purchased a pigeon from one of the many hawkers swinging braces of birds through the air, eddies of tiny feathers falling like confetti from the sky.

One chaotic stream of pedestrians, packed with eager, impatient families and their bleating, defecating animals, flowed north toward the Temple Mount. Another equally crowded, noisy stream of people flowed back, the cries of livestock replaced now by those of offspring, exhausted and hungry for the lightly seared meat clutched by their parents, remnants of whatever beast had given its blood for the family's sins.

Outside the temple complex, Roman soldiers kept the lines moving by clanging swords against shields and prodding anyone who loitered too long in one place. We shuffled our way forward, through the tide, buffeted by elbows and shoulders, trying to avoid the mines of animal excrement that dotted the street. Pressed upward on an incline of long, shallow steps, we popped through the Shushan gate, like a cork from a bottle of champagne, into an enormous plaza where the crowd was finally able to spread out.

I stepped into the shadowed lip of a gateway, leaning against the stone to steady myself. The entire experience of getting to the temple had been a blur of dizziness and disorientation, and I was grateful to breathe deeply for the first time in many minutes.

Yohanna came over and offered me some water from her goatskin, which I gladly accepted. "Crazy, isn't it?" she asked. "The first few times I was here, I wanted to run away screaming. Getting here, you feel overwhelmed by how little room you have to move in. Then when you arrive at the top, you're suddenly released into this wide-open expanse."

An ocean of space now surrounded us. The Temple Mount was mammoth in size, beyond anything I had ever seen. Picture twenty-nine football fields of polished white stone laid side by side and end to end, all surrounding and enclosing a nine-foot-high wall, within which the temple building itself gleamed in the sun. Against that wall, scores of merchants had set up stalls for the day's commerce. Pigeons, flapping about on tethered perches, were on sale to anyone who still needed the requisite offering.

Most numerous were the brokers who exchanged money, the money changers. Every Jew who came to the Temple was required under Jewish law to offer not just an animal sacrifice but a monetary contribution: the Temple's annual tax of half a shekel. But you couldn't pay the tax with whatever local currency you brought from home: the High Priest had decreed that the tax be paid in a particular kind of coin, a specific priest-sanctioned shekel. So pilgrims took their "filthy" native coins to a money changer's table and, for a hefty fee, received the equivalent in "pure" shekels.

Yeshua had made his way over to one of the money-changing tables by the time Yohanna and I rejoined the group. He held one of the sanctioned coins and examined it, while the merchant looked on warily.

"You understand money, Levi," Yeshua said, peering closely at the images on the coin. "Tell me what this coin is."

"That, Rabbi," said Levi, straightening his shoulders, "is a Tyrian shekel, first minted in Tyre over a century ago. Now, it is minted here in Jerusalem."

"But there are images on its faces," Yeshua scowled. "An eagle on one side, and on the other—"

"Yes, Rabbi, the other image is of—"

"A man. A man with Grecian features."

"—the Greek demi-god Heracles," Levi concluded.

"A god. A *pagan* god." Yeshua returned the coin to the merchant, an elderly turbaned man with a practiced smile and a haphazard set of teeth. "Tell me sir, you spend much of your time near the temple, do you not?"

"Indeed, sir, I do, indeed I do," said the merchant. "I am here for many years, since the days of our great King Herod."

"Since Herod?" Yeshua mused. "Were you here when Herod placed the golden eagle over the Temple gate?"

"Was I here?" The old man chuckled. "Any law-abiding Jew in his right mind was here, protesting that abomination."

"And it was an abomination because . . .?" Yeshua goaded him on.

"Because it was an idol, of course! 'Ye shall not make any likeness of anything that is in heaven above, or that is in the earth beneath.' Moses gave us that commandment directly from the Lord." The merchant pronounced the words sanctimoniously, shaking his head in disbelief at Yeshua's apparent ignorance.

"So, the likeness of an eagle on anything would make that thing an idol?" Yeshua asked.

"Yes, absolutely."

"As would the likeness of a pagan god."

"Certainly so!"

"Both of which images appear on this coin," Yeshua said. "Thus, by your own admission, this coin is an idol. And yet, you are selling it to others to pay their taxes."

The old man began to stammer and cough. "Well yes, but . . . the only reason I sell this—ahem!—this coin, the reason I, uh, make it available is because—ahem!—because the High Priest has decreed this coin as the only acceptable token. For, uh, the tax."

Sweat from the man's forehead had begun dislodging the edge of his turban, and he mopped his brow with it.

"The High Priest requires an idol to be used to pay the annual tax? Why would he do that? Does he not know the law?" A smile played over Yeshua's lips, as he watched this self-professed servant of Jewish law squirm. At the same time, his eyes darkened. Yeshua was not an intolerant man, but he abhorred hypocrisy.

"Well, of course he does," the merchant protested. "High Priest Caiphas probably understands the law almost as well as the Lord himself. And Caiphas is always looking to maximize the glory of our Lord. In fact, this coin is a perfect example. Because this Tyrian shekel," he picked up one of the coins and held it high so it could be properly admired, "is more valuable than any other coin in our realm."

"How so?"

"Most of the coins we use in Judea are a mishmash of metals—bronze, copper, a bit of silver perhaps. But *this* coin is almost *pure silver*! Over ninety percent!"

"Worth every extra penny you charge for it," Levi interrupted sarcastically.

"How much *do* you charge for it?" Yeshua asked. "How much would I owe you if I had kept the shekel?"

"Twelve drachms. Twelve drachms for one shekel, or—" the man gestured toward our group, "if you want to purchase enough shekels for everyone to pay their taxes, I can give you a better price."

"*Twelve* drachms!" Levi protested. "That is three times what the shekel is worth!"

"I am entitled to my profit," the old man insisted, crossing his arms.

That did it. That self-serving rationalization put Yeshua over the edge. Anger clenched his jaw and honed his tongue. Putting both hands on the money changer's flimsy table, he leaned forward to within a hands-breadth of the man's face and stared. Rattled, unwilling to meet Yeshua's gaze, the merchant shuffled backward until he was pressed against the wall. When Yeshua finally spoke, it was in a low tone simmering with rage.

"This Temple behind you, *this* is my Father's house. It is your Father's house too."

The money changer nodded rapidly, eager to appease the madman before him, desperate for Yeshua to go. But Yeshua had no intention of leaving.

"It is a house of prayer. It belongs to everyone here, *everyone*— Jew, Gentile, man, woman, rich, or poor. And anyone may enter, *anyone*. Not only those who bring an animal for sacrifice. My Father would rather see a goat give milk for a lifetime than meat for one meal."

Yeshua straightened up, keeping his hands on the table. By this point, he had attracted the attention of people waiting nearby, pilgrims who had stopped wondering what was taking so long, and now watched with curiosity this man who was apparently becoming enraged by a shekel.

To my dismay, I saw that he had also attracted the attention of two other groups—a gang of men being waved over by Judah, and even more alarming, a pair of Roman soldiers, who followed the brigands as they crossed the plaza.

"Yeshua!" I hissed. He paid no attention.

"My Father wants no part of your trade." Yeshua swung one arm toward the row of tables along the wall.

"Yeshua!" I called again, more loudly. I began pushing my way toward him.

"My Father cares not a whit for the silver in your coins."

Yeshua swept his left palm across the table, sending coins sprawling everywhere. The money changer cried out in horror, and scrambled to collect his revenue before anyone else could get it. The small crowd around Yeshua cheered, and the Roman soldiers ran toward us.

"My Father's house is not a house of *commerce!*" Yeshua flipped the table over, scattering its contents. At that moment, Judah's friends arrived and expanded the melee, turning over neighboring tables and encouraging others around them to join in. I did not yet see any swords, but I imagined they were concealed under the men's cloaks. It was definitely time to go. I grabbed Yeshua's arm and pulled him away.

"Come," I said. "It is not safe for you to stay."

"My Father's house is a place of peace and love," he murmured, distant and dazed.

Yohanna, Levi, and Ilana helped me hurry Yeshua out of the Temple complex. Just before we descended the stairs from the plaza, I heard Judah call out.

"Why are you taking him? Magda, bring him back! He must stay to lead us!"

Ignoring Judah's pleas, we rushed Yeshua down the steps, then formed a circle around him, lest he be recognized. Walking as quickly as we dared to avoid suspicion, we pressed through the throngs, past the stinking sacrifices, out of the stone city gate, and onto the road toward the Mount of Olives. There, finally, I felt safe. Stopping under the shade of an olive tree to rest, I sat before Yeshua and turned his face toward me. There were the eyes I recognized, deep brown and fluid, as much because of their shifting color as because there was water gathering at their corners.

"What is it, my love? What distresses you?" I asked.

"I thought I knew myself," he said, looking back at the temple complex. "I consider myself nonviolent. I have never had any desire to hurt anyone or cause a disturbance, at least not deliberately. But today . . . today, I really wanted to smash things apart. All those animals being led to slaughter, for no good reason; the hypocrisy and greed of the priests, demanding their silver coins, the thievery of the entire operation! I felt rage, Magda, real *rage*."

"That's normal," I reassured him. "All humans experience anger."

"But rage cannot be our path forward, can it? My Father's house . . . ." He tilted his head to one side, as though he were listening to something else. After a long moment, he continued. "My Father's house is a house of prayer, not violence."

"Surely there is room in that house for passion," I said. "Perhaps not a passion based on rage and violence, but one based on the desire for justice." I remembered my conversation with Judah in Capharnaum. Judah had insisted that there could be no kingdom of God without justice. But Judah equated justice with revenge and violence. There had to be another way.

Yeshua leaned back against the olive tree and closed his eyes. "Perhaps, Magda, perhaps. If so, you teach me. As you have been doing all along."

JERUSALEM

2

The people Yeshua encountered in Jerusalem over Passover fell into one of two categories: those who loved him, and those who wanted him dead. If this truth weren't so tragic, it might be comical. Here was a simple peasant preacher who scattered agricultural parables like barley seed, yet some people felt as threatened as if the Babylonian army were outside the city walls, risen from the dust of history to take them back into captivity.

I'll dive into the hornet's nest of who actually orchestrated Yeshua's death shortly. For now, let's just look at his enemies. First and foremost, there were the Temple priests. They saw Yeshua as a blasphemer trying to undermine their authority, and they were particularly vexed when he called them money-grubbing hypocrites. The priests also felt threatened by how much the masses adored him. In their hierarchical worldview, devotion and love were directly related to power—the more you had of the first two, the more you could grab of the last.

Herod Antipas, up in Galilee, was equally pissed off at Yeshua's popularity. He had been watching the numbers who flocked to Yeshua grow for months, and, while there wasn't anything *obviously* rebellious about Yeshua's words, Antipas wasn't stupid. He could see where all this talk about the rich becoming poor and the poor becoming rich was going.

Last but not least, there was Pontius Pilate. I put Pilate last because, unlike the others, he really had nothing personal against Yeshua. Pilate's biggest concern was the maintenance of law and order during Passover. When he heard the news of a rabble-rouser upending tables at the Temple, he sent reinforcements to deal with the fracas. They arrested a handful of Zealots: two young boys, barely able to shave, and a more seasoned rebel named Barabbas. Pilate planned on keeping them in prison until after the holiday, maybe flog them a few times to teach them a lesson. As for Yeshua, Pilate wasn't too worried about him. The preacher from Nazareth had quieted down after that first day, returning to the Temple to teach small groups of people in a remote corner of the plaza. Nothing harmful in that. Still, Pilate told his soldiers to keep an eye on him, just in case.

Remember, it was Passover. A holy time, not a time to be running around killing people. This rationale, along with the fact that the common people appeared to love Yeshua, gave the Temple priests pause. Because, let's face it, it doesn't look good to interrupt your slaughter of the sacrificial lambs so you can slit the throat of a prophet, no matter how false you think he is.

<hr/>

After the drama of our first day, we settled into a calmer rhythm. Each morning, we headed back to the Temple. There, on the expansive plaza, under the arms of an enormous hackberry tree with lime-green leaves just beginning to unfurl, Yeshua taught anyone who would listen. Initially, his audience was a smattering of men and women, mostly curious Jewish pilgrims who were killing time while they waited for the priests to kill their animals. By the end of the week, after word of the charismatic new prophet traveled, hundreds of people, Jewish and Gentile, crowded against each other to hear his words.

I set up a small table nearby, where, with Yohanna's help, I anointed pilgrims. Like Yeshua, I watched the number of my devotees grow throughout the week. This should not have surprised me as much as it did. Had I been in the habit of giving myself credit, I would have recognized that my anointment skills were now much more refined than they had been months earlier. Time and practice had made me an expert on touchpoints of relaxation in the human body—the scalp, the base of the neck, the shoulders, the upper shell of the ear, the inner wrists, the feet. My oiled hands moved over a person's skin for however long it took me to reach past their defenses and bond with their inner energy.

It was in Jerusalem that I experienced my first glimpse at how my anointment practice might yet evolve. The inner sanctum, that ecstatic spiritual space where I connected with others, always held me, my anointee, and Yeshua, if he was near. But on the Temple Mount, I began noticing the proximity of other spirits, people I had recently anointed. Their spirits hovered nearby when I was connected to someone else, looking longingly at our union like children gazing through the window of a toy store.

This was new, and I thrilled at its potential. If anointment could bring together, not just whoever was with me at the time, but people I had anointed earlier—well, couldn't such an experience be a catalyst for change? Couldn't it provide the foundation for the society of equality, tolerance, and love that Yeshua was always talking about? I was eager to explore how I might forge those broader connections.

Not all those who visited Yeshua at the Temple were open-minded or curious seekers. The Pharisees, for example. The smug, sanctimonious know-it-alls with their blue-striped tallits draped over luxurious, gold-fringed tunics. Windbags who claimed to understand every Jewish law, written and oral, as handed down through the centuries by our ancestors. Yeshua had had a few run-ins with Pharisees already, in Capharnaum and its surrounding villages, in which he challenged that group's blind obedience to strict written laws rather than adaptive moral principles. Frankly, these challenges had not gone well for the Pharisees. Yeshua argued circles around them.

Reports of such encounters must have gotten back to Jerusalem, because while Yeshua was there, Pharisee representatives came every day to question him on legal minutiae, trying to trip him up and reveal him as a fraud. Yet every day, Yeshua skewered them anew with the honesty and deftness of his thought. At the end of each interrogation, freshly chastised Pharisees left, worrying the fringe tassels on their shawls, and muttering to each other. The next day, a new pair of interrogators appeared. This ecclesiastical Whack-A-Mole lasted for three days before the Pharisees finally gave up.

One afternoon, a Pharisee raised a convoluted question that I really couldn't follow—something about a childless woman marrying one man who died, then marrying his brother (who also died), and multiple other brothers thereafter, *blah, blah, blah*, and the bottom line was: who would be allowed to have her in the resurrection prophesied by Daniel? Yeshua's response was, in a nutshell, they would all be like angels, and angels don't have sex.

As the Pharisee slunk away, I stepped over to Yeshua, to suggest that it was time to go home. His stance stopped me in my tracks:

he was standing ramrod straight, head bowed, eyes shut. His arms hung at his sides, fists clenching and unclenching. Wherever he was, it was not here.

If he was having another vision, like the kind in his night terrors, I decided then and there that he would not experience it alone. After all, I was his wife. Wasn't it my duty to help him bear the dark disturbances that plagued him? When sorrows and difficulties are shared, their burden is halved, my father always said. Also, I reasoned that I should learn what the danger to him looked like, so I could better help him avert it. Reaching for Yeshua's hand, I closed my eyes, ready to enter whatever ominous space he was in.

Yohanna later told me that the moment my skin touched his, a fierce hot wind blew across the outer Temple court, stirring up so much dust and fine debris that the two of us were temporarily shrouded from view. I didn't notice it, for I was being transported into an alternate reality—Yeshua's vision became my vision too.

In this dream-space, Yeshua and I stood on the peak of the Mount of Olives, under a foreboding sky that surged with dark angry clouds. Already, a storm erupted across the Kidron valley, and within the walls of the Holy City, a tempest of fire and smoke, of steel clashing against steel, of blood drawing blood into the parched dirt. Hundreds—no, thousands—of soldiers charged furiously through the streets of Jerusalem, while all around them the walls of the city blazed in a hellfire of destruction. I had no way of knowing what year it was.

"There are days of war coming," Yeshua muttered aloud. Then he shouted out, perhaps as a warning, "Days of war!"

"Days of justice!" My voice cried out next, compelled by some unknown force. Years earlier, I had been falsely accused of being possessed by demons, but this was the first time in my life that I understood what possession might feel like, for I had absolutely no control over the words coming out of my mouth. Yet the power or energy forcing my speech did not feel menacing. And despite the devastation unfolding before my eyes in this vision, I was not fearful. Although what I saw was horrifying and would, under normal circumstances, make me cringe or look away, I continued watching with what I can only describe as detached fascination. I was watching people die, people I did not know, some of whom I understood had yet to be born. Somehow, I intuited that what was taking place before me was an inevitable event in the future, not the past.

Yeshua's words and mine rumbled through the thick particulate air of the present world to our bewildered audience at the Temple, who saw nothing of what we saw. They shielded themselves from a dust storm, while we watched armies rush into a burning city from the north and west. One group of unarmed citizens was slaughtered, another was trampled to death by crowds seeking escape. In our vision, the dead began to pile high around the altar of the Temple, and their lifeblood streamed down its steps.

Yeshua stretched his hands toward the sky, still clutching mine. "All that is written shall be fulfilled. Jerusalem will be surrounded by armies . . . its desolation will be near."

Suddenly, the scene before us shifted, and, still in our hallucination, Yeshua and I stood outside the Temple, watching Roman invaders trying to gain access to the inner sanctuary. The soldiers' fury knew no bounds, so intent were they on ransacking the building. They pounded the walls with a battering ram again and again, wheeling their weapon to and fro with such bellows and roars that they resembled wild beasts more than civilized humans. Finally, one soldier grabbed a flaming piece of wood and, standing on the shoulders of another, flung it through a golden window into a hallway filled with jeweled wall-hangings and carpets. Within minutes the entire Temple complex was aflame.

Gazing on as the Temple burned, I felt Yeshua retreat. He turned to me with a pleading look, part exhaustion, and part abdication.

"Finish it," he said. "Show them what is coming." I remembered Deborah's words from Mount Tabor. His time was almost complete, she said, while mine was just beginning. Was this moment part of that transition?

A violent energy tore into and through me. Suddenly, I felt enraged at the hypocrisy and dishonesty of the Temple's keepers. The Temple should have been a monument to God's goodness, a celebration of love and equality, but it had been defiled with deceit and greed. And it was beyond redemption.

"All of *this* . . ." I cried, sweeping my arms in a semicircle around the inner Temple, "*all* of this will be destroyed! These stones will be *thrown down*! Not a single one shall remain."

I waited for a minute, as the vision before me slowly ebbed away. When I again spoke, my voice was calmer, more hopeful. "We are building something better now, something more inclusive. A social order where everyone is acknowledged equally and loved equally. Come." I swept my arm through the air again, more slowly. "Come join us in that effort."

Our listeners stood stunned. The wind died down, allowing the desert to settle on Yeshua and me. We blinked off the thin film of sand encrusting our lashes and looked at each other. The Temple stood behind us, unscathed.

I did not know back then that the vision Yeshua and I saw was the violent end to a Jewish rebellion that would take place over thirty years later, long after he had died. I would receive the news in the wild lavender fields of Provence, outside the tiny village of Sainte Baume. Yohanna would be with me, and she and I would hold each other and cry for the city that we had tried to save.

☙

At the Temple, Yohanna helped me pack up my oils and blankets, while Yeshua went to meditate in the shadow of the hackberry some distance away. From across the plaza, I heard a familiar voice.

"So it is certain to happen!"

I turned around to see Judah striding quickly toward me. None of us had seen him since our first day in the Holy City. We feared he had been swept up with his rebel colleagues that afternoon and was languishing somewhere in Pilate's Fortress Antonia on the north side of Jerusalem.

"Where have you been? We've been so worried." I gave him a cursory hug, the only kind he would tolerate. Deep folds under his red-rimmed eyes told me that he had not been doing much sleeping, and the stench of stale liquor and sweat told me where he had been.

"I've been trying to stay out of sight," Judah said. "I don't know if I was seen by any of the Romans the other day, but I didn't want to take that chance. Our leader Barabbas was arrested, you know."

The inferno of a setting sun raged against the gold Temple dome. I gave Judah a hard look. "Barabbas is a violent man. Your Zealots won't get anywhere with violence, Judah, you know that."

Judah glared at me, incredulous. "But you just saw the Temple's destruction. You said every stone would fall! How is that not violent?"

I had no answer for him. I didn't know how to interpret the vision.

"Magda, isn't it possible that the vision you saw was the Apocalypse? And that it will shortly be upon us?"

"I don't think so, Judah."

"No, listen to me, Magda, listen." Judah was getting agitated, and he glanced around the plaza furtively. "I have told the Zealots how important Rabbi Yeshua is, that he has extraordinary powers, extra-human capabilities—"

"Well, yes, but . . . ."

"And I have told them that there may be a moment this week when Rabbi Yeshua will be in trouble. I thought that moment was the other day when he turned over the money changers' tables. Remember I called to you? I wanted you to bring him back so we could start the revolution."

"Judah, I—"

"No, Magda, I know. I know I was wrong; I see that now. You and our Rabbi have just given me a much clearer picture of what is coming. I'm finally putting it all together in my head: Rabbi Yeshua told us that he will die soon. And I think that at that moment, when Rabbi is in greatest danger, God will intervene. God will save him! Or Rabbi Yeshua will save himself because he has divine powers." Judah's eyes were wide and eager, my own were squinting in disbelief. "Don't you see? God and Rabbi Yeshua will initiate the End of Days. And we, we Zealots, will be there to help, to fight with the armies of Heaven. Against the Romans. Against Pontius Pilate."

"Oh?" Yohanna had come closer to listen and could not contain the skepticism in her voice.

"Judah," I spoke quietly. "I believe what I saw today was a vision of the future, but I do not think it was imminent. I cannot say when the events I saw will happen or how they will come to be. And frankly, it is my hope that perhaps they can be avoided."

"If you don't know when those events will happen, you

can't say for certain that they *won't* happen soon," Judah insisted.

"That's true, but . . . ."

"Hah!" Abruptly, Judah turned around and saw a small group of men standing at the western gate. He ran across the plaza, pursued by his lengthening shadow. "I'll be back for the Passover feast!" he called over his shoulder.

That night, sitting outside Miriam's home in Bethany, I tried once again to convince Yeshua to flee. After all, he himself had said we were running out of time.

"My love, my dear Yeshua," I began, in the softest, most compelling voice I could muster. "Nothing is certain about how this week will end, is it? You have done what you came here to do, you have taught eager listeners every day. Your words will undoubtedly travel with them and continue to spread. We can travel too, perhaps to Syria, perhaps to Egypt. Now that you have delivered your message, there is no reason to stay here, where you are surrounded by enemies."

I couldn't tell if he was listening. He was staring at the sky with a dreamy, almost wistful look. Emboldened, hopeful that I might be swaying him, I continued, spinning out the fantasy I had been creating in my mind for so long.

"We can bring your truth to more people, in this land, and in others. We could even travel for a time with Marcus Silanus, we could learn how to ride camels. Imagine Shoshanna on a camel! Two stubborn creatures pitted against each other," I smiled at the idea, and to my delight, Yeshua chuckled too.

"We could continue wandering and teaching, or . . . ." Here was the heart of my dream. Yeshua's eyes were closed now, but I didn't think he was asleep. "Or we could find a town and stay. We could build a community. We could build a home. You would become a rabbi beloved by all, and I . . . ."

His voice was tender, relaxed. "Yes, dear Magda, what would you do in this fantasy?"

"Well, I could help you. I could continue my anointment practice. Perhaps Yohanna might join us. Perhaps—perhaps someday we might even be blessed with children, and I . . . ." The emotion I had been holding back threatened to break through. "If we had children, Yohanna could take over anointing while I devoted myself to them. And to you."

We sat next to each other in silence—I, buoyed by the imaginary world I had woven, and he . . . well, I could only hope the picture I had created was enticing enough for him to act.

"You would devote yourself to me?" he asked.

"Of course!" I insisted. "What greater purpose could I have in this world than to support you? And to raise our children, should we be fortunate enough to have any?"

"You would be a wife and a mother."

"I am already a wife, and I would embrace being a mother," I said. "Surely those are worthwhile roles in life."

"And you would prioritize this family of ours, if we had one, over everything else? You would give up anointing? You would abandon the work of bringing people together. "

It felt like an unfair question. It wouldn't be one or the other. My mother had been able to exercise her anointment skills occasionally while still prioritizing her domestic duties. Yet I recognized that my anointment practice, with its spiritual dimension, was different from my mother's. It required a certain mental focus from me, one that I might not be able to achieve if there were children running around.

Then too, there was the glimpse I had recently, up on the Temple Mount, of other souls or spirits waiting to join my space of connectivity during anointment. Might I draw them in over time, with more practice? What would *that* feel like, to unify multiple souls? Was I willing to give up that effort if necessary?

On the other hand, I loved him. Oh, how I loved him!

Yeshua watched me. Did he want me to say yes or no? Hesitating, I realized he had let go of my hand. In the end, I told him the only truth I knew.

"Yes. Absolutely, I would. Because I love you."

He sighed. Was it relief or resignation? "I know you do, Magda."

"I love you more than *anything* in the world," I declared. Now, finally, I allowed myself to weep. "Anything."

"I know that," he said, comforting me. "I know. And that is why I cannot go."

JERUSALEM

3

eshua's last supper was not the somber affair that has been painted for you throughout the centuries by grand masters like Giotto, da Vinci, Raphael, or Warhol. Such paintings were based upon the fabricated narratives of the Quartet, who peppered their descriptions of his final Passover meal with dire predictions of upcoming betrayals and the introduction of a primitive ritual in which Yeshua offered his actual body and blood for consumption.

Paul came up with that fiction, of course. Paul, the eleventh-hour Apostle, who wasn't even there. Cunning Paul, master of ritual and symbolism. Who else would have been able to introduce the idea of a sacrament in which ordinary bread and wine are magically transformed into a man's flesh and blood? A sacrament in which, when you eat that bit of bread and drink that sip of wine, you are *actually* eating and drinking from Yeshua's body? Crazy cannibalistic concept, yet there it lies, at the heart of the Catholic Church's catechism of divine forgiveness.

Marcus Silanus had arranged for us to eat our Passover meal at the home of one of his clients. Because this gentleman planned to dine with friends on the other side of the city, he generously agreed to let us use his kitchen and courtyard. His home was modest, but beautifully decorated with riches from the Far East: vibrant silk tapestries, lacquered wooden boxes, intricate jade, and ivory figurines, and, I saw with a twang of envy, a library that rivaled the one in my father's home. These treasures spilled out even into the courtyard, where a battalion of terra cotta warriors and horses stood at ease under a small grove of lemon and olive trees.

Most of our group went to the Temple with Yeshua on the feast day. Ilana had been feeling unwell all week, but she woke up that morning feeling well enough to take on the task of going to the market with Levi and Phillip to shop for the evening meal. That left Yohanna and me to prepare the table.

When Peter learned that I would be staying behind, he was overjoyed, for he hadn't had uninterrupted time with Yeshua for several days. He sought me out in the kitchen, where I was assessing cooking utensils and dishes. With my head deep in a crockery cupboard, I didn't hear him enter the room until he loudly cleared his throat. When I pulled my head out of the darkness of the shelves, he stared at me in silence for a few seconds, smacking his tongue against the roof of his mouth, as if he had to slap it into obedience to speak.

"Um, I am here to uh, to . . . well, to thank you, Magda," Peter said. He smiled uncomfortably, unused to finding kind words for me. "Rabbi says he will soon die. I don't want to believe him, but if it is true, I have so much more to ask him. Thank you for giving me the time today to do that." Pressing palm to palm, Peter bowed his head.

Part of me was disarmed by Peter's suppliant pose, yet I knew better than to let my guard down completely. "Well, it is Yeshua's time to give, not mine," I said cautiously.

"But his time and your time have become so intertwined it has been almost impossible to find him alone." Poor Peter could never quite contain his resentment and spite, even in a moment of gratitude. He closed his eyes and squared his shoulders, and I saw his lips move. Was he praying for self-restraint? It would have been a first. "In any case, I am grateful to have this morning alone with him."

My heart softened a bit toward this lunk of a man, whose jealousy had always stood in the way of our friendship. I knew that he loved Yeshua deeply. In that love, and in the fear of loss that accompanied it, Peter and I were exactly alike.

"Of course, Peter. I understand."

Thinking back on this private exchange in the days immediately after Yeshua's death made me believe that Peter's anger and resentment toward me was subsiding. I should have known better.

After Peter left, I sought out Yohanna. Throughout the week, I had not spent much time with her, and I felt in need of her level head and warm heart. We began setting up for our feast by dragging a heavy oak dining table from the house to the courtyard. I put myself in charge of the lighting, gathering candlesticks, candles, and oil lamps from various rooms, while Yohanna clipped boughs from a large cassia tree, which was unfurling yellow flowers like fingers of clustered sunshine. We reconvened at the table to discuss ornamentation.

"Should we place the flowers in a vase?" I wondered aloud as Yohanna placed her harvest on the tabletop. "Or should we arrange them along the center of the table?" I picked up one of the cut branches and buried my nose in its saffron pollen. "But it will be hours before we sit down to dine, and I wouldn't want these blooms to wilt." My fingertips hovered over the delicate petals. I imagined them dropping, curling into themselves, shriveling up.

"They are so beautiful. Don't you think they're beautiful? They shouldn't have to die—" my voice choked on the last word.

Yohanna took the branch and placed it back on the table. She held me close as I allowed myself to weep. I wept as Jacob must have wept on the road to Ephrath, when he watched his beloved wife Rachel die giving birth to his son. I wept as Ruth must have wept when her husband Boaz collapsed and perished, right after their wedding night. Now that I was finally facing the devastating truth that Yeshua would soon be gone, I felt that I was shouldering the grief of every woman who had ever lost, or would ever lose, a man she loved more than life itself. I would have given anything, *everything* to keep Yeshua with me.

"How can I live without him?" I cried, my diaphragm in spasm. "I cannot—I cannot imagine my life without him."

Yohanna shushed me and rocked me gently. Her thick mane of hair spilled over my shoulders, smelling of fresh grass and rosemary. Gently, she guided me to a bench in the garden. I sat down next to a terra cotta warrior who was kneeling on the ground, spear in hand.

"Magda, you cannot imagine your life without Yeshua, because it is unimaginable," Yohanna said, wiping my cheeks with the sleeve of her tunic. "None of us can think of the world without him in it." She sighed. "But he says—and I don't know whether to believe him—he says he will always be with us. You are closest to him. Can we believe him? Do *you* believe him?"

I had heard Yeshua make this statement to the group, when he shared the news of his impending death with everyone. Levi and Peter and some of the others had argued with him, but they could not change his conviction. "I have seen my fate, and I cannot alter it," Yeshua had said. "But I will never be far away from you. I will live on in your hearts."

Yohanna's question reminded me of the resting space Yeshua had introduced me to, way back in Magdala, when he first taught me how to meditate. A silent, reflective space, somewhere outside of reality and accessible only through quiet contemplation, where he and I met, gently joined through faint bands of energy, manifested as different wavelengths of light, gold or indigo. Unlike the space where I connected to people during anointment, this meditation plane contained only Yeshua and me, no one else.

"Yes," I told Yohanna, "I believe him completely."

She looked surprised at my conviction but nodded. "Then you must be present for him. Be present for him in whatever trials he may face. You are strong, Magda." Yohanna squeezed my hand, and I felt her heartbeat in her fingertips. "And remember, you have my strength to draw upon. I will be here with you. I will stay with you however long you will have me."

"Shall we grow old together then?" I sniffled.

"As old as the desert," Yohanna said.

The dinner was a triumph. Of love and fellowship. Of remembrance and instruction. Of meats and sauces. We had so much food, it felt like the entire market of Jerusalem had spilled over our table—there was pigeon and lamb, of course, fresh and pickled fish, apricots and melons, olives and figs, nuts and cheese and yogurt, and freshly-baked flatbread.

For years afterward, I thought of that evening meal as his last gift to me, to all of us. Because whenever grief descended upon me like a black ocean storm, I conjured the memory of all of us sitting together around the heavy oak table, bodies pressed against each other on two long benches, voices overlapping in jest and laughter. Food being heartily eaten, wine and water flowing in equal measure. Candle flames lengthening and reaching up toward their cousins, the stars.

Near the end of the meal, Yeshua stood with his goblet and held up his hand for quiet.

"In this holy hour," he began, "I am almost speechless with the love I feel for you all, my friends." His voice wavered. We waited silently. Every single one of us experienced a flood of emotion—adoration and euphoria—for the man before us. I saw extremes of tenderness and devotion on every face turned toward him. We were spellbound with love. Even Judah—who, I now know, was wrestling with more ambivalent feelings—was able, in that moment, to call upon a deep reservoir of respect and appreciation.

Yeshua continued. "I said 'almost speechless.' When have you ever known me to be at a loss for words?" He grinned, choosing to sail over the sea of seriousness in a balsa boat of gentle humor. We laughed with him, eager to be buoyant.

"I do not know what comes our way tomorrow, I know only what has come before and what is here now. What came before was a rich journey that I could never have undertaken alone. Your company, that of each and every one of you, was and is a blessing." Yeshua looked to his right, where Peter sat beaming with pride and passion. "Peter, my rock in loyalty. And in physicality. You, dear Peter, are a plinth of a man. Would that every place of worship had a foundation as steady as your legs." Laughter from around the table deepened the blush on Peter, and he tried taking up Yeshua's gauntlet.

"Rabbi, my legs will gladly carry you, should you ever tire," Peter said.

"As no doubt would John and James, those man-trees," quipped Judah. "Their height would give you a better vantage to spot your enemies."

Yeshua turned to Ilana and Levi. "I toast the two of you, a daily testimonial to the goodness of unified souls. To the power of family. And the creation of family." He beamed.

For a moment, Ilana looked confused, and she turned to Levi with an unspoken question on her lips. Levi shook his head, protesting, "No, I didn't say a word."

Yeshua's smile could not have stretched any wider. "You cannot hide the secrets of life from me. I know them all."

Yohanna and I exchanged looks, both of us simultaneously connecting the dots between Ilana's recent illness and Yeshua's words.

"You are with child?" Yohanna asked. Ilana nodded shyly and flushed with joy, as we leaped up to embrace her.

"Well," said Peter, clapping Levi on the back, "I am impressed."

In the midst of everyone's celebration of this good news, I saw Yeshua gazing at me wistfully. I felt a pang of anguish at being denied a similar future, but Yohanna's words echoed in my head: *Be present for him.* Resisting the pull of self-pity, I stood up to kiss him on the cheek. Yeshua brushed his fingers through my hair, sending pinpricks tingling over my scalp. I wanted to pull him away someplace private that very moment to test our child-making abilities, but he was not done talking.

"When I am gone . . . ." There were protests around the table, but Yeshua silenced them with an upraised palm. "My leaving is not an 'if,' it is a 'when.' You must prepare yourselves for this, as I have been trying to prepare all of us for some time."

Everyone's face slackened. Only Judah appeared strangely animated. When he first joined us for the meal, he reeked of ale. And I noticed that, throughout dinner, he drank more wine than he ate. Now he stood up, goblet in hand. Although unsteady on his feet, Judah spoke clearly, certain of his words. "But Rabbi, your life can still be saved!" he declared. "God is all-powerful, is he not? Your life could be saved by God! Or by you yourself!"

Yeshua raised an eyebrow. "If it is God's will that I die, then it cannot be God's inclination to save me. But you raise a rhetorical point, Judah. We do not know God's will."

"Right! Absolutely right," said Judah. "Which means that you cannot know your fate with certainty."

"No, but I have seen enough in my visions to convince me."

"But it is a possibility, surely, is it not? That you could be saved?"

Yeshua sighed deeply. "Judah, your imagination misleads you."

"No, Rabbi, it does not." Judah dropped to the ground to kneel at Yeshua's feet, gazing up at him as if by sheer intensity and earnestness he might change Yeshua's mind. "I have seen the kingdom of God you told us about in my dreams. Always, always, you are there. How could you not be?" Judah's voice shifted to a plaintive tone. "You cannot leave us, Rabbi. We love you. *I* love you. Do you not love me? Do you not love me enough to stay?"

The room was silent, perhaps because Judah had articulated a question on everyone's mind. I could sense Yeshua struggling to maintain composure.

"I love all of you, yes Judah, you included. But I fear that has little to do with what is going to happen."

"No!" Judah's tone shifted suddenly. "God will save you. And then God will usher in the new kingdom. And I am ready to help. As are others." He jumped up, intending to exit to the street, not realizing that his cloak had twisted around his legs.

Unceremoniously, he fell forward, bumping his forehead on a terra cotta cavalryman. The soldier stood impassive, as Judah rubbed a rising bump and winced. Embarrassment fueled his anger and pain, both of which he directed at Yeshua. "Why can you not admit that you might be wrong?" Wrenching his cloak behind his shoulders, he stormed away.

"I will go after him," said Phillip, rising from the bench, "to make sure he is safe."

"Wait just a moment. I have one final charge," Yeshua said. He looked up and down the length of the table, resting melancholy eyes on each of our faces. "You don't need me anymore. You are ready. I have taught you everything you need to know to go forward on your own, to spread my message. But," he pulled me close so that I stood shoulder to shoulder with him. "Some of you might, over the course of time, have doubts or questions about how to implement my teachings. I urge you in such cases to seek guidance. There is one here who can advise you." He put his hands on my shoulders. "Magda."

Nobody expected that pronouncement, least of all I. Instinctively I lowered my head, but Yohanna poked me in the ribs from where she was sitting. "Step up. Be present."

"Magda knows me better than anyone here on earth. And I do not say that to make any of you jealous." Yeshua stared directly at Peter as he spoke. "Listen closely: my love for Magda does not diminish the deep love I have for each of you. Can any of you doubt the capacity of my heart? Magda knows my heart intimately. She understands my words, not just because she has read them herself elsewhere, but because she *feels* them. They are a part of her. So let her be a lodestar to all of you, as you try to educate the world in love and tolerance."

Thus did I become his Chosen One.

Earlier that day, we had all agreed that after our supper, we would walk to Gethsemane, a wild grove at the foot of the Mount of Olives. Weather permitting, we thought about spending the night there. But first, I had a final task of my own.

Before leaving Capharnaum, I had purchased from Marcus Silanus a large flask of myrrh oil, which I brought with me to Jerusalem. I've already told you how my mother had used myrrh oil, years earlier, to help me heal. Its effect on me had been twofold: first, its mysterious, complex aroma revealed a gossamer world that lay far from the pain of my injuries; and second, it diminished the intensity of my physical pain. When I asked my mother about the second phenomenon, she confirmed my intuition.

"Myrrh is one of my favorite oils, because of its curative powers," she told me. "But what few people know, Magda, even those who use myrrh for healing and pain, is that its powers build over time. Your father once had a tooth that was rotting and had to be pulled, and he refused to go to the dentist. I gave him a myrrh oil rinse to use every day for a week, and when Marcus Silanus finally dragged him to the dental shop, he claims he never felt a thing!"

That story never left me.

I brought the flask to Jerusalem for Yeshua. He had told me nothing about the torment that lay ahead of him, but the unknown future frightened me. Yes, I was determined to shield him from all danger and pain, if possible, but myrrh was my back-up plan. If it turned out that I couldn't protect him from his fate, I could at least inoculate him against it.

All that week, I had been anointing him with a palmful of myrrh oil in the evening. After the daily stress of the Pharisees, he welcomed a deep tissue massage. Usually, I waited until bedtime to do my anointing, but on this night of toasting, some nagging suspicion told me not to wait.

I placed the myrrh container on the table. "I have a gift for you, Rabbi."

Yeshua recognized the flask and raised an eyebrow. "Now? You wish to present this gift now?"

"Yes, I . . . ." I didn't want to say what I was thinking, that I had a hunch that there might be pain coming his way in the next twenty-four hours, and that I wanted to prepare him. "Rabbi, we have just eaten a sacred meal. It is more appropriate for me to share my gift with you now than at any other time today."

"I see." He understood. "Well then, Magda, I am ready to receive it."

He stood, and I stepped onto the bench to reach the top of his head. The flask held a *chous* of liquid (somewhat less than your gallon today), of which I had, throughout the week, used less than one-eighth. For a moment I hesitated, not sure how Yeshua would react to the shower he was about to receive. *Be present*, I heard again in my head.

Anointment was my calling. I uncorked the bottle and poured.

The myrrh oil that Marcus Silanus gave me came from an herbalist in Parthia who used steam to distill its essence. As a result, the fluid was thicker and more viscous than any oil I had previously used. It flowed like honeyed syrup, saturating the air in musty balsam and cloves. Spilling out over Yeshua, the elixir swirled into his hair and slipped past his shoulders, washing him in Aurelian liquid. I followed its cascade with my hands, smoothing the balm into his skin, trying to ensure that each pore of his body absorbed as much of the healing salve as possible. I willed it to drench him, to cover him like a coat of armor and permeate his skin, so his blood could carry it to his inner organs.

He closed his eyes in appreciation, relaxing his body against my touch and breathing steadily.

Peter's rebuke interrupted my trance. "What are you doing, woman!? You are wasting an enormous quantity of precious oil! You have squandered funds that could have been used for many other things! Like buying food or clothing for those poor pilgrims we see every day."

Who was Peter to tell me what I could or could not do with my money? Like all of Yeshua's followers who had disposable income, I had given many of my funds to Levi, to bankroll the group's activities over the past year. But, with Yeshua's blessing, I had kept a small allowance for myself, for my future needs. It was this allowance that I had used for the myrrh oil. Anger and indignation trembled on my tongue, but Yeshua beat me to it.

"Peter, enough! This is *Magda's* gift to *me!* How can that offend?" he scolded. "Surely you do not bemoan her generosity? You should rather look to her kindness and compassion to guide your own behavior!"

"Also, if this is an extravagance," Yeshua continued, "why should not I receive it? I, the man whom she loves? I, who may die tomorrow? Why should she not anoint me before my death?"

"Rabbi, I . . . I . . ." Peter stammered.

"No, Peter. There will always be poor people among you, there will always be people that we could feed. But I, I will not always be among you."

There was nothing else to be said. I toweled the excess oil off Yeshua with a cloth, and we walked in silence to Gethsemane. It was the last time we would ever hold hands.

JERUSALEM

4

*I*f this were a Shakespearean play, now would be the moment to send in the fool. Because for me, the trauma of what took place over the next day remains as sharp as a Damascus sword. One reason I haven't spoken of it for all this time is that I fear reliving it. So I will approach the story aslant.

I'm going to treat Yeshua's death as a murder investigation.

History records that the Romans—specifically, Pontius Pilate—gave the order to execute Yeshua, but nobody really knows *why* Pilate did so. Who or what made Pilate decide to kill a man who was basically harmless, someone who hadn't violated any Roman laws, other than causing a little commotion at the Temple?

To answer that question for you, I have to go all the way to Rome. Because what happens in Rome doesn't always stay there—sometimes it travels across the sea to Judea.

Remember how I told you that Pontius Pilate was appointed by the Roman Emperor Tiberius? Well, the man Pilate *really* owed his position to was Lucius Sejanus, head of Tiberius's security detail, the man in Rome who made all government decisions.

You see, Tiberius was a reluctant ruler. He didn't want to stay in Rome, making tedious day-to-day decisions about how to govern his sprawling realm. He wanted to live year-round in his summer palace in Capri, chasing naked teenagers in olive groves, and leading a life of wanton debauchery. What was the point of being emperor if you couldn't do that?

Tiberius decided to appoint someone else to run his empire for him, so he could follow his lascivious dreams. That man was his bodyguard, the soldier Lucius Aelius Sejanus. The Emperor trusted Sejanus completely.

Big mistake.

As so often happens to men who get a taste of power, Sejanus decided, after a few months of being ersatz emperor, that he should be next in line for the job. To this end, he killed anyone that he perceived as possibly standing in his way to the throne, including Tiberius's son. Over time, the letters to Emperor Tiberius from family members and Senators detailing Sejanus's murders, power grabs, and political manipulations became impossible to ignore. Tiberius decided it was time for a purge.

And oh what a purge it was! The Emperor kicked things off by massacring the perfidious Sejanus, then throwing his body to a bloodthirsty Roman crowd, which tore Sejanus's corpse to pieces. After that, anyone who had so much as shared a glass of wine with Sejanus was summarily imprisoned, tortured, driven to suicide, or executed. The power shift in Rome was cataclysmic.

It took about six months for news to travel from Rome to Jerusalem. Sejanus was killed in October, which meant that Pontius Pilate received news about the annihilation of his friend and benefactor right before the Passover holiday. He heard about the rape and murder of Sejanus's young daughters, the castration of Sejanus's slaves, the imprisonment of Sejanus's barber. All of a sudden, Pilate became very, very nervous, because somewhere in

Rome, there was a paper trail between this traitor Sejanus and Pilate himself.

What did Pilate do? Well, the *last* thing Pilate wanted to do was make waves. Judea was enough of a backwater province that if he kept his head down and quietly did his job, he might escape Rome's notice.

But the upcoming Passover festival worried him. Emperor Tiberius, despite all his governance flaws, was ahead of his time in one area: religious tolerance. Tiberius had always insisted that administrators of Roman colonies respect the natives in the exercise of their religious beliefs. (His theory being that minimizing unrest would maximize productivity, and, by extension, Rome's tax profits.) If thousands of Jews were gathering in Jerusalem for their most sacred holiday, Tiberius would want Pilate to ensure that everything went smoothly. That is precisely what Pilate intended to do.

So why, you ask, bringing me back to our murder investigation, why would Pilate kill Yeshua, a popular Jewish prophet, if he wanted to stay under Tiberius's imperial radar?

I suggest to you that, in fact, Pilate had no desire to execute Yeshua, but he was expertly manipulated into doing so.

Who would do such a thing? you ask.

Who indeed.

Herod Antipas, King of Galilee, wannabe king of all Judea, got the news about Sejanus's downfall at the same time that Pilate did. Having done his homework on Pilate, Antipas knew about Pilate's connection to Sejanus. For years, Antipas had been fuming about the four-way partition of Judea after the death of his father, Herod the Great. For years, Antipas thought he deserved more land than had been bequeathed to him. Here, finally, was the chance he'd been waiting for.

Surely, Antipas schemed, the uproar in Rome could somehow be used to orchestrate Pilate's removal. If Pilate were gone, Jerusalem would be up for grabs. And if Antipas got Jerusalem . . . well, Jerusalem was the prize of Judea, nothing else really mattered.

The Passover holiday was a perfect opportunity. All Antipas had to do was orchestrate a major misstep by Pilate, something that would draw negative attention and Tiberius's disapproval. Something like arresting and executing a popular Jewish prophet.

Antipas began by infiltrating the Zealots with thugs who were loyal to him. Their orders were to start trouble near Yeshua, whenever and wherever possible, inciting enough violence that Pilate would have to arrest everyone.

Unfortunately, the embedded rabblerousers failed in their first effort. When Yeshua upset the money changer's table at the Temple, the pseudo-Zealots jumped in to increase the pandemonium. But they only succeeded in getting themselves arrested, while Yeshua somehow disappeared. Antipas had to spend a small fortune to ransom them before they were flogged. (The Zealot leader Barabbas was also arrested, but Antipas decided to let that cur languish in prison.)

A few days later, Yeshua denounced the Pharisees and the Holy Temple priests; after that, he foretold the destruction of the Temple. Surely, Pilate would arrest the man now, Antipas thought.

But no. Spies that Antipas had placed in Pilate's palace told him that Pilate wasn't concerned with Yeshua's predictions for the future, so long as they didn't foment unrest. He ordered his soldiers to arrest Yeshua only if the man actively threatened the Roman state.

Antipas scoffed. That would not do. That would not do at all. If Pilate's men were too namby-pamby to seize Yeshua on their own, Antipas would have to help them. But first, he had to get information about Yeshua's whereabouts. And he knew just where to go for that: the local taverns.

Phillip hurried after Judah while the rest of us walked to Gethsemane. He ran down the stone steps from Jerusalem's upper city, where we had dined, to the lower city, where the poorer classes lived and where, despite the holiday, he was certain to find several open taverns. After all, not everyone in Jerusalem was Jewish, nor did all Jews stay away from drink, even on Passover.

Phillip told us later that he located the right tavern only because two men staggered out of it just as he passed by. The basement room housing the bar belonged to an abandoned stone dwelling that was missing part of its thatched roof. Despite the heat of the previous week, its walls and floor were still damp with the last of the winter rains, making the staircase to its entrance slick and slippery.

Phillip entered the dank space to find it packed with men, mostly Gentiles. At the back of the room, in an alcove, four or five military men sat around a small table. Phillip supposed them to be mercenary troops, perhaps hired to help keep the peace during Passover, because their tunics and cloaks were white and gold, rather than the red and blue worn by Pilate's men. But when Yohanna later heard Phillip's description, she identified them as Herod Antipas's soldiers.

"Did they wear gold bracelets on their right arms?" she asked Phillip.

"Why yes, I think they did," he said.

"Then definitely, they were paid by Antipas. He makes everyone in his service wear a gold bracelet, to demonstrate to others that they are bound to the king."

Two more of these soldiers were sitting next to Judah at the bar, making sure his goblet was filled. Phillip took a seat a little farther down, far enough away to avoid calling attention to himself, but close enough to listen in on the conversation. Not that it was difficult to hear Judah's wine-fortified voice.

"We had a grand feash—a *feash*— " Judah struggled mightily to enunciate. "A *meal*," he finally capitulated.

"And where was this meal?" asked the stocky gorilla to Judah's right. His unibrow contracted and relaxed with his attention. At that moment, it had crept toward the man's nose, collecting in the space between his eyes like a snake waiting to strike.

"Where rich people live," Judah answered. "A good home. A good man, that friend of . . . of, uh, the trader man, Magda's friend, I forget hizh name."

"Is your rabbi still there?" The brow narrowed, coiled for attack.

"No, no, no. They're all gone, all gone. Praying. Praying in the garden. Rabbi told me to come. 'M going shoon, shoon . . . right after thish drink."

"A garden?" the soldier to Judah's left piped up. "Which garden?"

Phillip jumped off his stool. Too quickly, the conversation had steered into dangerous territory. No one needed to know where Yeshua was spending the evening, certainly not two mercenaries who seemed overly interested in that location. He reached Judah just as Judah's head nodded onto the bar counter. "Geth-shum," Judah muttered as he passed out. "Geth-sha-la-la."

Readers of the Quartet will know that Gethsemane was not, on that night, the restful haven we sought.

We arrived shortly after sunset and prayed together until the stars came out. It was a mild enough evening that Yeshua decided to spend the night, and we all separated, not too far from each other. I was determined to keep Yeshua in sight, because my fear for his safety had reached a crescendo that was hard to quell.

I spread out our blanket beneath an old Joshua tree. It gave me comfort to gaze at its branches reaching upward in every direction, its arms finding all those different paths to heaven. Peter and the Zebedees settled nearby, proclaiming their intent to protect Yeshua at all costs.

After ten minutes, all three were snoring loudly.

"A fine posse of bodyguards they make," Yeshua said.

I didn't answer. My heart was too heavy to make light of Yeshua's vulnerability. I didn't want him to feel my fear, he had enough to worry about. Silence was my best course.

But whom was I kidding? I couldn't hide anything from him.

"Do not be afraid, Magda," he whispered softly. "What is coming must be borne, it cannot be avoided."

"How can you say that? How can you ask me not to fear? I am terrified for you, *terrified!* What if our roles were reversed? What if you had to watch me suffer? Would you not try to avoid it?"

He gathered me in his arms, so close that I felt every beat of his heart in his chest.

"Do not ask me to imagine that," he said. "I can hardly bear the burden I have been given."

I made a great effort to swallow my fear, along with the small piece of anger I still kept, for his refusal to run away. He had made it clear to everyone that I would be the spokesperson for his truth and vision. I couldn't crumble now.

"Forgive me, my love," I said. "I can tolerate whatever comes. Whatever you must bear, of course I can bear it too. We will endure it together."

Yeshua sighed into my hair. "You have such strength, Magda. I knew it from the first day I met you. Every moment with you has been a blessing. I never anticipated that my purpose on Earth would be so pleasurable."

"And what is that purpose, Yeshua? You told me months ago that I wasn't ready to hear it. Am I ready now?"

"Soon," he said, leaning into me. "Soon."

It would be the last time I ever felt him against my body. For years afterward, up in Damascus and far across the sea in France, whenever I felt alone, I conjured the warmth and moisture of his breath on that night. The sweet and heady musk of his sweat, mixed with faint remnants of myrrh became a lasting memory for me of his physical being.

I must have felt reassured enough to doze off, for I was woken by the faint sound of scraping metal. I sat up suddenly, looking around. Yeshua was not with me. The noise came again, a slow and steady rasp. Like a sword being pulled out of a scabbard.

Jumping up, I rushed over to Peter and the Zebedee brothers.

"There is someone else in the garden," I hissed.

I did not wait for them but raced immediately to the spot where I hoped I would find Yeshua. An ancient olive tree, craggy and forbidding, located at the far end of the garden. It had been alive, Yeshua had told me, since the time of Moses. We had meditated beneath it earlier that week, on one of our walks from the Temple back to Bethany.

Indeed there he was, head bowed to the ground, deep in prayer under the shelter of those aged limbs. I rushed over and threw my arms around his body.

"Get up, Yeshua, get up! You must leave. You must leave *now!*"

He turned his head toward me and stood slowly, far too slowly. The pit that had been in my stomach all day expanded into a black chasm, as I understood: he was not going to run.

"Magda," he whispered, holding my face in his hands, washing them in my tears. "Thank you for showing me all your beautiful landscapes of love. Without you, this would have been for nothing." He kissed me then. A gentle kiss, soft and slow, unwavering and apologetic.

The small band of armed soldiers appeared out of nowhere and surrounded him, pushing me away, as Peter, James, and John came barreling toward us. None of us had weapons to fight for our Rabbi. We ran to the men holding Yeshua, intending to go along, wherever they might take him. Two of them, swinging their swords menacingly through the air, stepped forward to block our way.

"No," one barked. "He goes alone. King's orders."

If we needed proof that it was Herod Antipas's men taking Yeshua into custody, we had it with those words, Antipas being the only person within miles who called himself "king." But I didn't register the words then, I tried pummeling the brutes with my fists, while others from our group fought equally in vain. Until Yeshua called out.

"Enough! I must go." He allowed his arms to be bound behind him.

Yohanna came up behind me as I stood limp and helpless, watching Yeshua disappear into the darkness.

"Come," she said. "Get your shawl. We will follow."

JERUSALEM

5

We trailed the soldiers at a distance, as they marched Yeshua back into Jerusalem, across the old city and up to Herod's Palace. Heavy iron gates swung open into the maw of that leviathan structure to swallow up my beloved husband. We had no choice but to wait in the public plaza outside the entrance, so we spread our cloaks onto the ground, getting no sleep at all.

Herod's Palace had been built by Herod the Great, Antipas's father. It was an enormous building, built on a series of retaining walls and rising high above the ground so that everyone could comprehend the supremacy of King Herod and admire his riches. Two main residential buildings—each with its own banquet halls, baths, and guestrooms—faced each other across a grand marble quadrangle. Because Antipas lived up in Galilee, the Romans had appropriated the entire palace for Pontius Pilate's use. On the few occasions that Antipas visited Jerusalem—for example, on Passover—Pilate graciously allowed him to stay in the palace's north wing, while Pilate retreated to the south wing. Elaborate gardens, porticoes, and fountains, together with the wide expanse of the quadrangle, offered enough of a buffer to allow the egos of both men free exercise.

The night felt never-ending. After vowing that I would do everything in my power to keep Yeshua from harm, what, in the end, had I done to protect him? Nothing. I had completely and utterly failed him, and I spent every long hour of that night wrestling with my imagination of what he might be enduring.

It wasn't until months later, when Chuza called Yohanna to the city of Tiberias, that we learned the specifics of what happened inside the palace while we waited outside. Yohanna so detested Chuza by then that she was ready to ignore his summons entirely. But he claimed to have a finalized copy of their divorce decree, and she wanted the written record for her own peace of mind.

When Yohanna arrived in Tiberias, Chuza made her sit in a chair before him, while he strutted back and forth, waving the divorce scroll in the air, reveling in these last minutes of his control over her.

"He was quite the criminal, that delusional preacher of yours," Chuza said. "More important to the king than that baptizing fanatic we executed last year. A vexing thorn in the royal side. But we found a way to put him in his place." He leaned in toward Yohanna, seeking confirmation, or at least acquiescence. She didn't bat an eye.

"I'll tell you, I thought he'd put up more of a fight when we came to arrest him. Instead, it was like taking a child into custody, he didn't resist at all. Not much of a *man*, was he?" Chuza thrust forward his groin a few times. Yohanna tried to quell a wave of nausea.

"When I told the king we had seized him, His Majesty was already in bed. He told me to get the Temple priests involved, but they wouldn't come until dawn. I thought the king would want to see your preacher right away, but he must have had an enticing wench in his bed, because he dismissed me. 'Do what you want with him until the priests get here,' he said. Can you imagine? I was free to do anything, *anything*. And oh, we had *so* much fun with your rabbi!"

Yohanna cringed as Chuza laughed with perverted joy at the memory.

"First, we beat him, of course. All prisoners need to be knocked about—you don't want them getting ideas. Some of them fight back, but your preacher, he didn't flex a single muscle. He just stood there and took it. No wait, he *did* double over when Germanicus kicked him in the stomach. You remember Gerry, don't you? Big lug of a guy, probably three times the size of your preacher. And when Gerry slammed a fist into his head, preacher fell down. Somehow, though, he always pulled himself back up, no matter what we did to him. Resilient, I'll give him that. Probably a little stupid too, eh? I mean, why keep standing up, if it's only going to subject you to more beating?"

Yohanna felt her lunch rise up in her stomach, but she refused to show any outward reaction. Chuza pulled another chair over and sat on it backward, so he could glare at Yohanna while continuing to talk. He placed the divorce scroll on the floor.

"It must have been close to dawn, and we were all getting a little tired. It takes a lot out of you, you know, to beat a man continuously. Hurts the hands." Chuza made a fist and contemplated his knuckles. "By this time, your preacher wasn't standing anymore. We decided to give ourselves a break, because you know, he had to be able to stand for his morning trial. Gerry gave him one final boot, in that tender spot where men should never be kicked," Chuza winced sympathetically, "and we left him to ponder his future." Laughing hysterically at this last statement, Chuza stood to pour himself a goblet of wine, and Yohanna took the opportunity to hop up, grab the scroll, and run outside to her waiting carriage.

On the morning of the day Yeshua was killed, dawn made a hesitant entrance, struggling to find its way through the bits and pieces of desert that overnight winds had uprooted and kept aloft in the air. But once news of Yeshua's arrest made its way through the city, no curtain of dirt and sand was going to keep the people of Jerusalem at home. By the time daylight shifted the shade of gloom around us, a large crowd had gathered at the gate. Some spectators came out of sheer curiosity, others because they had heard Yeshua speak, or because they had been anointed by me, and felt connected to us. And a third group—comprised, I later learned, of Zealots and Antipas's henchmen—hovered nearby, there to ensure a particular outcome.

I didn't expect a trial. In my time, Roman rulers didn't conduct trials for non-Roman citizens. If you were a Jew accused of a high crime, your process was as summary as your execution. I was waiting at the gate simply in the hope that sooner or later, I would have the chance to see him again.

But it gradually became clear that some sort of proceeding would take place that morning. Shortly after dawn, a troop of Roman soldiers stomped its way across the palace quadrangle, boots echoing off the marble. They stopped to erect a portable dais just beyond the gate where we clamored, then retreated to two side gates at either end of the quad. Next thing I knew, they were intermingling with the crowd, presumably to keep us under control.

Within minutes, Pilate himself appeared from the south palace, followed by a flurry of Temple priests in white robes. Although I had never seen Pontius Pilate, I knew him immediately from the description my friend Ehud had given me years earlier—dark-haired, spindly legs struggling to support his heavy torso, a build reminiscent of a wild boar. Pilate was dressed in full Roman regalia of maroon velvet embroidered with gold, and he carried himself with a cocky confidence that could have been self-assurance or overcompensation, but in any case conveyed authority. Not a single crease on his face suggested that he was a man given to laughter.

Upon reaching the makeshift platform, Pilate perched impatiently on the edge of the velvet chair placed there for him, like someone already tired of the nonsense about to come his way.

"Bring out the prisoner!" he shouted.

That's when I saw what they had done. Yohanna had the presence of mind to stand next to me and hold my forearm as Yeshua was led out. His body was a riot of welts and cuts—some had coagulated, most were still openly bleeding—and a profusion of lumps and bruises reshaped and discolored the panorama of his skin. I inhaled sharply, feeling every cut and laceration as if it were my own.

He did not act like a man in pain. He did not stagger, but walked lightly, with his head held steadily forward and his gaze slightly above the heads of everyone around him. I dared to hope the myrrh I had poured over him had helped anesthetize him to his pain. Maybe too, whatever he had experienced overnight had taken him another step away from his human form, another step further from matter and closer to spirit.

"Yeshua of Nazareth," Pontius Pilate grumbled. "You stand accused of . . . ." He stopped and turned to the pretension of Temple priests gathered nearby. "What do you accuse this man of?" A low murmur animated the robes as they conferred. This was the only chance the Temple priests would have to rid themselves of a man who imperiled their religious authority. They had to muster a convincing argument for Pilate. Finally, a gnarled hand emerged from one of the robes, motioning for help to two nearby Temple guards. The guards lifted this figure onto the dais so he could whisper briefly in Pilate's ear, then returned him to the ground.

"King of the Jews?" Pilate repeated, looking mystified. He turned to Yeshua with a slight smirk on his face. "Do you call yourself 'King of the Jews'? *Are* you the King of the Jews?"

Tell him, I urged silently. Tell Pilate you are not a threat. Reassure him that you are no danger to Roman authority, and he'll let you go.

Yeshua's voice, when he answered, was listless, almost dreamlike. He seemed completely indifferent to his own fate. "You say that I am."

The priests' robes fluttered anew; again the gnarled hand emerged to demand access to Pilate's ear and was elevated.

"I know, I know, but what is that to me?" Pilate demanded. He flicked his wrist to be rid of the aged priest. The Temple guards complied. At that moment, someone in a white and gold cloak came hurrying across the quadrangle from the north wing of the palace.

"Chuza!" Yohanna murmured, recognizing her husband as he neared.

Now it was Chuza's turn to offer secret evidence, leaning over and murmuring to the governor. Pilate listened impatiently, scowled, and waved Chuza away. He took a few steps back and waited with the guards.

"So you caused an uproar at the Temple the other day, all because of a shekel?" Pilate asked.

Yeshua said nothing.

"And you foretold the downfall of Jerusalem? The massacre of all your people?"

Nothing.

"And the destruction of your very own Temple, your Holy of Holies?"

Still nothing.

"Have you nothing to say in your defense?"

Yeshua remained mute.

I'll remind you now of the metaphorical ice Pilate skated on— there was his friendly and professional connection to Sejanus, the reviled and executed Roman traitor. Also, Emperor Tiberius's mandate not to interfere with the Jewish people in the exercise of their religion, especially during their most sacred holiday. Pilate was not oblivious to this ice. He knew how thin it was. He was hoping that this smart-talking Galilean preacher would come up with a convincing story to explain the charges against him, giving Pilate some traction against the Temple priests. The last thing Pilate wanted to do was execute a sad-looking, harmless Jewish prophet. And during Passover, no less. Emperor Tiberius would most likely send him swimming with the fishes.

But the man who stood before Pilate stubbornly refused to help himself in his own cause. Exasperated, Pilate jumped off the chair and waved his right arm at the soldiers flanking the prisoner. "Take him away to be flogged, and then release him. That should be sufficient to keep him out of trouble." Temple priests be damned, Pilate probably thought. I won't risk my neck for them.

I was so relieved to hear this sentence that, unexpectedly I crushed Yohanna's hand, which I had been holding more and more tightly. Laughing and blowing on her fingers, she beamed at me, and we shared a fleeting instant of happiness. My hopes for the future danced again. Flogging was no picnic, to be sure, but it was far preferable to the alternatives I had imagined overnight.

Alas, our joy did not last long.

"No! Kill the traitor! Crucify him!" shouted a lone voice from the crowd behind me. Appalled, I turned to identify the unwelcome agitator. There, in the midst of a ragtag collection of pilgrims and Jerusalem citizens, stood a man I didn't recognize. He wore a gold bracelet on his arm.

"Kill him! Crucify him!" The man's exhortation was taken up by a rabble of voices. They drowned out all opposition.

Who were these people? I thought everyone loved Yeshua. All week long, Jews and Gentiles alike had flocked to hear him at the Temple, they had crowded around him in the streets whenever we passed through, eager to touch his robe or hand. Even now, most of the onlookers nearby looked as confused as I felt, wondering who was spreading this new charge.

It was Antipas's men, of course. Not the citizens of Jerusalem, nor the pilgrims, but men hired from other lands to do the bidding of the tetrarch of Galilee, and for a handsome sum. Herod Antipas, doing everything he could to manipulate Pilate into imposing a death sentence on his enemy, thereby hopefully hastening Pilate's removal. These mercenaries did not particularly care whether Yeshua lived or died. Or perhaps they preferred an execution, especially a crucifixion, seeing it as welcome entertainment. There was a grisly fervor animating their chant: "Crucify him! Crucify him!"

Then, somewhere from the depths of the crowd, came a new cry: "Give us Barabbas!" The voice was terrifyingly familiar to me. I had heard that voice broadcast the day's catch to the Magdala market. I had heard it wail in grief over the death of a beloved brother. I had even heard it, the night before, profess its love for Yeshua.

Looking around me in panic, I saw him standing nearby, at the edge of the gate.

"Judah!" I shrieked. "What are you doing? Why are you calling for Barabbas!?" I pushed my way past several people and tried clamping my hand over Judah's mouth, but he jerked his head and shoved me away.

"Don't you see, Magda? It is so clear to me! He has to be delivered in a dramatic way. So people will understand who he really is. And what could be more dramatic than for God to intervene and rescue him from the cross?"

I couldn't believe what I was hearing. "So you would have our Rabbi, someone whom you profess to love, undergo the torture of being nailed to a cross just so that some fantasy of yours might be fulfilled? And you think God would have Yeshua endure such pain before interceding?"

All around us, Zealots and Antipas's lackeys had taken up Judah's call: "Barab-bas! Barab-bas!" Judah stared at me, silenced by my words. His lips trembled as he wrestled with his feelings. When he finally spoke, it was in such a low tone that I could barely hear him over the din of the crowd. "It pains me more than you know."

"What if all your Zealot friends want is to get their leader out of jail? How can you trust their motives?" By this point, I was so angry, I was screaming.

"*Quiet!*" Pontius Pilate had had enough of everyone's yelling. The uproar ebbed to a low rumble. Pilate beckoned for the High Priest and leaned over the dais to ask a question. The answer made Pilate smile, for he had finally discovered a way out of his dilemma.

Under normal circumstances, Pilate would not have thought twice about putting Yeshua to death. The fact that Yeshua did not commit a capital crime did not bother him, for the preacher was certainly causing a lot of disruption, and Pilate could easily have labeled inciting rowdy behavior during the Passover holiday a transgression against the state.

But, as I said, Pilate was leery of doing *anything* to anger Emperor Tiberius, not with his own neck on a line that had been drawn by Sejanus. As Pilate was listening to the crowd's calls for crucifixion and turning this dilemma over in his mind, he suddenly remembered a custom his predecessor, Valerius Gratus, had told him about when he first arrived in Caesarea: the *privilegium paschale.*

The Passover pardon. It began with the Hasmoneans, rulers of Judea before Rome. The Hasmoneans had not been popular sovereigns. They threw people in jail for political dissent willy-nilly, usually without any fear of repercussion for their tyranny. But during the week-long Passover holiday, when thousands of pilgrims flocked to Jerusalem, the possibility of an uprising suddenly looked more real. So the Hasmonean kings instituted a tradition designed to pacify the people: each Passover, they granted a pardon to one prisoner, releasing him from jail so he could celebrate with his family.

This was the tradition that gave Pilate his out. After confirming with the High Priest that the custom was still recognized, Pilate ordered Barabbas to be dragged from prison and brought to stand next to Yeshua so that both men faced the crowd. It was hard to say which captive looked more pitiable. Both were covered in cuts and bruises from the beatings they had endured. The tunics of both men were dirtied and torn. But Barabbas looked like a man in fear for his life, eyes darting left and right, feet twitching, as he scoured his environs for possible escape. Yeshua, on the other hand, stood tall and silent, his deep brown eyes staring off into an unseen world. Pilate adjusted his cloak and stood on the dais, behind the two men.

"People of Jerusalem!" he called out. "It has been the custom among the previous rulers of this city to release, on this holy day, one prisoner who stands accused of a crime. I shall, in my magnanimity, honor and uphold this tradition today."

A great cheer erupted from the crowd. Everybody loved a good tradition.

"And I will go one step further—I will let you choose the man to be pardoned. Will it be Yeshua of Nazareth"—here, Pilate raised Yeshua's right arm high in the air—"Or will it be Barabbas?" With this, he lifted Barabbas's left arm.

Antipas had prepared for this moment. He could not have known that Pilate would invoke the pardon privilege, but it was always a good idea to prime the crowd with a bribe. Earlier that morning, Antipas had given his mercenaries small purses of gold, promising them even greater wealth if they did what he asked. He commanded them to disseminate the coins by chatting up nearby men, pressing a gold coin into their palms, and urging them to "Watch, and do what I do."

Now was their time. Antipas's henchmen began the chant. "Barabbas!" The name was taken up by scores of voices, which quickly became a roar. "Barabbas! Barabbas! Barabbas!"

Against this din, against this tsunami of sound, my own small voice, and those of Yeshua's supporters, barely registered. "Yeshua!" we called out with all the strength of our lungs, our vocal chords, our hearts. We might as well have been mute.

Pilate held up his hand for silence. He appeared surprised and a bit disappointed. "Stupid people," he muttered, loudly enough for me to hear. "Choosing a thug over a prophet." But he had given his word. After ordering a nearby soldier to remove Barabbas' shackles, he turned to Yeshua. He looked long and hard into my husband's eyes. Yeshua barely registered Pilate's presence, blinking only once and staring past the Roman. Pilate sighed and shrugged.

"Crucify him."

JERUSALEM

6

The Romans loved a good crucifixion. If you think they invented this torture, you're wrong—the Persians beat them to it, 400 years earlier. But Rome embraced crucifixion more thoroughly than Persia. It became the go-to sanction for slaves, rebels, and basically anyone who crossed the state. And being experts in brutality, the Romans did what they could to maximize the elements of pain and suffering.

First, they forced you to carry your own hundred-pound crossbeam to the execution site. You did this by bracing it against your back, which the Romans had usually flogged to a bloody mess in advance. Then you stumbled off to wherever you were to meet your end. In Jerusalem, crucifixions took place right outside the city wall, at a spot named Golgotha, where several sturdy vertical posts were permanently secured in the ground just for that purpose. Once you staggered up to Golgotha, your arms were nailed to the crossbeam you had been lugging. But contrary to what you might believe from the thousands of depictions you've seen of Yeshua on the cross, the nails did not go through your hands. No, palms were too flimsy, too delicate to support the weight of a human body for hours, plus there was a good chance you'd rip through those bones over time, freeing your torso. Not a scenario the Romans wanted to deal with. So they placed the nail through the much stronger bones of your wrists, severing the median nerve, causing searing pain and immediate metacarpal paralysis. As extra insurance that you wouldn't be twisting or squirming those hands free, the Romans also tied your wrists to the beam with a thick sturdy rope.

Once you were nailed and tied to your crossbar, the Romans raised it with ropes that ran along the vertical post. This pole had notches nicked into its sides and top, so the lifting could be accomplished in stages. And when the crossbeam finally rested in the uppermost notch of that post, your feet were placed on top of each other, so that the last nail, the longest one, could be hammered through both of them into the wood. Then you were left to hang, for however long it took for you to die.

Crucifixion was an agonizingly slow death.

Ironically, if you had been thoroughly and violently flogged, you were better off, because you'd die more quickly if you lost a lot of blood. And trust me, anything that hastened your death on the cross was a blessing. Because it could take as long as twenty-four hours to die by crucifixion alone. With your arms extended perpendicular to your body and bearing all of your weight, your chest muscles and lungs were perpetually hyper-extended, making it both difficult and painful to inhale. You constantly felt as if you were suffocating.

You'd be able to shift some of your weight to the muscles of your legs, by pushing up on your nailed feet and using them for leverage. The longer you could tolerate the excruciating pain of doing this, the easier it would be for you to breathe. Sooner or later, though, and certainly before dinnertime, the Roman soldiers would tire of standing guard over you, and they'd smash their truncheons into your legs to prevent you from using your leg muscles at all. You wouldn't last much longer after that.

I've given you this synopsis of crucifixion so that you know exactly what Yeshua suffered. There's no sugarcoating it. You don't get to look away. You want to know the truth of our story? Get used to pain and suffering.

࿐

After Pontius Pilate pronounced Yeshua's sentence, the guards took him away to be flogged. I did not try to catch his eye. From his demeanor throughout the trial, I could see that he was channeling his resources inward, withdrawing his consciousness into the world of spirit so that his body could bear what the world of man inflicted upon him. I didn't want to leave him alone, but the soldiers barring entrance to the palace plaza made it clear when I approached that there would be no passing beyond the gates.

"You! All of you!" barked the hairier of two armored men as he waved his sword at our group, "Begone, before we round you up as accomplices of this traitor!"

"Indeed," said his comrade, eyes narrowing, "The Nazarene rebel had a band of followers, did he not? Perhaps we should arrest all of you for questioning."

That threat was enough to scatter our men. They melted back into the crowd, hunching down and pulling their cloaks over their heads. No one wanted to go, but the risk of ending up in the next round of crucifixions was real. I didn't see most of the group again until my return to Galilee a few weeks later. Even Levi and Phillip, who were most loyal to Yohanna and me, left Jerusalem upon our urging. They took Ilana with them, despite her protests. She relented only when Levi suggested that the emotional turmoil she would experience by staying would not be good for their baby.

But I was not going anywhere. I had promised not to leave Yeshua, and I intended to honor that promise. Also, it was highly unlikely the Romans would consider a *woman* dangerous. A rare advantage for our gender.

I turned to Yohanna. "Do you think we can get to him? Where will they take him?"

Ever resourceful, she had an answer for me, for she had sent a messenger to Herodias as soon as Yeshua was arrested. Yohanna hoped that, if anyone could help us gain access to Yeshua, it would be Antipas's wife. But Herodias sent the messenger back, with her deep regrets. Antipas was keeping her in the dark. All she could tell us was where the Romans carried out crucifixions.

"We must go to Golgotha," Yohanna said. "The Place of the Skull."

Golgotha was aptly named. Situated northwest of Herod's Palace, this escarpment of rock rose next to the intersection of two main roads into Jerusalem, making it the perfect place to confront travelers with the consequences of wrongdoing in the Roman Empire. Wind and rain had, circumstantially, carved out two parallel circular indentations in the stone. From a distance, the craters looked like hollowed-out sockets, which, together with the sloping promontory that jutted out between them, gave the entire cliff the appearance of a human skull.

It was not difficult to find. Aside from its telltale topography, the wooden posts that formed the vertical axes of three crosses rose up from the horizon as gruesome landmarks to guide us. As we neared, I judged they were about twelve feet in height, and even from a distance, I could make out the brown pigment of blood staining the wood. Shuddering, I found a large rock off to the side and sat down. Yohanna joined me, and together we faced the road along which we knew Yeshua must come.

I tried not to think about what he must be enduring. What he was about to endure. I tried to clear my mind of fear. But that kind of fear—the impending pain of someone you love—well, it has Krazy-Glue sticky fingers, thousands of them, attaching themselves to every nook and cranny of your brain. All my years of meditation were no match against it. Yohanna was my only defense, for she was experiencing something similar. Holding on to each other, even if it was just by hand, gave both of us the strength to watch and wait.

We heard the crowd long before we saw him. A cacophony of wails and jeers, raucous laughter and clanking armor announced its approach. Six Romans in full military garb led the mob, which included Romans, Gentiles, and Jews. Some called out loud insults and taunts, others cried for mercy.

With all the dust that was stirred up as the company arrived, I did not immediately see Yeshua, but I noticed two other prisoners, each struggling under the weight of a crossbeam that had been lashed to his back with thick twine. The Romans had stripped them of clothes, to humiliate them as much as possible on their march through the city.

"Magda!" Yohanna called, pointing to my left. And there he was, my husband, our Rabbi, shuffling forward under his own heavy load, streaks of blood newly splattering the cuts and bruises I had seen earlier. I couldn't see his back, but I knew that it must be a shambles of slashed skin after the flogging Pilate had ordered.

The Quartet will tell you that Yeshua was too weak after his flogging to carry his own cross, and that another man, Simon of

Cyrene, stepped in to bear it for him. Not true. Remember, the men who supposedly recited this story to the Quartet scribes had all (except for Judah) fled to Galilee. So you have to take the Quartet's entire narration of the crucifixion with a block of salt, not a grain.

Yeshua bore his own cross that day. Yes, he was weakened by the assault of the scourge on his flesh, and by his subsequent loss of blood. But the myrrh oil that I had massaged into his skin all week had done its work. He told me much later that he felt the impact of the flogging, but not the pain.

I wish I could say the same about the nails. Myrrh is topical; it can only penetrate the skin and desensitize nerve endings to a certain depth. Yeshua felt every rusty jag of the iron spikes that impaled his wrists and feet. He did not scream in pain, but he let out a quiet groan as his flesh and tendons were severed. A groan of reluctant recognition—that the ordeal he had been fearing for months had finally begun.

I won't recapitulate the stages of his suffering on the cross because I've already given you a general idea of that horror. Yeshua was hoisted up when the sun was halfway to noon, so about nine o'clock in the morning by modern clocks. As soon as he was secured, the soldiers allowed the women—Yohanna, Miriam, our friend from Bethany, and me—to kneel at the foot of the cross. A small group of hecklers stood behind us, calling upon Yeshua to perform a miracle, daring him to save himself.

I was about to begin praying when I saw a petite woman make her way through the crowd, leaning on the arm of a taller, much younger man. From the similarities in facial features that I could vaguely discern through her muslin veil, he might have been her son. The man brought her to a spot right next to me, then quickly headed back to Jerusalem along the road.

I bowed my head away from her, intending to give her privacy, but she sought my attention. "Sister."

Looking up, I saw that she had pulled back her veil and gazed at me with deep brown eyes whose color and shape I knew better than my own. The only difference between her eyes and those of the man I loved was their depth—I could fall into Yeshua's eyes and travel forever, whereas these eyes closed me off.

Without having to ask, I knew that I was in the presence of Maryam of Nazareth, Yeshua's mother.

"Are you the woman from Magdala," Maryam asked. "The one who . . . who—"

"I am Magda," I answered. "I am . . . ." How I wanted to tell this woman I was Yeshua's wife! But I thought of the man who had brought her here, who might possibly be her son, James, whom I might then have to marry if . . . . I stopped myself from completing that thought, though the conclusion was now inevitable. "I am a devoted follower of your son," I answered.

Yeshua had told me very little about his mother. The only time he had ever spoken of her was the night he told me about his return to Nazareth to begin his ministry. When he tried to preach to the villagers and they drove him out of town, telling him to take his nonsense elsewhere, he said he had looked for his mother, hoping that she or another family member might come to his defense.

"I finally saw her at the back of the crowd, standing behind my father and brothers. Back at home, they had told me to stop my 'prophet nonsense,' as they put it." Yeshua's heavy sigh as he told this story was part frustration, part compassion. "My mother was crying that day because she loved me. But she could only love me as much as the men around her allowed."

The woman standing next to me now was somewhere in her

late-forties, and she had not lost any of the beauty that drew in her husband Yosef years earlier. But lines of worry cultivated her forehead and pulled down the corners of her eyes and lips, and there were as many white as ebony hairs beneath her veil. She held her body in a perpetual stoop, like someone trying to take up as little space as possible, making her appear much older than her years.

"I heard there was a trial," Maryam slowly lowered her body next to mine, and sat crouching on her feet.

"Were you not there?" I wondered why, if she had been in Jerusalem, she would not have come out to see her son.

"James told me not to go. He told me not to come here either, but . . . ." Maryam tilted her head back and closed her eyes to the sky, blinking away tears. "But I was able to convince him of a mother's need to be with her son in his final hours."

"Your presence here is a blessing to Yeshua," I said, trying to offer her comfort.

"Do you think so? Because I have failed him, I have failed him in every way a mother can fail her son." She sobbed.

I didn't know what to say, so I put my arm around her shoulder. That gesture of kindness unlatched her emotions.

"I always knew there was something odd about him," Maryam began. "He was unlike my other boys, so quiet and dreamy, always wandering off somewhere when he should have been working. No amount of beating from Yosef could change that behavior. And I—I could only stand by and watch. I could not protect him." Her shoulders trembled with grief and remorse. "One day, I suppose Yeshua had had enough, and he left. Just disappeared in the middle of the night, without saying farewell. I was beside myself, as you can imagine, not knowing where he was or what might befall him. But Yosef refused to let me dwell on the matter. 'We are well rid of him,' he said. 'A son who will not listen to his father is of no use to this family.' I was too afraid of my husband to go look for my son. And then, years later, when he came back—"

"*Shh, shh.*" I tried soothing her because Maryam was growing increasingly agitated. "Do not dwell on the past, for you cannot change it now. And what I hear in everything you tell me is how much you love your son. That never changed, did it?"

"No, no, I have always loved him!" she insisted. "I love him now."

"Then bring your thoughts and prayers to that place of love in your heart," I said, pressing her palms against each other.

With that, we both bent our heads to pray.

JERUSALEM

7

*A*s the heat of the day advanced, the small crowd of gawkers at Golgotha slowly began to break up. One by one, they headed back to the city, the entertainment value of watching men in agony having subsided and given way to hunger or thirst. Among the last to leave was a mysterious figure whose head was wrapped in a woman's shawl and who, prior to departing, came over to me and squatted.

"Magda."

"Judah?" I reached for the edge of his head shawl, but Judah batted my hand away.

"I fear for my safety, I cannot remain here much longer. But I *know* that our Rabbi will be delivered from his torment." Judah spoke quickly, his words rushing together in a torrent. He could hardly keep still, shifting uncomfortably from one foot to another. "The End of Days is upon us. You know, Magda, you saw it at the Temple. This is the beginning. It's now just a matter of hours, isn't it?"

I looked at him in disbelief.

"No, do not dispute the truth!" Judah grabbed onto my

cloak with trembling hands. "It *has* to happen, Magda, he *has* to be delivered! Because if he is not, if he dies up there on the cross, like an ordinary human being, then I . . . I will have been . . . it will have been my fault." His words faded off, and he began mumbling to himself. "But if it *has* to happen, why hasn't it? Why is it taking so long?"

Shaking off his doubt, Judah stood to go. "I cannot stay here, I must leave. But you, Magda, you can remain and bear witness. I shall withdraw to Bethany. When the skies open up and it is time for me to join the army of God, you will see me again. Today, we shall receive the justice we have been waiting for!"

Before I could respond, Judah ran off. Moments later, I saw him shuffling toward Jerusalem, glancing back at Golgotha from time to time, in case the Apocalypse should arrive sooner rather than later.

That left Maryam of Nazareth, Miriam of Bethany, Yohanna, and me to attend Yeshua's ordeal. Miriam of Bethany was a wailer. She grieved loudly, sobbing and howling, interspersing her cries with calls to God for salvation and sustenance. Some part of me envied her that public display of sorrow. Had I focused on my own anguish, I too might have screamed aloud to ease its hold. For my despair felt like a living creature, a desert sand boa coiled around my throat, cutting off my breath minute by minute.

Instead, I was preoccupied with Yeshua's pain, desperate to find a source of relief for him. The myrrh oil had done what it could. Now, every time Yeshua breathed, his entire body tensed, as he convulsed his thigh muscles upward, trying to snatch a mouthful of air in a desperate gasp. I could think of only one way to reach him. But I needed to wait for the right moment.

Of the six Roman soldiers who had marched out of Jerusalem with the prisoners, three returned to their barracks in Fort Antonia once all the prisoners had been secured to their crosses. The remaining three positioned themselves so that there was one soldier near each cross. In the beginning, they occasionally threw a few taunts and jeers at Yeshua. But as the crowd left, taking with it spectacle and audience, what remained were long hours of tedious suffering. Not a desirable post for the average Roman guard.

Sure enough, by midday, with the sun blazing overhead, the guards wandered to an overhang in the nearby cliff to get some respite from the heat. There they sat, sharing the latest army gossip and polishing their armor. They had no reason to worry about us, four women bent and huddled in fervent prayer for a man who the Romans could only hope would be dead before dusk.

This was the opportunity I had been waiting for, but I needed Miriam and Yohanna's help. Yeshua's mother was so deep in prayer behind me that I chose not to disturb her.

"Could you each move over a little bit?" I asked. "That way, if the soldiers glance up, they will see you kneeling on either side of the cross and will assume I am kneeling between you. The cross itself will block their view of me, so they won't know what I am doing."

"And what will you be doing?" Yohanna asked.

"Standing. So I can touch him."

Miriam of Bethany appeared confused, but she did not argue. The two women rearranged themselves as I had requested. I glanced at the soldiers in the distance. They were laughing at some joke, paying us no attention.

I stood. In my kneeling position, I had been unable to touch Yeshua's body, so tall were the crucifixion posts. But standing up, I was able to maneuver the fingers of my right hand under the arch of his right foot, the one that was closest to the post. I did so slowly, carefully, mindful of not doing anything that might jostle his feet and send an unnecessary jab of pain upward. I gave the cruel iron nail wide berth.

Gingerly, I placed my thumb on his instep and my second and third fingers on his arch. I knew from anointing that I could travel inwards here—physically, I could ease the stress in his spine, possibly even relax his heart and lungs, which must be under enormous strain. I hoped to minimize the physical shock he was in.

But I wanted more. I wanted my touch to bring him to our meditative space. I wanted to help him separate spirit from body and join me in the world of shimmering energy that we both knew so intimately. This was something he had been able to do easily when his body was relaxed. We had met and connected in that space countless times in the past. But when his body was under such extreme duress as now, when he was in the throes of constant physical torment, could he make that separation? I had to help him try.

I took a deep breath, unsure what would happen. I pressed my thumb against the top of his foot, my other fingers against the bottom.

Instantly a wall of pain slammed into me. A hurricane of agony, with unrelenting misery and crushing despair. I fell against the heavy post, bracing myself against its onslaught. *This* was what Yeshua had been enduring for two hours? How was he still alive? And how could I possibly break through this fortress of torture? I could barely breathe.

"Your time has just begun." I heard Deborah's words as if they had just been spoken. My time, I thought. What did I do with my time? I *anointed.*

Yeshua was between breaths of air, allowing the wave of torment to abate slightly. I took that break to feel around the pocket of my tunic for the small flask of lavender oil that I always carried with me. Pulling it out with my left hand, I used my teeth to unstop the flask, then poured its contents over my right hand.

More easily now, smoothly, and steadily, my fingers slid over the skin of his foot, reaching inward, upward, seeking him.

Amazingly, as quickly as it had descended, the pain evaporated. I found myself floating in that familiar beloved space that I had sought. The ethereal world of nothing and of everything, of wind and light and heat, energy in all its forms.

And there he was.

"Magda," he whispered. Had he been in his body, I know he would have embraced me, I know we would have kissed. But those days of physical intimacy were over. I would grieve them later. Right now, I was in this space with him, where we were pure spirit, pure lightness. I was practically delirious with relief, to be with the Yeshua I remembered, to know that he was no longer suffering, and to realize that I—I! with my anointment skills—had facilitated his deliverance.

I lost track of time. For all I knew, our union might have lasted for an instant or hours. Then, suddenly, I was torn out of that space, as I felt myself being pulled away from the cross. Abruptly, I returned to my body. As did Yeshua.

"Aaagggh!" he cried out.

Yohanna had pulled me away. She continued to tug desperately at my hand as I stood next to the cross, slightly dazed. Forcefully, she yanked me into my kneeling position.

"The soldiers are returning!"

The sun had slid much farther in its arc across the sky, now halfway between its apex and the peak of Mount Zion. One part of me rejoiced that Yeshua had been spared hours of agony, yet I fumed that his relief should be interrupted.

"What happened?" I asked, unable to disguise my annoyance. "Why did you . . . ?"

"I waited as long as I could," Yohanna said. "Look." She pointed at the road. There, galloping toward us at great speed, came a Roman commander, with the telltale red plume vaulting his helmet. An officer who was clearly in a hurry to get to Golgotha. No wonder the Roman soldiers scrambled back to their duty posts.

A moment later, I saw who it was—our friend Gnaeus Castus from Capharnaum, the Roman who had rebuilt our synagogue and attended our wedding. I didn't know how he had gotten the news of Yeshua's arrest and trial so quickly; perhaps he had his own spies in Jerusalem. Still, it would have taken several swift horses for him to cover all that distance with such speed. I wondered at his dedication but questioned his mission. Even if he was sympathetic to Yeshua, he couldn't betray himself to these soldiers. How could he possibly help?

We stood up and backed away, allowing Castus to guide his horse toward Yeshua's cross. Passing by me, he nodded so slightly that it would have been imperceptible to a bystander.

"This criminal is the infamous Yeshua of Nazareth, is he not?" Castus's tone was scornful.

Recognizing the voice, Yeshua moaned as he pushed up on his feet to breathe. He opened his eyes slowly and tried to turn his head toward the commander, who had positioned himself on Yeshua's left side.

"Yes, sir!" one of the guards answered. "This one dares to call himself 'King of the Jews!'"

"Some 'King of the Jews' he is, indeed!" laughed the soldier stationed at one of the other crosses. "Where are his armies? Why don't they come rescue him?"

Castus did not respond. He sought Yeshua's gaze. Yeshua sighed and dropped his head in a nod.

"What is happening?" Yohanna whispered, looking to the sky.

As Castus dismounted from his horse, the day suddenly darkened. A moment earlier, the sky had been cloudless. The soldiers shifted uneasily at their posts, unsure why dusk was falling in midafternoon. Castus acted as if everything were normal.

"I know this man from Capharnaum," he said, choosing his words carefully. "I have seen what he has done to people, I have heard the words he uttered aloud. And believe me when I tell you that I have good reason for what I am about to do."

Gnaeus Castus pulled his sword from the sheath he wore belted to his waist. Yohanna and I gasped, riveted to what was unfolding before us. Castus stepped up to the cross, and with one swift movement, he plunged his sword into Yeshua's side, just below the ribcage, and thrust it upward, into Yeshua's heart.

Yeshua's mother screamed and fainted. Yohanna, Miriam of Bethany, and I held each other tightly. All three soldiers were applauding Castus's bold move when the sky went completely dark and thunder began to roll across the Plain of Rephaim, booming through the Valley of Hinnom, echoing back and forth between Mount Zion and the city walls. The ground beneath us shuddered and a squall of cold air moaned over the skull crag of Golgotha.

All as I watched the life flow out of my beloved and pool into the dust.

Images of Yeshua passed before me: head thrown back in laughter, shaking out his blanket of curls; arms scooping up Peter's and Andrew's children, blessing them with his soft lips; feet stepping over the threshold of the Capharnaum synagogue, fulfilling its promise—"He is within." And eyes—oh, his eyes!—the all-embracing gaze that beckoned to me every night, tumbling me toward his heart, where I found my perfect home.

One final time, his eyes reopened. One last time, he pulled me in, whirled me back through our lives, as my tears mixed with his blood in the dirt.

Moments later, he was dead.

JERUSALEM

8

The next two days were a fever of grief and exhaustion.

Thank goodness for Castus, who oversaw Yeshua's interment. The fact that Castus was able to negotiate a burial at all was extraordinary, because crucifixion victims were generally not allowed that dignity. The Romans believed in scare tactics, so they routinely left crucified bodies hanging by the roadside as a warning to society to behave. Those bodies rotted slowly, pelted by dust and rocks from sandstorms, pecked down to the bone by hungry carrion birds. After a week or so, what was left of the bodies was tossed into the local trash pit in the Hinnom valley, where wild dogs fought over the skeletal remains. That was where the two criminals crucified next to Yeshua ended up.

But Castus made certain that Yeshua's body had a different fate, one consistent with Jewish tradition. He approached a sympathetic member of the priests of the Sanhedrin, Joseph of Arimathea, and asked him to petition Pontius Pilate for a proper Jewish burial. Amazingly, Pilate agreed. Maybe it was the lingering fear in Pilate's mind of how Emperor Tiberius would react to Yeshua's execution. If Pilate allowed the body to be buried in a manner consistent with the family's religious tradition, he could argue that he did what he could to honor the religious beliefs of a dangerous criminal. Joseph offered his own family burial tomb as a resting place, which Castus gratefully accepted.

I wanted to anoint Yeshua's body the day he died, but we had not brought the necessary herbs and oils to Golgotha, and Castus wisely insisted that Yeshua's body be removed quickly, lest the fickle public—who had so cruelly abandoned Him at his trial—suddenly remember their love for Him and cause an outcry. Castus assured us we would have our opportunity two days hence, after the Sabbath. In the meantime, the body could safely rest in the tomb, away from scavengers.

I looked at Yeshua's body as it lay on the linen shroud before they wrapped Him. It looked completely different, of course. Just a shell for an indomitable spirit, an abandoned husk for the seed of life. Where was that spirit now? I ached for it, when the linen was laid over his body, its edges carefully tucked beneath the corners of his elbows and heels. The ache deepened into a craving, when Yohanna and Miriam dragged me back to Bethany, and I crawled into bed alone. The bed I had last shared with Him. The blanket that covered both our bodies just two nights ago.

I stared at the small table next to our bed. There, on a placemat lovingly embroidered by our hostess, lay the dust-sprinkled figs and seeds that he had fished out of his tunic pocket before we left for supper yesterday. And the stone I had picked up at the edge of the Sea of Galilee, during one of our first walks together—had it been only a year ago? Had it not been a lifetime? A stone worn smooth by the caressing of years of lake water waves. I had given it to Him, because it fit perfectly into his palm. "A stone for all your worries," I had said. "Or all my dreams," he had answered. Now I took the stone into my palm and wrapped my fingers around it tightly before closing my eyes.

The Sabbath fell on the day after Yeshua's death. I spent it in bed, unable to rise. Every minute awake was an agony of loss and emptiness. The world outside the window looked washed-out and desolate, a barren wasteland. It felt irrelevant. The bedroom and its furniture were undifferentiated nothingness, pointlessly adorned with pillows and rugs. Why bother with any of it, I thought, when my purpose in life had vanished?

I did try, once or twice that day, to break out of my oblivion by meditating. Desperate, I entered the space he and I used to share in our reflective moments. Of course I was searching for his spirit. But he was not there. After all those promises that he would remain with me forever, that he would be with me even after his death, there was nothing. Our space felt as bleak as Golgotha. More than anything else, the realization that I was alone in that space engulfed me in darkness.

I thought I knew despair, after my rape, in those two years of isolation. But my earlier despair was nothing, *nothing* compared to the grief I felt now, a pitch-black shadow that annihilated light and hope, past, present, and future. What was the point, I thought, without Him to guide me? Without Him to hold me?

Mercifully, I was able to sleep, so that's what I did. I stayed in my bed for over thirty-six hours.

Yohanna, as always, brought me to my senses. On the morning after the Sabbath, she came into my room bearing a cup of tea, along with some bread, yogurt, and melon.

"You did not eat anything yesterday," she chided, sitting down on the bed, and placing the food tray on the floor.

"I was not hungry yesterday. Nor am I now." I stared at the wall, mindlessly counting imperfections in the stone.

"Magda, you cannot do this. You cannot give in to self-pity."

"I am grieving. I am entitled to self-pity," I hissed at the impassive dimples in the white-washed wall. How could Yohanna berate me? Why greet me with reprimands instead of comfort and support?

Heaven bless her, I think now. Had Yohanna been commiserative and soft-hearted, I might have stayed in bed for who knows how long—several days? A week? But she refused to coddle me. She knew that I had to walk *through* my grief, not crumble beneath it. Also, she recognized that I did not have the luxury of wallowing in sadness. Now that Yeshua was gone, someone had to step up. There were still many people who had not heard his truth, and even those who had heard him needed to begin establishing what he envisioned—communities based on love and equality. We, his followers, had to continue what he had begun. That was what he would have wanted us to do.

Yohanna reached over to the bedside table and picked up the hairbrush I kept there. She poked and prodded me into a sitting position. I kept my back to her, resentful that she wasn't being more sympathetic.

"You told me three days ago that you believed him when he said he would always be with us, remember?" Yohanna gathered my hair and began brushing it.

"But he's *not!*" I whirled around, knocking the brush from Yohanna's grip. "He's disappeared, Yohanna! I don't know where he is," I wailed.

"Just because we don't know where he is," she said, "just because we cannot see him, that doesn't mean he is gone." She picked up the brush from the floor and grazed it over my scalp.

Oh, Yohanna had such wisdom. She knew that combing my hair would calm me. The touch and rhythm of boar bristles sweeping over my head recalled my mother and the caretaking of my childhood. A different, simpler lifetime.

"You know, I have never been able to meditate as easily as you do," Yohanna said, brushing slowly and steadily. "There are days when I cannot quiet my mind at all, when even prayer is elusive. On those days, Yeshua's spirit feels very far away."

She moved the brush through the strands of my hair, softening and coaxing out knots. With each stroke, my muscles eased a bit of tension, and my heart pumped a wisp of hope. "But I know that eventually, I will find him. Because I trust in him. You trust in him too, Magda."

It took Yohanna and a hairbrush to recall my faith in Yeshua. It would take more than that to recall my faith in myself. But that day, at least, Yohanna got my ass out of bed.

"When we are done here, and when you have eaten your breakfast, let's go to Yeshua's tomb and anoint him properly," Yohanna said. "I've spent all morning preparing the herbs and oils. Miriam said she would like to join us."

"And Maryam, Yeshua's mother?"

"She's gone back to Nazareth. Her son James took her this morning."

We had to cross through Jerusalem to get to Yeshua's tomb, so it was late morning when we arrived. Immediately, we knew something was wrong. Before leaving the burial site two days earlier, fearful that someone might try to desecrate it, Castus and Joseph had maneuvered a large boulder in front of the entrance. Yohanna, Miriam, and I worried aloud, as we made our way back to the tomb, whether the three of us would have the strength to push that rock far enough aside that we might squeeze by.

We needn't have worried. The boulder had been rolled away. Yeshua's tomb was wide open.

With a cry of surprise, Yohanna and Miriam hurried into the cave. I hesitated. My grief was still so raw that I had wondered all morning whether I really had the strength to look at Yeshua's body again. And now there was this new shock. Did someone pillage the tomb? Had Yeshua's body been defiled? Had it been stolen? In the unfolding of the past three days, it felt like one twist too many. Before I knew it, my tears were flowing freely again.

While I cried, the air around me began heating up. It was early enough in the day that the sun, still lying low on the horizon, could not have been the cause. Inside my closed eyelids, dancing colors shifted from blood red to fiery gold to an all-bleaching white, as if a burning star had left the firmament and come to rest on my shoulder. In the instant before my eyes were forced open by all that light, I heard him.

"Dearest Magda."

I tell you truly, I have never, *never* been as happy as I was in that moment! I opened my eyes, and there he stood before me, in the body that I knew so intimately. Except that now his form was like a multi-faceted crystal, its edges shimmering like a thousand polished jewels, he was the source of all the heat and light that enveloped me.

"Oh!" I cried, leaping up, disarmed by my awe and, above all else, my profound relief. I took a step toward him, but he held up a hand, smiling apologetically.

"I wish I could touch you, Magda," Yeshua said. "But this figure that you see is not an earthly body, it is a silhouette, a shadow somewhere between body and spirit. You will understand one day, when you take this journey."

"Is that where you have been?" I asked. "Is that why I couldn't find you?"

"Oh, I ached for you, Magda, as you ached for me, believe me! But I couldn't come to you as I wished, not until now. I had to undergo the process of relinquishing my earthly body and all its desires."

"But not your love for me," I hoped aloud.

"That would be impossible," he smiled more widely. "My love, your love, our love, it is not of the body. It survives death. You know this, deep in your heart, don't you?" I nodded, embarrassed and ashamed that I had entertained any doubt.

"Unfortunately, I cannot stay here long, for I have work to do. As do you now." Yeshua opened his hands in a supplicating gesture, and his incandescence rippled outward, making everything around us fade in and out of focus.

"I shall continue your ministry, teach your words," I said.

"No. It is *your* ministry now, Magda. Your words, your wisdom. And equally important, your hands. You must begin building the kingdom we envisioned."

I looked down at my hands, which were shimmering ever so slightly. Either something was animating them, or all this radiance was affecting my eyesight.

"The world awaits your touch. Through you, it can be transformed."

I didn't feel ready to transform the world. But maybe I could manage a small village. "Where should I go?"

"Go anywhere you like." I felt waves of love and encouragement emanating from Him. Then, a moment later, a small push of direction.

"But first, you must return to Galilee."

MINISTRY

1

I imagine some of you aren't totally on board at this point. Not everyone buys the resurrection story. Who's to say I wasn't hallucinating? Underfed, overheated, probably dehydrated, certainly distraught—all the elements were in place for me to have a vision of my own fancy. I desperately wanted Yeshua to be alive, so he appeared before me.

Well, I'm not going to argue the point. *I* know what I saw, and *I* know I wasn't dreaming. But I also know that I'm never going to convince you, so believe what you like. Let me suggest, however, that if what I saw was nothing more than a figment of my imagination, that figment was remarkably persistent and equally visible to others. Over the next few weeks, Yeshua appeared repeatedly before everyone in our fellowship. Bravo me, for creating such a convincing hallucination and sending it out to roam. Or do you think everyone was dehydrated and distraught to exactly the same degree, conjuring up exactly the same ghost?

Yohanna and I returned to Capharnaum. During the long walk back to Galilee, she gave me other news, which she had withheld earlier because she didn't want to overwhelm me with grief. Judah, she told me, was dead.

"What!?" I stumbled in the road.

Once again, Yohanna had gotten her information from Chuza. Ever eager to badger his wife about the disintegration of her spiritual fellowship, he sent a servant to tell her in Bethany, the day I languished in bed.

I didn't think my heart had room for more sorrow. My mind immediately went to Ehud. He had lost his youngest son just a year ago, and now suddenly his oldest had been taken from him too. It was an undeserved woe for such a good man, someone who doted on his children. When Ehud visited me in my father's library, he always brought a family story with him—about the new house Moshe was building for his wife, or the inedible bread his granddaughter Tamar had baked for him. It pained me to think that Ehud's laughter, which had forged so many creases around his eyes, might now be silent again.

I wasn't sure I wanted an answer to my next question, but I asked it anyway. "How did he die?"

"He was found hanging from a yew tree," Yohanna said quietly.

The Quartet says that Judah took his own life. That's not true.

Yohanna also suggested that Judah committed suicide, but I rejected the idea. He had too much to live for—a loving wife and child back in Magdala, a large family that would have enveloped him and held him through the rest of his grief. Though Judah might have felt guilt and shame over Yeshua's death, I didn't think his spirit would have quit this world willingly.

No, the Zealots killed Judah.

Think about it. Judah managed to convince this group of

violent fanatics to hold off on whatever rebellion they were planning in Jerusalem until Yeshua revealed his divinity. He assured the Zealots that such a moment would come. When Yeshua upended the money changer's table on the Temple Mount, the Zealots thought it was time. They threw themselves into the fray, hoping Yeshua would bring down the armies of God to help. Instead, Yeshua disappeared, and their leader Barabbas was arrested.

Somehow, Judah appeased them. Yeshua was waiting for a more dramatic moment, Judah insisted. And nothing could be more dramatic than a man saving himself from crucifixion by stepping down off the cross. For the sake of Judah's younger brother, who had given his life for their cause, the Zealots gave Judah one last benefit of the doubt. They sent him to Golgotha and waited impatiently for the miracle he promised. Each hour of Yeshua's suffering on the cross increased their doubt and anger. When, finally, the Zealots heard that Yeshua had died, and that his body had been removed from the cross, with no angels coming down from heaven to restore him, they were furious. They hunted Judah down, found him sitting under a yew tree on the road to Bethany. That yew—tree of life and death, tree of weeping—became Judah's scaffold.

These are all facts I learned a few weeks later, from a young Zealot who had been at the scene and rued his involvement. The poor teenager was so racked with regret that he hunted me down in Capharnaum. Remembering me as a healer at Yeshua's side in Jerusalem, the boy asked me to forgive his sin of watching Judah die.

Yohanna gave me the news about Judah as we spread our cloaks on the floor of a cave outside Jericho, preparing to spend the night there. It was safer for us, two women traveling alone, not to camp near the road. From this elevation, we watched evening fall into the Judean desert, like a silk billowing to the ground, layer after layer of violet folding upon itself.

"What a callous world," I blinked through my tears, "that dares to offer beauty in the midst of all this grief."

"Maybe the world is not indifferent to us." Yohanna came up behind me and clasped her hands in front of my chest, resting her head on my shoulder to watch night fall. "Maybe it sends us reminders just when we need them."

"Reminders?"

"That sorrow always lives side by side with grace," Yohanna said. She kissed my hair. "That we do not bear our woes alone."

Early morning had just begun to sharpen the edges of the stone in the Capharnaum synagogue when I entered. I walked to the middle of the devotional chamber and stood surrounded by shadows, as the walls oozed gloom and inertia. When Yeshua was alive, there had been magic in this room, rekindled every day when he stepped over its threshold. Now the space felt cavernous. It was my job to fill it with hope.

News of Yeshua's death and burial had traveled to Capharnaum faster than Yohanna and I could walk. I looked at the familiar faces staring at me from the synagogue benches—among them, Yohanna, Ilana, Levi, Phillip, Andrew, and the Zebedee brothers, James, and John. Peter chose to stand. I saw loss and heartache, different degrees of despair. But I also saw commitment and loyalty, and it was these that inspired me. Surely these honest men and women, who so loved Yeshua, could succeed in spreading his message, even though he was no longer here to lead us. Our com-

pany was large, and if mobilized into action, we could travel far—
to Syria and Mesopotamia, Nabataea and Parthia, possibly even
farther east. I thought of Shoshanna and Marcus and their caravan and wondered where they were.

What the people in this room needed was a jolt of faith. I
could give them that, because other than Yohanna, no one knew
what I had seen at the tomb. I felt certain that hearing my story of
Yeshua's resurrection would rouse everyone into action.

Oh, I was so naive.

"We are all mourning our beloved Rabbi," I began. "Nobody,
absolutely nobody can replace him." I paused to give our sorrow
the space it deserved. We lowered our heads in prayer, as the
ascending sun sent more light into the room.

"Fortunately, nobody has to," I announced, breaking the
silence.

Bodies shifted on the benches, confusion layering itself over
grief. Peter stiffened, as if he was preparing for a threat. "What do
you mean?" he asked.

"I mean that Yeshua has not left us. I saw him four days ago."
There was skepticism on almost every face. To shake it off, I
raised my voice and shouted with excitement, "He is risen from
the dead!"

That did it. Everyone burst into clamorous chatter, turning to
Yohanna to ask if what I said was true. She nodded enthusiastically.
Beaming, I waited in the center of the room. I was eager to provide
all the details. The walls around me had now brightened. Even the
stone was rejoicing.

Peter didn't buy it. He was suspicious. He stamped across the
room like the raging wind of a desert haboob. "Impossible!" he
growled, shaking his head. "Castus told us that he placed our
Rabbi's body in the tomb. His *dead* body."

"Yes!" John agreed. "He said he blocked the entrance with a large rock."

"That is true," I said. "I was there for the burial, as were Yohanna, Miriam of Bethany, and Yeshua's mother. It all happened as you were told. But I'm talking about what I saw two days later, after the Sabbath."

Peter stopped less than an arm's length away from me. Striking distance, I thought, and took a step back. "You want us to believe that you saw Yeshua, walking and talking like a normal man, as if he had never been tortured, never been crucified?" I felt the moisture of the last word as Peter spat it out at me.

Months earlier, I might have been intimidated by this aggressive display. But today, I refused to be bullied.

"Yes, Peter, I saw Yeshua alive. And yes, he was walking and talking."

Peter remained unconvinced. "Tell me then, Magda, if what you say is true, why has he appeared only to you? If he has been alive for—what? Four days now, you say—why have none of us seen him? Surely he would want all of us to know of his transformation."

"He did. He does," I insisted. "That's why I am here. He asked me to come and tell all of you. To prepare you."

Peter guffawed, throwing his head back. The man was such a drama queen. "Oh come, you expect me to believe that the Rabbi I loved—and who loved me—would choose *you* as the messenger to tell me he was risen? I was the first person he chose to follow him. He called me his 'rock.' Why would he not appear to *me*?"

I could have been cruel then. I could have said, "Because he loved me more." But I didn't. I knew Yeshua would want me to spare Peter's feelings. And, with some surprise, I realized that I did too. I could see the man was hurting. Who was I to turn the knife in his wound? So I acted ignorant.

"I cannot say, Peter. That is something only Yeshua can answer." This response silenced his tantrum, at least for the moment. I took the opportunity to speak to the others. "Yeshua has said that he will come to Capharnaum to meet with everyone. I don't know exactly when. I thought he might join us here this morning."

Maybe Yeshua timed his arrival to enhance my credibility, because just at that moment, a great incandescence pulsed through the chamber. We shielded our eyes briefly in adjustment, and when we looked again, in the center of the floor, there he stood, looking as he had when I saw him days earlier. His bodily form was exactly the same as when he was alive, but he now glowed with a wondrous phosphorescence.

No one could stay seated. They crowded around him with questions, all of which he answered patiently. They marveled to see that his wounds—the flayed skin on his back, the holes through his feet—were healed. Of course, I knew that was because the form he occupied was not his earthly body. He had left that body behind, nobody knew where.

I kept myself at a distance during this reunion, content to watch him and be near him. I would never tire of his presence,

Yeshua would stay with us for several weeks. "Go spread what I have taught you," he said. "Tell everyone about the way of life we practiced—teach them love and tolerance, peace and equality. Urge them to dismantle their existing structures and build a new world based on our principles. Go to the towns and cities of Judea and Idumea, Galilee and Samaria. Go south to Egypt and north to Armenia. Go east with the caravans, and west with the ships over the sea."

"And if you have any question about how to forge a true connection," Yeshua said as he gestured at me, "whether that connection be to me, to God, or to another human being, Magda will show you. Let her wisdom be your guide."

He meant his last comment to be helpful. But Yeshua always underestimated the divisive power of human jealousy. Peter hadn't stopped resenting me since the first day Yeshua ordered him to leave us alone in Magdala. He wasn't about to admit now that I had more wisdom than he, regardless of what Yeshua said. The plan Peter had been shaping in his mind since Yeshua's death—going to Jerusalem to establish a church in Yeshua's name—did not include me. Peter could not tolerate sharing the stage with a woman.

One last fiction needs to be cleared up about these weeks that Yeshua was with us. It's a story invented by—need I even say it?—your "Saint" Paul. Paul (who was not there) points out that we would have encountered language barriers in traveling to all the foreign countries Yeshua mentioned. To eliminate this problem, Paul says, we were each visited by a "Holy Spirit," which descended upon us in a burst of wind and fire and gave us all the ability to speak in foreign tongues. This "Holy Spirit" supposedly manifested itself as little flames dancing on our heads.

Uh huh.

Look, if there was a flame flickering on top of my hair, I'd plunge my head in the nearest water cistern. So no, that did not happen. Just another fanciful myth created by Paul and his overactive imagination. We learned those foreign languages as slowly as anyone else, word by word, gesture by gesture.

At the end of his last day, Yeshua kissed each of us, one by one, a faint whisper of wind brushing over our faces. Then he walked off into the desert. He looked back only one time and called out, "You know where to find me." The others may have thought that was a message for them, but I knew better.

MINISTRY

2

*Y*eshua's message could have gone in dozens of directions. Any of us could have spread his word wherever we went. If the message had been truly delivered, and in good faith, based on the principles he believed in—love, equality, tolerance—well, the world today would be quite different from what it is.

Yes, you read that right. You'd be living in an entirely changed world if his ideas had been implemented. I'm not saying it would have been easy, I'm not saying there wouldn't have been resistance, but at least we would have had a chance.

Thanks to Peter, and especially, to Paul, that didn't happen. Let me be clear on this point since you've been tolerating my jabs at these two for quite a while. I don't think that Peter and Paul had any ill intent in establishing the Church that they did. I don't think they *meant* to undermine Yeshua's teachings. Much of what they taught, and much of what the Church continues to teach today, is absolutely consistent with what he embodied—love your fellow, forgive each other's sins, help those less fortunate.

But Peter and Paul couldn't wrap their heads around the two

most fundamental elements of Yeshua's teachings: radical equality
and radical tolerance. Radical equality, as I've said earlier, meant
that no one was better than anyone else. It meant that the beggar
who spent all day on the street in tattered rags, blocking your way
to market, equally deserved the food you were going to buy with
money that you worked hard to earn. Radical equality meant getting rid of inequitable power structures and eliminating hierarchy
however and wherever it appeared. It meant there was no need for
high priests and low priests and bishops and archbishops because
everyone had direct access to God within themselves. And radical
tolerance meant tolerating any and all beliefs that differ from your
own, not annihilating them through Crusades or Inquisitions, or
banning and burning.

The Church that Peter and Paul created did not adhere to
these principles.

🖋️

After Yeshua left us in Galilee, Peter gathered his wife and children
and shepherded them all to Jerusalem. A posse of apostles from
our original group joined him, along with the most committed
members of our congregation in Capharnaum. Only Yohanna,
Levi, Ilana, and I remained behind. We heard that, a few weeks
later, Peter was joined in the Holy City by James of Nazareth,
Yeshua's older brother. Dragging along poor Maryam, who depended on him for her care.

Wait, you say. Didn't James dismiss Yeshua and his teachings
when he was still alive? Didn't he join the rest of Nazareth in dri-
ving Yeshua out of town? Indeed, he did. Apparently, James had a
change of heart. When, at the moment your brother dies, in the
middle of the day, the earth suddenly quakes and the sky darkens

to pitch black, it might make you pause and reconsider. Maybe James saw the error of his ways.

Or maybe he saw something else. An opportunity to take advantage of a martyred prophet. To marshal his followers and create something. Something powerful. Something that James, being Yeshua's flesh and blood, might lead. Something that would give James, unknown peasant from a miserable backwater village, more stature than he had ever dreamed of.

⚜

Peter did not prevent Yohanna, Ilana, and me from joining his band of brothers in Jerusalem. Indeed, he invited us to come. "We'll need someone to assist with the chores," he told us. "To help Rivka and the girls cook and serve at communal meals." Oh, how I wanted to smack him when he said that to us! No—whatever he was planning to do in the Holy City, we wanted no part of it.

Levi, Ilana, Yohanna, and I decided to head north. Ultimately, we were aiming for Damascus, because Levi wanted Ilana to give birth in a city where we would have access to skilled midwives. But we had months before the baby would be coming, so we chose a route through the western edge of the Syrian desert, a parched, unyielding land very different from the fertile fields of Galilee. Here, the wind buffeted the ground so constantly that finer particles of dirt and sand had been blown away, leaving behind small pieces of gravel, pressed together into a kind of pavement. It made for easy walking, which was a blessing to Ilana, as she navigated the area with a belly that increasingly unbalanced her.

Levi, ever solicitous of Ilana's health, insisted we go slowly. Every half hour, he nagged his wife, asking how she felt, suggesting she take a rest. "I am *not* an invalid," she finally barked at him. "But if you don't stop pestering me, *you* might become one."

We approached villages as Yeshua had taught us. We greeted people, told them who we were, and invited everyone to assemble for a communal meal and our after-dinner story. Of course, the story we had to tell was now infinitely more dramatic, because it included Yeshua's crucifixion and resurrection. Ironically, the Romans couldn't have done Yeshua's message a bigger favor than to crucify its spokesperson. If the messenger was dangerous enough to execute, people thought, surely the message was worth listening to.

I was surprised how readily the communities we visited here, on the edge of the desert, embraced our message of equality and tolerance. In the villages we had visited around Galilee with Yeshua, we had occasionally encountered resistance to his ideas, especially in larger towns where there was a thriving middle class of merchants and traders, people who had become used to the special status that their economic success gave them. But the northern settlements—Serisa, Kabok, and others—were more recently descended from nomad tribes. Desert wanderers who had few, if any, authority or class structures. They were used to having to share scarce food and water, they knew that survival of the tribe depended on commonality of resources. In that context, everyone was already equal.

Three months into our travels, we arrived in Naveh, a tiny town south of Damascus. I had, by then, developed enough of a reputation as a healer that the moment we set foot in town, the people of Naveh begged me to help them. There was a young girl named Zenora, they said, who had been ravaged by a demon for two years. Apparently, Zenora's mother had died in childbirth when Zenora was ten years old, and her tiny baby brother lived only two days. Overcome with grief, Zenora's father could not face the responsibility of raising his daughter alone, so he disappeared one night and had not been seen since. An uncle who lived alone had taken the young girl in. But less than a year later, he threw her out of his house, saying she had become wild and unmanageable. He claimed that she had a demon within her, for she kicked and screamed whenever he or any other man came near. Because no family wanted to take the risk of bringing a demon into their home, the village had banished her to a cave, feeding her occasionally with scraps of food.

The villagers led me to Zenora's cave, well on the outside of town. No one wanted Zenora's demon too close to themselves or their children, lest the fiend be tempted to find a new host. Eventually, we reached a small dark hole carved out of an escarpment of basalt rock. The place was completely desolate, with a few anemic buckthorn bushes breaking the monotony of gravel and dust. Two hefty stone-workers volunteered to go in and find Zenora. Moments later, they dragged out a shrieking, hysterical young girl.

Now, you know me. I'm skeptical of the tag "demon-possessed." I always gave "demoniacs" the benefit of the doubt when it came to believing in the inherent goodness of the supposedly possessed individual. So I listened to the Naveans' story with skepticism. Which was confirmed the moment I saw Zenora—whatever this poor child suffered from, I thought, it was not a demon.

Thrashing before me was a feral, emaciated waif with tattered clothes and matted hair. Looking at her, I decided the only truly demonic thing about Zenora was the way she had been discarded by her people. Surely, the solitude alone would have made her halfway crazy. Then, as I watched the frantic way she clawed and scratched at the two men holding her, I knew the nature of her possession. Her panic and terror, not just at being restrained, but at being touched, the way she recoiled from the physical proximity of their skin to hers—all of it felt viscerally familiar, evoking a muted memory buried deep within me. This girl had been physically assaulted.

I approached her slowly, whispering her name like a spell. "Zenora, my child, Zenora, dear beauty." My softness took her by surprise. She relaxed ever so slightly, until one of the brutes picked her up and threw her over his shoulder.

"Where do you want her?" he barked. She bucked and squirmed and finally bit him on the shoulder. "Stop that!" he yelled, slamming her body down on a rock. Stunned, her body went limp.

"What have you done?" I cried, running over to the girl, and placing my hand just above her mouth. Thankfully, she still breathed. Yohanna was waiting in the crowd, holding our oils, and she hurried over, as I began gently running my hands over Zenora's scalp.

"Chamomile and lavender," Yohanna said, handing me two small flasks. "To soothe and relax."

"Exactly what I would have chosen."

Zenora's breathing became deeper and more regular as I poured the oils over my hands and worked them into her body. Head, face, torso, arms, belly, and legs. I asked Yohanna to help me roll her over, and to hold Zenora's head in her hands. Neck, shoulders, and spine. What I discovered, as I closed my eyes and let myself roam into her being, was a girl whose trust in other people had been violated, a girl steeped in shame and worthlessness, as I had been so long ago. It was my job now to assure her of her value and her virtue. I gave her my love, unequivocally and unconditionally. I did all of this through the prayer my fingers traced and retraced over her skin.

When I was done, Yohanna and I stepped away. Zenora lay

quietly on the rock for a minute, before sitting up and rubbing her eyes. I made everyone else wait at a distance. Zenora scanned the small crowd that had come to watch my efforts, finally resting her eyes on me. Holding my gaze, she got up and knelt on the ground. And bowed her head.

For the rest of that day, as we moved about town, spreading word about our evening meal and purchasing food for it, I noticed Zenora watching us at a distance, always from behind a wall or a tree. When I was able to catch her eye, I smiled at her, and she immediately disappeared. That night, word about Zenora's transformation having traveled fast, the entire town of Naveh turned out to join us for supper. Thanks to the last-minute generosity of several well-stocked kitchens, we did not run out of food.

It was Yohanna's turn to preach. She told the story of the friendship between Yeshua and Yochanan the Baptizer. Yohanna explained that they both lived their lives according to their belief in a kingdom of God that was at hand *now*, one that could be lived *now*. But for the kingdom to manifest on Earth, we all had to love each other and to understand that no one was better than anyone else. We had to recognize the divinity within ourselves as being the same divinity within others. If enough of us came to that belief, she said, society could be transformed. Because power feeds upon perceptions of difference, Yohanna said, total equality for everyone undermines power structures. And that was why, she concluded sadly, egalitarians like Yochanan and Yeshua had to be killed.

Mouths were agape at the end of her lesson. Suddenly, we were bombarded with questions, too many to answer fully in just one evening. We were asked to stay on for a few days, and homes were offered for our comfort.

As I lay on a rooftop next to Yohanna that night, I heard light footfalls scampering up the ladder from the courtyard below. They scurried across the thatch. Suddenly, a small figure appeared next to me, squatting beside my blanket. The night was overcast, so I could not make out her face, but the sharp angles of her body gave her away.

"Zenora?"

A crack of moonlight pushed its way through the cloud cover to light up the girl's cautious, imploring smile. She pressed her palms together, raised them to her cheek, and bent her head against them.

"Of course you can sleep here," I said, lifting my blanket to make room. She scrambled beneath it and curled up next to me, laying her head in the crook between my arm and my chest.

That was how I came to adopt my daughter.

MINISTRY

3

*A*s my narrative now heads to Damascus, I must introduce you to Paul. I won't call him *Saint Paul* or *Paul the Apostle*, because he was neither, not in my book. The Paul I knew was an ordinary man—an ambitious, religiously-fanatical man. The religion didn't matter, the fanaticism did.

Peter and the other disciples met Paul before I did, when they returned to Jerusalem after we parted ways. At that time, Paul was using his birth name, Saul. (He later changed his name for reasons that will become obvious.) As Peter's new church in the Holy City attracted converts, one of its most ardent followers was a pious man named Stephen. Like Yeshua, Stephen denounced the money-grubbing Temple cult and the Jewish Sanhedrin priests who upheld it, and like Yeshua, he was arrested for blasphemy. The Pharisees, staunch advocates for strict adherence to Jewish law, deliberated on what punishment to give Stephen. They turned to Saul for advice. That's right, Saul was, in his early years, one of the most zealous Pharisees around.

For those of you who don't know, Saul was a Roman citizen. More importantly, he was a Jew, a learned and very devout Jew. In fact, being devout was one of Saul's defining characteristics. The object of his devotion mattered far less than the intensity of his devotional fervor.

As far as Saul was concerned, it was blasphemous to claim, as Stephen did, that the recently-executed Jewish peasant, Yeshua of Nazareth, was the *Christ* or *Messiah* predicted by the prophet Daniel. Stephen's crime of heresy, Saul thought, offered a perfect opportunity to send a message to the young communities beginning to adopt similar beliefs: Worship this nonsense, and you will die. To bring this message home, Saul pressed for Stephen to receive the harshest possible punishment: stoning.

As a manner of execution, stoning was only slightly more merciful than crucifixion, primarily because—depending on the enthusiasm of the participating crowd—the victim died more quickly. The condemned was placed in a hole just deep enough to hold his body while still exposing his head. Participants in the stoning—and there were always plenty of them—gathered rocks of just the right weight, heavy enough to maim but not kill outright. The goal was for the victim to succumb slowly, after suffering an appropriate amount of pain. Stephen lasted less than half an hour.

Pleased with Stephen's extermination and impressed with Saul's anti-Christian bloodthirstiness, the High Priest in Jerusalem sent Saul north to Syria, to sniff out and snuff out all fledgling Christian communities. He told Saul to arrest the heretics he found and send them back to Jerusalem for questioning and trial. Off Saul went on the road to Damascus, with a few thugs in tow, to help him corral his targets.

Now keep in mind, as you hear the next piece of Saul's story, that what happened on the road to Damascus is a tale told by Saul that has never been corroborated.

As Saul was walking along the road, contemplating his up-coming persecutions, a blazing light suddenly shone down all around him from Heaven, making him fall to the ground. A loud voice called out, "Saul, why do you persecute me?" When Saul asked the voice who it was, it claimed to be Yeshua, and it told him to go to Damascus and await further instruction. But Saul had been struck blind, so he had to be led to Damascus by his comrades.

When I first heard this tale, I had serious doubts. It didn't sound like Yeshua's way of doing things—the dramatic lighting, the mysterious instruction, the sudden blindness. Plus, none of the men Saul was traveling with ever came forward with that story. You'd think that if anyone else had seen such a vision, they'd be sharing it left and right, running to the nearest Christian commu-nity, totally converted. Nope, not a one.

Of course, I sought out Yeshua for confirmation, the next time I meditated. I asked him whether Saul's tale was true. My beloved husband clucked sympathetically. "Oh, Saul, what am I going to do with you and your stories?" Enough said.

It's not that I think Paul was *lying* about his vision when he wrote about it. I'm sure he saw *someone* or *something*. He probably fell to the ground too. Maybe he even went blind for a little while, who knows? But looking at the entire event in hindsight, and with the benefit of modern medical knowledge, I've come to this conclusion: Paul was an epileptic, and on the road to Dam-ascus, he had an epileptic seizure. It all fits—the loss of muscle control, the falling down, the ecstatic vision, the temporary blindness (not terribly common among epileptics, but it does happen). And I'm willing to bet that some, if not all, of the other "visions" he brags about in his never-ending letters were related to seizures too.

I also think that something more calculated was going on, in that overactive brain Paul carried around. By the time of his "conversion," Paul had been traveling north for some time. He had seen firsthand the strength and conviction of the followers of this new religion that would be called Christianity. Stephen's death had proven that at least some of these believers were willing to sacrifice their lives. The small Christian communities that Paul found on his way north to Syria were equally fervent in their faith. Paul was reluctantly coming to the conclusion that maybe, just maybe, the new religion was here to stay.

What to do? Should Paul continue to arrest, try, and execute *all* of these followers? Stephen had already become a martyr back in Jerusalem. Should Paul run the very palpable risk of creating even more martyrs, who would most likely encourage even more converts to the new faith? Maybe the answer wasn't to try to beat them, if beating them was a lost cause. Maybe the answer was to join them.

Paul's ambition saw an opportunity here, the opportunity to shape a religion, to get in on the ground floor and design its governing principles. He knew that none of the men back in Jerusalem had written down anything about their time with Yeshua. The ones he had met already—Peter and James and the Zebedee brothers—were glaringly illiterate. That gave Paul, a highly educated man who swung a vicious quill, the opportunity to create a record that would outlast all of them.

But Paul faced two problems. First, there was his reputation as Saul the Pharisee, zealous persecutor of Christians. Easily solved, Paul thought, by a quick name change. Heck, it didn't take more than one letter. More problematic were all those disciples who had known the living Yeshua. Apostles like Peter and the Zebedee brothers were acknowledged as elders by other Christians in their community because of their intimacy with the prophet in his lifetime. Unfortunately, Paul had not known Yeshua. If he was going to have any authority, he had to put himself on equal footing. Hence the transformation of Paul's epileptic vision into a personal visitation from Yeshua, with a personal message and subsequent personal instruction. Paul elevated himself from being an ordinary follower to someone *special*, someone *chosen*, someone *singled out*. He couldn't wait to tell everyone about it.

⁂

With Zenora in tow, Yohanna, Levi, Ilana, and I arrived in Damascus shortly before Paul's transformation. One of the merchants of Naveh had kindly given us a donkey for our trip north, because Ilana had only a month to go in her pregnancy. She was so heavy with child that everyone feared she would drop the baby en route. But sitting astride Pontius Pilate the ass—our little group joke— Ilana made it safely to Damascus, with the baby still happily kicking her internal organs. We were able to find a small house and had just settled in when Ilana went into labor.

Ilana was lucky to have the solicitous attention of a group of women, who all encouraged her to scream out loud whenever she needed to. Yohanna had supervised a number of births at Antipas's palace, and our closest neighbor in Damascus, a woman named Tamar, had ten children and considered herself an expert. I had no experience at all in childbirth, so I focused my efforts on keeping Levi calm.

Poor Levi. Nobody suffered more during the day and a half that Ilana's body worked to bring a new soul into the world. I don't mean to minimize the pain of Ilana's labor, but at least she had a purpose. All Levi could do was pace, because he refused to leave the house. We told him it would take hours, and urged him to distract himself in town, but he refused.

"If Ilana is stuck here, then so am I," Levi said, pressing his lips together so firmly they paled. At first he walked a straight line, back and forth between the chair we had set outside the closed bedroom door and the kitchen table. A carafe of water sitting on the table tempted him to drink a glass every half hour, just so he would have something to do. But all that liquid required elimination, and after reluctantly exiting the house several times to relieve himself, Levi poured the water out of the pitcher.

When Ilana's labor intensified and she began screaming with her contractions, Levi shifted to a circular pacing pattern. I took a break from the bedroom to check on him and found him muttering in prayer as he wore an oval groove into the dirt floor.

He stopped briefly when he heard me come out. "Magda, how is she?"

"She's doing well, Levi, as well as can be expected for a first birth. It is a difficult process."

Levi's nervous energy drove his feet back to the dirt moat he was making. "Yes I know, I know, but I didn't expect it to be *this* difficult." He followed his trench over to the wall, pausing only to straighten a tapestry, which hung more crookedly after his effort. I suspected he had been "straightening" it all day. "She cries out so often, I fear for her. Is that normal, how often she screams?"

"That is normal, Levi."

"But Magda, I … I am afraid. I love her so much. What if she dies? What if she dies, Magda? I don't know how I would live without her."

My heart stumbled in its rhythm, touching the grief that still lived there. You would *survive*, Levi, I thought to myself. You would survive because you'd have no other choice. But your life would be forever poorer for her absence.

"She is strong," I said aloud, putting my hand on his shoulder. "She will be fine."

And she was. Two hours later, Ilana delivered a healthy, squalling baby boy. When we finally let Levi into the bedroom, he ran over to Ilana, knelt next to the bed, and covered her face with kisses.

"*Motek, motek,* my love, I am happy to see you too," Ilana laughed. "But don't you want to meet your son?"

"My son . . ." Levi whispered, staring with awe and wonder at the swaddled cocoon she held up to him. "What shall we name him?" he asked, nestling the bundle against his chest.

Ilana had talked to me earlier about the name, and my eyes were wet as she told him. "Yeshua."

MINISTRY

4

We might all have lived happily ever after in Damascus had not Paul come to visit our home during a Greek lesson. Months later—when it was too late to change the consequences, when Yohanna, Zenora, and I were bobbing in an open boat in the Mediterranean Sea, praying for a gentle wind and benevolent currents—I wondered at the power of our one small Greek alphabet exercise. Because when Paul saw that women were learning Greek, the language of written records, the language of scribes, he imagined a future where women could read and write their own version of events. There is nothing more dangerous to a tyrant crafting his own version of history than an oppressed minority with access to ink and paper.

But even if I had known then that the Greek lesson would trigger an alarm for Paul, that it would set into motion the events that got me expelled from my homeland, I wouldn't have stopped teaching. (In hindsight, I might have taken it underground, or to some cave in the nearby desert, where we could chalk our *etas* and *psis* in peace.) I had always been committed to educating women, and now I had my own girl to teach, Zenora. Yohanna and Ilana were eager to join her.

"Think of *omicron* as a rock." Yohanna drew a circle on her wax tablet, as she and Zenora practiced their letters in our courtyard. Our formal class had just ended, and Ilana was headed off to the market with Levi. "And *sigma* as someone peeking out from behind the rock." Yohanna extended the top edge of her circle. "*Zeta* is just a *xi*," she drew a curlicue *xi* with a foot hovering over it, "that's been stepped on."

Zenora's giggles skipped through the spring air, prompting little Yeshua, or Yosh, as we called him, to leave the puddle he had been filling with sand. The three-year-old ran under a bower of flowering bougainvillea, fuchsia and tangerine tendrils reaching through the air to pet him as he passed. When he got to Zenora, she lifted him onto her lap, and he clapped his hands, trying to grab her stylus, sending bits of mud flying.

"Ah! Yosh is telling us it's time for a snack," I said. Zenora handed me the squirming boy.

Heading to the pantry, I marveled at the life and the family we had created. It was, to be sure, not the family I had imagined in my fantasies when Yeshua was alive, but it was still rich and deeply satisfying. Yohanna and I shared this house with Ilana and Levi—several rooms arranged around the open courtyard—allowing all of us the privacy we needed to stay sane.

Zenora and I shared a bedroom, at her request. Having crawled under my blanket every night back in Naveh, she had no intention of relinquishing that spot, though she was now a young teenager and might have sought her own bed. Of course I welcomed her. The softness of her body next to my own and her quiet snores throughout the night were wonderfully soothing. My bed had felt cold and empty since Yeshua's death, and maternal love was a powerful bedwarmer.

I still met Yeshua daily when I meditated, and that time with him went a long way toward stemming the grief I felt at his physical absence from my daily life. My love for him had been so all-encompassing that I had to rechannel it elsewhere. So I directed it at Zenora. I came to think of her as the child we never had and taught her as Yeshua had taught me. It was surprisingly easy, because she was a clean slate. As a young orphan, she had no learning to speak of. As an abandoned and isolated individual, she had no one filling her head with prevailing social prejudices. And as a victim of abuse, she had a deeply wounded heart, one that was particularly empathic to the pain and suffering of others.

"You know that Zenora is becoming just like you," Yeshua said to me one day.

"Like *me?*" I was taken aback. "I was just about to say she reminds me so much of you."

"Oh, maybe so, when she meditates," Yeshua said. "But the other day, she was playing mancala with one of the neighborhood boys, and he secretly pocketed one of the stones so he could win. He thought he had fooled her, but she figured it out and gave him a well-deserved slap across the cheek at the end of the game." He laughed, remembering. "Just like you! Same fire, same outrage at wrongdoing!"

I would have felt overwhelmed with the expectations of motherhood, had not my friends stepped in to help. As a practical matter, when Yohanna, Levi, Ilana, and I decided to live together in one home, we agreed to share child-raising responsibilities for Zenora and Yosh. Not only did this arrangement keep us all more level-headed, it gave us the opportunity to spread Yeshua's teachings to nearby neighborhoods. We opened our courtyard for communal meals twice a week and watched them become increasingly popular. In the two-plus years that we had been here, attendance at those meals increased from a handful to scores of people.

But our greatest success in Damascus came through our anointment practice—two of the rooms in our home were dedicated to it. In one room, Yohanna and I recreated the herbal chamber where we had spent so much time in Capharnaum, replenishing and expanding our store of oils. In the other, we set up benches and blankets, incense and candles. This was where Yohanna, Ilana, and I actually laid our hands on the people who came to us for healing.

I continued pondering my role in Yeshua's ministry. Over and over, I considered Deborah's words—"You have the power to connect them." Yeshua was annoyingly deflective when I sought insight from him as to what Deborah meant.

"What do *you* think Deborah meant?" He asked.

"If I knew what she meant, why do you think I'm asking you?"

"Magda, when a prophet gives you her prediction, the only one who can discern her true meaning is *you*. I can offer theories or guesses, but it will be *your* actions that reveal its significance to you."

"My *actions*?" I felt like I was being particularly dense.

"What do you do?" Yeshua prodded me.

I thought for a moment. "I anoint people."

"There you are," Yeshua said.

I remained confused. Yeshua had taught me that God could be found within everyone. I knew that people *felt* that divinity—their own and mine—during anointment. In that moment, however, I was only connecting their spirit to mine, and to Yeshua's. I was not connecting them to anyone else. Then it came back to me, that time in Jerusalem—when I had anointed on the Temple Mount, I had sensed other spirits hovering nearby. I wondered whether there was some way to pull those spirits in when I was anointing another.

One morning, I resolved to make that attempt. I was anointing a young woman named Esther, who complained of cramps and back pain. When I reached the point where our souls united, I paused, allowing myself to drift, feeling her energy merge with mine, both of us resting on waves of shifting light and bracing warmth.

I murmured a prayer of supplication. Earlier that day, before Esther arrived, I had anointed Abel, an elderly man who suffered from rheumatism. Like many of the people I healed, he was overcome with gratitude at the end of our session. "If there is ever anything I can do for you," Abel croaked, leaning on my arm as I helped him to the front door. "Just ask."

Remembering his promise, I consciously sought him. My mind repeated Abel's name and asked him to join us, focusing on the energy I had felt from him hours earlier. And what do you know? In that space where I was lingering with Esther, we suddenly felt the presence of another. I knew Abel immediately. Awestruck, the three of us swayed as one.

Later that day, Abel came to our courtyard at the evening service, and he saw Esther standing in a group of ladies, chatting. Without hesitation, Abel limped over to her and tapped her shoulder. When she turned, the joy of kinship already lit her face, for she had recognized him by his touch.

Watching this, I almost fell to my knees. I felt empowered and magical, like your comic heroine Wonder Woman, the Amazon lady who summons lightning bolts of energy by knocking her golden bracelets against each other. Could this power of connecting people at their most inner and fundamental levels—uniting souls to each other—be the key to the radical equality Yeshua had spoken of? Was this the beginning of God's kingdom on Earth? If so, I intended to begin transforming society right then and there.

Alas, my efforts would soon be cut short.

The first week we opened our doors in Damascus, we had perhaps two or three visitors to our fledgling ministry. Within two years, our weekly total had skyrocketed. Every day, we gathered for evening prayers, after which one of the four of us taught in the courtyard. Soul by soul, voice by voice, Yeshua's message of radical equality and love was being heard and internalized. My anointment skills—especially the feeling of bliss and harmony that people carried away with them—were praised throughout the city and beyond. Eventually, word reached the ears of Paul.

I hadn't given Paul much thought after hearing about his conversion years earlier. I knew he had gone north to set up a church in Antioch and was baptizing and preaching to his own followers. As far as I was concerned, Syria had room for more than a few preachers, and if he wanted to carve out his own niche based on whatever he thought his vision told him, that was fine by me. I never expected him to show up at my house.

Yet there he was, with a colleague, in our courtyard. Yohanna heard the knock on our front door and, not having any reason to be fearful of two strangers who professed an interest in our spiritual community, she invited them in. Zenora saw a chance to take a break from her studies and quietly disappeared. The strange voices in the courtyard brought me out of the kitchen area, still holding Yosh, who was sucking on a dried fig and digging his fingers into its sticky flesh.

Before me stood two men who could not have looked less alike. The one closer to me was quite short, and I knew immediately, from the fine silk tunic visible beneath his woolen cloak, that he was a man of means. He was almost bald, which did his disproportionately large head no favors. The shiny sphere atop this man's body was balanced by a belly plump enough to part the sides of his mantle and expose two strangely curved legs. These bent outward at the knees and gave him a rocking gait whenever he walked, like a ship tossing back and forth on disordered waves. He took a few tottering steps forward.

"Greetings! I am Paul of Tarsus, citizen of Rome, Beloved Apostle of Yeshua of Nazareth, the Risen Christ and Messiah, Descendant of the great King David." The well-oiled words rolled out of his mouth like the fish that used to slide out of my friend Ehud's nets back in Magdala—so many you could hardly grab onto them.

Paul's companion, a young man about Levi's age, also stepped forward. Although most men were probably taller than Paul, this fellow towered over us all. As if apologetic about his height, he kept his shoulders stooped and his head bowed. "And I am Barnabas of Antioch," he said, "humble follower of the Christian faith. We are grateful to you for your hospitality this morning." Paul of Tarsus, citizen of Rome, I thought, could stand a few lessons in humility from his colleague.

Yohanna motioned for the men to take a seat at the table, while she and I settled ourselves on the opposite bench. Yosh sat on my lap, eyes intently watchful, sweet-sticky fingers now plugging his mouth for comfort.

Paul cleared his throat. "You have no doubt heard of my ministry. By the grace of God and our Savior Yeshua of Nazareth, the Christ and Messiah, I have established the preeminent Christian community here in Syria." Yohanna kicked me lightly under the table. "What you may not know, and what is of particular relevance to you, is that I have been given the *exclusive* authority to preach to the Gentile people."

In fact, I did know something about the subject Paul was raising. I had heard about a schism between Paul and the

Jerusalem crowd led by Peter and James. There was, apparently, a difference in opinion about who should be allowed to practice this new religion called Christianity. Peter and James took the position that the only people who could become followers of Yeshua's teachings were Jews. Their reasoning was simple, if simple-minded: Yeshua was Jewish, all of his closest followers were Jewish, and most of the crowds who came to hear Yeshua in the synagogue at Capharnaum were Jewish. Thus, the new Christian religion should be limited to Jews.

Either it did not occur to Peter and James, or they simply did not care, that this position was contrary to Yeshua's teachings of equality and tolerance. Yeshua would never have excluded anyone who wanted to follow him. In his lifetime, he brought his message to Gentiles as well as Jews. Nor would he have insisted that there was only one way to believe. He knew, from his understanding of the religions farther east, that there were many paths to the truth, and that they looked remarkably similar. Be that as it may, Peter and James held fast to their conviction that non-Jewish individuals, whether Gentile or pagan, could not become Christians.

Imagine Peter and James's surprise and concern when they learned that a man named Paul was preaching indiscriminately up in Antioch, to Gentiles as well as Jews. This would not do, they decided. They called Paul down to Jerusalem pronto.

After much bickering they offered the following compromise: Paul could continue his approach, however misguided, of allowing anyone to join his church, provided that, if a person was not already Jewish, he or she must first convert to Judaism. At first glance, it seemed reasonable and simple. It wouldn't be too difficult for people to practice the Ten Commandments and keep the Sabbath. But Paul immediately saw the sucker punch at its heart: circumcision. For any adult non-Jewish males, this was a practically inconceivable sacrifice, especially in an age without anesthesia.

I have to admit to laughing out loud when I heard about the proposal. Ilana and Yohanna shared my amusement. One evening after dinner, the three of us playfully recreated the Jerusalem meeting between Paul and Peter. Our loud bursts of laughter brought out Levi, who had just bathed baby Yosh and demanded to know what was so hysterical.

"We could tell you," Ilana said, "but it might be more fun to act it out for you."

"Excellent!" Yohanna agreed. "I'll play James, Magda can be Paul, and you, Ilana, you get to be our good friend Peter."

Levi sat down on a blanket and placed Yosh beside him. Our audience, modest but appreciative.

I grabbed a small melon from our fruit bowl, wedged it between my thighs, and hobbled back and forth, wagging my finger through the air.

"Listen, you two," I said as Paul, "you keep saying you want to spread this new religion, this Christianity. I tell you, the fastest way for us to gain new followers is to make the religion available to *everyone*, Gentiles as well as Jews."

"Nope, can't happen," Yohanna barked as James. "Those stinking heathens will defile our religious spaces. They'll seat their pig-eating bodies on our benches, walk their idol-worshipping feet across our floors. Think of the extra cleaning that will require. We'll have to scrub the benches and floors daily. And we'll have to repurify ourselves too, just by sharing that space with them. All in all, it's going to be a lot of water."

"Wait, wait, I have a great idea!" Ilana puffed out her chest to mimic Peter. "Let's let the Gentiles in, but first make them Jewish!"

I squinted and tilted my head. "Uh, what do you mean, 'make them Jewish'?"

Ilana continued brightly. "You know, make them follow the laws of the Torah. Keep them from eating catfish. Stuff like that."

"Well, fine, but is that all you'll need? What about the other requirement? What about . . . ." I waited. Paused for dramatic effect. "Circumcision?"

"Circumcision?" Ilana massaged her chin with her thumb and forefinger, looking pensive.

"Circumcision," I repeated.

"Circumcision!" Yohanna belted out and stomped her right foot. "Circumcision is a *must!*"

"Well, circumcision is going to be a problem," I said. "You know how attached men can be to their foreskins. And they might be just the tiniest bit squeamish about someone taking a knife to their penis."

"Nonsense," Yohanna walked over to where Levi and Yosh were sitting. "Let's ask this Gentile right here. Sir, how would you feel about someone chopping off part of your penis?"

Levi looked aghast and pretended to faint, falling over backward. Yosh squealed with delight.

Sitting across from Paul in our courtyard that morning, I couldn't help but smile, thinking back on our little skit. I had heard that, in the end, Paul persuaded Peter and James to relent. He convinced them to let him spread Christianity *his* way, to non-Jewish Gentiles up in northern cities like Antioch. Back in Judea, Peter and James would continue to limit Christianity to Jews.

But for Paul to say now that he had been given *sole* authority over the conversion of *all* Gentiles—well, that was a leap. A leap based not on facts but on what I saw as egotism and willpower.

Before I could say anything, Paul blathered on. "I have heard reports that you are also preaching the words of Yeshua, the Christ and Messiah. Moreover, that you and your friends are doing so on a daily basis. In the beginning, I was not overly concerned about these unsanctioned activities, but as it appears your followers are growing at an extraordinary rate, I must now intervene and ask— by whose authority do you instruct others on the doctrines of our Savior? I have not given you such permission."

Oh my goodness, I thought, what a pompous jackass.

"I did not know I was required to answer to anyone in order to teach what Yeshua taught," I said. "When what I am teaching is exactly the same as what he spoke to us."

"What he *spoke* to you?" Paul's eyes widened.

"Yes, when Yeshua was alive, words came out of his mouth, and we heard them." There was sarcasm in my voice, but it was wasted on Paul.

"Ah, you had the opportunity to hear our Savior and Messiah preach! How lucky you were."

"Indeed, we were very lucky to be his disciples."

"*Disciples!?*" Paul snorted. "Oh no, you are mistaken, you couldn't have been disciples."

"Because?"

"Because you are women!"

Little Yosh chose that moment to blow a raspberry, spewing bits of fig all over the table.

But Paul was still talking, adding fuel to the fire I felt beginning to simmer within me. "I recently traveled to Jerusalem, and all of the disciples I met there—Peter, James, John, Andrew—all were men. And they told me about several others who had originally traveled with our Savior and Messiah, who were spreading his teachings to other lands. Again, all men. No one ever mentioned a woman disciple."

"And yet, miraculously, here we are," I said, waving my arm toward Yohanna.

During our conversation, I focused my attention so much on Paul that I didn't notice Barnabas studying the wax tablets lying on the table. The young man picked one up and peered closely at it, eyebrows rising. Leaning toward Paul, Barnabas whispered a few words.

"Greek?" Paul sputtered. He shook his head in disbelief, took the tablet from Barnabas, and then scowled. "You women are studying *Greek?*"

Yohanna had had enough. Reaching across the table, she wrested the tablet from Paul's grasp and gathered others still on the table. Sitting back with her arms clutching the wooden frames, she glared at the men, her green eyes narrowed, like a snake ready to strike.

My patience was equally thin. I was ready to usher this odious little toad out of my house, or better yet, give him a silencing kick in the backside. "Indeed, you have interrupted our morning lessons," I said, standing up and shifting Yosh to my hip. "And it's time we returned to them." Sensing my tension, Yosh looked up at my face. He stopped licking his fingers.

Barnabas stood up quickly and bowed. "Of course, of course."

But Paul took his time. "I must tell you that this visit has unsettled me more than I expected. I will consult with Peter as to your authority to teach the Christian faith, and you will certainly be hearing from me on that matter." He shook his head at Yohanna and me. "In my community of Christians, women do not transgress the boundaries that God set by trying to learn languages beyond their capabilities. They know the places established for them by men."

Paul swirled his cloak around his body and seesawed over to the front door, where Barnabas waited for him. Again, a whisper passed from Barnabas's lips. For a few seconds, Paul froze in concentration. Then a smile spread slowly across his face.

"One final matter," he said. "I am concerned about the reports I have received of strange rituals with mysterious unguents taking place in this house."

"Strange rituals?" Yohanna repeated, confused.

"Mysterious unguents?" I asked. What new accusation was this man fabricating?

"Oh, don't deny that you are taking people into a room and muttering incantations over them while rubbing their bodies with unknown creams," Paul accused.

"I'm sorry, but are you referring to our *anointment* practice?" I asked, unintentionally raising my voice. Yosh, whose head had been pivoting back and forth, like a small sparrow on the alert for danger, began whimpering. Yohanna took him from my arms and shushed him against her shoulder.

"Perhaps you call it 'anointment,'" Paul sneered. "But I have heard reports of transformations in personality that are suggestive of witchcraft."

"*Witchcraft?*" The accusation was absurd. I didn't know whether to laugh or rant. But Yosh reacted for me, letting out a loud howl that mushroomed quickly into a screaming jag. "I think it is time for you to go," I said.

"Yes." Paul sidled his way over to the door, the smile still plastered on his face. "I encourage you, however, to keep in mind what we have discussed today. As a Roman citizen, I can tell you that witchcraft will not be tolerated. However . . . ." He toddled a few steps closer to me, and I took the same number of steps back. "It may be possible we can come to an arrangement, once we both see the situation clearly."

"I cannot imagine coming to any arrangement with you. I think I understand the situation clearly enough," I said.

"I assure you that you don't." And with that, Paul was finally out the door.

Ministry

5

I should have exercised greater caution after Paul's visit. But I felt defiant, determined to demonstrate to him, and to the world at large, that a woman could do everything Paul wanted to deny her—preach, read, and yes, write.

"Beware those rebellious instincts of yours," Yeshua told me, when I vented my irritation, sending little cyclones of anger through our energy field. "They might get you into trouble."

"I'm not going to let some portly man with an ego bigger than he is tell me what I can and cannot do in my own house!" I retorted. "Are you honestly asking me to submit to that polliwog's authority?"

"Of course not, I don't ask for the impossible," Yeshua teased. "All I suggest is that you exercise some caution, because Paul does have friends in high places."

So yes, Yeshua warned me, but I didn't heed his advice. At least, not enough. Caution is a virtue that eludes me.

I continued my Greek lessons in our home, expanded them even, encouraging anyone among our followers with interest to join us. Yohanna convinced me that it would be prudent to tell our students not to broadcast their learning to the world at large, and everyone agreed to practice their studies when they were alone and unobserved.

On the days that it was my turn to teach our community, I shared stories and lessons from some of the Eastern religious scrolls I had read back in Magdala, those that echoed our message of love and forgiveness, tolerance and equality. Once or twice, I brought out my own manuscript and dared to read from it. That was probably the straw that broke the back of Paul's patience.

The manuscript was a project I had been working on for several years. Back in Naveh, when I was training Yohanna and Zenora in the art of anointment, I told them that the first step in connecting with another person's spirit was to be in touch with your own. Yeshua had guided me through the complexities of self-discovery during the countless hours that we spent in meditation. The Eastern spiritual discourses that my father had obtained for me gave me a firm understanding of the process of surrendering my ego, but with Yeshua, I gained practical, firsthand insight. I learned that discovering my true self was like eating a pomegranate: First, you had to peel off the leathery protective rind, the outward self that you presented to the world. Then, you had to dive into a crevice where the seeds were hidden, picking off the sticky, inedible pith—the trappings of the world, all the false beliefs and shiny things that your ego attached itself to. And oh, there was so much pith! Then and only then would you have access to the ruby seeds of who you really are.

As I walked Yohanna and Zenora through this method, I realized it would be a good idea to write it all down. I myself could only teach so many people—perhaps a written account could help others in the future. My goal was to prepare a simplified road map to spiritual access. Bits and pieces of this work have been found over the years. Your modern historians have given it the title,

"The Gospel of Mary Magdalene." Seems a bit grandiose to me, but I won't complain.

Because Paul's visit unsettled me—he had, after all, called me a witch—I worked quickly to finish this project over the next several weeks. The ink on it was barely dry when I received a message from Jerusalem.

"Peter has sent for me," I said, as our family gathered for dinner.

"What?" Ilana was distracted by the mess Yosh was making of a piece of bread and a bowl of hummus. "What does that mean, Peter has 'sent for you?'"

"I imagine it means he wants her to come to Jerusalem," Levi said. He held Yosh up in the air so Ilana could wipe his face and hands with a cloth.

"Ridiculous!" Yohanna said. "If Peter wants to talk to you, he can get off his throne and come here himself."

Zenora shook her head at me as I passed her a bowl of cooked leeks, but I put a spoonful on her plate. "True, I could refuse to go. But a part of me is ready to make a gesture of goodwill, to put our past squabbles behind us."

"Squabbles, please remember, that were instigated by Peter, because he cannot tolerate women," Yohanna said. "Why would you subject yourself to that kind of disdain once again?"

"Why does Peter dislike women?" Zenora asked. "Doesn't he have a wife and daughters?"

"That's such a good question, Zenora," Yohanna said. Thinking I wasn't looking, she scraped the leeks off Zenora's plate to her own. I frowned, but Yohanna simply shrugged and smiled back. "And yes, he does have a wife and daughters. We can only hope he is kinder and more respectful to them than he ever was to us."

I sought Yeshua's advice on the question of whether I should answer Peter's summons.

"I don't know why he wants to see me after all this time," I mused. "Unless maybe he's finally ready to talk to me about some of my spiritual insights? Maybe it's an opportunity for Peter and me to align our communities. What do you think, Yeshua? Should I go?"

His answer was maddeningly unhelpful. "Whether you stay or go, Magda, the outcome will be the same."

"What does that mean, Yeshua? What outcome are you talking about? You sound like those seers who gather shekels at the market and promise to tell you your future, then say, 'All will be as it should be.'"

He tried to appease me with a dazzling display of light beams.

"I will not be mollified," I grumbled.

"Oh Magda, just because I am dead doesn't mean I can suddenly see and understand *everything* that will happen to you," Yeshua said. "There are some things I know about your destiny, but those events have not yet transpired, and may not take place for quite a while. The day-to-day minutiae of your life—well, those are as much a mystery to me as to you."

"What's the use in loving the spirit of a dead prophet then?" My heart was softening toward him, as it always did. "If he can't see the future?"

"Because the love is out of this world."

⚱

I did go to Jerusalem in the end. As Yeshua predicted, the result would have been no different had I stayed in Damascus. Paul wielded power wherever he went. That was the reality of Roman citizenship. And of membership in an elite Jewish sect, the Pharisees. (Just because Paul called himself a Christian didn't mean he gave up his Pharisee brothers, nor they him.) Paul had plenty of Roman and Jewish strings at his disposal if he wanted to get rid of someone.

Yohanna refused to let me go alone. And in a moment of prescience, I allowed Zenora to join us. I told myself Zenora should see Jerusalem, because she had never been there, but some part of me also feared that if I didn't bring her along, I might never see her again.

Before we left, I hid the papyrus I had been working on in my belongings. I had made only one other copy of that work, which I took to a scribe in Damascus for copying. Fearing Paul's spies, I offered the old man a premium in return for his promise to keep the project secret. Levi agreed to retrieve the copies when they were ready. To this day, I have no idea what Levi did with those copies, but I know some of them ended up buried in the earth for safekeeping from the Church's heresy-seekers. You may have heard of the one or two that eventually found their way to light, at Nag Hammadi and elsewhere. There are others still hidden.

Our journey to Jerusalem was uneventful—no dust storms, no brigands or bandits, just long days through fields of wild wheat and hawthorn, and quiet nights under a sky quilted with stars. Barely one week after parting from Levi and Ilana, Yohanna, Zenora, and I found ourselves in the entranceway of the small house where Yeshua had shared his last meal with us. Apparently, the owner of the house had embraced the new Christian religion and donated the house, with all its contents, to Peter and James for their use.

As I crossed over the threshold, memories of that last evening with Yeshua descended on me like small mallets sounding a singing bowl—deep and intense at first, then radiating out in ever-wider rings, softened and subdued, so I could appreciate the riches they offered. I looked into the courtyard. There stood the cassia tree, its blooming season over, limbs still proud and vibrant. There was the bench where Yohanna had reminded me that Yeshua would always be with us, and where we had pledged ourselves in lifelong friendship. I was sorry to see that the army of terra cotta warriors had disappeared—perhaps their services were now required elsewhere.

In my last visual sweep of the outside space before I entered the room where Peter and James waited, something slowly came into focus. Lights, a collection of lights, tiny flames flickering here and there in the air. Were these echoes of the candles that I had collected and placed around the courtyard and on our table that fateful evening? I had lit scores of candles that night, enough to burn down a modern cathedral. Yohanna had even raised some concern about the quantity and whether they might be a fire hazard. No, the flames I saw now were fewer, and more distinct, each glimmering at a particular spot around a rectangle that outlined where our table had stood. Their number was equal to the number of our fellowship who had dined with Yeshua that night.

I stared at this spectacle, soaking it in. I was reminded of the unity of our group, the bonds we had made with each other through our shared devotion to a remarkable man. We had been, and ever would be, tied to one another by that experience. Fortified by this memory, and carrying a new warmth in my heart, I went inside.

The room where Peter and James chose to meet us had once been the living area of the house. It felt strange to walk into a chamber that I remembered as cozy and welcoming, with richly upholstered furniture and crystal lamps and mahogany tables. Because now, the entire space was bare. Only the walls remained adorned as they had been earlier, with vibrant tapestries depicting scenes from the Torah: Moses receiving the Ten Commandments, Abraham about to sacrifice Isaac, and David slaying Goliath.

My eyes were drawn immediately to the far end of the room, where Peter and James sat on silk-upholstered chairs, like kings awaiting petitions from their subjects. In the three years since I had last seen him, Peter had not changed much, except that the belt around his waist now had a harder time containing his belly. At the front entrance, we had passed by a collection of covered food trays—perhaps Peter and James encouraged edible offerings in lieu of money for their new church?

I had not been told that Paul would be present, but I wasn't surprised to see him standing behind the two chairs, his round head barely reaching the top of James's seat. Ever restless, Paul shuffled back and forth between the men like a horsefly.

James was the only person in the room I had never met. I had wrongly imagined he would favor Yeshua. But physically, James no more looked like my beloved husband than a donkey resembles an Arabian stallion. Harsh as that sounds, the truth is that everything about James was different from Yeshua—his build was heavier, his hair was thinner, his lips were tight and drawn. Yeshua had been so vibrant, brimming with a life-force that touched everyone he met. But James might as well have been a mummy, so vapid did he appear. His eyes, when I finally caught them, looked empty and dull, with about as much depth as a puddle.

James spoke first, in a languid drawn-out voice. "Miriam of Magdala, rightly have you answered our summons and appear now before us. We called you here to—"

Oh no, I thought, time to set the record straight. "To be clear, James, I have not come here under any sense of obligation, either to you or to Peter. As far as I am concerned, you have no authority over me, nor I over you," I said. "I come, rather, as a colleague in ministry, a fellow declarant of the words and teachings of Yeshua of Nazareth."

Paul muttered something to Peter, who nodded and put a restraining hand on James' arm.

"Miriam—" Peter began.

I turned my attention to Peter. He appeared more tired than I remembered, though perhaps it was his proximity to the energy-sapping James. I reminded myself that I had shared Peter's company for over a year. That he was as devoted to the love of my life as I was. And I still carried the vision I had just seen in the courtyard, all those tiny flames burning in unison. For a moment, all the animosity I harbored toward Peter disappeared. I stepped forward, arms outstretched, ready to embrace him.

But he did not stand. Instead, he extended his arm, palm upraised toward me. I stopped.

"Miriam—" he said again.

I tried shrugging off the slight. "Why this formality, Peter?" I asked. "After all the months we spent together in Yeshua's company, I would think we might call each other friends. My friends call me Magda."

"Miriam," Peter repeated, for the third time. "Our colleague in Syria, Paul of Tarsus, tells us that you are practicing your own ministry up in Damascus, with disturbing success. In fact, Paul tells us you gather more followers daily than he does in Antioch. We are worried about how you are spreading the words of our Christ and Savior, the Messiah Yeshua of Nazareth—those words should be consistently taught."

"Everything I am teaching originates in Yeshua's words. I heard the same words you heard," I said.

"That may be true, but our brother Paul tells us that you encourage women to assume roles that we in the Jerusalem Church reserve for men. For example, you are teaching them to read and write Greek? If nothing else, surely this is a terrible waste of time."

I clenched my teeth. Behind me, Yohanna reached her hand between my shoulder blades and began tracing a circle to calm me down. I took a few deep breaths before I spoke.

"You may remember, Peter, that Yeshua taught us that all people are equal, men *and* women. Do you remember that? Do you remember how Yeshua made the men of our group relieve Rivka and Naomi of their serving and washing duties at mealtimes?" I tried to stare Peter down, but he maintained a distant gaze, staring beyond me to the back wall of the room. Someone must have taught him that trick. "Just as men can do many of the same things as women, women can do the same things as men. If women want to learn Greek, they should be permitted to do so. Yeshua would agree with me."

Paul whispered furiously into Peter's ear for the next minute or so. Finally, Peter spoke again. "Miriam, you twist the words of our Rabbi. He said that all *men* were equal to each other. He meant all *men* are equal to other *men*. It was a statement of social and economic equality. It had nothing to do with women."

This was too much. Was Peter deliberately lying, or had he misunderstood Yeshua's message so completely? Or had time and distance from Yeshua's ministry allowed Peter's inherent misogyny to rewrite his memories? Was Paul providing Peter the intellectual support he needed for these statements? Before I could object, James interrupted.

"This argument is beside the point," James opined. "So few women have the mental ability to learn Greek."

"I'm learning Greek," Zenora announced. She stepped forward, bunching her veil into her fists. For a moment, I saw the spitfire child I had met years earlier. Indignation straightened Zenora's posture. "And I lived much of my life in a cave, which you could say puts me at a disadvantage. It definitely didn't help my mental state."

"And you are who, young lady?" James leaned forward.

"This is my daughter," I said, pulling her toward me and standing slightly in front of her. "Her name is Zenora."

"Your *daughter?*" Peter was incredulous. "How is that possible? You are not married."

I paused, because I considered myself still married to Yeshua—to me, he lived on. But Jewish law would have declared my marriage over upon his death, so I made my next statement in good conscience. "I am not."

Peter and James looked confused, as they pondered the possible social arrangements that could have provided a single woman with a fifteen-year-old child. Becoming impatient, Paul tried to move things along.

"We have much more serious business to discuss here than the composition of your family, Miriam." Paul hobbled over to where I stood and shook a finger at me. The very caricature of an ineffective nag.

"It has come to my attention that you have in your possession some sort of document, and that this treatise makes an extraordinary and deeply troubling statement. Is it true that you are teaching your followers that they can access God on their own?"

So Paul had been spying on our ministry. He knew about my papyrus. "They can," I answered.

"Miriam, surely you understand that people need priests to guide them to God. Men who have been selected for their faith and conviction," Paul insisted. He looked back at Peter and James, who were nodding vigorously.

Peter jumped in next. "Our religion has always had priests, as you know. Priests who have been chosen and blessed by our God as his special and sole intermediaries to humankind. Your treatise will, at the very best, confuse people. At worst, it is heretical."

"Heretical!?" I barked at him. "How can you label anything 'heretical' when you haven't even read it? My treatise is based entirely on the teachings of Rabbi Yeshua, the man you claim as the figurehead of your new religion, so how could it be heretical?"

Peter opened his mouth, but I wasn't done yet.

"I can forgive James's and Paul's ignorance about Yeshua's teachings because they weren't in our fellowship. They didn't *live* his beliefs every day, as we all tried to. But you did, Peter. You were there every day when we gathered for our hour of meditation in the synagogue. Did you think that was a time for napping?"

Peter rose from his chair, incensed. "Don't mock me, Miriam!"

"It's not my intention to mock you, Peter, but why are you ignoring what Yeshua tried to teach us, and what he wanted us to teach others?"

Paul had been pacing to and fro during my little tirade, and now broke in. "You are not the only one to whom the Messiah spoke, Miriam. Nor are you the last."

Was Paul really trying to compete with me in the sphere of who knew Yeshua best? I would run circles around him in that contest.

"Paul of Tarsus." I decided to abbreviate the extensive title he liked to give himself, both because I didn't want to waste an entire minute uttering it and because I couldn't remember it all. "I will not dispute what you claim to have seen on your journey to Damascus, when you say you were visited by Yeshua, other than to point out that none of the other travelers with you that day saw what you saw." A long strand of uncut hair fell off the dome of Paul's head and poked at his left eye as he vehemently shook his head. Undeterred, I continued, "But my friend Yohanna, who is with me today, can confirm that, during his last meal with us before he died, Yeshua named *me* as the person who best understood his heart."

Yohanna squeezed my hand and stepped forward. "Yes, he did. Rabbi Yeshua called Magda the 'lodestar' of his teaching."

"Peter knows this too," I said. "He was there."

Paul turned his head to Peter so quickly, the rebellious strand of hair slapped his cheek. "Peter, is this true?"

Peter began chewing the inside of his cheek, until James repeated the question. "Peter, *is this true?*"

"If . . . if . . ." Peter stammered, "If our Rabbi said such a thing, I cannot remember it." What a cowardly dodge.

Paul, Peter, and James huddled together to confer briefly, then stood up as one, while James delivered the verdict they had reached. "Miriam of Magdala, you leave us no choice but to command you to stop your ministry in Damascus and to hand over all copies of the pseudo-religious treatise you have authored. We will review its contents and determine whether you will be permitted to resume your activities in the future."

I could have predicted that outcome, had I played out everything I knew about Paul. Looking back, I realize that I must have honestly believed he wouldn't go as far as he did. I didn't see myself as threatening. But Paul did. Paul could see, as I could not, that the history of Christianity had arrived at one of many critical forks in its path, and that he and I wanted to proceed in entirely different directions. He was determined to steer the religion his way. And he was ruthless enough to try to eliminate competitors.

I could not do what they were asking. Not only was my ministry my life, it was the fulfillment of my dedication to Yeshua. Stepping away from it, regardless of the circumstances, would be a betrayal of him. "What if I refuse?" I asked.

"If you refuse, you put yourself and your family in jeopardy," Paul interjected, gesturing toward Zenora and Yohanna. "Remember my warning to you about your other activities. Those that could interpreted as immersion in the dark arts. The punishment for witchcraft is severe."

Witchcraft, my ass. It was an anointment practice, and he knew it. The allegation was ridiculous, but he wasn't letting go. I would never give up anointment—it was essential to my self-definition and to the future of the people I touched. Still, for just an instant, I drifted in fear, looking for Yeshua's spirit to ground me. Instead, I heard Deborah's voice: "Your time is just beginning."

I would not falter. "Gentlemen," I said, gathering my mantle, "I cannot accommodate your wishes. My heart and my spirit command otherwise."

And I turned and walked out. Yohanna and Zenora followed. When we were outside the house, out of sight of the men, Yohanna let out a quiet shriek and hugged me. "I was so afraid you might give in," she said. "Paul was really piling on the intimidation."

"What do you think they'll do next?" Zenora asked.

"I don't know," I said, pulling her close. "But I don't think we should wait around to see."

As we headed down the street, arms linked and pace synchronized, Paul came stumbling after us. "I beseech you to reconsider, Magda!" he called out. "You put yourself in peril!"

Was he concerned about the moral transgression he was about

to commit? If so, I wasn't going to make it any easier for him, for any of them, by giving in. If they were intent on pursuing whatever unscrupulous path they were contemplating to get me to stop my ministry, they would have to plow forward. I would not yield.

MINISTRY

6

If I thought Pontius Pilate's influence on my life would end with Yeshua's death, I was wrong. Herod Antipas's expectation that Emperor Tiberius would sack Pontius Pilate for killing Yeshua went nowhere. It took a later misstep by Pilate—the massacre of a group of unarmed Samaritans—for Tiberius to call Pilate back to Rome. By that time, three years after Yeshua's death, the Emperor was too tired to appoint a replacement.

With no prefect in the Holy City, local magistrates stepped in to handle judicial process. Any criminal charge—including the crime of witchcraft—that would ordinarily have been investigated and tried by the prefect now rested in their hands. Those hands, it turned out, were grubby, and their ethics were slick.

Paul knew his audience. As a Roman citizen, he had the right to bring a charge of witchcraft against anyone. Immediately after his last warning to us in the street, Paul hurried over to the local tribunal with accusations against Yohanna and me. He thoroughly greased all the necessary palms, then trampled upon our right to defend ourselves by arguing that if we were allowed to appear in person, we would certainly influence the procedure through magic.

To reassure the magistrate as to the righteousness of his cause, Paul presented trumped-up evidence of our alleged witchcraft rituals. Citizens of Jerusalem came forward to attest to my activities in the healing corner I had set up years earlier, outside the Temple where Yeshua preached during Passover. They spoke of my strange-smelling potions, handed to me by Yohanna, my accomplice. They spoke of my manipulation of bodies, how I pressed my brewed philters into skin and sinew, to ensure their absorption. They spoke of the dazed look on the faces of people leaving my table.

Of course, none of these witnesses had ever subjected themselves to my anointment, so no one could testify to the nature of the transformation undergone by my so-called victims. But the magistrate did not need that evidence. He didn't really need any evidence, other than for show, for his ruling had been determined hours earlier, when the bag of money promised him by Paul appeared on his desk. By the end of the day, Paul procured an order banishing us from Judea and all neighboring lands.

We were ignorant of it all until it was too late. Yohanna and I had debated whether to spend the night in Bethany or leave immediately for Damascus. Neither of us felt safe in Jerusalem after Paul's threat, but I was emotionally exhausted after the day's events. What we did do immediately was to send a warning to Levi and Ilana, telling them to begin packing up all our belongings. If Paul kept us from preaching in Damascus, we would become itinerant ministers again, hardly the worst fate we could imagine.

When Levi and Ilana learned several days later what ultimately happened to the three of us, they took Yosh and their broken hearts into hiding, and waited for the next caravan to arrive in Damascus. Marcus Silanus and Shoshanna, ignorant of the drama that was transpiring in our world, had sent advance word that they would be arriving on the camel train from Tehran. I wish I could have been there to see that family reunion. I wish I could have thrown my arms around Shoshanna one more time, or kissed the craggy cheeks of Marcus Silanus.

⁂

The three of us hurried back to Bethany, to the home of our friend Miriam, whom we hadn't seen since that tragic Passover week. Hastening through Jerusalem and up the Mount of Olives, I was reminded everywhere of my last days with Yeshua—here was the Garden of Gethsemane, where I last felt his breath against my skin; there was the dusty path through the olive orchards, which we had traversed together countless times. I kept expecting to walk through a trace of his scent, or to hear his deep laughter on a breeze. By the time we reached Miriam's house, my tears were flowing as freely as the day he died.

That night, I lay with Zenora and Yohanna in the same bed I had shared with him. It was a tight squeeze for three people, but I was grateful to have two loving souls cushion my heavy heart. My ache for Yeshua—usually a manageable, dim woe—flared up like a carnivorous animal newly provoked by the smell of raw meat. Not wanting to wake my bedmates, I cried silently. Zenora, God bless her youth, could sleep through anything, but Yohanna wrapped me against her body and sang a quiet lullaby, kissing my heaving shoulders in between every verse.

That tenuous shelter did not last. In the middle of the night, a violent banging jolted us all awake. Miriam stumbled through the front hall, pulling a blanket around her shoulders, just as a group of Roman guards slammed the door open, splintering its frame. I quickly reached for the papyrus that contained my gospel, which I had taken from my clothing before getting into bed, and resecured it against my body. I vowed to defend this hidden treasure with my life.

The soldiers clamored past Miriam toward the back of the house where Yohanna, Zenora, and I huddled against the back wall of our room. There was no escape. The only window was just below the roofline, too high for us to reach. And the door led into the hallway down which we could already see the soldiers stomping toward us. I grabbed Yohanna's and Zenora's hand in each of my own before we were surrounded and hustled into the hall.

Prodding us with spears, the soldiers forced us out of the house and into a horse-drawn covered wagon that waited by the road. Miriam stood on her threshold, screaming hysterically for help. But her effort was futile and succeeded only in drawing her neighbors to their front doors, their arms crossed in resignation or palms pressed together in prayer, shaking their heads ever so slightly at yet another exercise of random Roman violence against Jews.

The horses were lashed into motion, and we jostled against animal hides stretched over the sides of the wagon, as it lurched forward at a brisk pace. For a long time, we said nothing to each other, bumping first along a dirt road and later over the paved stone roads that encircled Jerusalem. Poor Zenora wept uncontrollably with fear, and I drew her against me, as much for my comfort as hers. Yohanna stroked Zenora's back, quietly murmuring prayers.

Initially, I assumed we were being taken into the Holy City, perhaps for the witchcraft trial Paul had threatened, but when I looked out the back of the wagon and saw the walls of Jerusalem recede into the distance, I was puzzled.

"We're heading west," I whispered to Yohanna. "Away from the city."

She shrugged and pulled me back into the bed of straw and mats that would become our only defense against the nonstop jolts of the road. "We have no control over where we are going," she said. "We might as well try to rest until we get there."

"There" turned out to be the port city of Joppa, where we arrived three days later, bruised and disoriented. Yohanna and I had speculated at length about our fate during those days in the wagon. We concluded fairly quickly that, whatever was about to befall us, Paul was responsible. It didn't surprise me at all, then, to see Paul's sidekick Barnabas waiting for us, as our carriage pulled up just outside the town walls. Though it was nighttime, I recognized him from his shape—tall thin beanpole with shoulders slouched in misgiving.

The soldiers shuttled the three of us onto a sandbank below the pier where Barnabas stood, and they took up position behind us, in case one of us tried to flee. Barnabas was nervously shifting his weight from one foot to another, muttering to himself and shaking his head. I allowed myself a glimmer of hope. Whatever he was about to do to us, perhaps he could be persuaded against it. He did not look like a man who was resolute in his purpose.

Upon seeing us, Barnabas immediately looked down at the scroll he was holding. Carefully, and without raising his head again, he unfurled the parchment and scanned its contents.

The tribunal order that Barnabas finally read aloud in a halting voice proclaimed both Yohanna and me guilty of engaging in sorcery and witchcraft. We were to exit the land of Judea immediately and permanently. But this was not all—a standing order from the Roman consul in Syria, the tribunal reminded us, extended the reach of all exiles to include any Roman province east of the Mediterranean Sea.

I stood in shock. Here was a punishment that I had neither

expected nor imagined, even in my most fearful nightmares about Paul. I knew that exile from Judea was a remote possibility because exile was always a dish on the feast table of Roman penalties. But exile from all Roman provinces that surrounded Judea? That would include all of Syria, as well as Phoenicia, Idumea, and Egypt. I turned to Yohanna and saw her eyes watering. We were both slowly realizing we might never see Ilana and Levi again.

Where were we to go?

As if he heard our unspoken question, Barnabas stepped to the left, allowing us to see more of the narrow pier. It was too dark to make out the vessels that bobbed along its sides, but the soldiers took Barnabas's movement as a cue to urge us forward, nudging us with sheathed swords toward a small boat that was tied abeam to the far end of the dock.

The craft before us looked, to my eyes, barely seaworthy. Its weathered and battered hull had visible cracks that I hoped were superficial. But it was the same type of fishing boat that I had watched sail on the Sea of Galilee—an open scow, just under thirty feet long, with two benches spanning its width, and a mast with a square sail. Ehud's boat, which I had waited for day after day as a child, had been only slightly smaller. I was grateful now that I had relentlessly pestered my parents to let me join Ehud on his boat. When I was ten years old, they finally agreed, and Ehud had taken me out on the lake for a full-day excursion. He showed me how to predict the wind and harness it for maximum speed, and how to maneuver the boat with the rudder. Then he demonstrated exactly how to catch fish, first using a net and then with a hook and line.

Standing in the gloom, I said a silent prayer of thanks to Ehud—what he taught me that day, though a distant and vague memory, might serve us now to keep us from starvation. That knowledge, together with my faith that Yeshua would watch over us and guide us to safety, kept me from panic.

I stepped onto the boat and found a pile of woolen blankets under the benches, one of which I wrapped around a shivering Zenora. She was exempt from the tribunal order, of course, but Barnabas seemed not to notice her. I would have torn the beard off every man present with my bare hands rather than be separated from her. She, fortunately, felt the same. There were a few other provisions stored under the benches—several loaves of bread, a supply of fresh water, an oar, a fishing net, and other fishing gear. When I saw the last items, I breathed a sigh of relief. But I was still ready to rip into Paul, which I did the moment Barnabas approached.

"What a coward Paul is, sending you to do his dirty work," I said.

Barnabas flushed with embarrassment. "My colleague Paul of Tarsus was, er, called to Antioch on a matter of . . ." I saw his mind searching for something convincing, "urgent spiritual import."

"Well, I hope for the sake of all the souls in Syria that he's had his fill of sending women and children to unknown fates," I snarled. "And I hope you've paid these soldiers well," I waved toward the armed men. "Lest they tell others about the shoddy little boats that the great Paul of Tarsus chooses for those he condemns."

Barnabas could only continue stuttering. Clearly I had touched a sore spot. "I . . . I don't think there were any other crafts available." He cast a glance up and down the pier, to confirm that a more luxurious vessel was not moored nearby. I watched his conscience struggle with his devotion to Paul. Slowly, the devotion began to prevail.

"But you know," Barnabas shook his head, gathering courage, "he did warn you back when we visited Damascus. It was you who chose to continue your blasphemous activities. And when the magistrate found both of you guilty the other day, Paul argued strongly in favor of your exile rather than your execution. So in a way, you should consider yourself lucky. Because your life was spared. And I am permitting you to bring your daughter."

I gave Barnabas a long hard stare. "Those who are dishonest in little are dishonest in much," I said, paraphrasing a line from one of Yeshua's favorite stories. "If you cannot be trusted to take care of God's true servants, Barnabas, how will you ever be entrusted with his riches?"

Barnabas opened his mouth to respond but could not find an appropriate reply.

Indeed, there was nothing more to say. I suddenly felt eager to get away from this man and everything he was associated with. As I bent to untie the bowline, Yohanna went astern to unfurl the aft line from its piling. Picking up a wooden oar, I pushed our boat off the pier.

Slowly, we drifted to the harbor entrance. To the northeast, beyond the Plain of Sharon, lay Magdala and my parents' home, which I now knew I would never see again. Silently, I sent my mother and father a farewell prayer.

Dawn was beginning to part the drapery of night. A gentle breeze fluttered the furled canvas on deck, urging us to fly out and away. "There are souls in the wind," Ehud told me the day he took me sailing. "A sailor never feels lonely." I pulled on the halyard to raise the sail, and I did not look back again.

Epilogue

The stars nearby have dimmed. Yeshua is unhappy.

"That's it? That's where you're ending the story? Drifting out to sea in an open boat?"

I hate it when he sulks.

You want the rest of the story? Okay, here's the nutshell version: By the grace of God and Yeshua, we landed in southern France. There, we—Yohanna and I, and later Zenora and her children—spread Yeshua's message. There, I began my own ministry, the one Deborah had foretold: I brought people together, anointed them, and united them. Slowly, the egalitarian communities we had tried starting in Damascus began taking root in France. We taught men and women how to read, how to meditate, how to find and embrace their own souls, and how to find and embrace God. The kingdom of God gained a small foothold in that corner of the world as we moved through it.

Across the Mediterranean Sea, however, Peter and Paul's hierarchical church established its own tenacious roots. Over time, it stretched its greedy tendrils beyond Rome, reaching north to Gaul, south to Egypt, east to Mesopotamia. Inevitably, it slithered its unctuous way westward, around the shore of the sea. When my beloved French communities refused to bow to its beliefs, the Roman Catholic Church crushed them. By then, I had long been dead. All I could do was watch from up Here.

Someday, I'll give you the details of the last years of my life—

how Yohanna and I lived to be wrinkled old crones. How she died before me, and my heart broke for the second time in my life. How, after her death, I retreated to a cliffside cave, so I could look out over the hills that reminded me of home. How Zenora and her children brought food up that steep precipice, their spirits like angels floating toward me. How, one day, I too died and came Here, where I was reunited with Yeshua forever.

The people of that region dug up a pile of old bones they claimed were mine. They took "my" skull and plated it in pure gold, and they placed a desiccated femur (also "mine") in a case of glass. Every year, on my feast day, their ancestors parade these relics up the cliff to the cave where I ended my days. It's quite the show.

All of that is a story for another time. Right now, I'm feeling peeved and irritable, thinking back on my exile. Also, that label good old Pope Gregory slapped on me. The prostitute tag that stuck for over one and a half millennia.

I'll bet if you were to ask any random person today who Mary Magdalene is, they'd give you a blank stare. Or, if they do recognize my name, they'd say, "Mary Magdalene? Wasn't she a hooker?"

All of it pisses me off.

"Hang onto that anger," Yeshua tells me. "It will be helpful when you go back."

"You keep talking about *me* going back," I grumble. "Why aren't *you* going back? You're the Christ. *You're* the Messiah."

"Ah, the Messiah. About that . . . ."

Suddenly Yeshua musters a thousand rays of light, and stars begin exploding around him, like midnight fireworks at Disneyworld. When the spectacle calms down, a galaxy is swirling around us—we're at the epicenter of a luminous whirlpool.

Yeshua's tone is serious.

"Magda, do you remember who first called me *Messiah*?"

"Well, that was Paul, wasn't it? Before Paul, I don't remember any talk about a *messiah*, certainly not in our group." I think back on our followers. So many people wanted to believe in Yeshua's promise of a new world. Sure, there were cynics outside the group who scoffed, even one or two crackpots who insisted *they* were the messiah promised by the prophet Daniel centuries earlier. But Yeshua never claimed that title for himself.

No, it was Paul who brilliantly effected that transformation.

"Paul made you into the ultimate, *capital M* Messiah," I say. "He said you came to save everyone, no matter what religion they were. Clever strategy, really: Paul wanted to get *everybody* under the roof of his new church. The Jews would follow you because you were the messiah promised by Daniel. And the Gentiles could latch onto you as a fresh messiah offering them salvation."

"Paul knew how to build an empire," Yeshua admits. "But I think he had good intentions for his church."

"Did he, though?" I ask, annoyed.

Sometimes, I want to smack Yeshua for his persistent belief in the goodness of all people. Mostly, I share that belief. But I can't abide two-faced people. Especially people who have deliberately and unnecessarily hurt me. People like Paul.

"Let's not rehash our old argument about Paul," Yeshua says. "Tell me, Magda, what does *messiah* mean? What are its root letters in Hebrew?"

"What, we're doing a remedial language lesson now?"

"Humor me."

I feel like I'm five years old again, sitting in front of my father in his library, waiting for morning instruction.

"As you well know," I say, "*Messiah* means *anointed*, and its root letters are Mem Shin Chet."

"Excellent. And as I'm sure *you* know, those three letters also form the root of another word." He pauses, waiting for some sign of recognition from me. When I give him nothing, he continues. "That other word is 'anointer.' The one who anoints."

He gives me a moment to digest this before he asks: "Do you see it now?"

Anointed. Anointer. Overlapping scenes swirl forward from the galaxy still spinning around us.

I see the prophet Daniel scribbling letters onto vellum by candlelight. Gray hair bleaching into white, his head bobs over his quill as he writes with an urgency compelled by amazement.

I see a sprinkling of phosphorescence around Daniel, from which a clarion voice issues. The angel Gabriel. There will come an *anointer*, says Gabriel, who will establish God's eternal kingdom. A woman, Gabriel emphasizes. Because God's kingdom is life-giving.

Daniel is astounded at this message, the word and its implications. *Anointers* in daily Jewish society are women. Only on rare occasions do male priests anoint kings or other priests. By and large, anointment is seen as a domestic female activity, so everyone would understand the word *anointer* to mean a woman. Still awestruck but dutiful, Daniel pens the word *anointer* onto the vellum.

I see Daniel overseeing a scribe. The scribe hesitates, quill poised over Daniel's original. "'*Anointer*?'" the scribe asks. "Surely, sir, you mean *anointed*, as in king or prince or priest. Surely God's kingdom will be established by a man of importance? By the one who is *anointed*?" Daniel shakes his head, stands firm. But Daniel cannot go everywhere his words go, and other scribes feel free to edit and substitute. After all, they reason, both words have the same root letters.

I see stories being told at night, after dinner, and around an open fire. Stories based on the sacred writings. People huddle near the flames in animal furs, listening to bards tell tales of their common ancestors, a special tribe of people, God's chosen. The Torah. The Ketuvim. The Book of Daniel. The bards, all men with little, if any, education, never doubt that the word Daniel intended was *anointed*. Some scribes have added in the word *prince* to make it clear that God's kingdom will be led by someone royal.

Sexism triumphs, and a female messiah is lost.

I try making sense of these images. Everything churns around me. Yeshua comes nearer, settles the chaos. Suddenly, all is still. "Magda, I was never the Messiah."

I turn to him.

"You are," he says.

The world feels upside-down.

"I was sent to find you and keep you safe," Yeshua says. "I was supposed to prepare you for your role, to help you develop your abilities. To till the soil with *my* ministry so you could begin sowing the seeds of *yours*. I never expected to fall in love with you, that was not part of the plan, but you . . . you . . . ." He falters.

"Are you going to say I seduced you?"

"Of course not. But you *were* ravishing—accomplished, intelligent, honest. And so beautiful. Indeed, it was impossible *not* to fall in love with you. Quite impossible."

He drifts closer.

"I watched you grow. I watched you mature into who you were meant to be. I saw your healing abilities expand and your spirit flourish. Over time, I fell even more in love with you. At some point, the crucifixion dreams began. Before we fell in love, before we were married, I hadn't understood an untimely death to be part of the plan for me, but suddenly, I saw it every night, right behind my closed eyes. It was terrifying."

"But why would being in love with me mean that you had to die? That makes no sense."

"Because, Magda, I stood in your way. As long as I remained on Earth, as long as we loved as fiercely as we did, you prioritized me over everything else. Do you remember when we were in Jerusalem, and you tried convincing me to run away? You said that we could build a home somewhere, and that you would devote yourself to me and our children? And that, in placing our family ahead of all else, you would give up anointing?"

I do remember that conversation. Back then, I thought it was a test. I didn't realize it was an execution sentence.

Yeshua continues. "In that moment, I understood why I had to die. I had to get out of the way of your destiny."

I snap back. "What *destiny* was that? I accomplished *nothing* in the end. First, I lost you. Then, I lost my homeland. And then, after I successfully brought our message to France, after small towns began shifting toward the kind of 'kingdom' we described— after all that, those beautiful towns were destroyed. Everything, *everything* I did in my lifetime was wiped out by Peter and Paul and their ravenous Church."

The galaxy of stars that once enclosed us has now evaporated. Yeshua is subdued.

"I've had many conversations with the Source about this, Magda. Maybe we were too late. Maybe our message failed because the power structures on Earth were already too firmly entrenched. Humans are mesmerized by power. They always have been and always will be." He sounds like a father watching his children steal cookies from the cookie jar. Disappointed and sad, knowing that he will have to punish them. "People won't give up power until they have to."

"If that's true, then how is now a better time?" I demand.

"Those power structures you talk about have had two thousand more years to dig in their heels. And remember, my process is slow. I can only anoint one person at a time." Mentally, I try tallying the number of people who live on Earth. "We're talking *billions* of people!"

"Over eight billion," he admits. "I didn't say it wouldn't be challenging."

A deep dark energy rumbles in the distance. "I have spent much time trying to convince the Source that it is still possible to save humanity," Yeshua says. "Right now is our last opportunity. Because right now, they are tumbling toward extinction."

The energy beyond us rolls like the beat of a kettledrum. It feels strangely like a summons.

"The Source has agreed to let you go back," Yeshua says. "But you're going to need something to get their attention."

"Like what? Are we talking lightning bolts and thunderclouds? Will they erupt from my fingertips? Or will it be something more extreme?" Images flash by: hurricanes, tsunamis, torrential rains; lakes, seas, and oceans all gushing upward and outward, sweeping over the Earth, engulfing entire cities, skyscrapers toppling, thousands of flickering lights suddenly extinguished.

"No, no floods," Yeshua glides in front of me, blocking the vision. "No indiscriminate worldwide annihilation."

"Right," I say, thinking of Noah. "Been there, done that."

The distant energy has moved closer and is now pulsing on our periphery. Yeshua nods to some unspoken question.

"The Source wants you to check in now. An arsenal awaits your disposal."

"*Uh huh.*" Perhaps I'll be hurling asteroids. Small enough to cause local damage but big enough to get noticed. I try not to think about individual people—mothers, fathers, children. I am grateful that all the people I loved in my lifetime are Here now.

Yeshua approaches, begins to merge his energy with mine. "I believe in you, Magda. If there is anyone who can save them, it is you."

I look down at the Earth. That jewel floating in darkness.

"Why do you care so much about these people, Yeshua? After everything they did to you? And everything they have done to each other?"

"You know the answer to that question." I feel his peace, warmth, and light. His love for all those souls. His love for me.

"Because they are a part of us," I say.

"Exactly."

I watch the planet sparkle as it rises above its own moon, bleached paisley clouds waltzing over an expanse of blue ocean.

It *was* a beautiful place to spend a lifetime.

I am the Messiah. I have no idea how to begin.

But, whatever.

"Okay," I say. "I'll go."

Acknowledgments

First and foremost, enormous thanks to Brooke Warner of She Writes Press for taking a chance on this book, and to the entire team of talented people who helped it come to print, especially Addison Gallegos, Julie Metz, and Lauren Wise.

The teachers and students of the University of Iowa Summer Writing Program gave me insight and encouragement throughout this writing journey. I am particularly grateful to editors Robert Anthony Siegel and Kelly Dwyer for their meticulous feedback and helpful suggestions, and for making time in their demanding schedules.

For invaluable advice on issues of religious and cultural sensitivity, I am indebted to Sam Schindler and Brunella Costagliola.

My "village" of readers is a procession led by the ever incisive and whip-smart Pamela Toutant. This book grew, chapter by chapter, through the discerning eyes and diligent pens of Pamela and the small group of dedicated writers that gathered at her home once a week. It was a writing group that I cherished.

Many, *many* thanks also to the countless friends and family who provided feedback and support along the way: Marianne Green, Katinka Werner, Rudolf Werner, Beth Werner, Stephen Klineberg, Kathy Edmunds, Benson Forman, Kendall Guthrie, Katie Bluth, Timna Zucker, David Finegold, Ryan Spiegel, Bill Dodge, and Bill Wescott.

Finally, I would be lost without my nest—Geoffrey, Julia, Anna, Emily, Dan, and Arpam. Thank you for all the light you bring to my world.

About the Author

Photo credit: Damon Bowe

URSULA WERNER has been writing for over twenty-five years. She has published one novel, *The Good at Heart* (2017), and two chapbooks of poetry, *The Silence of the Woodruff* (2006) and *Rapunzel Revisited* (2010). When she is not writing fiction, she works as a part-time attorney. She and her husband live in Washington, DC and are trying to entice their three daughters to live nearby.

Looking for your next great read?

We can help!

Visit www.shewritespress.com/next-read
or scan the QR code below for a list
of our recommended titles.

She Writes Press is an award-winning
independent publishing company founded to
serve women writers everywhere.